More praise for THE LAST BIZARRE TALE

"For anyone wishing to rediscover or discover the work of David Madden—
and that should include not only aspiring writers but all lovers of great
literature—*The Last Bizarre Tale* is the perfect place to start . . . yet another step
toward a wider public recognition that Madden is a master craftsman and
an American storyteller of the first rank. I was nailed to the wall by the
autobiographical 'James Agee Never Lived in This House.'"
MARK POWELL · author of *The Dark Corner*

"In these stories, David Madden proves himself a master of the brilliant
narrative left turn, the oddly illuminating digression, the swoop you never
expected. No one else writes stories quite like these, and they are a revelation."
CHARLES BAXTER · author of *Gryphon: New and Selected Stories*

"Here's a gathering of serious fictions to delight serious readers. Madden's stories
are wide-ranging and richly varied. Manifest in voices that occupy a span from
the conventional authorial to the eccentric, style here leans toward the lyric, but
is never unrestrained. His characters' epiphanies become the reader's, created
through crisp dialogue that is always on the money. A number of David Madden's
stories are indeed bizarre, but never gratuitously so. If there is a common subject
or theme, it is the writer's and the reader's imagination. Madden's fictional worlds
are grim and gritty in their depiction of human nature and history, but humanity
persists, redeeming the possibility of redemption. Whatever the milieu, the felt
presence of place grounds the author's examination and exploration of the real
world, which is what these fictions ultimately deliver."
GORDON WEAVER · author of *The Eight Corners of the World*

"David Madden is a true master of fiction – one of our most
adept creators of memorable characters and unforgettable voices.
The Last Bizarre Tale is a wonderful collection. These stories display
the full range of his skill and the grand sweep of a remarkable career."
MARK CHILDRESS · author of *Georgia Bottoms* and *Crazy in Alabama*

"The twenty-two spellbinding stories collected here were written over the past
sixty-six years of David Madden's remarkable writing career, and they demonstrate
the amazing range of his talents and the extremely wide angle of his vision.
Madden's inventive use of point of view allows his myriad memorable characters—often characters who live somewhere on the edge—to speak for themselves
in a rich variety of voices. In a time when linked story collections are so popular,
The Last Bizarre Tale offers the multiplicities of an anthology collection—the best
form to present Madden's innovative fictions. Because David Madden's prodigal
imagination knows no bounds, *The Last Bizarre Tale* will soar into readers' hearts."
ALLEN WIER · author of *Tahano*

Fiction by
David Madden

NOVELS

The Beautiful Greed

Cassandra Singing

Hair of the Dog

Brothers in Confidence

Bijou

The Suicide's Wife

Pleasure-Dome

On the Big Wind

Sharpshooter

Abducted by Circumstance

London Bridge in Plague and Fire

SHORT STORY COLLECTIONS

The Shadow Knows

The New Orleans of Possibilities

THE LAST

BIZARRE TALE

The paper in this book meets the requirements
of American National Standards Institute / National Information
Standards Organization specification z39.48–1992 (Permanence
of Paper). It contains 30 percent post-consumer waste and is
certified by the Forest Stewardship Council.

Library of Congress Cataloging-in-Publication Data

Madden, David, 1933–
[Short stories. Selections]
The Last Bizarre Tale: Stories / by David Madden;
Edited with an Introduction
by James A. Perkins. — First Edition.
    pages   cm
ISBN 978-1-62190-052-8 (paperback)
I. Perkins, James A., 1941- II. Title.

PS3563.A339A6 2014
813.54—dc23
2013039694

THE LAST
BIZARRE TALE

Stories by David Madden

Edited with an Introduction
by James A. Perkins

The University of Tennessee Press | Knoxville

to Robbie, my wife,

to Blake, my son

to Nicole, my granddaughter

CONTENTS

❋

INTRODUCTION

Reading David Madden

for Half a Century

✳

I am standing beside the great stone outdoor fireplace on the gallery of Canaras Lodge with a group of fellow writers at the inaugural *fiction international/ St. Lawrence University Writers' Conference* on Saranac Lake in New York. We have just listened to David Madden's evening fiction reading and talk on the craft of writing, and we are discussing some of his ideas when David walks by.

"Tell us a story, David," says Beth Anton, a rising sophomore English major at St. Lawrence, repeating the words David earlier said a writer likes to hear most.

He stops and, from memory, tells us most of the story "In the Bag" that will not appear in the *Southern Review* until 1977. When he gets near the end, he stops, prompting some of us to wail, "What happens next?" — the words a writer next most likes to hear.

"I don't know yet," David says, and he walks off toward his cabin.

✳

That happened in 1974, but my first encounter with David Madden was in the fall of 1960 at Centre College in Kentucky, where he was teaching a full load of courses in the English Department, and I was finishing up my core requirements on my way to a career in the law. I heard Madden read from his recently published first novel, *The Beautiful Greed*, at a required convocation, but, since he seemed to just tell stories like my relatives back home, for the most part, I was not drawn to him. I never had a class with David Madden, but I have spent my life, since leaving Centre College, reading his work and learning the craft of fiction from him.

By my senior year, Madden had moved on to the University of Louisville, and I had given up on the law. He taught at Kenyon College and Ohio University before moving to Louisiana State University as writer-in-residence. He is now the LSU Robert Penn Warren Professor of Creative Writing, Emeritus. I went on to study literature at the graduate level and wound up at Westminster College, a small liberal arts school in New Wilmington, Pennsylvania. Since I had been hired to teach creative writing and had never had a course in it, after reuniting with Madden at Saranac, I turned to his books to learn my craft. I read *Cassandra Singing* (1969), *The Shadow Knows* (1970), *Brothers in Confidence* (1972), and *Bijou* (1974) before our next meeting. Besides beginning to learn the craft of writing, I learned a great deal about human nature and myself by reading about eccentric and marginalized characters pushed by circumstance to make hard decisions to survive in a world that usually was unaware of their plight.

❋

March 12, 1975, I am in a large lecture hall at Carnegie Mellon University in Pittsburgh. Madden is reading a marvelous passage from his newly published novel *Bijou* in which the grandmother is telling Lucius and Bucky the story of the death of Harl Abshire, a famous bank robber. It is an almost perfect example of the Southern oral story-telling tradition that his grandmother taught him by example and that is at the heart of Madden's craft. After the dramatic reading, Madden signs my brand new copy of *Bijou* "To Jim, Who made a surprise appearance in Saranac and Pittsburgh. Where next?"

❋

"Where next" turned out to be Youngstown State University, where Madden appeared as the featured speaker at the annual English Festival and led a workshop on teaching creative writing effectively. The presentation was based on Madden's long-time, careful reading of fiction that also led to such books as *Writers' Revisions, A Primer of the Novel for Writers and Readers,* and *Revising Fiction*. By then I was beginning to see that Madden is a force of nature, keenly present and focused, who puts his whole being into whatever he is doing at the moment.

⁂

It is April 19, 1976. David Madden is at Westminster College. I have brought him here to give a reading. But it is not a reading. Madden is presenting, from memory it seems, a dramatic dialogue. But the two speakers, Pete and Wayne, are controlled in what they say by the mute cinematographer/editor, Fred, who is showing rough cuts for a documentary about poverty in Eastern Kentucky. The story, "The Singer," is a complex narrative, but Madden delivers it so that it is clear, understandable, and forceful. The audience is still, barely breathing. And when it is over they are wrung out and totally impressed.

⁂

During the late 70s, the 80s, and the 90s, Madden continued to publish fiction, and I continued to read his work and learn from it: *The Suicide's Wife* (1978), *Pleasure Dome* (1979), *On the Big Wind* (1980), *The New Orleans of Possibilities* (1982), and *Sharpshooter* (1996).

I next saw Madden at the South Atlantic Modern Language Association meeting in Atlanta in 2000, at which time he agreed to cooperate with me on a collection of critical essays on his work. Part of that cooperation was a two-day interview at Madden's Baton Rouge home in January of 2002. At some point in the interview, I asked Madden about Reatha Dameron, a character in his story "The World's One Breathing." I was fascinated by the pregnant Reatha Dameron, who is kissed in the parking lot of the A&P in Hyden, Eastern Kentucky, by Harl Abshire, an escaped criminal and her former sweetheart. She drops her groceries and hugs her nine-year-old son to her belly. Harl shoots a deputy sheriff, runs down to the railroad crossing and jumps on a passing train. A bystander asks her, "Did he kiss you?" She says, "Tasted like Pabst Blue Ribbon." I urged Madden to write more about Reatha. "If you like her so much," he said, "*you* write the story." I have. And I included Madden as a character in the tale.

"There was a little guy in a black trench coat that night firing off flash pictures one after another. A week or so later, Betsy Tinker handed me a clipping from the *Harlan Daily Enterprise* as I walked out of church. I have it right here."

She reached into her big leather bag and pulled out a yellowed and folded newspaper clipping. It was part of the front page of *the Harlan Daily Enterprise* headlined, "Abshire Evades Capture Again." The lead article was written by a staff reporter who came over to Hyden the next day, but the photos — one of deputy sheriff Billy Ray Sherman dead on the ground with sheriff Elrod Clevenger bending over him, one of Reatha standing in the parking lot, with her son hanging on her skirt, a ripped grocery bag pressed against her stomach, doing little to hide the fact that she was about seven months pregnant, one of Kenneth McLain banging on the door of Ran's Red Bird bus (That one had the cut line "national television figure witnesses event.") — were all credited to David Madden.

An edited version of that interview (along with one by my co-editor Randy Hendricks) appeared along with eight essays by fiction writers and critics in *David Madden: A Writer for All Genres* (2006). Shortly after that volume appeared, I invited Madden back to Westminster for a reading.

⁎

It is October 22, 2010, Westminster College again. Madden is reading from his just published novel *Abducted by Circumstance*. As usual, he is putting considerable pressure on his audience. It is a difficult narrative, the female protagonist imagining the actions of a woman she believes to have been abducted. In the audience, I am uncomfortable. I have read the novel, and I am able to follow the thread of the story, but I fear that the other auditors will be lost. Then suddenly, Madden ends the reading. There is a silence, and then serious and enthusiastic applause followed by audience questions that convince me that they get it. They get it all.

As part of that interview, in Baton Rouge in 2002, Madden told me a story that illustrated his focus on the power of the art of fiction.

A teacher met me in the hall one day and said, "I'm sick, this is the last day of my class, I can't prepare them for the exam. We were going to review the novel they read for today. Would you take the class for me?" He says, "I assume you've read Ernest Gaines' *A Gathering of Old Men?*" I said, "No, but that's okay, I'll teach your class. Trust me." I started asking the students technical questions . . . What's the structure of this novel? What's the point of view? Which character is the most important character? They alternate among five or six different voices. Well, which one is most reoccurring? And what happens when this one is juxtaposed next to that one? Every single question was grounded in a technical term, none of which they had been taught. Except I'd explain it if it was really difficult. And they said, "This is the best class we've had so far. We're totally confident going into the exam." Because nobody'd ever nailed the damn thing down — the art of fiction. It's always the meaning of it all.

This passage from the interview might serve readers as a way to approach the stories in this volume. Madden is always interested in the techniques of fiction, and point of view is always the first technique he considers, then style as it evolves out of point of view.

In nearly half of these stories, including "Who Killed Harpo Marx," "The Master's Thesis," and the title story, "The Last Bizarre Tale," Madden employs a third-person, central intelligence point of view that allows him to maintain control of the narrative by filtering everything through the perceptions of a single character, thus revealing that character's experience. As Madden tells us in *Studies in the Short Story:*

> The writer presents only what the character sees, hears, feels, thinks, knows. . . . It is as if the author were paraphrasing in the third person what the character would say *if* he were telling the story in the first person. Usually the author adjusts his style and vocabulary to the age, mentality, and social situation of the point-of-view character.

> Many writers favor the third-person, central intelligence point of view because of its great advantage that the reader consistently experiences everything through the character's own mind and emotions with the greatest intimacy and intensity.

In this volume, Madden also employs a combination of his own memoir abruptly juxtaposed to an imagined episode (in "James Agee Never Lived in this House"), first-person narrative (in "A Piece of the Sky"), dramatic monologue (in "By Way of Introduction"), a dramatic dialogue (in "The Singer"), the format of a television documentary (in "Second Look Presents: the Rape of an Indian Brave"), and semi-omniscient point of view (in "Seven Frozen Starlings").

For each of Madden's stories there is an ideal reader (or auditor). That reader is an alert, serious reader of literature (not just someone imbibing formulaic fiction), and one capable of filling in blanks, taking leaps, and making decisions based on an assessment of the characters presented. That reader is an active collaborator with Madden in the creation of the story, and that means that Madden makes demands on his readers; but he earns their effort.

This volume is a dense forest made up of very different trees. The trees are a variety of southern hardwoods that have survived the rapaciousness of clear cutting that has turned the southern forests (read: contemporary southern literature) into a pulp wood lot. They are certainly not ornamentals, the flowering fruit trees of the sort you find in well-groomed, suburban yards. These are not the sort of stories you would find by Cheever or Updike. Mostly these are not the sort of characters you would find in corner offices, commuter trains, or at the mall on a weekend. A good many of Madden's characters are late-night, back-alley, marginal, maimed, hardscrabble characters, characters pushed by unique circumstances to reveal their essential natures, either good or bad.

Each of these stories (with four exceptions) have appeared previously in literary quarterlies. Two of them, "The Singer" and "Second Look Presents: the Rape of an Indian Brave," Madden used as chapters in his 1980 novel *On the Big Wind*. One, "The Headless Girl's Mother," was first published as a chapter in a serialized novel titled *Hair of the Dog*, which Madden wrote in 11 days sitting under a tree up Hot Holler Road just east of Boone, North Carolina, after a year at Yale Drama School. Other stories developed out of longer versions of some of Madden's novels; for instance, "A Demon in My View" is part of a sequel, not yet published, to *Bijou*. For Madden, process is as important as product, and one can learn as much about the process of writing as about the human condition by a careful reading of these stories.

Of the four stories that have not appeared in print before, the most recent in this collection is "Lying in Wait." Presented totally in dialogue, it is one of the most experimental stories in the volume. The reader is urged to read it carefully, paying close attention to the shifting content of the dialogue and to the continued calm demeanor of the interrogator in response to the increasing nervousness of the other speaker.

"These stories," Madden has said, "were written from 1947 to 2008." If you are someone interested in the craft of writing, I suggest reading these stories in the order in which they were written and reading them with Madden's *Revising Fiction* as a close companion. Here is the order of composition of the stories in this volume: "Seven Frozen Starlings" (1948), "A Human Interest Death" (1953), "Hurry Up Please It's Time" (1956), "The Master's Thesis" (1961), "The Singer" (1964), "A Piece of the Sky" (1966), "The Headless Girl's Mother," and "Over the Cliff" (1967), "A Secondary Character" (1972), "Wanted: Ghost Writer" (1973), "Second Look Presents: The Rape of an Indian Brave" (1975), "James Agee Never Lived in This House" (1987), "A Demon in My View" (1988), "A Walk with Thomas Jefferson at Poplar Forest," and "The Last Bizarre Tale" (1991), "The Retriever" (1993), "By Way of Introduction" (1996), "She Always Had A Will Of Her Own," "Who Killed Harpo Marx," and "Lying in Wait" (2008).

⁂

It is February 12, 2013. My wife and I are in Madden's unusual house in Black Mountain, North Carolina. We are talking about this introduction.

"I think you should just tell readers about our interactions over the years and about your reading of my work," says Madden, "just as it happened, nothing too scholarly."

"I like the idea."

"Good," says Madden. "Now that that is settled, let me show you something."

He leads us out the back door to a two-car garage divided into two large rooms lined floor to ceiling with 5,000 books and 150 file boxes full of manuscripts and notes that he is on the verge of selling to his alma mater, the University of Tennessee. "I'm deep into three novels, a screenplay, a book about civil war worldwide throughout history, a ground-breaking book called

Myriadmindedness, and at the moment deepest into a memoir, *My Intellectual Life in the Army.* And over there are the books I read at Fort Jackson and in Alaska in 1954 and '55."

As I said earlier, Madden is a force of nature.

James A. Perkins
NEW WILMINGTON, PA
APRIL 16, 2013

A PIECE

OF THE SKY

I never hit the streets of Knoxville in my Honda till after dark. Even then, I'm afraid somebody's going to notice that under this outfit and these goggles is a clerk in the town's finest bank. I've got one strike against me already — divorced at 22. But riding relaxes me, so I take a chance.

That night I went to see a re-run of *Gone with the Wind*. It let out late. I didn't have anything to do, so I started walking around. Then I was over on Market Street walking along looking at the vegetable trucks parked in the dark, and I was about to climb on my 'sickle, when I got a feeling I wanted to go down that long corridor into the bus terminal and stroll around easy-like and look at the people and maybe flip through a few magazines and listen to the dispatcher call out the towns.

Inside, I headed straight for the men's room and tripped over a woman's foot. It snapped her out of a doze and her chin slid off the palm of her propped-up hand and the biggest blue eyes I ever saw flew open. I muttered sorry and went on in the men's room.

And when I came out, that woman was the first thing I saw. Wide awake, smoking a cigarette, looking, not staring, into space, her legs crossed, one hand resting lightly just where the hem of her powder blue dress touched her knee. Her shoes were blue, too, and even the suitcases on the other side of her feet. Her arms were out of her coat, dark blue, and it set back a little off her shoulders, the satin lining glossy under the lights. I leaned against the pinball machine and looked at the rest of her. Blonde hair that was probably naturally blonde and the blue eyes with the dress and no lipstick. She had a good shape.

I walked across the waiting room and sat down in a phone booth, the door slightly open to keep the light off, and automatically felt in the coin return. It was empty.

She got up the way I never saw a girl get up — not a girl, she was really a woman of about twenty-nine — in that terminal. She wanted a Coke. She smoked and sipped and then she got bored, very bored, or maybe it was just now showing after a long wait and that doze I startled her out of. She reached down beside her where the magazine rack was and pulled out a *Harper's Bazaar*.

I ambled over there, nervous, hot in the jacket, weak in the knees, my heart pounding, why I don't know, since I never in my life picked up a girl, and I sure as hell didn't have nerve to give *her* even a straight look. I flipped through a *True* and tried to glance at her, but I was too close to hide it. So I didn't even see her close up. But I noticed the waitress was looking at her, on the verge for a long time of saying something to her.

Then I remembered that this place was tougher than most about reading the magazines when you obviously weren't going to buy. I wanted to warn the blue lady. The waitress couldn't see me where I was. It really bothered me to imagine that woman being embarrassed by this bitch with a bashed-in chin and heavy penciled eyebrows. So I shifted around to where the waitress, wiping the counter, could see me.

She came over. "Can I help you?"

"Thanks anyway. Just looking."

"Where's your library card?"

When they start that routine, I always get mad. They sound like they just made up the cute question that's supposed to hit the nail on the head. I pulled out my wallet andshowed my draft registration card.

"Where's *your health* card?" I asked.

She blushed and stomped toward the back the way a stupid employee will do when they're looking for the manager to sic on you.

The lady in blue was blushing too. She got up and stooped over enough to put the *Harper's Bazaar* back in the rack.

She smiled at me when she straightened up. I smiled back and put the *True* beside her *Bazaar*.

"I was going to buy it," she said, "but when I sensed she was trying to scrape up enough gumption to say something to me, I felt silly."

I didn't know what to say. "Maybe you'd better get it anyway, if you got a long wait. Let me buy it for you."

"Thanks anyway. I'm too between things to get interested. Four hours before I can get a bus to Athens."

"Georgia?"

"Tennessee."

I saw the waitress lead the manager toward the front from a back booth. He bobbed his head up and down like he was straining to see me over the heads of a crowd of people.

"She got the manager after me. I told her off."

I turned and walked out without glancing back, but wasn't going to run. So I stood there, my back to the long dark tunnel to the waiting room, expecting to feel his big hand on my shoulder. What startled me was a gentle little tug at my leather sleeve by a small hand in a blue glove.

"Four hours is a long time," she said.

"You ever ride a motorsickle?"

She smiled like she thought I was kidding her, and then she laughed. A red neon sign blinked in her open mouth. "Will you wait for me?" she asked, in a voice that meant a few minutes.

"Yes, but I mean it about the motorsickle."

"You do?" She tilted her head and looked at me, her hands clasped just under her breasts. "That would be wonderful."

"That skirt's awful tight."

"Can I manage?"

"Oh. Yeah, far as that goes. Look, I want to avoid somebody who's in that drug store, so suppose I walk up the street there? I'll just amble along where you can see me."

"I'm just going to check the suitcase."

I put my hand on her clasped hands. "You will —" but I didn't finish because I knew by her eyes she would. Anyway, she put both hands over my hands for a second and then turned and went in.

I strolled up toward Market Square and the farmers' trucks. She was quick. The third time I looked back she was coming across against the light. I guess the word is elegant. I never saw a woman walk like that except in a movie, and then, of course, it looked phony. But here it was coming across

Gay Street at midnight. I listened to her sharp high heels get louder as she came up to me on the corner, and four or five feet away I heard her breathing hard, and when she got right up to me, she swallowed. She took my hand and we started to walk. The only light around besides the 40-watt bulb at the corner of this end of the market house was the white brightness of the Gold Sun Cafe. As we turned down Market, I slipped the glove off the hand I held and stuffed it in my pocket. Her skin was so soft I felt on the verge of buckling at the knees.

The 'sickle was parked between two flower wagons, one of the canvas awnings over it. When I unveiled it, and she saw it sitting there dark between the trucks, she stepped back a little and bent forward a little, her hands in her coat pockets and made a faint *oh* sound like I'd produced it by magic. I felt like I had. Some magic had sure produced her.

I put the canvas back over the rear of the truck, then stuck my hand behind it and pulled out a rose. The stem was cold, and after she sniffed it and put it to my nose, the flower itself felt cold. Out in the street, made narrow by the hoods of the trucks and the Dempster Dumpsters along the brick wall of the market house, she had a hard time getting on behind me in that dress.

"I'm going to have to pull my skirt pretty far up. It's pretty late, isn't it?"

"Not many people out."

She settled on the buddy seat, and her arms slid around my waist. I didn't look back at her legs.

We rode and rode and she hugged me tight and hooked her chin over my shoulder to get the wind full force and I felt her long blonde hair whip against my cheeks and across my eyes. We went out Kingston Pike. Among all those fine houses, I thought she'd feel more at home. Then we cut off and wound down and around Cherokee Boulevard, where some even better houses were and where, in the spring, the dogwood was famous. At the big fountain, where the boulevard turned at a bend in the river, I stopped.

I kicked down the stand and walked around in the middle of the deserted boulevard. Off to the right, the river was wide below the high bluffs, and the moon was on the water, and on the left, up under the big trees, were the fine houses spread wide apart, only a few lights.

She whirled around near the fountain in that coat, and as she whirled it turned into wings of blue. The fountain wasn't flowing, but there was a little rainwater catching the moon and some soggy dead leaves around the bottom. I went over to her and put my hands on her cheeks. "Feel," I said.

"You feel," she said, smiling.

Our faces and our hands were ice cold. She had a glove on one hand, and even it was cold, but the bare one stung my cheek.

"It's gorgeous out here. If it were a warm night, wouldn't it be more than you could stand?"

"*They* stand it every night," I said, nodding at the acres of high living.

I slid my arms around her waist under her coat, and we were so tight up against each other that she pulled her coat around us both. Our faces rubbed together until the chill wore off. I stepped back and looked at her.

"What a blue lady you are. You're like a piece of the sky."

"And you're like a piece of the earth."

"And don't neither of us have to talk this way, if *you* feel —"

She nodded and I kissed her before she could stop nodding yes.

I led her by the hand over to the 'sickle. She just slightly pulled back, but the taut feeling was good. I looked out over the river. "Nobody would believe us with you looking like an angel dropped out of the sky and me looking like a lump of the earth come alive."

She didn't laugh. She opened her mouth and kind of threw back her head and a little breathy sound throbbed up out of her throat.

Suddenly, a loud horn sounded very deep and long. She reached for my hand so quickly she pushed my little finger and I jerked back with the hurt. Then a big white light swooped across the trees at the bend in the river, show-ing three willows and a huge private boat dock and a garage and a swimming pool and a patio. Then the light swung over us and leveled out on the river and we saw red and white lights behind the big one.

"River boat," I said.

She made that same little *oh* sound, like I'd produced *that,* too. I laughed, and the horn blew over me. She was hugging my neck when the horn stopped. We watched it go by and saw a man standing in the lighted doorway below the cabin, but the wheelhouse was dark. The low barges full of sand slid forward on the water, and the white light played over the bluffs where two kids came out of a cave and waved their flashlights. Then the horn gave four short honks. The light moved on, and it was dark where the kids were.

"They've got the place," she said. She stood facing the river with her gloved hand behind my head and her bare hand in her overcoat pocket.

"I know one."

I got on and she got on behind me, and I heard her dress go up over her legs just as I struck the motor. And flying in the wind going back up the boulevard her blue coat must have looked good.

The tug made me think of it. That deserted houseboat under the Gay Street Bridge. They'd run all the others off the river as unhealthy and a hazard to the inhabitants and the river traffic, but one man stayed on until one day he got run down by a bus in front of the Tennessee Theatre, and nobody had bought the houseboat or sunk it or what in the two months since. So I rode down Front Street, where the slums are, my light off to keep from attracting attention. Where I turned off into the high dead grass and bushes there was the old Chisholm Tavern up on the hillside behind us that was deserted if we couldn't get into the houseboat. It was a path no wider than my tires between the canes that grew there, but they were pushed back from people coming down to the spit to fish. And then we were out in the open on the huge thumb of gravel and silt, where the Front Street people spend their Sundays fishing and playing horseshoes and just sitting. The moon was bright out there, and the houseboat was still, green and white in the moonlight. The lights of the bridge overhead were fuzzed over with enough mist to soften them, and beyond the trees the uptown all-night lights glowed one tender pink. Across the river up toward the city water reservoir, the huge meat packing company was dark.

On the gravelly bank was the long, wobbly plank that got you onto the porch of the boat. She started to reach down for one end, but I told her not to. I didn't want to see her stoop over and the elegant blue coat fall into an awkward shape. I wanted her to stand there in the moonlight the way she was, her gloved hand holding her bare hand just under her breasts. I got the plank placed and held her hand as we went over the water to the porch.

I felt the floor give under my feet. It was double what I already felt in my knees. There was a heavy padlock on the door and a NO TRESPASSING notice with a note penciled in red: "Otis Claypool is watching this houseboat for us.

Signed, Earl Bob Hocutt." The man the bus struck down on Gay Street in front of the Tennessee Theatre. Maybe Claypool was still watching it for him. She put her hands on my shoulders and read it, her cheek against my ear.

I took her hand, and we walked around the porch that extended around the house, and on all four walls was nailed one of the notices and the same note in red at the bottom.

It looked like kids and plunderers had left the place alone.

"I don't think we should violate his privacy," she said, her head covering part of the notice there at the back door now.

"He's dead."

"Oh."

"But I once sat with him around a fire over on the spit, and I think he liked me. He told me all about himself and that he had lost his wife to cancer in Memphis and had taken to live in a houseboat because the sound of the river running beneath him soothed him. I remember two things he said. 'I don't mind that the river is full of filth. The *flow* is clean.'"

She made that faint *oh* sound. It was almost like a vapor that you could hear. I never heard a sound that wasn't a word, and such a look as went with it, that expressed understanding so completely.

"And the other thing was that the thing that made him sad about his house, which he loved, was that there was no love in it, no woman, that the river itself was certainly a woman, but alone in bed at night that wouldn't do, knowing that. The thing that put a chill on the place was that the warm touch of woman love had never been there."

She started to make that *oh* sound again, and I put my mouth over hers, and the tips of our tongues flicked at each other.

I tried the windows. They wouldn't budge. Then I leaned against the railing and just stared at the back door and held her hand. Suddenly, she pulled away and looked at the lock.

"It's not locked," she said, and I heard a snap. Then the door pushed open, and beyond where she stood in the door I saw the moon come through the four-paned window.

I shut the door behind me. It was fully furnished and neat. Where the moonlight hit the floor the wood was smooth, and I reached down and touched it with my finger and it was clean.

The bed was big, antique oak with just sheets on it. She stood with her back to me, and then she came over to the pool of light and turned a picture so she could see it better.

"He was a Negro?"

"I forgot. Yeah. He was a very nice man."

"He had a nice Negro wife."

"She died . . ."

"Yes, I know."

I went to the window and stared at the moon. Then I heard the long, deep honk of the riverboat, and the light swept through the front door window. It waved around the room and made it look like we were underwater. It was chilly in there but not cold. I guess the sun had been on the tin roof all day long. I turned her around so her face was toward the moonlight.

"But now I can't see you," she said.

"I need to see you more than you need to see me."

"Do you really need to see me?"

I didn't say anything. I pushed my fingers through her hair and pulled her face up to mine and we kissed and her arms went under my jacket and her fingers played over my ribs. Behind my back she pulled off the glove, and I heard it fall on the floor. I pushed back her coat, and she pulled her arms out. It fell heavy, spread out by the bed where there was a round rag rug. I undressed her in the pool of moonlight with the riverboat searchlight wavering over the walls. She kept her blue eyes on me and didn't help me and didn't reach for me, but moved perfectly with me as I undressed her body. She was perfect. I had seen hundreds of pictures, but she was perfect. The riverboat light blending with the moonlight, but flowing over her from different angles and over different angles of her body, made slow moving shadows over her that set her off in relief and made her seem to move while standing still. She was not ashamed. She acted as if she was used to it, but *she* didn't flaunt her body. She revealed it, even though *I* had disrobed it. I watched her go to the bed.

"Turn away," she said. "Nobody looks good getting into bed."

I turned my back and took off my clothes. On her body my hands had been graceful, but unbuckling and unbuttoning and pulling off my clothes was awkward. The river barge honked passing, and I heard the motor chugging as I walked over her coat and put my knee on the mattress. She was under the sheet, one hand holding the other on her belly. I pulled back the sheet and slid under. When my hip touched hers she turned, and I turned to meet her body and our arms went around each other and our lips came together and our mouths blended. She did not smell like perfume. She smelled like wind and flesh. I covered her body with the tip of my tongue and smelled her flesh. She was the most alive living thing I ever touched, the one place where my tongue touched setting the whole surface of her body to quivering. She said *oh, oh, oh,* without cease, and never above a whisper, until I kissed her on the inside of her legs and up and sunk my tongue in her navel.

Then she kissed me the same way and sunk her tongue in my navel, and when I went in she tried to say *oh,* but her breath stopped for a moment as though it had left her body.

❋

When it was over we lay on the bed, tangled, and listened to the river.

"I must go," she said, finally.

I was startled. Listening to the river run under us, I had felt it would go on forever. No, goddamn it, I don't mean that. I mean that that time on the bed seemed without beginning or end, that it was just itself and that there was nothing else.

She dressed and I watched her. Then I got up and helped her put her coat on. She looked up at the moon while I dressed. We left without touching anything but the picture and the bed. I locked the lock, and when we got on the bank, I pulled off the board and shoved it quietly into the river and watched it slide like that sand barge down the river under the Gay Street Bridge toward Cherokee Boulevard.

She got on behind me, and I didn't look at her legs, but I glanced back to see what the coat looked like. She asked me to go around back where the bus would be waiting. When I slowed for a stop sign on the four a.m. street, she asked me to let her off a block from the station.

"I want to watch you, wait with you."

"No. I don't want you to see where I'm going."

"You said Athens."

"Only for an hour. And then I go on."

"Where?"

"No. Please let me off."

I pulled over to the curb, and she got off and straightened her dress.

She stood there with her hands that way, and I wanted her the way she was looking at me to say *oh*, but she just reached down and kissed me and as she drew away said, "Goodbye," in a way that was as final as any human could make it, but that was full of all that we had had. It was so perfect that I didn't try to stop her or try to draw it out. It was so perfect that it spoke for both of us. So she walked down the dark sidewalk toward the lights of the terminal, where one bus was pulling out, and I sat there silently and watched her disappear.

I rode around. I went back out Cherokee and stopped at the fountain and leaned on the rim and stared at the pale rainwater and the sodden leaves. The warmth of her flesh was gone. I was cold. I felt my face, and then I put my hands on the cold stone and suddenly a hardness like ice formed in my throat.

In the early morning dark with the sound of the river running by the bluff, I felt terror. It was a pure, cold terror that flattened up against me like a cold stone wall that chilled through my body and made a spiderlike crawl of ice dash up and down my back. I would never see her again. It was a new kind of terror. I had never felt it on the 'sickle. It was like a birth of the mind, a thing of flesh bursting up out of my mind and slipping down over me like a hood. I wasn't afraid because it was dark by the river with those rocky bluffs looming across the water. I was terrified by the realization that I had made love to a woman the way I had always hoped making love would be — pure and simple and a clean thrust of passion, ebbing like a pain of sheer rapture — and now she was gone, leaving nothing behind but . . . I put my hand in my jacket pocket. Her blue glove didn't make me feel soft and sad and good that I had something to remember her by. It was like a glove used to strangle a laughing child. I threw it into the river.

I wanted the person I had begun to know. It was a natural, clean, good and pure start. But it had ended there. Maybe I ought to be thankful that at last I could make love to a woman without fear or shame or disgust. Maybe I should be thankful it didn't go on and on until our lives became messed up together and I knew her and she knew me so well that the lovemaking could never again be as vivid as it had been. But I wasn't. I cried with rage and helplessness. I had nothing of her but the sweet smell on my hands that the rubber handgrip on the 'sickle had already corrupted and the sound of that *oh* she breathed, but from the start it was part of the lovemaking that was over.

I raced back to the bus terminal. There was only one bus and it said: San Francisco. I asked a baggage man if he had seen a beautiful girl in blue board a bus and he said he sure had. When I asked him which way the bus went to Athens, he just reared back and looked at me. "Man, that Athens bus left four or five hours ago. I didn't pay no attention to which bus she got on. Didn't see her get on. The gates was full and I was shoving baggage. All I seen was her. One of the prettiest white girls I ever saw."

I looked upstairs in the waiting room and asked an old lady to check in the ladies' room to see if my sister in blue was in there, and she came out and said no. I looked up and down Gay Street, and a Lonsdale bus stopped, empty, and opened the doors, thinking I wanted to get on.

"Sorry," I said and went back into the terminal and back down to my 'sickle.

SHE'S ALWAYS HAD A
WILL OF HER OWN

❄

I wish I could live the rest of my life in the dark — no more sunrises, no more sunsets.

She pushes the blanket down with both feet, blots out the sliver of sunrise between the sill and the blinds.

Just her and me.

Another jet taking off shakes the window glass, makes the blinds shudder. *Father is one of them.*

But she will *come out. Into the sunlight, into rooms full of harsh light, and she won't be just mine anymore.*

Mother slams the refrigerator door, protesting the jet's intrusion into her kitchen.

"Jessica! Rise and shine! Oatmeal's piping hot!"

Getting out from under the blankets, she senses herself and another exposed to the chill, simultaneously, her feet and another's feet touching the floor.

She pees, breaks wind. *Does she, too?*

She is hoping she will not show as she is coming down the stairs. *Just us, you and me, as long as I can.*

"There you are." From the bottom of the stairs, Mother looks up at her. *Does she notice?*

At the table, she plunges the spoon into the bowl. *Here it comes, for you and me.*

Mother sits down across from her, *them*, sets down her mug of black coffee. "Anything special happening at school?"

"Math test."

"Math." Mother shivers.

Another jet is shaking all the shakeables in the house. Mother grits her teeth, hunches her shoulders, looks up at the white ceiling, turned gray from the cooking of many military families, imagines the belly of the jet. "Probably that noisy jet pilot father of yours."

"More, please?"

Mother eagerly gets up and fills the bowl. "Does my heart good to see you eat so heartily lately."

Some of it puked into the sewer system, some of it still in her stomach, she leaves the house, warmly wrapped against the sub-zero weather. *Glad you're warm.*

Waiting for the bus, she remembers the photographs of Elmendorf Air Force Base, of Anchorage, of Alaska projected onto the screen in history class yesterday.

Stepping up into the bus, she is aware that in all that vast whiteness, she lives her life, *our life now*, in confined spaces, moving from her room to other rooms, out and into this bus, out into homeroom, into the five other class-rooms, and then the sequence in reverse. Small spaces, like her womb.

Father in his cockpit.

Mother in her kitchen.

All of us in Alaska. But only in moments of transit from one confined space into another.

Alone with her is what she wants to be.

Deep into the math test, she remembers Nakisha coming in from next door, showing Mother her bare belly, saying, "Feel, feel it kick?" And stroking her belly often while she sipped coffee.

She feels so much that she and she are one that she never touches her own belly.

Chad's head hovers over a math problem.

He will look at me one day and wonder why my clothes fit so tight. Then he will look the other way.

She smiles. Being in Sex Ed together had made no difference.

She remembers other girls last year and this year, some leaving school, ashamed, some brazening it out. *What's her name sitting over there by the window.*

But they were all older, mostly seniors, almost women. *Maybe I'll be the only fourteen-year- old, except for that one Eskimo girl in the sixth grade. I liked her. They called her "That klutch."*

She looked over at Chad, chewing his ballpoint again. *Is a father a half a person?*

The two of us are one.

Out of the five rooms, she (*we*) stepped up into the belly of the bus again. Into the living room of the house again. Up into her own room.

"You're so quiet up here all by yourself. Other kids come home, rush to their rooms, lock the door, and ramp up their music. You never play music or even shut your door. Odd, but okay by me. And you aren't reading. What? Are you meditating or something?"

"Something. Yeah, something."

"There's a blinding snow storm outside your window. See it?"

"Yeah."

"The shades are down, Jessica."

"Oh."

"Your father is grounded in Fairbanks. Peace and quiet for a while anyway."

Father doesn't look at Mother much either.

She looks at her mother's belly. *Me in there once upon a time.*

Mother is standing there outside us.

The snow confines father in some small space, smaller than the cockpit.

She is in me. I am in her. We are one.

"Well, whatever. Enjoy yourself. Supper soon."

Listening to Mother's footsteps going down, she imagines her own footsteps, superimposed, going down heavier with *her* one day too soon.

Turning out the light, she remembers a doctor probing her when she had a urinary infection.

Nobody is going to touch you, us.

We will live as many days as we can in the dark.

Her time comes early.

She has a will of her own.

Sunlight off snow glares into the room.

❋

"She has always had a will of her own, Father."

"Jessica, I will say this again. As long as that little hellion lives in my house, she will abide by my will and by the will of the God who created her, whether she goes to church or not."

"Father, she's only fifteen. You have to give her a little space."

"Space? She's got all of Florida out there, and she seems to be covering each acre of it."

"She's no runaway."

"She's run off from home five times since she was twelve, no, eleven, for god's sake."

"She always comes home, she never stays gone long. She's an adventurer."

"I let her stay out until ten, and she's still not home."

"Do you want me to take your Jeep and go out and look for her? If you do, I will."

"When are you going to get your Chevy fixed?"

"Pay day."

"Take my Jeep. Go get her. I'm going to bed. I'll give her a good talking to bright and early in the morning before I hit the driving range."

"Fair enough, Captain."

"Can that. You know, you could have done with a little more willfulness yourself."

Driving around Orlando, Jessica remembered the day of Tanya's birth, Mother saying, "God willing, her coming so early will not be a danger to her."

And Jessica saying aloud, "She has a will of her own."

That became a mantra between them until Mother divorced "that noisy jet pilot" and married a bush pilot, of all things, and went to live in a snow-covered town north of Fairbanks. She reminded her once in one of her few letters from up there, "Well, honey, not to worry. You know as well as I do that she has always had a will of her own."

When Tanya was five and Father retired and bought a little house in Orlando, he reluctantly let them go on living with him in two rooms in the back of the house. "We'll be fine."

And they had been. As long as they were together, they were always fine, whether Tanya wandered or spent a few hours a day in "that noisy jet pilot's retirement home," as Tanya called it, picking up the phrase her grandmother passed on to her in a birthday card message.

Yes, give her some space, Father. But I wish she didn't need it so badly. Something in her seems to need it badly. Not like me.

Jessica still wished she could live the rest of her life in the dark, no more sunrises, no more sunsets. In a room, in the dark, like the fluid dark of the womb, but not herself in a womb. Tanya in her womb. Tanya, whose fifteen-year-old womb may even this instant, in a dark room somewhere — no, on a beach under palm trees somewhere — be lurching to take into itself a rush of semen. Tanya, who took the dark only in stride, and rushed from sunrise to sunset into the light, from the blue sky, from the blue Atlantic, from the blue eyes of underage lovers like herself.

"Don't you be so damned possessive," Father often said. But the other thing he said most often was, "You are too goddamn permissive."

"You seem to be saying, Father, that I am transfixed between the two terms of a paradox."

"Don't dump that literary crap on me, girl."

Her master's thesis on *Paradise Lost* squatted in a drawer somewhere, neglected as her career had been neglected. Neither her quiet Mother nor her noisy Father had encouraged her, nor had their failure discouraged her. *My limbo is my own creation.* Tanya, half her creation, had always mattered far more than her taking the next step, work on a doctorate so she could teach, when Tanya went out into her own wild blue yonder.

Is that her? Looks like her from the back. Yes, that's her.

"Tanya, wanna get in the car?"

"Sure, Mother, but that's not a normal car. That there is an aggressive Jeep."

Tanya jumped in beside Jessica.

Jessica now felt really there, in the Jeep.

Maybe someday we will be one together again. Somehow. Somewhere.

Meanwhile, Tanya, her hair orange now, wore that outfit, blaring to the world, "Look at me, I am not like everybody else, and I am on the move, from space to space."

Not if you are knocked up, honey.

Jessica dreaded that more than anything in the world. She had forewarned her long before Sex Ed, with its abstinence credo. After Tanya, Jessica had dreaded pregnancy even after marriage, even at twenty, even after divorce at twenty-five, even now at thirty.

Possessive, Father? You are damned right. But not wanting to be too possessive, permissive to some extent, hoping that Tanya would thrive on that paradox, that neither would be too oppressive, knowing very well that Tanya, from the trauma of the day of her birth to the prolonged suspense of her adolescence, had a will of her own.

"Not *thy* will, you little shit," her father told Tanya, a tinge of affection in his commanding voice, "but the will of the Almighty God."

Retired, he had discovered that he had time now not only for golf every morning but for God every Sunday and even for Wednesday morning Bible study with eleven of his Republican, country club golf buddies, a few of them former pilots, both bomber and jet.

Oddly, from childhood, every Sunday, without fail and without complaint, even these days, Tanya had traipsed along with "my noisy jet pilot grandpa" to church, Episcopal though it was.

Jessica fondly teased her. "Church tomorrow, kid."

"I know."

"But do you know Jesus?"

"You agnostics give me a pain in the butt."

Well, her tone is amiable.

"Seriously, do you truly believe in all that — those —"

"No, but if it will make my noisy old pilot grandpa happy . . ."

"Would you go to the Unitarian church, if it would make your quiescent old mother happy?"

"Will Jesus be there?"

"Don't be so sarcastic. That word being from the Greek, meaning —"

"The tearing of flesh. I wasn't born yesterday."

"Are you pregnant?"

"I don't know. Are you? Twenty-nine is not too old to get knocked up."

"When I was your age, I was abysmally ignorant."

"But you can't get knocked up on your own, Mother. Did you know that?"

"No, I didn't know that. How *come* I can't?"

"Puns. That takes me back to Middle School."

"Don't run away again, please."

"Don't get knocked up, don't run off from home. Grandma says I have a —"

"I know, 'A will of your own.' It's just that I love you."

"Too much maybe for your own good."

Don't leave me. Don't say that to her. Keep that, along with everything else, to yourself.

The next morning, Sunday, Father came in to the kitchen, sat down at the table prepared for him, ate without a word.

Jessica and Tanya looked at him and at each other, back and forth.

"Fore!" yelled Tanya, long and loud, tapering off as if a little white ball were zooming over the table.

On his last bite, the noisy old jet pilot jumped up. "You can both just kiss my rusty!" He stomped out to the Jeep.

"I think we made his day." Jessica put her hand on Tanya's knee.

Tanya ran after her grandpa.

Almost in a panic, Jessica ran out to the Jeep where Tanya sat beside Father.

"May I come with you, Tanya?"

"You'll have to ask the pilot."

"Will you promise not to sneer at us getting up and down like you did the last time?" Father looked straight ahead.

"That was when Tanya was three and I was still a child myself."

"That's got nothing to do with it. Get in and behave yourself."

Jessica surprised herself, that she was actually hanging on every word of the homily, about the indweller, the Holy Spirit.

"He —"

Or She.

" — lives within you every moment of everyday, for he is the Indweller, comforting you, guiding you."

In the Jeep, she sat quietly, letting the words sink in, without trying to verbalize what they meant in her life, knowing they somehow described the well-remembered experience of her childhood pregnancy.

"She's biting her tongue." Father looked straight ahead at the road.

"I think she wants to be alone." Tanya was looking at her.

Jessica did not respond.

In bed, Tanya was looking up at the ceiling, the overhead light glaring into her eyes.

"Tuck me in, Mother."

The last time she had tucked her in was three years ago, on her twelfth birthday.

In the doorway again, Jessica switched off the light. "Pleasant dreams."

"You, too, Mother."

Going down the hall, Jessica was aware that Tanya had gotten up and opened her door and turned on her little bedside lamp, too dim for reading, and wondered what that half-opened door and that light were meant to comfort.

Jessica craved total darkness but left her own door open, listening to Tanya turning over and sighing deeply again and again, exposing her ears to Father's fitful snore.

She tried to force the blinds to shut completely, but tropical moonlight filtered through slits and lay, patterned, across her legs.

Tanya turning and sighing, perhaps silently weeping, Father snoring — *and, oh, Mother in Alaska trying to sleep in that season of no night* — Jessica wracked her brain to understand why the Indweller, the Holy Spirit, aka the Holy Ghost, comfort and guide, despite the monotonous voice of the priest, had so profoundly, wordlessly affected her, silenced her. Into her consciousness rose words sufficiently clear to declare to herself that she was experiencing nothing religious. She was experiencing, with the force of sheer intuition, a sense that Tanya had been, in Jessica's childhood months of pregnancy, the Indweller, and that their secret communion, unbroken throughout the nearly 240 days and nights, was the comforting darkness of what the noisy old jet pilot and his "brothers and sisters in Christ" called the Holy Spirit.

LIGHTS

✺

"*So late?*" She came so close to him the acrid smell of polish that was drying in a purple sheen on her long fingernails made him gag on the aftertaste of two boxes of Milk Duds. "*Don't you just love these long rainy afternoons in New Orleans when an hour isn't just an hour — but a little piece of eternity dropped into your hands — and who knows —*" As she reached out mechanically to touch his shoulder, he knew the electrical charge he'd always anticipated, giggling, his skin rilling, in the damp room in Charleston, would not be in her fingertips here. Did Bill feel it when she touched *his* shoulder? "*— what to do with it?*" Only her fingertips now, heavy, on his shoulder.

She knew all her lines now, lines he'd learned even before she did, and he knew all his light and sound cues. Is this the way it always is — the night before opening night, all the magic gone, the excitement, leaving only fear? He'd been through all the phases many times before, but now his mother was playing Blanche, the part she'd always dreamed of, in *A Streetcar Named Desire*, the play she loved most — she'd taken him to see three productions and the movie version six times — and Tim had expected not to have to suffer through the cold fear again. "*You-uh-didn't get wet in the rain?*" Thunder shook the window pane. He laughed, knowing such coincidences always broke her up.

But she licked her lips, swallowed. "Oh, if it does that tomorrow night, I'll —"

"*No, ma'am, I stepped inside.*" The way she stared at him, he knew she'd forgotten her line. He fed it to her. "*In a drug store? And had a soda?*"

"No, that's enough. Go out and play."

"In the rain and thunder and lightning?"

"Okay, wise guy. Go look for yourself somewhere in the building."

"Maybe I'm not the one that's lost." He pulled the light cord; the room went dark.

"How do you know until you look?"

Out in the hall, he smiled. "'*How do you know till you look?*' That's a good line."

But he didn't feel like looking for himself. He wished the rain had trapped him in the rehearsal building where he might finally see Harlequin in costume for a run-through. He wished she had let him go to the company's main theater to see the last performance of the one about the crazy family. He felt sad that the next time he saw the grandfather character, he'd be a whole different person. "When you're as old as the grandfather — who is played by a kid not much older than you are — you will have seen maybe five different actors play the part, and you'll have missed two or three hundred others." He expected her to say things like that, and almost every day, she did.

He couldn't get used to the width of the long hallway in this old inn. Wide as the ones in all the schools he had attended. Lightning suddenly lit up the tall black window at the end, showing him the blowing rain and the Shenandoah Mountains. "*You will please clasp your hands together at the back of your neck, Mr. Spade.*" Not as good as last night, just as she was about to drop off to sleep.

She'd turned on the bedside lamp. "Just checking."

He wished he could do Bogart's voice for himself as well as he could Peter Lorre for *her*.

"*Is she coming?*"

"*I don't think so.*" Harlequin and Colombine, still at it. They too would open tomorrow night, a world premiere in the main theatre.

"'*What makes you think she*' — oh, hell!"

"Did I throw you?"

"No, it's okay. I —"

Tim felt suddenly seen, there in the doorway.

"*Is she coming?*"

"*I don't think so.*"

"How do you know she's not coming?"

"Woman's intuition, my dear Harlequin."

The next door down the hall was closed. Most of them were in the two theaters, doing shows, or watching each other, or caught in the rain somewhere.

In the john, Bill was shaving, wearing jock shorts.

"Hi, Tim."

"Hi."

"Got the lights all ready to go for tomorrow night?"

"Yeah, I think so."

"You're doing great."

He shrugged, spread his arms, let his hands slap his thighs, sighing loudly, and got his laugh from Bill, who always encouraged his Harpo Marx routines.

"I just did your lines."

"With your mother?"

"Yeah."

"Can't wait to read the reviews."

"Yeah . . . Well, if you got it — "

"Flaunt it."

"See you."

"See you."

All the other doors were closed. Out or asleep. One door at the other end stood open on an empty room. His back to the black window, he stood, his arms held high, Harpo as a grinning monster. Lightning cast his shadow far down the hall and he enjoyed the way his hands resembled claws. Bill stepped out of the john into the last glimmer of pulsing lights just as thunder rattled the panes.

"Scared the — ! Don't you have a bedtime coming up real soon?"

"Good grief!" He passed Bill opening his door and in the middle of the hall went down the staircase. Three minor players in *Streetcar* burst through the front door, wooden produce market baskets over their heads, drenched in rain, holding their shoes, and slapped their bare feet up the wide stairs past him. "Hi, Tim!" "Hi, Tim!" "Hi, Tim!" and were upstairs before he could think of an ad-lib response to deliver.

He prowled the downstairs hallway. Invited in where four of them were drinking, smoking, laughing, lacing their talk with lines from plays already produced, in rehearsal, or in production, he fidgeted on the edge of a cot, feeling the Harpo mania rise in him, Harpo in *Coconuts*, reacting to boring after-dinner speeches. Each time another actor began, Tim got up, his mouth twisted in excruciating boredom, hissing heavily, hunching his shoulders, and slouched, arms dangling over to the punch bowl, doing wilder and wilder drunk bits, finally letting his head fall innocently on Deborah's shoulder, as if asleep, then suddenly biting her ear, and when she screamed, he began soulfully playing the harp, rising, backing out of the room amid laughter and applause — a routine for which he felt he was justly famous.

Upstairs again, he flushed the toilet, then flushed all the others, and snapped off all the lights.

Janet exited George's room. Clutching her dressing gown at her throat drew the satin material taut over her buttocks, as she slipped down the hall to her door, faded inside. Her husband Paul was probably bowing to applause in the main theater as the curtain fell on the last night of *You Can't Take It With You*.

He went back into the bathroom and locked himself in a booth by the window, listening to the rain on the glass, and waited. He smelled George's cheroot cigars and listened to the booth latch open and catch, and saw his shower clogs under the partition. After a long time, George finished and flushed and went out. As Tim followed, he saw Janet come out into the hall and go into the ladies' room.

✳

The mauve kimono his mother wore as Blanche lay over the foot of her cot. Cigarette smoke still hovered over the room. He unscrewed the cap on the polish bottle and inhaled deeply, making his nose sting, his eyes water, the tip of his tongue taste sour.

He lay on her cot, aslant. "Do I have to tell you *everywhere* I go?" She had never said that to him before. Maybe she had often thought of it and finally this place had made her say it. "I have my own life to lead, you know. Or *do* I?"

Do I?

Where *is* she? He opened the window. By the front porch light, he saw only a few feet of the yard. The rain hadn't slackened, but the thunder only rumbled, off in the mountains, and no lightning ripped the sky.

On her cot, again, sleepy, he couldn't sleep. Looking up into the dim light bulb, he heard each sound, distinctly, and tried to locate it in the rooms, upstairs and down. He listened for her walk coming down the hall, stopping outside the door, as he had listened in many rooms all over the country. Charleston before this one. The night she came home with the news she had waited for all her life, she woke him with wet, Scotch-laden kisses from his pretense of sleep.

"He said I was miscast as Stella, that I was born to play Blanche. Haven't I told you since you were old enough to listen to me that I was born to play Blanche?"

"Is it on the Great White Way?"

"No, darling, but *on the way* to the Great White Way. Summer repertory in an old theater in the Shenandoah Mountains of Virginia. Where Patricia Neal got her start."

Last night, after the run-through for time, she sat in the dressing room staring into the mirror. "I'm too old even to play Blanche." The depression he had seen coming many times before, in dressing rooms he'd lost count of, had hit her right on schedule, as if cued, and with it, the pains in his stomach had hit him.

But as he had listened to her read the play aloud in that chilly room over the Chinese take-out in Charleston, and watched the scenes take shape here in the old church converted into a theater, he'd finally seen why she'd often said, "You know, darling, the part I was born to play is Blanche DuBois."

Staring up into the 40-watt bulb, letting it hurt his eyes, concentrating until he smelled each of her scents in the room at will, he watched her play Blanche Dubois, from curtain up until curtain down, his lights, his sound effects enhancing every movement, every gesture, every word, thinking, If only you could smell Blanche, too, and touch her, still alert for the sound of her walk coming toward their room.

※

He sat up. The rain had stopped. He heard nothing. Her kimono lay twisted under his sneakers.

Bill was the only one of them he knew well enough to wake up at two o'clock.

"Bill, have you seen my mother?"

"Not since dress rehearsal. Tim, it's two o'clock."

"I know." The girl he saw in Bill's bed was Melissa, the ingénue in *You Can't Take It With You.*

He listened at the director's door. Breathing heavily, Jonas slept.

Hearing a door open — Mary was leaving Fred's room, slipping, afraid of being seen, into Mickey's — afraid of being taken for a peeping Tom, he ducked into the men's room.

She might be rehearsing with the Stanley character. He listened at Stanley's door. He didn't recognize the female voice. His heart beat so fast and hard, he couldn't hear other sounds. His sneakers muffled his own movements as he stopped at every door, expecting to hear her laugh.

Downstairs, he looked into or listened at each of the rooms, then went outside where crickets and frogs were loud. Remembering what one of the actors had told him, he touched a tree trunk and all the crickets stopped, but the frogs didn't. When he took his hand away, the crickets started again. When Tim asked him how it worked, the actor had said, "Just nature, that's all."

The rehearsal hall was empty. There was the tree he had helped build and the traveling trunks for the new experimental play about Harlequin.

The sight of a light in the costume room started his heart up again. Certain she was in there, searching for a better dress for Blanche's last scene — she hated the one they had given her — he walked past the false tree, between the trunks, over the chalk marks for blocking to the doorway, and stopped.

☼

Running back to the room, hoping his mother would be there waiting for him, he was shocked to realize that he had not been prepared after all for the sight of a man and a woman actually making love. Carl and Gloria looked like two different people.

His heart pounding, he opened the door.

"*Well, well! What can I do for you?*" Wearing her slip, the kimono on a hangar over the curtain rod at her back, she used Blanche's cigarette holder. The smoke was fresh. She had not been back long.

"Nothing."

"'*I'm collecting for The Evening Star.*'"

"Maybe *you* are, but I'm not."

"You're supposed to say, '*I'm collecting for* The Evening Star' so I can say, '*I didn't know that stars took up collections.*'"

"Yeah, well, where you been?"

"Where *you* been all my life?"

"Cut it out."

"That's Jack Benny's line."

"I don't care if it is. I got my own lines. Where have you been since —"

"Look, who's eleven years old around here? Who was gone when I looked in at two thirty in the morning?"

"I was in the costume room."

"In the costume room. What for? With whom? Mary said she saw you sleep-walking or something downstairs."

"Well, what was she doing in Fred's — no, Mickey's room?"

"*What?*"

"Turn out the light. It hurts my eyes."

"Not unless you're a moth. I haven't seen a light that weak since you were born."

She pulled the string and he put his hands over his ears to shut out the sounds as she got into bed.

"Hey. Hey, kid. Hey! Do Peter Lorre for me. Hey! You asleep? Goodnight, darling. . . . Poor thing is so tired . . ." Her yawn sounded like a stage yawn. But in a few minutes her sleep was real.

When light warmed the window sill just under the hem of her hanging kimono, he was still seeing Gloria and Carl in the costume room, still trying not to imagine his mother in some other room. "Your father was the world's worst actor," she had told him, years ago. "Oh, yes, he was an actor all right." In eleven years, Gloria and Carl would have a kid his age. But would Carl still be with them?

❁

"Are you all right, Tim?" Maurice whispered from the doorway.

He nodded, without turning from the little window where he stared down at his mother.

"*Come here, I want to kiss you, just once, softly and sweetly on your mouth!*"
She crossed quickly to the young man character.

"You missed '*the blue piano.*'" Maurice seemed irritated.

Watching his mother kiss the young man while people sat all around her, their laps, hands, legs, and feet in warm light spillage, their faces in shadows he made, he reached back, let the tape roll, faded in "*the blue piano.*"

"What happened, Tim?"

He shrugged, listening.

"*Now run along, now, quickly! It would be nice to keep you, but I've got to be good — and keep my hands off children.*"

The pains in his stomach were not for her. In the light he had made for her, she knew she looked fabulous.

As Carl, playing Mitch, kissed her forehead and her eyelids and her mouth, he twisted the knob viciously, bringing the polka tune up loud enough to cover her sobs of gratitude and drown out one of her greatest lines: "'*Sometimes — there's God — so quickly!*'"

Maurice reached over Tim's shoulder and faded down the bright lights that drenched her as embarrassed applause died down, making her walk off a fully lit stage at intermission.

"What the hell's come over you, Tim! Dress rehearsal you were perfect!"

"Your mother is on the verge of hysterics!" Jonas came charging in. "Maurice, I told you he's just a kid! He shouldn't —"

"Where's Joe?"

"Plotting lights for *The Death of Harlequin.*"

"Get him over here! Tim's sick or something. You sick, kid?"

He shook his head.

"Should I get Joe? We got five minutes to send over there!"

"I can do it."

"We're trusting you, Tim. Your mother's counting on you. Without you, she could fall on her face tonight — *in front of all those people.*"

"Besides which, Carl will kill you if he has to chase that spot once more."

"Tim can do it. Let's go."

Jonas and Maurice went outside the booth, started down the ladder.

He heard Jonas say, "Maurice, this is a professional company."

"Well, I wanted to give the kid a chance."

"You mean to give *you* a chance with his mother."

As he brought the lights up on Stella putting flowers on a table set for supper with a birthday cake, he wondered whether they *knew*, just by looking at her. "You can always tell," a boy had said in the latrine in one of the schools. "It shows. They look different."

His mother waited for her cue in the dark behind the flat. When she came out of the bathroom, a towel like a turban around her head, he dimmed the light on the door, and she broke character to look up at the light booth.

Mechanically, mindlessly, pretending he was a robot, he made all the moves he had rehearsed.

"*I've been onto you from the start!*" Stanley walked into the bedroom. Tim broke out in a cold sweat.

"*Don't come in here!*"

The pain in his stomach so fierce he tried to keep from fainting, he forgot to cast the "*grotesque, menacing shadows.*" With the panic of an actress who has been thrown by the unexpected, she lurched for the telephone and jiggled the hook as Stanley went into the bathroom and closed the door.

"*Operator! Operator! Give me long distance, please!*"

Tim filled the night "*with inhuman voices, like cries in a jungle.*"

But the timing and rhythm of his manipulations of "*shadows, lurid reflections*" along the wall was awkward, inept. He forgot to make the back wall transparent until the prostitute had already rolled the drunkard. When the audience saw the drunkard struggling with the prostitute, they were confused. Tim blew a policeman's whistle and they stumbled off.

When Stanley came back in and put the receiver on the hook, Tim didn't start "*the blue piano*" and "*the locomotive.*" She could not crouch, could not press her fists to her ears until it went by. Seeing the panic in her face, Stanley jumped her line, and when she went back and delivered hers, he got lost. As they tried to recover and get through their dialog, Tim drowned them out with "*the blue piano*" and jungle voices. She smashed the bottle on the table and Tim blacked out all the lights. Stanley jumped, panic in his voice, to "*Oh! So you want some roughhouse! . . . Tiger — Tiger! . . . We've had this date with each other from the beginning!*"

Tim killed the sound and left the house black. He felt the urge to run, but the blackness nailed him to the chair as the beat exceeded rehearsal count, and the audience rustled and coughed apprehensively. The door to the cramped booth opened behind him, giving a bump to his chair that he felt this time as a shattering jolt. He stared into the dark, recognizing Jonas' scent. Maurice fumbled for the lights, made a mistake, covered it. *"Sound of water can be heard running in the bathroom."*

"Drew an inside straight and made it, by God," said Stanley, inevitable against catastrophe, doomed to say it, all over the world until the end of the world.

His own behavior so shocked and bewildered him that he did not move. The final scene played out, and he hardly breathed.

"This game is seven card stud." BLACKOUT.

As the applause dwindled, he began to pant. Hearing the commotion of the audience getting up to leave, he jumped up and squeezed out of the control booth before Maurice could turn to him.

She was crying hysterically as he swept past her and ran out of the former church building and down off the hill and past the company's main theater, where *The Bat's* first performance was still playing, and into the woods on the slopes behind the town.

※

As he pushed open the door, she turned out the light. Well-timed, and no coincidence. The realization that she had provided him with darkness to cover his embarrassment and that she couldn't then be very angry with him started tears of gratitude and relief. Undeserving, he eased across the room and sat on his cot, wincing at the loud creak of the springs. He sensed how lucidly awake she was, how patient.

"Why did you *do* it?" he waited for her to say. Or "Why did you do that to *me?*" Or "How could you do that to your own mother?" Walking in the woods, he had asked all the possible questions and answered them, and just hearing in his head his lame excuse, "I got sick," made him feel queasy.

He heard her breathing, wondered if he only imagined it, or confused hers with his own. The beating of his heart made him lie down, but the mattress seemed to pulsate. He wanted to say "I got sick" without waiting for her question, but he couldn't utter the line.

"Okay, Harpo, spill it."

He'd hoped she'd say something like that — Harpo being mute — to dispel the darkness and everything in it. Of all the characters that over-populated their life together, he loved Harpo most, not just to amuse her, to do a bit with her, but because Harpo was real, his zaniness made sense, and he looked forlorn. Tim didn't want to *be* Peter Lorre or Bogart.

"Wanna buy a duck?"

She did Groucho better than any *man* he ever heard. He wanted to play that scene in the dark, as Harpo, in Chico's place. But would that work? The material could be reshaped, couldn't it? As Harpo, he lay awake in the dark, his mouth a cherubic smile, his eyes, bugged.

⁂

When he awoke, he looked at her cot, neatly made. His was mangled and moist with struggle and sweat, and smelled of fear.

When he was unusually effective in one of his routines, she often said, "What'll you do for an encore?"

"I have always depended on the kindness of strangers." Why had that line made him hate her last night? He sat up on the edge of the barracks cot. He had punished her impulsively last night, ruining her opening night performance in the play that had waited for her at the end of many highways and rooming house and hotel-motel corridors. He still didn't know why. He expected that one day, he would, but somehow, somewhere, sometime between her hysterical tears backstage and his near dawn entrance, *she* had understood. Turning out the light when she had heard him at the door had been a statement, sign language. Her empty cot, well-made, that she often left unmade, sign language, too. He let that sink in, and hoped he would at least feel what it meant before he saw her again. But what then? What could he say for himself? Maybe she would let him be Harpo today, let him take her hand and use it for a leg rest. As Harpo, he could leave this room, wander, and be mute, and so survive this long day.

In the dining hall and during the day, he moved in orbit around her, caught her glances, but stayed beyond speaking range and ear-shot. And ducked farcically to avoid Bill and Jonas and Maurice and the casts of the two shows running and the two in rehearsal.

An hour before the doors of the old church opened to let the *Streetcar* audience in, he climbed into the hot, cramped light booth and pantomimed working the lights for the show as gracefully as Harpo plucking his harp.

Maurice slammed the door in against the back of the chair, obviously startled to find someone sitting there. "Oh, my God, I don't believe this. Tim! Up — and out! Do you hear me?"

Tim nodded, smiling, his eyes bugged.

"Then move it!"

He shook his head, smiling, his eyes bugging larger.

"Listen, you little jerk!"

Tim made a frowning, bugle-mouth face.

Recognizing the Harpo routine, Maurice tried to smother a giggle. "So you want to wreck her performance again tonight?"

Tim shook his head no, smiling, and mimed harp-playing.

Someone walked under the elevated booth.

"Jonas? Are you there?"

"Yeah."

"Speak to you a minute? We've got this little problem."

He left the booth, climbed down.

Tim heard only Jonas' parting comment. "Just don't let *her* know that little monster is up there."

Maurice came back inside the booth and huddled in the corner.

"Okay. For *her* sake. But one false move, kid, and you won't leave this booth alive."

It went so smoothly that at intermission, Maurice said, "Okay, Tim, okay. Fine. You are forgiven. *She* forgives you. If I knew it wouldn't throw her, I'd leave you alone up here, but I've got to stay so she'll think it's me up here. Pretend I'm invisible."

I don't want her to know I'm up here, either, Tim started to say. But the silence enhanced his sense of exhilaration. He remained mute.

Scene Nine, in which Mitch confronts Blanche. She was great — so that meant that to everyone else maybe she was at least good, almost certainly not mediocre, and definitely not bad. Well, she was fabulous.

"But what'll you do for an encore?" At the end of the summer run, what *would* she, having done the role of her dreams, of a lifetime, do? Would agents swoop down out of New York and discover her? Or the movies? Or television? Or just another summer stock director? Or would she take him bravely by the hand and set out for another city known to have a strong little theater? "Little?" He didn't like the word.

"I don't think I ever seen you in the light." Mitch was about to snatch the paper lantern off the light bulb, expose her to the cold light. It was all so predetermined, precise, and inevitable.

He shrank from the moment. He would soften the white light the script notation demanded.

No, to change anything, even out of compassion, would cause another catastrophe. Blanche wasn't his mother, anyway, was she? She was, and she wasn't. But at this moment, his mother was an actress, and by being true to the actress's expectations, to the artist's vision, and the director's rehearsals, he felt lucidly, he could help her most — by exposing Blanche. He could put his love into that. The actress knows what is coming, but the character does not, and in a way he couldn't focus, his mother was neither.

Mitch ripped the paper lantern from the bulb.

"I don't want realism," said Blanche. Mitch laughed. *"I want magic! Yes, yes, magic! I try to give that to people. I misrepresent things to them. I don't tell the truth, I tell what ought to be truth. And if that is sinful, then let me be damned for it! — Don't turn the light on!"*

Mitch crossed to the switch, snapped on the light, stared at her. Blanche cried out, covered her face. Mitch snapped the light off again.

When she reached the moment in Scene Ten when he had plunged her briefly last night into hell, her face showed, only to his eyes perhaps, a faint sense of apprehension, but when that moment faded, she ended the rape scene as rehearsed. And when, toward the end of Scene Eleven, Blanche said, *"Please don't get up. I'm only passing through,"* he resisted his natural inclination to respond to the parallels life readily provided and merely admired how well she delivered the line, had delivered it as herself in many cities and situations over the years.

The final line was his favorite because it was so frankly a cue to the light man to go black. *"This game is seven card stud."*

As she took bows to such applause as he knew she would thrive on for days, he motioned to Maurice, who was, or perhaps was not, his mother's lover, to take the controls. Elated to have been in control for awhile, he backed out of the booth, saying, "Don't ever tell her I worked lights tonight," as if Harpo had finally found his voice.

WHO KILLED

HARPO MARX?

✳

Having resigned his position as WQLX-TV's evening anchor to write a novel at long last, having lost everything in the divorce settlement soon afterwards, having hitch-hiked for the first time since his college days to return to the rented room in the house in Ogunquit, Maine, where he came to die twenty years ago after breaking up with the girl who eventually became his wife, having exhausted his savings, having wadded up the new landlord's curt eviction note, missing his son, wishing his feet were not so cold, he was staring out the window into the iced-burdened tree tops when he saw below the front door of the house next door open.

Out stepped the elegant — even when she wore ice-fishing togs — neighbor lady, carrying two huge suitcases easily. Coming out close behind her, her husband exposed his hairless head to the sub-zero wind chill.

She twisted around, gave him a look, and waited while he went back inside and came out under a furry hat that diminished the human look of him. Leaving the door open, he followed his younger-looking wife to the snow-covered car.

Fumbling with the suitcases, he only got in her way as she hoisted them into the trunk.

Pointing at the passenger door, the wife gently pushed her husband toward it, turned gracefully back toward the house.

From the high window, he watched the lady lock the front door and walk, twirling the keys, back to the car. The door open, she looked around as if in command of all she surveyed, looked up, saw him at the window, waved almost dismissively, got in, and drove herself and her husband away.

The next morning, he re-read the new opening line of "Powder Burns," based on all the women he had known from junior high on. "You shape-shifting son-of-a-bitch," she snarled, "with you, it's always the same old story."

As the line sank in, he stared out into the treetops where the ice was cracking and falling, melting and dripping, then down at the neighbor woman's driveway where the morning paper was missing.

A knock at the door was even louder than yesterday.

"Yes, what is it?"

"It's you, sir. *You*, who don't pay your rent. Pack up your computer and your toothbrush and vacate, my man."

"I just need to finish revising this chapter, sir, and then, I promise, I will be out of here."

"No, what you need, my man, is to hit the stairs in five minutes. I'll be standing down there, looking up to see."

He listened to the landlord go down the stairs, landing his feet loudly, like exclamation points at the end of his final sentence.

His St. Vincent de Paul battered suitcase loosely filled, he left the room, leaving the door open.

The landlord stepped politely aside to let him pass.

Walking briskly to keep warm through Ogunquit, as if he were touring the little resort town the tourists had deserted in September, he remembered every moment of that week he first walked here, thinking of killing himself. The more he had thought, the more a play took shape in his imagination. It was among the few things he had left stored in Indiana, along with a slew of other memorabilia of various kinds and types and degrees of sentimental and intellectual value.

The wind off the Atlantic drove him into the fortress-like library, the few cafes and other businesses until they all closed as early November darkness set in and lights came on in the houses of the natives set among the more numerous shut-up houses of the summer people. He was seriously pondering the good and bad consequences of gently breaking into one of the summer houses to keep warm but stopped to think about the fact that the electricity would have been cut off, leaving the heating units dead.

Up ahead was the two-story house where he had finally gotten into his novel in that very same room where years ago he had thought he was suicidal, having lost Brenda, but where he had finally realized he was only melancholy and in that state of mind wrote that unproducable play, "The Idealists."

Evicted, he walked toward the house next door.

Just as he had supposed, the back door was locked tight. But, of course, the window next to it proved to be evidence of small town trust. He raised it smoothly, the only sound a whisper.

The shades were down in the bedroom, so no one would see the attractive glow of the electric heater.

In case his old landlord could see the light, he unplugged the refrigerator before opening the door to feel around inside for something, anything to eat.

"Ravenously" he "devoured" the hard butt of a loaf of salami. The beer was one of his favorites, but he had to hold it to the glow of the heater to see that it was indeed Miller, but Lite.

The phone was live. TV too then, but he wouldn't risk that.

Taking a hot shower in the dark was a neat new experience.

He had to find and spread another blanket to make the bed cozy.

"How you all doing?" He turned to his left and then to his right, home to the wife and the husband, but the bed was wide enough for the three of them, king-size.

As he reviewed the events of the day, other literary words and phrases came to mind, some of which he spoke aloud, liking "the ring" of them. They lulled him into a "deep sleep."

In the middle of the night, coughing and sneezing fits woke him.

Throughout the next day, he moved freely about the house, thankful that the lady had drawn all the shades.

Walking from room to room, to pump himself up, he declaimed "Powder Burns!" and recited the opening line several times in several TV announcer voices, made hoarse by his cold.

The husband seemed to have no desk, but the wife's narrow, shallow desk, where she paid bills and probably wrote letters, worked fine.

Day after day, the writing went very well, literary words and phrases coming to him as he moved about the house and as he lay in half sleep and even in dreams, so that he woke with them "on the tip of his tongue," mostly unusable, such as "defang that glass of water."

His cold passed, a mild one.

At the end of his most productive day, he dropped down upon the bed and into what he would have perhaps called "a profound slumber."

Dreaming of Brenda and Shane speaking to him, words he couldn't quite make out, he asked, "What?"

"I said, what are you doing in my wife's bed?"

He looked up at the husband, who leaned over him, one knee braced on the edge of the bed. Snow powdered the shoulders of his outdoor coat.

"What? Oh. Me? I'm — well, I'm, just resting . . . Sort of . . ."

"Richard, are you talking to yourself?"

"I don't think so, darling."

"Then —" The wife appeared in the doorway, one arm still in her coat. "What are you — *Who* are you?"

"I found him just lying here."

"You look exhausted." The wife slid the rest of the way out of her coat and gracefully draped it over the foot of the bed, covering one of his feet.

"Yes, I am. I'm just a writer, Mrs. —"

"Seacrest. Seacrest, like the hotel in — Never mind. Don't get up. I need something in that drawer."

What she needed was a .22 revolver. But she wasn't pointing it, holding it at her side, but the grip and the trigger finger just right.

"Explain yourself, sir." She said it as if drawing upon a line from a repository.

He explained himself to her satisfaction, but she kept the revolver in hand, as non-threatening as a lily plucked from her garden —"in the spring."

He listened as she verified his story on the phone with her neighbor next door.

A lucid image of his vacant room on the second floor of the house next door came to mind.

"We're having a light supper. That is, if you haven't eaten us out of house and home."

"There are all those frozen dishes."

"They will do. Come help, but keep your distance, Mister Writer."

"You can call me Philip."

"I do not feel so inclined. Richard, he's left your favorite untouched."

The teriyaki beef with vegetables was pretty delicious for frozen food, but the table manners left something to be desired, the revolver lying by her side like an irritable aunt visiting.

"Now, let's get serious. What is your next move?"

"Can you give me a little time to think? I'm broke, with no prospects."

"I'll let you shovel the walkway." Richard smiled, shrugged.

"Richard, my dear, we are talking."

Richard nodded, acknowledging the fact.

"I appreciate the light supper, and I will now pack up and vacate the premises, as they say. First, may I use your bathroom?"

"You certainly may, and then we must bring this really charming episode to a close."

"You talk the way I sometimes write."

"I'm teasing you, Philip. I'm just a country girl from Eastern Kentucky. We've now made our summer home our only and final home."

She looked to be no older than late fifty. The husband maybe five years older.

He lingered in the bathroom. Through the window above the bathtub, he saw the wife, revolver still in hand, delving into the trunk of the car.

When he opened the bathroom door, the husband was standing outside, so close his nose was only inches away, his very blue eyes electric with a kind of scientific intelligence.

The husband took Philip by the hand and led him to a handsome door that opened upon a dingy flight of stairs that creaked all the way up into what proved to be a low-ceilinged attic, everything in it as neatly organized and arrayed as the furniture in the rooms below.

"Let me show you my pride and joy. She says it ought to be covered."

Richard removed a cloth, revealing a painting on an easel.

"And there you see my father, a gift from my mother. Do you see?"

"Oh, yes. And the resemblance to you. 'Uncanny.'"

"I loved my father very much. My mother, too, of course. It was a gift from my mother when I was ten, don't you know?"

"Yes, I know. You told me. And I am glad you showed it to me."

"Are you up in the attic again, Richard?"

Richard slowly, lovingly draped the portrait of his father.

"Richard?"

"He's up here with me."

"Will you two please come down?"

"She wants us to come down, Richard. We're on our way down, Mrs. Seacrest."

"I saw you on her bed, and I wanted you to see my father. I never called him daddy."

Richard's wife stood at the foot of the stairs, one hand holding the door open wide, the other holding the revolver, even less threatening, her arm across her breast.

"He wanted to show me the portrait of his father."

"Yes, I know. Richard, if you would like, there's a cup of hot chocolate on the kitchen table. But do say goodbye to Philip."

As Richard's handshake got firmer, the blue of his eyes shone more and more electric, intelligent. Without a word, he turned crisply and went down the hall toward the kitchen, passing the wife's wide bed where Philip had slept so soundly, memorably.

Turning to Richard's wife, Philip realized that in his contented rambling through the house, he had seen no other bed.

He wondered who Richard was talking to in the kitchen.

"Whoever painted that portrait of your husband's father was very talented."

"Talent and arthritis do not go hand in hand." Richard's wife smiled bitterly, holding up her right hand, afflicted obviously with arthritis.

Richard's voice came from the kitchen more loudly, garbled.

Mrs. Seacrest softened her voice. "I painted it twenty years ago for our son's birthday. A perfect resemblance, if I may say so myself. When our son moved to Thailand with a position in the state department, he left it with us for safekeeping."

"Not Richard's father then, but—"

She nodded and laid the revolver on the polished corner table.

"Aren't you even going to say goodbye to me?"

"Richard wants you. Do you mind? Then you can go, and with our blessing."

She took his hand, and he felt some bills along his palm.

"That lady in there won't tell me, afraid it will only upset me, but you are new here, so maybe you will tell me, Mister Writer, before you go, please tell me, Who killed Harpo Marx?"

As he rode the Greyhound bus, Maine south, he mulled it over.

JAMES AGEE NEVER
LIVED IN THIS HOUSE

✳

1980. That was the year the poets died. Elegant, silver-haired George P. Elliott, of a heart attack. Malcolm Braly, ex-con turned writer, killed at an intersection, a week after I first met him. James Wright, whose ambiguous line, "I have wasted my life," I had quoted to my students to enhance James Agee's confession, in a letter to Father Flye, "Meanwhile I am thirty and have missed irretrievably all the trains I should have caught."

The year the poets died, I was visiting writer at the University of Delaware in New-ark. Encouraged to teach whatever I wanted to, that winter of 1980, I took on the daunting task of reading *Let Us Now Praise Famous Men* with fifty sophomores. I had always wanted to explore similarities and contrasts between *Let Us Now Praise Famous Men* and *Moby Dick* and *Walden*. I asked them to consider Ishmael's first-person narration as only a device — we soon forget him and it is Melville's searching voice we follow. Look, I said, at the Agee-like polarities in the "Cetalogy" chapter and, soon after, in "The Whiteness of The Whale" chapter. Like Agee, Melville often talks to the reader about the mechanics and difficulties of writing the book — the whale Melville pursues is the book itself. Then we looked in *Walden* at the "Economy" and the "Solitude" chapters as *Famous Men* sort of polarities. The extrovert Melville of *Moby Dick* and the solitary Thoreau of *Walden* are combined, I suggested, in the Agee of *Famous Men*.

My fifty students at Delaware (all non-English majors) resisted Agee. They weren't interested in Alabama sharecroppers back in the mid-1930s, and they were certain that Agee was interested more in *himself* than in those sharecroppers. Melville gave them fits, too. Moby Dick the whale was lost, for them, in a dead sea of whale lore and nautical jargon. Thoreau's simple two-year experiment in his cabin in the woods by the pond made simple sense. A good place to go off by yourself and watch a lot of television without being bothered by parents for class deadlines. As for Walker Evans' photographs in Agee's book, they could not see what he saw in such faces.

I was discouraged. Maybe if I could persuade them of the relevance of *Let Us Now Praise Famous Men* to a decade closer to 1980. . . . I read to them from my own book *Remembering James Agee* where Robert Coles, the social psychologist, tells of rereading *Famous Men* very carefully — with voter registration workers and Vista volunteers doing field work in the South in the early sixties — feeling close to Agee, but arguing with him. "I never during the years I spent in the South allowed myself to be separated from *Let Us Now Praise Famous Men* . . . when hundreds of college students, and not a few of their younger teachers, flocked South to stage sit-ins and run 'freedom schools' and so often, repair evening after evening to a line or two of James Agee's prose." "Who's Robert Coles?" a young man in the back row asked. Suddenly, the hundred or so desk chairs that had been piled haphazardly at the back of the enormous room they had put me and my class in became a metaphor for the class, which had only five more meetings to go.

That early March weekend in my drafty summer cabin below the confluence of the Elk River and Chesapeake Bay, I intended to escape into my own work. I was just starting a Civil War novel called *Knoxville, Tennessee*, now, nine years later, renamed *Sharpshooter*. Finished, it is now giving New York editors as much trouble as *Let Us Now Praise Famous Men* gave my Delaware students. I don't mind thinking that reading and rereading *Let Us Now Praise Famous Men* over the past thirty years influenced the ten years' writing and rewriting of *Sharpshooter*, in which I use many contrasting techniques and satisfy no more expectations for a Civil War novel than Agee did for a study of sharecroppers.

I had no class on Fridays, so I tried to write about the sharpshooter who shot General Sanders from the tower in Bleak House on Kingston Pike, but the ice had broken up on the bay just outside my window, and although the white dog no longer walked out on the ice and howled, the geese were flying over, and I was sad about the deaths of my poet friends, one after the other, and missing the woman I loved, my wife, and I kept seeing Agee in the sharecropper's house in Alabama, starting his book in the very house that was as much his subject as its inhabitants were — "It is a late summer night, in a room of a house set deep and solitary in the country; all in this house save myself are sleeping; I sit at a table, facing a partition wall . . . writing, with a soft pencil, into a schoolchild's composition book . . . just now, I am entirely focused on the lamp, and light." That's my image of Agee writing *Let Us Now Praise Famous Men*, in Alabama, in Frenchtown, Brooklyn, Manhattan. A night writer, he inhabited his subject like sleep. The ruminative quality of his writing is best described in his own phrase, "the seining of experience."

And so, bright and early Saturday morning, without first taking my morning run through the little fishermen's village because one of my neighbor's three Dobermans had broken loose and bitten my hand a few mornings earlier, I reached for my camera and set out northward in my 1962 Dodge Dart for Frenchtown, New Jersey, on the eastern shore of the Delaware River where, they say, the current is unusually treacherous.

The landscape was brown and the sky gray, but I felt some comfort in the lure of the image of Agee writing in a pool of kerosene lamplight at a table in the kitchen of what I was certain would prove to be a ghost-white house like the one he lived in — "successfully disguised from myself as a child" — in Knoxville, Tennessee, like the one in that photograph where his hand clutches that porch post in a movie still for Stephen Crane's "The Bride Comes to Yellow Sky," for which he wrote the screenplay, and in which he had a minor role as the town drunk. Maybe I would show that movie to my students, so they could see Agee, alive, and hear his voice. His compelling voice. Maybe I would ask Helen Levitt, the photographer with whom he made the documentary movie *In the Street*, to lend me her print of Agee's other documentary *The Quiet One* — the only print that has Agee's own voice narrating his script. No, no, no, my tone of reverence has probably alienated my students. I should tell them of my own hate-love responses to Agee.

I have had a long struggle with Agee. I have had more ambivalent, tangled feelings about him than about any other writer, except Thomas Wolfe. When *A Death in the Family* came out in 1957, I was still a student, living a block away from Agee's childhood home, writing a novel set in Knoxville. That Agee was then the famous Knoxville writer I dreamed of becoming made me hellishly jealous. Ironically, it was Agee's editor David McDowell who published my own novel a decade later. Over the years, in my awareness of the many parallels between his life and work and my own, I frankly resented but reluctantly admired James Agee. When McDowell invited me to attend Agee Week at St. Andrews in October 1972, I didn't want to go. But then Edmund White asked me to write a page or two about the celebration for the *Saturday Review*. Before I went up there I reread some of Agee and decided, "I don't like Agee." But when I came back to Louisiana I wrote 170 pages about Agee Week.

I deliberately did not call my editor, David McDowell — who had been a student at St. Andrews when Agee visited his old teacher Father Flye there just before going to Alabama — to ask for the address of the house in Frenchtown where Agee had plunged most deeply into the making of *Let Us Now Praise Famous Men*. I drove up and down the few streets of Frenchtown, confident that I would intuitively recognize the very house where he and Alma Mailman took refuge from *Fortune* magazine and New York City and with only an enormous bed, a rocking chair and a table, lived in sin and played rambunctious duets on the piano and made drawings of each other's faces and made a pet of a house mouse and kept two goats.

I parked my car and walked, and scrutinized each house closely, until I saw, next door to an odd-shaped white cinder block building, a ghostly white house. *That's it.* In that very house James Agee wrote *Let Us Now Praise Famous Men*.

I felt his presence luring me across the street, up the cracked walk to the porch steps. A sense that the house was empty made me feel as if I were already inside, walking slowly from room to room, the Agee aura filling me with a sense of communion — forty-two years ago alive now in me. But through the glass in the door, I saw signs of occupation. No one responded to my knock.

The building next door housed the fire engine and a public library downstairs and a church upstairs. All three were shut up tight until one o'clock for the public library (full surely of all Agee's books and files of information on his year spent in Frenchtown, writing one of the great classics of American literature), until Sunday for the church, and until a fire broke out for the volunteer firehouse.

To verify my intuitive recognition of Agee's house, I started walking, looking for a Frenchtown native to accost. From the next cross street, which paralleled the Delaware River, I saw the town newspaper building up ahead. The front door stood open to the first fair day of March — the sun had come out. Nobody sat behind the seven or eight desks, except, way at the back, a young man, a little older maybe than my students, reading a paperback, cocked back in a straight chair, his feet propped up on a desk.

"Say!" I said, startling him. "I wonder if you could give me a little information?"

"Well, I'll try to," he said, keeping his place with his finger.

Certain the newspaper had done stories on Agee's sojourn in Frenchtown, I asked, "Could you tell me exactly which house Agee lived in?"

"Who?" I was close enough now to see clearly the look on his face.

He could see, I'm certain, the contempt on my face. "Agee. James Agee, one of the most famous writers in America, *known all over the world*, and I *thought* I could come here to the newspaper to find out *exactly* which *house* he lived in."

"In Frenchtown?" Now I was uncertain what *his* face and voice expressed. "Yes."

He jumped up, letting his chair slam down on its legs. "*James Agee* lived *here* in *Frenchtown?*"

"So you know who Agee *is?*"

"I was reading *A Death in the Family* when you walked in."

Well, this was certainly the kind of mystique I had hoped to experience in Frenchtown.

"I just happened to pick it up in a junk store because I liked the title."

"Then you *don't* know who James Agee is?"

"Never heard of him, but this book is *the* greatest book I ever read. All that boring junk I had to read in English class to get through journalism school, why don't they let you read books like *A Death in the Family!* Just think, I'm sitting right here in Frenchtown reading this book and the guy that wrote it actually — it's a real fact? — *lived* here in Frenchtown?"

"Yeah, right around the corner, I think. I'm not positive.

"Jesus Christ Almighty!"

"Not only that, you know that part up front, 'Knoxville, Summer 1915'?"

"Yeah. Yeah, one of my favorite parts."

"Well, he finished revising that when he was living here in Frenchtown. But what he mainly worked on the year he spent here was *Let Us Now Praise Famous Men.*"

"Never heard of *that* one."

"Well, take them one at a time."

And then, while he stood there, his index finger keeping his place, I told him about Agee — not everything, but packing into thirty minutes as much as I could, and throwing in the fact that in 1936, when Agee went down into Alabama, I was a three-year-old child living on Forrest Avenue a few houses over from his home place, and other Knoxville parallels. I told him about the movie version of *A Death in the Family*, *All the Way Home*, and that a scene was filmed in front of the Bijou Theater. "I wrote a novel about being an usher there in 1946," I told him, "and one time this tall, dark man in a rumpled suit walked in before *The Postman Always Rings Twice* started and asked the manager could he walk around, that he used to come here with his father, and that yesterday while he was writing a movie review for *Time* magazine he had been seized by a terrible nostalgia for the Bijou and had impulsively gotten a plane and come down from New York City. 'Sure,' said the manager, 'Lucius will show you around.' And Lucius takes him backstage and way up in the Negro balcony, and he runs his fingers over the walls, the drapes, the seats, and takes sudden, deep breaths. And Lucius watches him walk out into the bright August sunlight. And I am hoping the reader will suspect that the man is James Agee. But I cut that scene out of the novel."

And I told him that the novel I was starting to write now was also set partly in the Bijou when it was a hotel and that General Sanders, wounded by a sharpshooter, dies there, in the bridal suite, where, I imagine, the dome of the Bijou theater is now —

But he, I could see, was now ready and eager to return to *A Death in the Family*, so I asked to see his newspaper's file on Agee, and he was certain they had none, but he called the town librarian at home and asked, "Marion, does the library have a file on James Agee? *James Agee.* You know, the guy that wrote *A Death in the Family.*"

I whispered loudly, "And *Let Us Now Praise Famous Men.*"

He nodded, listening to Marion. "Well, there's this teacher here who's a writer, wants to know where James Agee lived here in Frenchtown. Did *you* know — ? Oh. OK. But no file? Well, hey, listen, I want to check out some of his books for myself. What do — Huh? Wait a minute. We don't *have* any of his books? Well, he's really good, Marion. You owe it to yourself to — OK. She said they don't have anything, they just keep in stock what meets their patrons' demands, but she said it's at 27 Second Street."

He let me speak to the librarian. I asked her, "Does anyone *live* there?"

A lady, it turned out, lived there alone, now that her husband had died, a year ago. "But nobody answered my knock." The librarian said she would call to see if the lady was home. "Ask her if I can come over and see the house where Agee lived? I'm — writing a book about him."

When the librarian called back, she said the lady said, "OK, come on over."

"Tell Bobby," said the librarian, "that I promise to try to sneak in an Agee title one of these days."

I told him.

"If you'll wait till somebody comes back from lunch," the young man said, "I'd like to see it, too."

"Well, it's sort of a private thing, you know?"

Bobby liked that. "Yeah, see what you mean."

So I stood in front of 27 Second Street, and it was the same white house my intuition had been drawn to, right next door to the library that met the Frenchtown public's demands, but that, in the future, would have to reckon with the young reporter with his fingers stuck in *A Death in the Family*.

So I walked up on the porch and knocked, and the door opened so quickly I imagined that the lady had been standing there, looking out at me through the curtains.

"Hello, my name is David Madden, I'm writing a book on Agee, and I sure appreciate your letting me see —"

"I just said I would so you'd come *back* here. I want you to go back and tell all your friends to stop coming up to my door allatime and knocking and knocking to be let in, cause I won't have it no more. Not no more. Never. And if you all don't quit, I'm going to nail me a sign — JAMES AGEE NEVER LIVED IN THIS HOUSE. You all can just go find somebody *else* to torment."

. . . I felt like slamming the door in that little runt's face, but I won't be mean, if I can help it.

Lord, Bobby, I've run clean out of tablet paper. I seldom go out, but I *will*.

Kal Kan. I need to feed that stray cat if it's ever going to kill that mouse. So when I go out for my Kal Kan is when I'll get me some more writing paper.

Well, here I am with more writing paper, and I will tell the rest of it.

First, this fresh tablet makes me want to tell you again that I *am* sorry I never let you do it, and maybe when you finish reading this you will understand. There's lots I still don't comprehend my own self. But like I first wrote, it had go to where I couldn't endure it. I would be standing in the kitchen trying to remember what it was I come in there to do, and that knocking would startle me so. Or I'd be watching my stories on T V like I do every livelong day, even when John was still with me, and here they would come-a-knocking. Imagine how *you* would feel. Or I'd go to the door to look out to see if it had started to snow yet, and one would be peeking into my living room like a raccoon. It gave me the red ass, if you'll pardon my French, because you know I never talked that way in front of you — *or* John, or nobody. My daddy back in Harlan would, though. And all my brothers. But not my sweet momma.

Well, to get on with it, they would park out front and stare and every *one*, seemed like, would pull out a camera and start taking pictures of my house. Well, John's *people's* house. My house now, of course, but it still seems to me like it's John's people's house. And some were real sensitive. After I run them off, they would park way down the street like I was blind or a fool one, and then stroll back on by and pretend to snap a bird in a tree and then drop down quick as a wink on the house, and I hate to think some of them is sitting at home laughing at a picture of me come flying out that front door.

Hate, Bobby. It was hate. And I hate to say it. But the Lord knows I *did* hate *all* of them James Agee people, and more than *them*, I hated the very *name* James Agee. Now you know, Bobby, the Lord can't abide a body that hates, and me hating a man I never laid eyes on, that never spoke a word to me. Lord, honey, he was dead and gone to his maker more than ten years before John got his disability and took me out of Harlan to live in his home place. And every day, I thank God for you, Bobby, that I ain't still yet afire with the hate of that man. Not, Lord knows, that I can find any love in my heart for James Agee, but to be free of all that hate is a blessing.

I had even come to where I hated John too for letting them in the house. We had no more than opened the doors — and raised the winders — to let out all that stale air, for it had been shut up for six years since his ma and pa died, when that knocking commenced. And John — you never knowed John — bellered out the way he always did, "Come on in, whoever you are! My house is *your* house!" And before he could hobble on that broke hip and cane down the hall, I could see a big man with piercing eyes, grinning, smack in the middle of the living room before I had even had time to feel like it was mine. I heard his deep voice all the way in the kitchen where I stood with my arms folded, not ready yet to meet neighbors, you know. Fresh out of Harlan, the only home I ever knowed. But he wasn't no neighbor. Boomed out that he was a friend — I didn't catch his name then of course — of James Agee. Said he was his editor. Newspaperman was what I figured. I never read a book I wasn't forced to. I'd rather sit and stare and daydream. Or listen to my stories on the radio like we used to could or watch my stories on the TV. John said this big man with the wall-shaking voice had one finger bent in his handshake, so of course John took to him right away, and he showed him all over the house, me ducking out of sight from room to room as they roved, and *up* in the attic, and *around* the house. And that big feller went out to his car and come back in with a bottle, and him and John kept talking and kept talking, and I was left out. I didn't like it then, and I never *did* like it. I have not even remembered *that* time until now, sitting here at the kitchen table, trying to explain it to you.

Well, what happened was that John let them in, each one that come a-knocking, until he fell and broke his other hip, had to take to his bed in November of 19 and 77. He would yell from his bed, "Come in, whoever you are! My house is *your* house!" and tell me to open the door, and when I wouldn't, he'd say, "*Now, why* do you want to act like that?" I couldn't say. I just did.

But I sort of did know later on, after I didn't *have* John no more and they would come. It was because they was the only ones that *did* come. I didn't *have* nobody that wanted to come to see *me*. All my folks was far away in Eastern Kentucky, and their letters all told of who had died and which ones had got married and which ones had babies, but mostly who died. My brothers roamed far from home and their sons even went to Vietnam, but none of them ever darkened *my* door. And me and John never had no children, so it was just us. And I was always very content just with John — from the word go. It was just that even in our Harlan home whenever he would yell out, "Come in, whoever you are! My house is *your* house," it would fly all over me.

And so, when I looked out that first day after the snow was gone and the cold spell broke and I seen that little runt pull up in his old-model car and get out and reach back in and pull out his camera, it was *one too* many. And I went and hid in the back of the house and I saw in my mind, plain as that kitchen stove, a big ol' sign —

JAMES AGEE NEVER LIVED IN THIS HOUSE

And he just *kept* knocking. The others did, too, but this one had his own special knock. I don't mean like some smart aleck going knock, knockety, *knock-knock.* I mean like he had some kind of right to be let in. You know, like if *you* was to get sick of New York City, Bobby, and come home to Frenchtown and come over to see me like you used to.

So after I had given that little call-him-what-you-want-to a piece of my mind, I *did.* I went straight to the kitchen and took out an old brown sack and dug out an old stub of a lipstick and made me a sign — JAMES AGEE NEVER LIVED IN THIS HOUSE. STOP KNOCKING AT MY DOOR. But I never could nail it to the front of the house. My neighbors would know for sure I was a raving maniac.

And so they kept coming, and the devil sunk his teeth into my heart, and hate was all I knew. Couldn't eat. Couldn't sleep. Didn't go *out* for fear they would break *in* while I was *out.* I couldn't even keep my mind on my stories on TV. I just walked these floors and stood and stared and I'd sit down, I'd get up and I'd lay my head down, and I'd have to get up and walk like I was a ghost turned loose in the house.

Because he was *in* the house, and I knew no way to get him out. One day, I let myself in for it by wondering, well, now where would this man have picked to write those books? John knows, I'll ask *him,* but quick as a flash, I remembered John was no more. I was surprised at myself even for wondering. I could have opened the door when the next one of them Agee people knocked and asked, but I never did.

One night they had a writer come on Johnny Carson to show off his book and try to get people to buy it. He looked like the boogerman, with big ol' bug eyes and a trimmed black beard, and told how he talked to everybody that ever knew the murderer and how he proved in the book that the police framed the man. Them knocking for James Agee made me see the face of that man on the TV. But one of them yelled, "We just want to see where James Agee wrote *Let Us Now Praise Famous Men*," and that sounded more like one of these ministers that writes books, that the TV preachers bring on their shows. Where I couldn't stop saying James Agee in my head, now I couldn't stop saying out loud for all the world to hear, "Let Us All Praise Famous Men." Which ones? George Washington, the Father of our Country? Abraham Lincoln that freed the slaves? President Kennedy who that little Communist killed? Jesus? No, he's not *famous*, he's just our God in Heaven. Praise which ones? If you had never told me, Bobby, I would never have knowed who. Because Alabama tenant farmers don't mean nothing to me. Why didn't he come to Bloody Harlan if he wanted to tell how poor people live? My daddy could have showed him what dirt and death is. It seemed to me like the one who got the most praise was James Agee — or else why all that knocking on my door?

But the name in my head and me saying "Let Us Now Praise Famous Men" like I was hypnotized was nothing to what come later. It was monotonous, but I could stand it. I made myself get out and go to the store first thing one morning, and I got to looking at Old Man Steuben and figured he must have been here in 19 and 38 when John's pa rented out the house. They had moved to Patterson by then. So I come right out and asked him is he remembered back in 19 and 38 when John's pa rented the house to a writer. Well, if it was more than I could endure to have James Agee and his book rattling around in my house, how do you reckon I felt when Mr. Steuben come out with, "You mean — and his Jewish girlfriend, don't you?"

If I had knowed that that was all it took for her to move right *in* with him, I might have knocked before going into my own house. A house of sin if they ever was one. Maybe in my own bed, that was mine and John's. But then I remembered we brought our bed with us down from Harlan. That still didn't help me to sleep. Them two being there was what drove me into the streets more often, where I would be more likely to run into people like Mr. Steuben that might tell me things I prayed never to know.

And sure as you're breathing, one morning I stepped out my front door and a heap of rags throwed down on the porch commenced to scream bloody murder. It was a body in a sleeping bag on one side of the door, and a girl come wiggling out of a sleeping bag on the other side. "We hiked into Frenchtown at three a.m., and she said we shouldn't wake you," the boy said. "James Agee never lived in this house," I told him, and they looked so like it was the last judgment that I took pity and brought some coffee out to them, and they shared my last cigarette right there on my front porch for all the neighbors to see.

That's when you caught me, Bobby, and begged me for the third time by phone and in person to let you write what you called a photo-essay on "the house where James Agee wrote *Let Us Now Praise Famous Men*." I didn't like your looks either, sorry to say, so I went inside. But that boy and girl and you digging it all up started people coming up to me when they caught me out, telling me things, just as if they thought I was dying to know.

This lady that never would even speak to me all the years me and John lived on that street — sail right by me on her way into the church next door — told me with a curl of her lip, "They were white trash. They moved in, him and that woman, with only a great big old four-poster bed and a rocking chair, the bed so big they couldn't get it upstairs into John's poor mother's bedroom, and you know, of course, where they put it." I said, no, I didn't, and I did not *want* to know. "*In the kit-chen*," she says, tight-lipped like some old gopher. I already hated James Agee and now I hated that hateful old lady.

I didn't hate that girl he had brought with him because I figured she couldn't help herself. Because by that time I had pieced together what he looked like and how he acted and how he talked, and I thought to myself, I *thought* so. But I didn't realize what it would do to me to walk into the kitchen, which was the only part of John's people's house I ever felt at home in. Catty-corner between the wall and the stove, with my table at the foot, set James Agee's four-poster bed. It was unmade, but at least they weren't in it. I'm not teasing you, Bobby, it was there — just in a flash — and then it was gone. Laying in my own bed that night upstairs, I couldn't sleep. I knew it wasn't down there — I'm not a crazy old lady — but I went down there just to look for myself. It was just the kitchen. It was when I was *not* in the kitchen that I saw it in the kitchen, and them in it, mostly asleep. I went in there less and less. They drove me out of my own kitchen. Not her. I didn't blame her. It was James Agee being a writer, always writing things down in huge books like those company store ledgers in Harlan — and at my own kitchen table — that made me keep on seeing that bed in the kitchen and them in it, mostly just sleeping.

Now, Bobby, I know you know everything there is to know about James

Agee and his ungodly books because ever since that little runt come rolling into Frenchtown and got you started, you ain't quit. And now you and him is two of a kind. But I promised to explain why I would never let you write my story or take my picture while you still lived here and why I ain't changed my mind in all the years since. Oh, I *have* changed, but my mind is made up not to tell it to the whole world, unless you break *your* promise not to put this letter in one of your books.

Next, it was the goats, and then it was the hobo, and then it was James Agee with that ribbon in his hair, and then somebody came at me with the mouse, and that was what made me start feeding that damned stray tomcat — excuse my French. I'd just get used to one thing when here come somebody with something else. How they brought in a piano and tormented the neighbors. And a victrola and blasted the windows in everybody's house with their Beethoven. I couldn't stand even being told about it, because all *they* had to do was tell it and go on.

The goats. James Agee had to have him a goat, to cut the grass, I reckon. They say it ba-ba-ed so much, he couldn't write his book. So being smart, like most city folks, he got another goat to keep it company. Two goats ba-baing didn't do his bookwriting any good either. So James Agee turned his goats over to the butcher. But that didn't stop Agee's goats from waking *me* up after I would finally go to sleep.

Then they took in one of those hobos that used to come through here — and I remember them hanging onto the coal gondolas passing through Harlan — to give him a roof over his head. But in only a few weeks they moved out, and left that ol' hobo sitting in John's people's living room, eating a baloney sandwich by candlelight.

That girl didn't want to kill the mouse that lived between the walls. She even fed it and let it run over her bare toes and soon there was five of them. In Harlan we killed them. But when they moved out, she caught them in a box trap, and they took those five mice with them in their car to their new house — probably up in one of those penthouses because I was told they only *dressed* like poor white trash, but if you ask me, I lived all my life around poor white trash, and none of *them* ever acted like James Agee and that girl. So when I heard about the mouse was when I started feeding that stray tomcat, Kal Kan. He never caught one, he just cut into my cigarette money.

The tomcat never comes around anymore, and the goats have quit, but sometimes I dream about that hobo, that he's still in the house, his stomach growling for an old baloney sandwich. I'm afraid to say it, but he's kindly company sometimes.

You was who saved me, Bobby. From James Agee's name in my head, me always whispering "Let Us Now Praise Famous Men," resentful, that bed in the kitchen, those mice, those goats, that hobo, the knocking at the door — oh, and I almost forgot, Agee greeting the church ladies at the door with a ribbon she had tied to his hair. From the hatred. That night you called me up to ask me to forgive you, to ask me to wish you well, that you would never again pester me to see the house where James Agee wrote it because you were shaking the dust of Frenchtown from your feet and going to New York to become a famous photographer. You said you had always felt ashamed for trying to destroy my privacy, and that you couldn't leave without telling me and asking my forgiveness. For some reason I said, "Come tell me to my face," and when you hung up, I opened the front door so you wouldn't knock, and when I heard your foot hit the porch, I turned off my story and opened the screen and let you in, and it was the freest I ever was since when John was with me. Now why do I say that?

And you should have seen your face when I said — before you could even open your mouth to say what you had come to say — "Tell me about James Agee before you go."

And you sure did, Bobby, and you didn't go until after midnight, so that as I drifted off into my first sane sleep in years, I pictured you rolling into New York City right when all the lights were going off.

The next day I stepped across the yard to the public library. That lady that unlocks the door every day almost dropped dead. She said thanks to you they had one book by Agee, *A Death in the Family*, that you had donated. It still had your name in the front. I checked it out.

I skipped my stories and tried my best to read it. I couldn't. For the longest time I couldn't get past the title to even open the book because I know I'm tough but I do miss John, even so, even now. When I got to that little part at the front about Knoxville way back yonder in 19 and 15, I couldn't figure out what he was saying. It's not it was bad, it was just not my kind of book. Listen to *me*. I do good if I read the Bible my granddaddy put in my hands the day *he* died.

Yours wasn't the only name in it, Bobby. They put a card in a pocket in the back, and people had wrote their names above where I had wrote mine, and there was dates the lady had stamped in beside each name. I read those names and the dates over and over and wondered if they read the book from cover to cover. *I* never did. I meant to. They called me up to bring it back, but it was yours, so I kept it, until the library lady knocked about six months later and demanded it or she would report me to the mayor of Frenchtown. I didn't want to let her have it, but I did.

And then one day when I heard that knock and knew one of them was out there, I realized I didn't feel any hate for James Agee anymore.

And here you come again, Bobby — after all your Christmas cards and after those two visits that meant so much to a lonesome old lady — to start it all up again with your long letter. I never heard of *Vanity Fair* and I don't care. Has that little runt been after you again?

When I didn't answer your letter, you called me up last Sunday and said you didn't understand why I still wouldn't let you take pictures. I promised to tell you why and now I have done it.

And in case you want to know, Bobby, yes, I forgive you. I forgive Agee. Maybe that girl does too. And I forgive everybody. Because now there's nothing *to* forgive.

But I can't be like John and beller, "Come on in, whoever you are! My house is *your* house!" Because finally it really *is* my house. All I've got. Even if I did have to sell some of the furniture to get by. And one of these days I might finally nail that sign to the front of my house. JAMES AGEE NEVER LIVED IN THIS HOUSE. I can't help it if they do go around calling me "The Woman Who Hates James Agee." It ain't true.

A SECONDARY
CHARACTER

Leona wanted only to take a look at Paul Gaddis. One of the other guards pointed him out. Standing in the corridor, glancing at his wristwatch, a black taxi of the twenties behind him in the sculpture garden outside, he did not look familiar. A furred old lady who was asking him the time nodded and moved away, revealing Salvador Dali standing in bright March sunlight, looking into the face he had made famous. Unextravagantly, Dali was calling his wife's attention to some feature of the old taxi, artificially rain-drenched from 11 to 6. Though Leona was used to recognizing celebrities during her infrequent visits to Manhattan, seeing Dali and his model in the flesh just as her eyes had fallen on the man she had been tracking, startled her. But she realized that nothing could be more predictable, more natural, than to glimpse Dali, and, naturally, his wife at the Surrealism Retrospective.

What still struck her as odd was the fact that Paul Gaddis (whose real name, she had learned only a few hours ago, was Eric Furst) worked as a guard in the Museum of Modern Art. As she began to scrutinize his face, he strolled into a gallery, cupping his elbows in his palms. She followed, one of her own palms sweating against the jacket of his novel, wrinkling the slick red paper. Even with the front of the book turned toward her fur coat, she was afraid he might recognize it by the battery of eulogies on the back. Pretending a knowledgeable scrutiny of the Dadaist typewriter before her, she glanced back at him. His blond hair, gray streaked, was longer than the hair of the other guards, and he wore a beard. As though aware of being observed, he seemed to be sucking in his belly.

Earlier, as she boarded the Staten Island Ferry, she had not expected the name, Eric Furst, when matched with a face, to recall a forgotten acquaintanceship. But back about 1953, maybe thirty pounds lighter, beardless, hair trimmed, what *had* he looked like? The jacket of his novel offered no photograph.

Feeling the delayed effect of his cold blue eyes, she turned again, hoping they would take her back to a time when she had at least *met* him. A different guard, stalling on the threshold of retirement, stood in the doorway.

Leona stepped briskly into the corridor. Paul Gaddis was walking intently through a congestion of spectators packed along the glass wall to stare at Dali and his wife, who were moving slowly away from the black taxi deeper into the sculpture garden.

Where the crowd thinned, Paul Gaddis was almost skipping. Perhaps to avoid betraying the fact that he had recognized her and was trying to escape, he wasn't looking back. She had intended only to observe, not to confront him, anticipating the possibility that he might recognize *her*. Now that apparently he had, Leona impulsively followed him through the lobby, out into the street.

The sun had gone. The wind made her slit her eyes and turn her face into her fur collar. At the subway entrance, she dropped Paul Gaddis' novel. A young man in a Nehru jacket stepped on it, backed up, picked it up and handed it to her, saying, "Hey, man, aren't you Joan Crawford in disguise?"

Unable to speak, she shook her head and watched him go down, buoyed past Paul Gaddis in a springy walk.

Leona reached the turnstile just as Paul Gaddis stepped into the 7th Avenue Express. As the doors slid shut behind her, Leona was glad she had struck out on impulse after him because she had discovered only where he worked, not where he lived — and wrote.

Standing, Leona kept her back toward Paul Gaddis, who sat, she saw, in the glass of the door, under the subway map. He seemed aware of her, but not intent upon eluding her. Perhaps she had only imagined that he recognized her. Still, three o'clock was a strange time to quit work.

When Paul Gaddis got off the subway, Leona followed him. As he ascended against the gray sky, he looked back down at her, more curious than disturbed — clearly not afraid. As rain struck her upturned face, Leona regretted only an instant wearing the fur coat, for things like that didn't really matter anymore. But she slipped the hand that held the novel through two buttons, protecting the thing that had brought her the greatest misery she had felt in fifteen years, exposing, because of it, the coat that had given her more pleasure than any of her other possessions.

Leona did not know that people actually lived in the financial district, within sight of the Brooklyn Bridge, the Statue of Liberty, and Staten Island, until Paul Gaddis inserted a key into a door just off the pavement.

"Please! Mr. Gaddis! Mr. Furst! Don't go in!"

Leona ran across the slick street, shaking her head, scattering rain from her eyes and mouth.

Paul Gaddis stood in his open doorway. He seemed fascinated by the sight of her, charging up to him.

"For Christ's sake, you really *were* following me, weren't you?"

"Yes. Did you recognize me?"

"*Every*body looks familiar to me."

"Who am I?"

"Joan Crawford, like the kid said."

"Why did you run away?"

"If I had known I was running away, I could answer your question."

"Then why did you leave the museum at three o'clock?"

"It's not every day my daughter gets married."

"You have a daughter?"

"Half a daughter. My ex-wife must take the blame for the other half. The blue eyes are mine, but what Leona sees with them has been conditioned by her moth —"

"Leona!"

"Where?" He looked into the hallway. "Where?"

"That's your daughter's *name*?"

"Something wrong with it?"

"I'm Leona Richards — Leona Claypool."

"You don't have to decide right now. Come on in, and we'll give George a rub-down."

"George?"

"What's-his-face with the drenched fur." He reached out at the fur, flicked little sprays of rain against the door. Then he opened the door wide, and she stepped into the vestibule.

"Excuse me while I collect my fan mail."

Had he published other novels then? Leona watched him in the dim room pull, viciously, three manila envelopes and other material out of his mailbox. "I'd like to shove that postman through a keyhole! Stuffs my stuff in here so I have to retype it!"

"Are you going to talk to me?"

"I got a wedding, lady."

"You *do* know me, *don't* you?"

"I live upstairs."

His arms full of mail, Paul Gaddis led Leona up three flights and stopped at a door freshly painted white.

"Would you hold this junk, please?"

She put her arms out; he dumped the mail. He unlocked the door, stepped aside, and she entered his apartment and put his mail down on a table just inside. Feeling the fur coat start to slip off her shoulders, she caught it by the lapels. "I'll keep it on."

"I *thought* you called me Gaddis just now!" Turning, she saw him reach for the novel — she had put it down along with his mail. "Jesus, lady!" He grinned like a kid. "You chased me down just to get my autograph or something? Jesus, I thought —"

"Do women usually follow you home from the Museum?"

"Once. One did it once," he mumbled, thumbing through the novel. He appeared overwhelmed to have a reader of his novel in his apartment fifteen years after its almost simultaneous appearance and disappearance. "Jesus Christ! What about that! What about that? I'm — by God, I'm speechless!"

Behind Paul Gaddis, three shelves were packed tightly with the glossy red spines of his novel. Nauseated, Leona grabbed his wrist and shut her eyes, hard, trying to keep from swaying.

"Give me a drink."

"Sure, lady!" She felt him guide her backward into a chair. "You feel okay?"

Her eyes still closed, she felt him go away from her, and then she sensed that he was close to her again.

"Here you are."

She opened her eyes and took the drink in both hands. In his other hand, he was still holding her copy of his novel against his chest, light from the kitchen making his museum guard's brass badge wink. The absurd feeling that he held in a convulsion of wonder the only copy that had sold made Leona turn in his mangled chair to scan the walls, hoping to see three thousand copies on the other shelves. She saw only about a hundred copies of the novel. She drank his whiskey.

"Are you Miranda O'Connor?"

"No. My name is Leona Richards now." His eyes showed no hint of recognition.

He looked again at the open book. "Your name isn't here. Harvey Gross's name is struck out with a fine line of brown ink and there's Miranda O'Connor written beneath with a flourish. Marked down from $3.75 to 59 cents. I thought I bought up all the remainders in Manhattan. What about that?" Then he saw something that made him snarl. "Goddamn review copy!" Was he looking at the reviewer's marginal scrawls? "Gross sold it, then *she* bought it — or was it *you?* — from Martin's book store in Richmond, according to this little seal."

"Mr. Gaddis — Mr. Furst —"

"Make it Gaddis."

The suggestion in his voice that he was condescending to an admirer who had almost fainted from the thrill of meeting him at last made her feel nauseated again.

"Are you only pretending you don't recognize me? Or have you so easily forgotten?"

"I don't understand."

"Does the name Leona Claypool — my *first* husband's name — mean nothing to you?"

"Well, I *do* love coincidences, and my daughter's name *is* Leona."

"Please turn on a light so I can see you."

"Oh, sure, Mrs. Claypool."

"Richards." Leona took another drink of his whiskey.

Paul Gaddis turned on a beaded Tiffany lamp that stood on his desk, highlighting strange dents in the wood as though he had more than once tried to beat it to death.

"Is that where you do it?"

Laughing abruptly, he turned back toward her, with an expression confused between a leer and embarrassment. "Where I *do* it?"

Leona stood up and looked into Paul Gaddis' cold blue eyes. "Leona is, as you know very well, not only my *own* name, and your daughter's name, but Leona is also the name of the heroine of your novel."

"That's right! That's right! I mean, she's not exactly — no, she isn't the *heroine* of the novel, but she's certainly an important secondary character in a kind of running subplot."

Startled, Leona realized that "Leona" *wasn't* the heroine of the novel. She couldn't remember the name of the girl who was. Leona's story had unfolded simply as a counter-plot to the —

"Where did you know me before, Mr. Gaddis?"

He began to look a little uncomfortable, as though something was coming warmly into focus deep in the blue darkness behind his eyes.

"I can't remember *you*, either. Maybe it's the beard. You're a little heavier, aren't you?" When she took another step toward him and he leaned backward, Leona realized that she had backed him against his desk.

"Than when?"

"Than whenever it was I knew you. We *did* know each other, didn't we?"

"Mrs. Richards, I never set eyes on you before today — when you came down the corridor at the museum."

"You noticed me even then?"

"I was watching your face when it dawned on you that Salvador Dali in the flesh was actually standing in the garden."

"Was *that* why you noticed me?"

"That and the fur coat. You *do* something to that coat. You look hunted in it. You look very neurotic in it, and you made the fur coat look neurotic, too."

"You're writing all this down in your head. I can see it in your eyes."

He laughed and slipped into a severe chair that might have come from a New England attic, still holding his novel, his finger marking the place where the names and the prices and the book store seal were. "The fur excited me, and I wanted to see if you would follow me into the gallery, so I went in there, and you followed me, and kept looking at me, but then Max comes up and tells me he's relieving me so I can go to Leona's birthday — I mean wedding.

She's getting married. I'm invited, see, and I want to look nice. Take my time. And here *you* are, stirring up the past."

"Stirring up *your* past!"

"Try to be calm, lady."

"How about *my* past?"

"Oh, my god! *Now* I get it!" He jumped up and took long strides that put the desk between them. Dull pencil points, red and black, stuck up out of a beer can. "Listen, Mrs. Claypool, I've *been* this route — twice, in fact. Ghost writing's not only not in my line, but it nearly put me in Bellevue the last time. In fact, the *first* time, it got me shot at. But I don't want to go into that. I don't want to go into anything. I —" She was staring at the black plastic hood, glistening in the lamp light, that covered the typewriter. "No, that's not it. I can see in your face that's not it, either. What the hell *do* you want? Not just a lousy autograph. I can see that, too. But what?"

"I want to know why you wrote about me in that book."

He cracked the book in the middle and looked at the pages. "In *this* book?"

"When did you know me? Show me a picture of yourself without the beard."

"I have a phobia about pictures. They wanted one for the jacket, but —" He was staring at her, as if getting her into focus. "Listen, lady, I'm pleased you got so involved in the book; I see you identified with Leona — and I can understand that with your name also being Leona — if it is — But, listen, I've got to make the Bronx by subway before four-thirty and it's raining violets outside, so, if you'll —" His nervous laugh convinced her that he was putting on an act.

"Don't give me that kind of treatment, Mr. Gaddis." Leona stood up and stared at him across the bright, dented surface of his desk. "I've come from Staten Island to see you — Well, I just meant at look at you first in the museum, to see if I could recognize you, and then when you disappeared, I went after you. Otherwise, I would have — *maybe*, I would have waited. I don't know."

"Listen, I'll —" He began dashing into the corners of the room. " — loan you — my umbrella. I'll *give* you — my umbrella. The ferry — Where *is* the damn thing?"

"I know where the ferry is. I haven't ridden on it since last summer because

I detest Manhattan. I have a lovely home on Staten Island, and a lovely child, and a husband I don't deserve —"

"I'm sure you do, and I'm sure you will understand that I have to get out of this crummy uniform and jump into a tux and get uptown for my daughter's — you being a mother, you ought to under —"

Her hands pressed against her face to conceal her tears, Leona felt him guide her backward, but as she sank into the chair, her awareness of the grip of his palms under her elbows became so keen that she rose abruptly and rushed into a cramped bathroom, vomiting into the dark.

"Can I help you?" His voice seemed to come from another apartment.

Leona flung her arms backward repeatedly, weakly, to keep him out. Sudden light and the dizziness kept her in the bathroom a few moments longer. Into focus came an inflated black umbrella, dripping in the white bathtub. Then more clearly, she saw that her own vomit had exploded into a psychedelic design on the dome of the umbrella. The dripping stopped even before she slapped the light switch.

"Look, you sit there a second and finish that drink while I start getting ready, and when you feel you can handle it, please take my umbrella — it's here some place — and make a dash for the ferry."

"You think I'm neurotic, don't you? You think I'm making all this up — to get the attention of a writer whose novel has excited me or something. You even think I may be psychotic, don't you? Tell me, tell me what you're thinking, so I'll know how to talk to you."

"Neurotic maybe — frankly — but psychotic, perhaps not. If I had all the time in the world I might find out."

"How long did it take you to find out the first time?"

"What *are* you talking about?"

"When you wrote about me in that novel."

"Listen, just because your name is Leona —"

"Why did you name your daughter Leona?"

"If someone had asked me that casually, I might not have been able to answer, but with you sitting there in my favorite chair stirring all this up — I named her Leona after my character, out of sentimentality over my first novel, and I loved that name when I wrote about her, so I named my child Leona."

"Where did you *get* her?"

"What?"

"She's adopted, *isn't* she?"

"Mrs. Claypool —"

"Why do you call me that?"

"You said it was your name."

"*Then.* Not now. But you called me Claypool because —"

"I must admit you're scaring the hell out of me." He was backing away from her toward the dark corner where the red jackets of his novel got brighter as his pale blue uniform coat came nearer the shelves. "If you could see your face —"

"I'm not talking about my face. I'm talking about me and about my baby."

"You've got a baby?"

Leona got up out of the low chair again. "Goddamn you, will you stop talking like that? You know who I am; you know what you wrote; you know *what* baby!"

"You said you had a lovely home and a lovely child and a husband you didn't deserve. Have you had a baby on the sly or something? I mean, it's none of *my* business — I don't even know how all this is happening to me."

"The baby I killed! The baby I killed!"

"Take it easy, lady. Will you take it easy, please? Women have to sometimes. Sometimes they just have to. I understand. You even love your husband, I can see that, too. But you're going to have this other man's baby, so you have to do it."

"No, in the book, in the book — I mean back in 1953 when Walter left me and I went into the garage with Brenda and we sat there in the car and —"

"Lady, can I *call* somebody for you?"

"Just get away from those books and sit down and talk to me, and tell me how you know all this. I don't think I ever knew you, but somehow *you* knew everything about *me*. And you wrote about it in your novel and I read it, and you brought it all back, everything I had gotten rid of — not *forgotten* exactly — but through analysis. *Please* sit down." Paul Gaddis sat on the edge of his desk. "I had a very successful analysis just after it happened. After I was released from the hospital, I went to a private analyst, and then — Are you listening?"

"Yes, I can listen a little while, but I really must —"

"For god's sake, are you still thinking I'm neurotic?"

"No, no, I mean — Well, what can you *expect?*"

"But you did it, you did it deliberately. You wrote about something that really happened. Exactly as it happened. And I can't tell whether you're pretending now or not. But when you said you had a daughter named Leona, that — Well, I always wondered whether Brenda *really* died. A neighbor saw us go into the garage and when we didn't come out — but you *know* that. You wrote about it. On that typewriter." The sight of it made her stop. "Why don't you let me see it?" He stared at her, not comprehending. "No. I don't want to see it. Keep the hood over it."

"I can't deny that a similar story is there in the novel." The book lay on the floor near her foot. She kicked it aside. "But I do swear to you that I've never met you, Mrs. Richards. Your name is Richards now?"

"All right. All right, Mr. Gaddis. Maybe you didn't ever know me. You don't look familiar to *me*, either. But maybe you knew somebody who knew me, and maybe he *told* you about me and Brenda, and Walter. You even used my name. You can't put it all on coincidence. Oh, you changed Brenda to Barbara and Walter to Jack, but — and Claypool to Clayton, but — Don't look at me as though you're about to *call* somebody. If you'll just sit still and listen to me, I'll show you that I'm not sick. I'm upset — No, I'm not just upset, I'm on the verge of a nervous breakdown over that damned novel of yours. You owe me an open mind, and when I've made it all clear, after I've laid it all out for you . . ."

"Then what? I can't unwrite what I've written. I can't track down all 367 copies that sold, and the 1233 that went out on remainder."

"It sold only that many?"

"Maybe less," he said slowly, seeming to think that she looked disappointed. "It was the first thing I ever published, and the last. Look."

He pulled out the desk drawers and the drawers of the three filing cabinets that sat between bookshelves along the wall. She stood still, imagining the drawers crammed full of manuscripts. On those reams and reams, perhaps the other real lives were recorded. She felt faint again. His fingertips as he reached for her wrist made her flesh feel like clay.

"You had no right — Don't touch me — to do it. You're a criminal. Why aren't you in jail?"

"Listen, lady, why don't you just go to hell?"

"I *am* in hell."

"Because, listen to me, I've worked hard all my life to create a world to *share* with people, and if nothing else, I've earned *self*-respect. Oh, hell, don't make me say crap like that. Go home. Go back on the ferry to Staten Island and let me go to my daughter's wedding. She doesn't deserve this."

"Why did you let her live? They told me she was dead. I couldn't leave the hospital to attend her funeral, and I never saw Walter again. *Tell* me, Mr. Gaddis. Did she really live? Did that neighbor — Mr. — Mr. — Mr. — ?"

"Mr. Morton?"

"That's what *you* called him. Well, no matter — did he save us *both*?"

"In my novel, you — her mother, I mean —"

"When you said you had a daughter eighteen —"

"*Have* a daughter."

"It hit me that —"

Sometimes his eyes stopped everything, as if turning her into a photograph. Now he got the picture. He understood. "Jesus. Jesus, Mrs. Richards. I guess I *was* treating you like a sick woman. That was the easy way of handling you. I didn't know what to say or do so — But I'm trying to believe you now and not explain it all so easily. I guess every writer worries, or is even a little fascinated by the possibility of one of his characters knocking at the door one day — I mean, the real person that he really knew and based his character on. But what makes it so hard with you coming here this way —"

"Then Brenda did live and you're a friend of Walter's. Or did you just go to an agency and — ?"

"No, that's not what I was about to say. What I'm saying is that — You see, it's really very odd because all the characters in that novel are based on real people. I mean, I was actually afraid for a long time that they *would* raise hell with me, so I was a little glad at first that the book didn't sell."

"Then was it Walter who told you about me?"

"Please. What I'm trying to tell you is that of all the characters in the novel, only Leona is pure fiction."

Leona stared into his eyes — they were trying to transfix her again. She walked distractedly around the desk to make his eyes move. "Oh, listen, Mr. Gaddis, you can't hand me that." She bent down and picked up the book. "I saw it, *didn't* I? The truth. Your Leona, your daughter, is my child, my Brenda, isn't she? Isn't she? Don't you lie to me! I have a *right* to know!"

"*Do* you? Is that so? You gassed her, didn't you?"

Leona threw the book at his eyes. Instantly, her own head was ringing. He backed away, his hand upraised, and she saw something break loose inside him, and he struck her again and again. "Leona! Leona! Leona!" he screamed, almost weeping, almost hysterical. He slapped her until she felt too numb to see or feel the blows.

He stood over her, panting, the guard coat jerked open. She looked up at him from the floor. The brass badge rolled out of her hand and spun near Paul Gaddis' novel and clattered as it settled.

"Listen, you, I hated that Leona the whole time I was writing that stuff — fifteen years ago, for god's sake — and I made her up, you furry bitch, I made her up, every hair on her head, and the baby girl and the husband who walked out on her, and she was the *only* character I made up. She was mine. And as I created her, I hated her with every breath I drew, line by line. The reviewers said she was superfluous, unconvincing even, she didn't belong in the damn novel; she was a subplot, excess, a creaky device, all *that* kind of crap, the fact being that I felt her more intensely than *any* of them, than any of those people I actually grew up with in Pittsburgh. And now you come here and tell me I got her from your husband, or that I knew you sometime in your life or some damned thing."

Leona watched him cross the room to a small table by the bookcase where the copies of his novel were shelved. Not until she saw the telephone in his hand did she realize she had heard it ring.

"Yes, I'll be there. Don't worry."

"Let me speak to her?"

He turned to Leona, the telephone no longer in his hand. "Speak to who?"

"That was Brenda, wasn't it?"

"That was nobody."

"What's her number? I want to talk to her — no, I can't. I can't talk to her yet."

"You're bleeding. Look, I didn't really mean to hit you so much. You got just like her, and you brought it all back, those nights in Ohio where I was a graduate student, trying to write a thesis on Robert Browning, for god's sake, and finish this novel, too. And I put all my hatred of everything — the university, Athens, Ohio, the threat of the army, all that, into Leona." On his knees, he bent over her. "Come on, let me help you up."

Leona clung to him as he pulled her up and guided her over to his bed in the corner. She caught the odor from the dark bathroom.

"Want to take off that coat and rest a while?"

"I can't make love to you."

"No, I don't mean that." He pulled the coat off. She felt naked. "Really, I'm going to my daughter's wedding, just like I said, and I'm getting a late start." He took off the guard coat and tossed it across the fur at the foot of the narrow bed.

"Everything here is so small."

"I'd take a taxi, but I don't have the cash."

"Take it out of my purse. It's all these books — everything shrinks."

"I can't take your money."

"I want you to be on time."

"All right. I'll pay you back. Write down your address before you go. And take that umbrella. I think I tossed it in the tub after yesterday's rain. You're in no condition to get a cold. This has been very upsetting for you. I'm so sorry I hit you. I'm getting sick."

"Then you believe me? I mean, that everything is the way I said?"

"Just like in the novel? Exactly?"

"Yes, except that you let Brenda live."

"Well, listen, maybe I read about it. And *forgot* I read about it. Did it make the national papers?"

"I don't know — What's that odd noise?"

Paul Gaddis listened, looking around the room and then up at the ceiling. She saw the leak and pointed and he walked over near the desk. "Right into my dress shoe." He shoved the beer can that held the pencils under the leak and came back to the bed, carrying the shoe.

"It happened in 1953?"

"Yes."

"I was in Ohio, going to school. That's where I met Kay. We had to get married. And I was writing the novel, and we named my child Leona."

"But you hated Leona."

"Kay was the one who named her. So I named the mother in the novel Leona."

"You hated the baby?"

"Listen, I hated Kay and the baby and myself and Athens, Ohio, and the world. I hate my own shoes." He shook rain out of his dress shoe.

"*I* didn't hate *anything*. I was happy. Walter and Brenda and I had everything. Everything we wanted. It was perfect. A house, a life full of social —"

"Where was this?"

"You put it in Pittsburgh, but it was Rhode Island. I moved to Staten Island when I met Frank Richards. And it started all over again."

"What? Being happy and perfect?"

"Yes. Just as though nothing had happened. The analysis. I was — the doctor said I was his most perfect patient. I didn't *forget* what I had done. I adjusted."

"Did you tell whatshisname?"

"Frank? Yes. And that's what I mean. He's a good man, and I love him, and I don't deserve him, but I didn't think about it until I read your novel. I went to this Unitarian church bazaar in the neighborhood last week. I bought coffee cake and a plate of fudge and some jewelry made by Narcotics Anonymous — and ten novels, ten cents apiece."

"They sold you Miranda O'Connor's copy of my novel for ten cents?"

"I began to hate this woman with my name, until I realized that you were writing about *me*. I had to find you and make you tell me about Brenda."

"And I have. She was a figment of my imagination, just like her mother. And my own real daughter is getting married, and I love her very much. I even like her mother now. In fact, last night I made love to her."

"On this bed?"

"She called me and said she was coming over."

"Has she remarried?"

"Yeah. To an artist. He was the one got me the job at the museum. We all like each other. Of course, if he knew I made love to Kay last night, he would cut my throat. Took off her clothes coming in the door, and we made love and cried the whole time, and it was the best we ever had — better than when we had Brenda — the power of suggestion, Mrs. Richards — Leona. So my life is a wreck; I'm thirty-seven and a failure as a writer, but I'm going out in this lovely burst of glory — liking my ex-wife and loving my daughter and almost liking her husband. And meeting a lady who tells me she was the bitch in my book. Are you listening?"

"I hurt. I'm beginning to feel where you hit me. It hurts."

"I'm sorry."

"Do you have a small mirror?"

"Maybe. You don't want to look at yourself."

"No."

"Shut your eyes, Leona, and rest."

She closed her eyes and felt his lips kiss her dry eyelids, and then the pressure of his knees on the mattress released, making the springs sway, and when she opened her eyes a little, the light was out and the bathroom door was closing.

Listening to the water rush into the tub, she dropped off to sleep.

"Did you hear me?" She opened her eyes. "I'm going now, Leona." Silhouetted in a tuxedo, the bathroom light behind him, Eric Furst held Leona's purse in his hands. "I'm borrowing ten. Okay? About what I made in royalties!" Sensing that she didn't think it was funny, he stopped laughing. Getting him in focus, she saw that he looked very impressive in his tuxedo, but somehow transformed beyond mere clothes. "These cabs scalp you."

"You've shaved your beard!"

"I promised Leona. She and Gary have renounced hippie-land, and are going to Eastern Kentucky with VISTA. So I did it for her — as a gesture. Fresh start. *Tabula rasa.*"

"Don't go. I can't be alone."

"Get on the ferry and go home to your perfect husband and child and house. And, believe me, I don't mean that sarcastically."

"Stay."

"No, baby, you know better than that."

"Do you still hate me?"

"Do I still *hate* you?"

"Leona. You hit me so many times, I thought —"

"Maybe I do. Maybe I would like to make love to you and miss my daughter's wedding, so I could hate you for that, and ruin your perfect life — deliberately, the way my novel did, accidently. But I know that's what *you* want, too."

"What is it I want?"

"I think you want to give your husband cause to suffer and hate you so you can be punished for Brenda all over again, because you escaped that first time through temporary insanity, and then analysis, and then the good life on a platter, and it's tearing you up."

"It all came back when I got to that scene in the garage where you let Brenda live."

"I can imagine. And believe me, baby, I know how it must feel. But my own life is loused up enough, and whatever else happens to me, whatever new hell I bring on myself, I'm going to have this one lovely moment with my daughter. I may never see Leona again." He went to the door, limping. "This wet shoe makes my flesh crawl." Eric Furst stood near the door, about to leave.

"I want you to stay."

"I'm late. She'll be looking for me."

"I'm staying."

"Then do. I'm going." His tone was compassionate; he didn't want to hurt her.

"I may still be here when you get back."

"As Joan Crawford used to say, 'Don't tempt fate.'"

"I may follow you home tomorrow."

"Tomorrow's my day off."

"And be like that woman, the other one who followed you because she loved your eyes."

"How'd *you* know that?"

"I loved them, too, but I didn't know it because they looked cold."

"You're just talking to yourself, Leona. You want this to happen so you can degrade yourself."

"You don't have to *say* that. I can read it, in all those copies."

He turned around and looked at the three shelves of copies. "Obscene, isn't it? I had a lot of friends in those days, but I'm still stuck with over 100 copies. Goodbye."

"I want you." He opened the door. "I want you, Eric." He shut the door.

The room was chilly. She heard the rain drip from the leak in the roof into the beer can on the floor. She pulled the fur coat up over her and lay back on the bed, shoving her bare feet under Paul's guard jacket. Shocked wide awake to the fact that she had not finished Paul Gaddis' novel, she sat up. She had stopped at the point when the neighbor revived Brenda by administering artificial respiration, mouth to mouth. The shock had made her stop reading.

Leona got out of bed and picked the book up off the floor and stepped in the water that had overflowed the beer can. On the bed again, she flipped through the book to the turned-down page. By the gray light from the rain-streaked window, she read:

> The limp child opened her eyes and looked up into the stranger's wrinkled face and murmured, "Mommy, Mommy. Where's my mommy?"
>
> "She's gone away, little girl," said the old man, the taste of the child's candy-flavored lips on his own mouth. "She's gone on a long visit and she's asked me to take care of her little girl."
>
> Relieved that the child believed him, he stood up, his joints popping from having bent over the child so long, and began to walk away from the garage and the car where Leona sat, slumped over the wheel.

The novel did not end there. She flipped through two more chapters, concerning a young woman named Katherine, and came to the end with no further mention of Leona.

Lying back on the bed where Eric Furst had made love to the mother of Leona, Leona dropped the book on the floor. Lights from somewhere outside came through the window, casting watery reflections over the wall where the three shelves of remainders sat neatly against each other, glimmering as though they were brand new, as though if she got up from the bed where she was sinking into sleep and opened one of them, she could smell the new paper, and if she touched the words on the page, the ink would be wet.

HURRY UP PLEASE

IT'S TIME

◌

I was ambling out of this art gallery on 53rd Street, a few blocks from the Mecca of modern art, and there she was. I had my hands crammed down into my pockets, one of them all the way to my knee. Last summer on Fire Island I somehow managed to subconsciously culture a wart on my loose-cartilaged knee cap, so I had punctured a hole in my left pants pocket, the better to scratch it with, so that I can be seen walking around Manhattan with a limp and a scratch, a limp and a scratch. I was wearing a trench coat, which made me feel like Humphrey Bogart when I passed a mirror. It was a chilly October evening and the pavement was wet from a gusty shower, which explains my presence in that particular museum. An autumn windy rain, a itchy wart and an hour of cubism . . . nothing could have depressed me more.

And there she was walking toward me from Sixth Avenue, cradling a miniature grandfather's clock in her arms, wearing a brown suede jacket and a green corduroy skirt, her tawny hair splattered back over her ears like a leprechaun.

It was by her ears that I recognized her after twenty years. I'm quite serious — she had the most exquisite ears I've ever seen. They were a sheer delight of form and contour, and the slightest glimpse of them, pink and wet, thrust me into a flood of remembrance so vivid, so nostalgic that as she passed me I *knew* it was Greta.

"Greta! Greta La Fonda! It's Dorish!" But she continued to walk with that lazy rhythm in her gait, a sort of list to the left that rather disconcerted me. Of course, I could have been wrong, but not about those ears. Too many Sundays

72

in the orphanage, when we were so bored to death we could sit together or lie on a divan together and contemplate an object for hours, had I examined her ears, with the sunlight bright as honey on them, or the cold stare of the winter light leaping up from the snow and sprawling over us in a dank room where we lay hidden from the others.

So I followed her slowly, planning what I would say to her now in this different time. She went down into the subway at Broadway and 50th. Just as she stepped down from the sidewalk, she slipped on the wet pavement and lost her balance. I was already at her elbow, so I caught her and set her aright with perfect co-ordination. But the turn of her head, the brilliant flash of recognition on her face did not come as I had anticipated. The only movement was a visible tightening of her arm grasp around the antique clock. I could hear it ticking, a sound like water dripping into a tin cup in an empty room. . . .

And I remembered the Christmas morning when everyone but she and me and a few others had been taken into the homes of childless couples in the city for the weekend. Having grown tired of our uninteresting toys, we had taken the dorm mother's clock from her dresser and had disassembled it piece by piece with quiet, whispering care, patience and engrossing fascination. And fantastically enough, we almost effortlessly put it back together again — not because we feared old Miss Pruitt, which we did, but because we wanted to hear the sweet ticking again, its absence having frightened us a little. Just as we put the face back on, the alarm went off and Miss Pruitt pounced on us suddenly out of nowhere as if waiting for the signal of our doom. After that we always trembled when we passed her door, and the bald face of the clock mocked us from the black mahogany dresser.

As we waited for the dim yellow eye of the loping 7th Avenue Local to appear far down the track, I leaned with feigned nonchalance against the Chiclet machine and gazed at the chewing gum wrappers and cigarette butts displayed below me like discarded years. I glanced now and the Greta who stood at the edge of the platform, so close to the edge and with such a look and posture of continued movement forward that I wanted to walk over and take her arm.

But the image of her suddenly stepping off in front of a subway with that tall clock in her arms struck me as ludicrous in the extreme. Yet she always had that look of being in one spot but just on the brink of stepping off into another. That sort of thing had captured my attention years ago so that when I was with her I did a great deal of looking at her with a kind of anticipation, though she never did anything extraordinary.

I looked at her now. She was very tall — willowy, I suppose, like a girl sketched by Dali, clock and all, only not in that rather humiliated, amoebic shape. Even at seven years old she had been unusually tall, four feet three of skin and bone, and three feet of light brown hair, her ears peeking through of course. She was much taller now, but there was the same thin face and sharp features with the very fragile mouth. Her lips were always very grave, except for her rare smiles, which were frightening in the ferocity of their brilliance.

I followed her into the subway and sat down across from her. I hoped she would finally recognize me, but she continued to stare fixedly. So I sat there, my legs crossed, scratching my wart, waiting, remembering that day in another October, our last autumn together, when she was eight and I was nine, and we began to separate — or so I thought.

The orphanage was in Manhattan, squeezed in on both sides by brownstone apartment buildings. The back yards were no larger than family plots and some of them were rather humpy in those days. Greta was sick one week with the measles and so they wouldn't let me near her, but during the night I would slip up the drain pipe and in the window and we'd talk until she fell asleep of the things we'd do when she would be well again.

But during the chilly days I'd sit on one of those grassless humps under a scrawny, black, naked tree. From there I could see over the top of a rotten wooden fence. The odor of the wet wooden fence had a heady tang in the sharp air if you were bored and lonely enough to concentrate on it. Sometimes I talked nonsense into a rusty tin can just to hear my voice roar, like in a seashell, with an almost adult richness and depth that made me feel even lonelier. I was looking for all kinds of designs, patterns, shapes of animals and humans in the various textures and surfaces the day I saw the window with the shade up and the lucid four o'clock sun splashed over it.

I could barely see the figures moving beyond the reflected glare. One of them came closer to the window. It was a girl about nineteen years old, wearing a blue sweater and a darker blue skirt. She stood a moment, arms akimbo with her back to the window, and moving through the dimness came a young man toward her, his red hair tousled, one hand scratching his head, the other in his pocket. He ambled as one who moves in casually to join a conversation. For a few moments he stood before her smiling, and took the hand out of the pocket and brought it up to rest gently on her shoulder, still mulling his hair. Suddenly she turned her face sideways, laughing with her eyes closed, and hugged his arm with both of hers, the sun holding the two in a golden sheen of warmth and brilliance.

And then he put his arms around her and held her a long time, swaying slightly, ruffling her long hair with one hand and running the other across her fanny. That struck me as peculiar behavior. I watched him fiddle around with her skirt and saw it slide down over her hips as he pulled her to him more tightly. And then he took her by the hand and led her away from the sun-struck window and into the darkness of the room. I strained my eyes but could see only dark movement. Then a cloud obscured the sun's glare, and I saw clearly through the cold window. They were both naked and playing some sort of game, which I couldn't figure out even though I watched until it grew too dark to see.

I rushed back to the orphanage, climbed the drainpipe, and pecked on the window that was beside Greta's bed. In an excited, rushing whisper, I told her what I had seen. But she looked at me with hurt confusion, as though I were playing a silly game with her. Yet she laughed at a few of the things I told her they had been doing, burying her face in the pillow to muffle the sound. I was a little peeved with her lack of enthusiasm for what I considered a mystery of human behavior quite enthralling to watch.

The next day she was released from the infirmary and we met at noon in the dining room. She appeared very excited now that we could be together again, but I ignored her and walked away. She ran after me and asked what the matter was, and I told her that I had more interesting things to do than piddle around with a child. But she followed me to the fence, then waited silently beside me, wondering what I was staring at. They were asleep on the bed with blankets over them, something I didn't find interesting enough to disclose to Greta as being my special secret.

But when the girl opened her eyes and sat up in bed and leaned over and put her mouth over his ear, I prodded Greta in the ribs and pointed at the window. She had to put on her hideous glasses to see. She was so awed by what transpired that she couldn't speak, while all I could do was laugh. That was the first time I ever saw her mouth show any expression besides that graveness and those rare smiles.

For two weeks we went every day to the fence and watched the boy and the girl in their ordinary activities as well as that one activity which so entranced us. Greta never spoke while that was happening but she called my attention to every little thing the boy did to or for the girl otherwise, like: tying her apron strings, zipping up her dress or handing her a cup of coffee as she stood gazing out the window, and once he even playfully combed her hair, and another time she sat by the window in her slip, painting her fingernails, and he blew on them and then kissed her so hard that her head pressed against the window and her hair spread out like a fan.

In very small ways I found Greta imitating her. Like one time in art class in school at the orphanage, she colored her fingers with red paint and looked at me as though she expected me to blow them dry, but Miss Pruitt caught her and pulled her roughly to the sink and stood over her like the leaning tower of Pisa while Greta scrubbed them clean.

Then two weeks after we discovered them, we saw the thing that affected both Greta and the girl so profoundly. The girl was sitting by the window, her elbow on the sill and her head resting in her hand, running her finger listlessly over the glass with her other hand, which also held a handkerchief. Her face was red from crying.

Suddenly, the door opened across the room. He came in wearing a straw hat and a happy-dan sort of suit. She ran to him and flung her arms around his neck, but he pushed her away from him, and after placing his hat over the bedpost, began to put some clothes into a suit-case, while she cried and tried to put her hand on his arm. Shortly, he put his hat on again and with suitcase in hand started for the door. But she had locked it and was running across the room to the window when he caught her by the neck and struggled with her. She managed to raise the window slightly with her free hand and put the one holding the key through the opening. Greta was holding tightly to the rim of the fence, on the verge of tears. Then a loud, shrill scream split the air. He had slammed the window on her fingers and both the girl and Greta had screamed at the same instant.

I did not go back the next day. I had not only lost interest but Greta had asked me to let her go alone. She went back alone five days in a row, and I began to miss my playmate, so on the sixth day I followed her and quietly sat beside her. The girl was lying on the bed, motionless. After two hours she hadn't moved in the slightest, and I brought this fact to Greta's attention, hoping she too would recognize the dull monotony of it all and come away to play jack-rocks with me. But she said blandly, "She hasn't moved for the last four days."

"She's been lying there like that all this time?"

"Yes. She's asleep, dreaming of him."

"She never gets up to eat or go out?"

"No. She just lies there asleep and never moves."

"Well, why do you keep looking at her?"

"I don't know." I jumped up and walked away in disgust.

A few days later, Miss Pruitt sent for me. A woman was there who was interested in adopting me. She was a fat woman with a black mustache. All the time she was talking to me I felt real panic. She looked me over and said yes, she'd take me.

I wasn't to leave for a few days yet but I had to find Greta and tell her. I found her sitting in the same position as the last time. A soft rain was falling and the sky was very dark and violet-colored though it was only three o'clock. Her hair glistened with the rain and her ears were pale. I could smell the strong odor of rot in the wooden fence. The girl lay on the bed the same as before, barely visible in the darkness of her room. Looking at her I completely forgot why I had come, because I was suddenly scared. Nobody sleeps that much, and if they do they turn over once in a while or curl up. The dress she wore was the same as on that day when the boy slammed the window on her fingers and the door on her life.

I ran back to the orphanage and told Miss Pruitt what I had seen and what I thought about it. She immediately telephoned the police.

I returned to Greta because I didn't want her to see what would happen when the police came bursting through the door so I grabbed her by the wrist and pulled her away rather violently. She screamed, "You're hurting my fingers!" But I hadn't touched them.

The next day Greta returned to the fence and I followed. The room was empty. Everything was gone. I watched her cry. She wouldn't let me come near her.

I had often gotten into moods when I would reject her. Now that she was rejecting me, I felt the numbing sting of it, and finally I rather cruelly yelled, "She's dead! Why don't you stop acting so crazy?"

But I didn't expect her answer. "She's not dead! She just went out to buy a clock so she can look at it while she waits for him." I thought that was the craziest thing I'd ever heard in my life so I just turned around and got the hell away from her.

We didn't speak at all after that. I didn't even tell her I was going away. It was as though I wasn't around. She walked around with a blank expression on her face and her eyes staring. I couldn't stand to look at her but I had an awful lonely feeling not being able to talk to her.

A few weeks later the fat lady returned. She took me with her to New Jersey. She wasn't so bad after all. But when I was old enough I got the hell away from her.

Now Greta was a woman of twenty-eight, and she was walking in front of me down a street of browns tone apartments with a clock in her arms, seemingly oblivious of everyone and everything, certainly of me. I tried in my mind the beginning of a conversation with her. "May I help you carry the clock, Greta?" "I was just taking it home to take it apart. Will you help me? Remember?" I couldn't imagine a likely flow of talk, and decided to delay speaking until she arrived at her destination.

Of course, her husband might have been nearby, thus calling for uncomfortable explanation, but for some inexplicable reason I felt that she was something of an old maid in corduroy. In my mind our conversation continued. "Yes, I was married but it didn't last long. He left me for another woman." And I would soften the tension with, "I haven't married, myself. I'm married to my art. A woman is just a worry-wart for an artist like me." Then she would laugh that completely shattering laugh of hers and I wouldn't be able to speak and the grandfather's clock would probably chime about then.

Then she slowed down at the corner building and climbed a short flight of steps. I was quickly at her elbow again, half expecting her to drop the black mahogany clock when she fumbled for her keys. "Please allow me to hold your burden while you find your keys, Miss."

Not looking at me, she smiled rather uncomfortably, and began to rummage through some things in her pockets. She had her hand full of some sort of junk. As I watched her picking through it for her key, I noticed that on the fingers of one of her hands were fresh bruises and old scars. An object fell from her hands and she turned to catch it.

At the sight of the small rubber ball used in jack-rocks games bouncing slowly down the steps and rolling into the gutter, a nameless panic seized me and I looked around with the kind of fear one feels just prior to the clearer realization of the exact nature of the danger. My frightened glances revealed a familiar sight, unseen for twenty years. Across a vacant lot to the rear of the buildings on the next street over, I could see the miserably familiar drainpipe and the window to the infirmary, and a few buildings down, the fence, the tree and the grassless mound of earth.

I half expected the clock to chime in my arms at that moment, but it had stopped ticking altogether, and Greta was ascending the steps again with the key in one hand and the ball in the other, bruised one. She looked up at me, full into my face and then she really saw me for the first time. Her eyes seemed almost to tremble but a slow smile moved across her lips. She reached out and softly laid the palm of her hand on my wrist, the fingers lightly touching the black mahogany.

"Hello, Greta. How have you been?"

"I've been asleep, dreaming of you."

Maybe I'm a coward, but I just turned and leaned the clock against the door and walked quickly away.

THE SINGER

✲

Thank you, Reverend Bullard. Your introduction was exaggerated, of course, but I won't say it made me mad. Ladies and gentlemen, I want to say first what splendid work your church has been doing. And I'm speaking now not as a P. R. man but as a citizen and a Christian. As the reverend was saying, the church must play a role in the important issues of this changing world of ours. Now don't anybody go away and tell it on me that Pete Simpkins talked here tonight like some radical. Politics is one thing, and the hard facts of social life is another. You can't legislate morality. But now you *can* educate people about the facts of their state government and where it's not doing right by the people. So "Christian Program on Politics" is a good, 100 per cent American name for what you're doing in this election year. Now with the ward your church is in, I don't have to guess how most of you folks have voted for the last half-century, but tonight I just want to *show* you some of the mistruths that the present administration is forsting upon the people, and you can vote accordingly. Because this movie I'm going to show you — which I was in on making — is to show you the truth, instead of what you read in the papers, about how they're wiping out poverty in eastern Kentucky.

You know, in spring, when the floods aren't raging, in summer they isn't a drought, and in the fall, when the mountain slopes aren't ablaze, eastern Kentucky is beautiful. In the winter, though, I don't hesitate to call it a nightmare landscape: nature hides herself under a mossy rock and you see the human landscape come into focus, especially in *this* winter's record cold and hunger. We took these movies all this summer and fall, off and on, up the narrow valleys, creeks, and hollers of the counties of eastern Kentucky: McCreary, Owsley, Bell, Breathitt, Perry, Pike, Laurel, Lee, Leslie, Letcher, Clay, Harlan, Knott, Floyd, and let's see, Magoffin, Martin, Whitley, and Wolfe.

So let me show you what we saw in eastern Kentucky. Now, you understand, we're in the early stages of working on this movie. We got a lot of work and a heap of fundraising ahead of us yet, before we can get it in shape to release to the general public on TV and at rallies where it can do the damage. So, Fred, if you're ready to roll . . .

Wayne, you want to get up here with me, so if there's any questions I can't answer, maybe you can? Come on up. You had more to do with this project than I did. As the reverend told you, ladies and gentlemen, Wayne was our advance man. We sent him ahead to prepare the people for the cameras — set things up. I got my poop sheets laying on the pulpit here, Wayne, else I'd let you see how it feels to stand in the preacher's shoes.

You're doing fine, Pete.

Then let's start, Fred . . . Ha! Can you all see through me okay? Those numbers show up awful clear on my shirt. I better scoot off to the side a little. Now, soon's those numbers stop flashing, you'll see what the whole national uproar is about. People better quit claiming credit before it's due, just because they're trying to win an election.

Now these washed-out shoulders you can blame on the Department of Highways and Politics. Coming down the steep mountainsides, you have to swerve to miss holes that look to been made by hand grenades, and then around the curve you try to miss the big trucks. Hard freezes, sudden thaws, and coal truck traffic too heavy for the roads they travel can tear up a cheap narrow road. But if the administration kept its promises to maintain certain standards of construction . . .

Folks, that's not an Indian mound, that's a slag heap. Something else that greets you around every curve: slate dumps from shut-down mines and saw-dust piles from abandoned wood-pecker mills, smoldering, thousands of them, smoldering for ten years or more. The fumes from these dumps'll peel the paint off your house. A haze always hangs over the towns and the taste of coal is in the air you breathe. That smell goes away with you in your clothes.

Good shot of one of those gas stations from the 1930s. Remember those tall, skinny, old-timey orange pumps with the glass domes? This station was lived in for about twenty-five years before it was abandoned. They don't demolish anything around there. Plenty of room to build somewhere else. Look at that place. You know, traveling in eastern Kentucky makes you feel you're back in the '30s.

Ah! Now this is a little ghost town called Blackey.

I think this is Decoy, Pete.

Decoy. And I mean, there's not a soul lives there. But plenty of evidence a lot of them once did. You get there up fifteen miles of dirt road. Millions of dollars were mined out of there. That's the company store, there's the hospital, post office, jail, schoolhouse — turned coal camp gray, and may as well be on the dark side of the moon. See the old mattress draped over the tree limb, and all the floors — see that — covered with a foot of wavy mud that's hardened over the summer. That crust around the walls close to the ceiling marks the level of the flood that bankrupted what was left of the company. Ripped couches in the yard there, stink weeds all around, rusty stovepipes, comic books, romance magazines, one shoe in the kitchen sink, the other somewhere out in the yard under the ropes where they've hacked the swing down. Rooms full of mud daubers building nests, dead flies on the sills, and half-eaten spider webs. And over the crusts of mud in the houses and in the yards is strowed about a bushel of old letters from boys that joined the services out of desperation or hoping for adventure, and photographs the people left behind when they fled to God knows where. So it's just out there in the middle of the wilderness, doing nothing. Decoy.

Here we are in a typical eastern Kentucky town. Harlan, wudn't it, Wayne?

Hazard.

Hard to tell them apart. Well, next time we show this thing, God willing, it'll have one of the biggest TV announcers in Louisville narrating.

See the way the slopes of the mountains kindly make a bowl around Harlan? Houses cover the hillsides — just sort of flung up there. No streets or even dirt roads lead up to some of them. Swaying staircases and crooked paths go up to those porches that hover above the road there. Go along the highway, and see washing machines and refrigerators parked on the front porches. See high up, just below the clouds, that brown house with the long porch — just clinging to the cliffside? Houses like that all over, deserted, some of them just charred shells, the roofs caved in under tons of snow, the junk spewed out the front door.

Now *this* you see everywhere you go — old folks sitting on the front porch in half-deserted coal camps. On relief, on the dole, *been* on the dole since the war. That old man isn't near as old as he looks. Worked in the mines before they laid him off and idleness went to work on him like erosion. Wife got no teeth, no money to get fitted. Dipped snuff and swigged RCs to kill the pain of a mouth full of cavities till the welfare jerked them all out for her. And there comes the little baby — right through the ripped screen door — grandchild the daughter left behind when she went to Chicago or Cincinnati or *Detroit* or Baltimore, which is where they all go. Didn't they say this baby's momma had it, Wayne, just had it, so they could collect on it?

Yeah.

And another girl, under twenty-one, had four babies and drew on *all* of them. Why, the government takes an interest in her that no husband could hope to match. Look at that baby's little tummy, swollen out there like a — Fred, you shoulda held on that one.

And this is a general view of how high the mountains are. *Way* up high . . . (What *was* the point of that, Wayne?)

(I don't know.)

See that stream? Watch. . . . See that big splash of garbage? Fred, did you get a good shot of that woman? *There* you go! She just waltzed out in her bare feet and tossed that lard bucket of slop over the back banister without batting an eye.

Even the industries dump —

Well . . . And that stream — Big Sandy, I think. See how low it runs? Well, every spring it climbs those banks and pours down that woman's chimney and washes out every home along that valley. See the strips of red cloth left hanging on the branches of the trees? Like flagging a lot of freight trains. And rags and paper and plastic bleach jugs dangle from the bushes and from the driftwood that juts up out of the riverbed mud. In the summer those banks swarm with green, but don't let it fool you. See how wavy that mud is? And that little bright trickle of poisoned water. Fish *die* in that stuff, so leave your pole at home. And stay away from the wells. Lot of them polluted.

This is a trash dump on a slope high above Harlan where whole families go to root for "valuables." Look like bats clinging to a slanting wall, don't they? But if you go in among them, why, seems like it's just a Sunday family outing.

Most of the graveyards are up on a hill like this one, to escape the floods, I guess. But living on the mountains, maybe the natural way of thinking is up. Look close under that inscription: it's a photograph, sealed in glass, showing the deceased sitting in the front-porch swing with his wife, morning-glories climbing the trellis.

With that red sky behind them, those kudzu vines crawling all over the hillsides, dripping from the trees, look like big lizards rising up out of the mud. Come around a bend on a steep mountain highway and they've crept to the edge. Those kudzu vines are the last greens to go.

Here we are up in the mountains again. (Who said to shoot the scenic overlooks, Wayne?)

(Nobody. Fred loved to shoot the view, I suppose.)

(That'd be fine if this was called "Vacation in Eastern Kentucky.") Now, this part, Wayne, I don't remember at all.

This is Cumberland. You were still asleep and Fred and I went out for coffee and passed this big crowd — Wait a minute . . .

Actually, folks, this is the first time I've had a chance to see the stuff. I told Fred just to throw it together for tonight. The real editing comes later.

Just a bunch of miners standing on a street corner. You might take notes on some of this stuff, Fred, stuff to cut out, and, ladies and gentlemen, I hope *you* will suggest what —

Good Lord, Fred!

(Watch your language, Wayne. I saw it.) Fred, I think you got some black-and-white footage accidentally mixed in. Folks, please excuse this little technical snafu, but as I say we wanted to get this *on* the screen for you, get your reactions, and I think Fred here — He's worked pretty hard and late hours, these past three weeks especially, and we only got back to Louisville a few days ago. . . . Ha! Ha. Fred, how much of this? . . . As some of you folks may know, Fred is mute.

Now this, ladies and gentlemen, is the girl some of you have been reading about in the *Courier*. And the other girl, the one leaning against the front of that empty pool hall, is —

Wayne, I don't think — I'm sure these fine people aren't interested in hearing any more about that little incident. Listen, Fred, that machine has a speed-up on it, as I recall.

I think he brought the old Keystone, Pete.

Oh. Well, folks, I don't know how long this part lasts, and I apologize for Fred, but we'll just have to wait till it runs out.

In the meantime, what I could do is share with you some facts I've collected from eyewitnesses and that my research staff has dug out for me. Barely see my notes in this dim light. The Cumberland Mountains are a serrated upland region that was once as pretty as the setting of that old *Trail of the Lonesome Pine* movie. It has a half-million inhabitants. But there's been a twenty-eight per cent decline in population of people between the ages of twenty and twenty-four, and an *increase* of about 85 per cent old people. In some counties about half the population is on relief and it's predicted that some day about 80 per cent of the whole region will be drawing commodities. There's about twenty-five per cent illiteracy for all practical purposes, and those that *do* get educated leave. And something that surprises me is that there's only about fifteen per cent church affiliation. All in all, I'd say the poverty is worse than Calcutta, India, and the fertility rate is about as high, seems like to me. In other words, the people are helpless and the situation is hopeless. The trouble with this administration is that they *think* a whole lot *can* be done, and then they claim credit even before they do it, to make *us* look bad. We don't make no such promises. Because we see that the facts —

I think a lady in the audience has her hand up, Pete.

Ma'am? . . . I'm sorry, that old moving-picture machine makes such a racket, you'll have to speak louder.

Pete, I think what she asked was, "Did any of us get to talk with her?"

With who? Oh. Ma'am, that really isn't what this movie is about. We went in there with the best color film money can buy to shoot poverty, and where Fred got this cheap black and white newsreel stock —

I think it was from that New York crew.

Now, Wayne, this is not the place to drag all *that* business in. We came here tonight to show what it's like to live in the welfare state where all a body's got is promises instead of bread to put on the table. *I* know. I *come* from those people. Now there *are* some legitimate cripples, caused by explosions, fires, roof-falls and methane gas poisoning in the mines, and some have been electrocuted and blinded and afflicted with miner's asthma. But a majority that's on relief are welfare malingerers who look forward to getting "sick enough to draw," and whose main ambition is to qualify for total and permanent disability. For those people, all these aids, gifts, grants, and loans are the magic key to the future, but I see it as what's undermining public morals and morale. That's the story I was hired to get, and as I remember that's the story we *got*, on those thousands of feet of expensive color film. And if —

Well, now we're back at the heart of the matter. Her we are on Saturday in Hazard.

Pete.

What?

I think *that's* Harlan.

Wayne, I was *born* in Harlan.

Well, Pete, there's that twelve foot pillar of coal in the middle of the intersection, which you told us to shoot because it belonged to your childhood.

Fred's got the whole thing so fouled up, he's probably spliced Hazard and Harlan together.

Okay. . . .

Now the shot's *gone.* That, as you could see, folks, *was* the bread line. The monthly rations.

I guess Wayne was right, after all. Says WORK, THINK, BUY COAL, painted right across the top of the town's highest building.

Here you see a mother and her four kids standing beside the highway, waiting for her goldbricking husband to row across the river and pick her up and take the rations and the donated clothes over to the old log cabin — caulked with mud, see that, and ambushed by briars and weeds. That's their swinging bridge, dangling in the water from the flood last spring that he's too lazy to —

Now this is *really* the kind of thing we went in there to get. That's not a desert, that's a dry river bed those two women are crossing. What they're lugging on their backs is tow-sacks full of little pieces of shale coal that — Now see that steep ridge? You can just barely make them out on the path now. See that? See that man under the bridge? A little too dark . . . Get down under there, Fred. *There* we go! Squatting on the bottom of that dry river bed with his five kids, actually rooting in the dirt for pieces of coal no bigger than a button that the floods washed down from the mountains. Whole family grubbing for coal, looking toward winter. Sunday. Bright fall morning. Church bells ringing in Harlan while we were shooting. Kids dirty. Noses and sores running. Don't that one remind you of pictures of children liberated from Auschwitz? Look at the way he stares at you. I offered to *buy* the man a truckload of coal. What he said, I won't repeat. Who's he talking to now, Wayne?

Fred.

Sure got a good close-up of him, Fred. The eye that belongs in that empty socket is under tons of coal dust in some choked-up mine shaft, and when he lifts those buckets and starts to follow the women, he'll limp.

Black and white again, Fred! Now where did this stuff *come* from? Who's paying for this waste?

That other crew, Pete, when they went back to New York, they practically gave it to Fred in exchange for a tank of gas.

(Wayne, I wouldn't be surprised if Fred put up as much as he made on the whole expedition.)

(Frankly, I think he did.)

Fred, shut off the dang picture and let the thing wind ahead by itself.

This is the old machine, Pete.

(I don't understand how he could make such a mistake. Anybody can see when they've got color and when —)

Pete, young man in the back has his hand up.

Yes? . . . Listen, son, I don't know one thing about that girl. In fact, I'd be happy to forget what little I *do* know. All three of them, in fact, and the motorsickle and the whole mess. . . .I'm sorry, you'll have to talk louder. . . . (Wayne, you should have *previewed* this movie!) Now, son, I don't have a thing to say about that girl.

(Well, somebody better say *something*, Pete. It's only human for them to be interested.)

(Then *you* tell them. You're as bad as Fred was — *is*.)

To answer your question, young man. No one has yet located the parents of the two girls. These shots show them walking along the highway between Whitesburg and Millstone. The smoke you see is coming from one of those slag heaps Pete was telling about. It's the first light of morning before the coal trucks begin to roll. Later, on down the road, one of those trucks, going around a hairpin curve, turned over and slung coal almost 200 feet. That's The Singer, as she was called, the one with the guitar slung over her shoulder, and there's the friend, who always walked a few steps behind, like a servant. These black and white shots were taken by the crew from New York. I don't think *they* were mentioned in the newspaper stories, though. But they crossed paths with the girls in Wheelright, Lovely, Upper Thousand Sticks, Dalna, Coal Run, Highsplint, and other towns along the way. Yes, Reverend Bullard?

What did he say?

He said no smoking on church premises, Pete.

Oh. Sorry, reverend. Nervous habit, I guess.

> Somewhere in here is a shot of the preacher who started it all. Soon after people started talking about The Singer, he described himself as God's transformer. Claimed God's electricity flowed through *him* into *her*. The day they found the girls, he put it a different way — said he was only God's impure vessel.

Ladies and gentlemen, I would like to focus your attention on a really fine shot of a rampaging brushy fire that —

> Hey, Fred, I didn't know you got those girls in color!

Okay, Fred, okay, okay! Just throw the switch! Lights, somebody! Lights!

> Fred, Pete said to cut the projector off!

Folks, I apologize for Fred, but I had no way of knowing. Fred, this is what I call a double cross, a real live doublecross, Fred! You promised that if I'd hire you back, you'd stay away from that New York outfit and those two girls.

> (Pete, aren't you doing more harm than good by just cutting the thing off?)

(This stuff don't belong in the picture.)

> (Just look at their faces. They want to know all about it, they want to *see* every inch of film on that reel.)

(This ain't what I come to show.)

> (She couldn't be in *all* of it. We didn't run into her that often, and neither did that New York bunch.)

(It's distracting as hell.)

> (The poverty footage is *on* the reel, too, you know.)

(You *want* to tell them, don't you? *He* wants to *show* them and *you* want to tell all about it. Admit it.)

(Look, Pete, it's only natural —)

(Yeah, like looking for a job when you're out of one. Go ahead. Tell them. If Fred wasn't a mute, he'd furnish the sound track in person.)

Folks, this is just our little joke tonight. We thought we'd experiment. You know, give you a double feature, both on the same reel.

Here, Fred got a shot of the revival tent in Blue Diamond where she first showed up about five weeks ago, early in September. That's a blown-up photograph of Reverend Daniel in front of the tent. Sun kind of bleached it out, but the one in the paper was clear.

That's the old company store at Blue Diamond and the photographs you see on the bulletin board there are of miners killed in the war. Maybe one of them was The Singer's brother.

The tent again ...

The way people tell it, Reverend Daniel was preaching pretty hard, lashing out at sinners, when he suddenly walked straight to the back, pointing at a girl that he said he knew wanted to be saved because she had committed a terrible sin that lay heavy on her heart. And standing where the tent flap was pulled back, dripping rain, was this girl. Thin and blond, with the biggest eyes you ever saw.

Good footage on that wrecked car in the creek, Fred. You know, the young men go to *Detroit* to work awhile, get homesick and drive some broken-down Cadillac or Buick back home and leave it where it crashed in the river or broken down in the front yard, and the floods ship it on to the next town. Hundreds of roadside scrap yards like this one where cars look like cannibals have been at them. Good panoramic shot. Fred's pictures are worth a thousand words when he's got his mind on his work.

And here's Fred shooting the mountains again. Couldn't get enough of those look-offs.

So there she stood, a little wet from walking to the tent in the rain, and Reverend Daniel led her up front, and pretty soon he began to heal the afflicted. They say he was great that night. Had them all down on the ground. He laid hands on them, and there was speaking in tongues, and those who weren't on the ground were singing or doing a sort of dance-like walk they do. And when it was all over, he went among them with his portable microphone and asked them to testify.

Then he came to *her*. And instead of talking, she began to sing. A man that lived nearby was sitting on his porch, and he said he thought it was the angels, coming ahead of Gabriel.

She sang "Power in the Blood" for an hour, and when she stopped, Reverend Bullard — excuse me — Reverend *Daniel* asked her what she suffered from. And when she didn't speak, he said he bet it was rheumatic fever, and when she still didn't speak —

Moving on now, we see a typical country schoolhouse. In the middle of the wilderness, a deserted schoolhouse is not just an eyesore, it's part of the country. When people live on the front porch, relics of the past are always in view, reminding them of times that's gone — the era of the feuds, of the timber industry, of the coming of the railroad, of the moonshine wars, and of the boom and bust of coal.

Ha! Fooled you, didn't I? Thought it was deserted. Ha. There's the teacher in her overcoat, and the kids all bundled up in what little clothes they have. See that one girl with rags wrapped around her legs in place of boots? That's the reason — gaps between the boards a foot wide. And believe me, it gets cold in those mountains. Now what's the administration going to say to the voters about *that* when they go to the polls in November? They claim they're *improving* conditions.

From the highway, you don't often see the scars in the earth from the strip mines and the black holes where the augers have bored. I suppose those New York boys are trying here to give you an impression of the landscape The Singer wandered over. On the highways, you may pass a truck hauling big augers, but to watch the auger rig boring, you have to climb steep dirt roads. That's where The Singer and her friend seem to be going now — not on purpose, I don't think. Just aimlessly wandering, those New York boys following close behind with their black and white. Now, who's *that* girl? Oh, yeah, the one that starred in *their* movie. What was her name? Deirdre. . . .Back to The Singer again. Going on up the winding road, and those black eyes staring at you out of that far hillside — auger holes seven feet in diameter. The dust those trucks stir up barreling down the mountain is from spoil banks that get powder-dry in the summer and it sifts down, along with coal grit, onto the little corn and alfalfa and clover that still grows in the worn-out land. With its trees cut down by the stripping operation, its insides ripped out by the augers, this mountain is like some mangy carcass, spewing out fumes that poison the air and the streams.

Where these augers and the strip mining have been, snows, rains, floods, freezes, and thaws cause sheet erosion, and rocks big as tanks shoot down on people's cabins. This used to be rich bottomland. Now it's weeds, broomsedge, and thickets. Don't look for an old bull-tongue plow on *those* hillsides. And the big trees are gone. Of course, the blight got the chestnuts, but what do you call *this*?

Wayne, let's keep in mind the money that helped make this movie possible.

Well, this, friends, was once called Eden. Some people have reason to call it dark and bloody ground. There's places that look like the petrified forest, places like the painted desert, but it's a wasteland, whatever you call it, and the descendants of the mountaineers are trespassers on company property that their fathers sold for a jug, ignorant as a common Indian of its long-term value. And they can't look to the unions any more. The UMWA has all but abandoned them, some say, while the bulldozers that made that road and which drag that auger apparatus into place for another boring every hour continue what some people call the rape of the Appalachians. . . . I'm sorry, I didn't hear the question?

Young lady wants to know what happened next.

Next? Oh. You mean about The Singer? Oh, yes. Well, the story, which we got piece by piece, has it that when the girl didn't speak, Reverend Daniel got a little scared and looked around for someone that knew her.

In the entrance to the tent, where The Singer had stood, was another girl — black-haired, sort of stocky, just a little cross-eyed, if you remember the picture, but pretty enough to attract more men than was good for her. She didn't know The Singer but was staring at her in a strange way, and several boys in leather jackets were trying to get her to come away from the tent and go off with them.

Now this is a shot of the girls drinking from a spring that gushes out of the mountain with enough force to knock a man down. Her friend sees the cameraman and steps behind The Singer to block her from the camera. Those New York boys would barge right in without blinking an eye.

Well, Reverend Daniel did find someone who knew her and who said there was absolutely nothing wrong with her, physically or mentally, that when she saw her the day before The Singer was just fine. That made everybody look at Reverend Daniel a little worried, and he turned pale, but an old, old woman began to do that dance and speak in tongues and when she calmed down she said *she* knew what had come over the girl. Said she had what they call —

Now here we see the Negro section of Harlan. Notice —

Just a second, Pete.

The old lady said that the girl had got a calling, to sing for Jesus. And The Singer began to sing again, and the girl that travels with Reverend Daniel *gave* The Singer her guitar, said, "Take it, keep it, use it to sing for Jesus." Then *she* took up the tambourine, the whole tent began to shake with singing, The Singer's voice soaring above it all, and listen, ladies and gentlemen, before that night nobody in that area knew a thing about her singing.

You pass this condemned swimming pool and that graveyard of school buses and go over a concrete-railing bridge that humps in the middle and there you are in the Negro slums. The cement street turns into a dirt road a country block long, and the houses are identical, and the ones that haven't turned brown are still company green. See, the street is just a narrow strip between that hill and the river that floods the houses every year. At each end, wild bushes reach up to the tree line. At the back steps, a steep hill starts up.

There's no blackness like midnight dark in the Cumberland Mountains, but the white man can walk this street safely. No one wants to discourage him from buying the white lightnin' and the black women. And here we are inside the dance hall where the Negroes are having a stomping Saturday night good time. Awful dim, but if you strain a little . . .

Want to let me finish, Pete?

Then The Singer walked out of the tent and they followed her up the highway, but she kept walking, higher and higher into the mountains, and the people kept falling back, until only one person walked behind her — that black-haired girl with the slightly crossed eyes.

You through?

Sure, go ahead.

(They just *missed* the greatest shot in the whole movie.)

(They saw it, Pete.)

(The hell. They were listening to *you*, 'stead of looking at the *move-ee*. For an Ohio Yankee you sure act like you know it all. Now when *my* part is on, *you* shut up.)

(Fair enough, Pete.)

More of the black and white. . . . Shots of The Singer at a coal tipple near Paintsville. Truck mine. No railroad up this branch, so they just pop-shoot it with dynamite and truck it out.

Anyway, what would happen was that The Singer and the other girl would walk along and whenever and *wherever* the spirit moved her, The Singer would sing. Just sing, though. She couldn't, wouldn't, anyway *didn't* speak a word. Only sing. And while she sang, she never sat down or leaned against anything. Hardly any expression on her face. Sometimes she seemed to be in a trance, sometimes a look on her face like she was trying to hide pain, sometimes a flicker of a smile, but what got you in a funny way was that the song hardly ever called for the little things she did, except the happy songs, "I Love to Tell the Story," or "Just As I Am," you know — those she'd plunge into with a smile at first, until she would be laughing almost hysterically in a way that made you want to hug her, but, of course, nobody, not even the kind of women that'll take hold of a sweating girl full of the Holy Ghost and drench her with tears, really dared to. No, not The Singer. She wasn't touched, that I know of, though people sort of reached for her as she passed. But then sometimes you'd feel that distance between you and her and next thing you knew she'd be so close in among people you could smell her breath, like cinnamon. She had ways of knocking you off balance, but so you only fell deeper into her song. Like she'd be staring into your eyes, and her lids would drop on a note that was going right through you. Or, coming out of a pause between verses, she'd suddenly take three steps toward you.

They walked, they never rode. They walked thousands of miles through those hills, aimlessly: through Sharondale, Vicco, Kingdom Come, Cumberland Gap, Cody, along Hell-for-Certain Creek, and up through Pine Mountain.

And here we are in a jailhouse in Manchester. Handle a lot of coal around there. And these boys you see looking through the bars are teenagers the sheriff rounded up the night before. Out roving the highways in these old cars, shooting up road signs. They loved having their picture taken — a mob of little Jesse Jameses.

Now, I ask you: can the administration just *give* these youngsters jobs?

Winding road . . . coiled up like a rattlesnake. See where those boys — WATCH FOR FALLEN ROCK. Just shot it all to pieces. Most of them will end up in the penitentiary *making* road signs.

Now in this shot — in Hellier, I think — The Singer has wandered into a church and they've followed her. And off to the side there, among the parked cars and pickup trucks, you can see the other girl, leaning against the door of a car, talking to some men and boys. Can't see them for the car. There. See them? Talking to her? Well, that's the way it was, after awhile.

A boy told one of the young men on the New York crew that he was outside the tent at Blue Diamond that first night, and that the black-haired girl was going from, truck to truck, where the men were waiting

for their wives to come out of the revival tent and the young boys were
waiting for the girls to come out. But this girl never made it in. They
always waited for her outside, and she went with all of them. And
then — I don't know who or where I got it — the girl heard the singing
and left the cab of a coal truck and went to the entrance of the tent,
and then when The Singer went out to the highway, she followed her.
Then after about a week —

Oh. Go ahead, Pete.

Folks, here we are, back on the track, with a shot we were afraid wouldn't
come out. Good job, Fred. A carload of pickets waiting to join a caravan.
Eight young men in that car, all of them armed. You can hear them at night,
prowling up and down the highways in long caravans, waking you up, and if
you look between the sill and the shade by your bed, you can see lights flashing
against Black Mountain under the cold sky, full of stars.

And here we are swinging down the mountain-side. . . . Some of the early
September shots before this record cold drove people indoors. We just suddenly, in the bright morning sunlight, came upon this train, derailed in the
night by dynamite. Don't it look like an exhibit out in that big open space, all
those crowded porches huddled around on the bare hillside?

Going along the highway, you can expect to find anything in the yards, even
in front of inhabited houses. See that car? Pulled up by a block and tackle
tossed over a tree limb — looks like an old-time lynching. This man's taken
the junk that the floods leave on his porch — sometimes on his roof — and
arranged a *dis*play of it all in his yard.

You look up and see those long porches, hanging over the road, seems
like, clinging to the steep slopes, and what it reminds *me* of is little villages
in Europe when I was in the army. Whole family sitting out there, on the
railing, on car seats jerked out of wrecks on the highway, on cane-bottom
chairs salvaged from their cabin home places far in the mountains, talking
and swirling RCs and watching the road. For *what*?

Well, for *her*, wouldn't you say, Pete? Word of her singing ran ahead
of her, and since nobody knew where she'd turn up next . . . One
time she even walked right into a congregation of snake handlers
and started singing. But not even that brazen New York crew got

any shots of *that*. And sometimes she'd walk right out of the wildest woods, the other girl a little behind, both of them covered with briars and streaked with mud.

Here — somewhere along the Poor Fork of the Cumberland River — Fred seems to be trying to give an impression of the road, the winding highway The Singer walked. Pretty fall leaves stripped from the branches now. Abandoned coal tipples, bins, chutes, ramps, sheds, clinging to the bare hillsides like wild animals flayed and nailed to an old door. Those stagnant yellow ponds, where the rain collects, breed mosquitoes and flies the way the abandoned towns and the garbage on the hillsides breed rats. You may leave this region, but the pictures of it stick in your mind like cave drawings.

Here you see The Singer and her friend walking along one of these mountain roads again.

Too bad those New York boys couldn't afford color. A light morning rain has melted most of the snow that fell the night before. This is along Troublesome Creek and they've already been through Cutshin, Diablock, Meta, Quicksand, Jeff, and Carbon Glow, Lynch, and Mayking. By the way, the reason the girls are dressed that way — style of the '30s — is because they're wearing donated clothes. Remember the appeal that came over television and filled the fire stations with clothes after last spring's flood?

These artificial legs were displayed in a window near our *hotel* next to the railroad depot in Harlan. Nice, hazy Sunday morning sunlight, but *that*, and this shot of a pawnshop window — little black-muzzled, pearl-handled revolvers on pretty little satin cushions — reminds you of what kind of life these people have in the welfare state. And those windows piled high with boots and shoes beyond repair are something else you see at rest on Sunday in Harlan.

There they are in front of a movie theater — What's that showing? Oh, yeah, an old Durango Kid movie. Fred and I saw that in another town — Prestonsburg, I think. Never forget the time she walked into a movie theater and started to sing right in the middle of a showdown in some cowboy shoot-out, and one big lummox started throwing popcorn at her till the singing reached him and he just left his hand stuffed in the bag like it was a bear trap.

Anyway, as I was telling before, the other girl, after about a week, took to luring the men away from The Singer because they began to follow her and bother her and try to start something with her, so the friend had to distract them from her, and ended up doing the very thing she had tried to stop herself from doing by going with The Singer. They say The Singer never seemed to know what was going on. She'd walk on up the highway or on out of town and the other girl would catch up.

See how they just nail their political posters to the nearest tree? Sun sure bleached that man out, didn't it?

Here, Fred got a shot of the New York movie crew getting out of their station wagon. Three young men and a girl. Looks like somebody scraped the bottom of a barrel full of Beatniks, doesn't it? The local boys and men kept teasing them about their beards and they tried to laugh along, but finally they would get into fights, and we'd come into a town just after they had gone, with the police trying to get people out of the street, or the highway patrol escorting the crew into the next county. They came down to shoot what they called an art movie. They told Fred the story once and I listened in, but I can't remember a thing about it, except that this girl named Deirdre was going to be in it. She *was* in it. Yeah, this is one of the scenes! Shot her *in front of* a lot of things, and she would kind of sway and dip around among some local people — just like that — and everybody — Yeah, see the big grins on their faces? And the director kept begging them to look serious, look serious.

That's one of *yours*, Pete.

Shots of old men in front of the courthouse. . . . Young boys, too. . . . No work. Bullet holes around the door from the '30s. Bad time, bad time.

What those guys did, Wayne, was make everybody mad, so that when *we* came rolling into town, they were ready to shoot anybody that even *looked* like he wanted to pull out a camera.

Yeah. Always pointing those loaded cameras at things and running around half-cocked, shoot, shoot, shooting.

Then they ran into The Singer and her friend, and — Yeah, this is the one, this is actually the *first* shot they took of The Singer. First, this is a close-up of *their* girl — Deirdre — you're looking at, long stringy hair, soulful eyes. One time they even put something *in* her eyes to make the tears run. And in just a second they'll swing to catch The Singer. That's it! See the camera jerk? The script writer saw The Singer on the opposite corner and jerked the cameraman around. Here you can see The Singer's friend standing off to one side, on the lookout for trouble-makers — front of a little café in Frenchberg. Cameraman got her in the picture by accident, but later when the director caught on to what she was *doing* with The Singer, he hounded her to death. Made her very angry a couple of times. Deirdre in *his* movie though —

Pete . . .

What's you want?

Your part's on.

Well . . . that's, as you can see . . . the garbage in the streams there . . . kids with rickets . . . brush fire in the mountains . . .

I was about to say about the folk singer from Greenwich Village — Deirdre — she got very angry too, over the way the movie boys took after The Singer, so she threatened to get a bus back to New York. But after they had listened to people tell about The Singer in the towns they came into, not long after she had gone on, and after they had tracked her down a few times, and after Deirdre had heard her sing, she got so she tried to *follow* The Singer. Deirdre ran away from the movie boys once, and when they caught up with her the black-haired girl was trying to fight off some local boys who thought Deirdre was like *her*. But she wasn't. Not after The Singer got to her, anyway. I don't know what Deirdre was like in New York, but in Cumberland Mountains she heard one song too many. I never saw her after she changed, either. Finally, the New York boys had to lock her in a room at the Phoenix Hotel in Salyersville and one stayed behind to watch over her. Wish we had a shot of that hotel. White, a century old, or more, three stories in front, four in back, little creek running behind it. Three porches along the front. Sit in a broken chair and watch the people go by below. If you're foolish, you sit on the rail. If you leave the windows open in the room at the back, you wake up covered with dew and everything you touch is damp.

Pete.

Shots of another abandoned shack . . .

Go ahead, Pete.

They can see it okay. . . . .same old thing . . .

Oh. Now *that's* Reverend Daniel, the one that ministered to The Singer in Blue Diamond. He'd moved his tent to Pikeville and that's where we saw him, and got these shots of his meeting. Promised him a stained-glass window for his tent if he'd let us, didn't we, Wayne? Ha! Anyway, next time we saw him was a week ago, just before the accident, and he told me how he had offered to make The Singer rich if she would sing here in Louisville. Told her people all over Kentucky had read about the wandering singer for Jesus, and that he could make her famous all over the world, and they could build the biggest church in the country, and stuff like that. She just looked at him and walked on. He pestered her awhile, but finally gave up after about six miles of walking. Wayne, you saw him after it happened, didn't you?

Yeah. He blames himself. Thinks he should have looked after her. As though God meant him to be not just a transformer but a guardian angel, too. He'll never put up another tent as long as he lives.

And that girl — Deirdre — that come down from New York, she could be dead for all we know. The boy that was guarding her —

Said he shouldn't have told her about what happened on the highway.

Slipped out of the Phoenix *Hotel* somehow and vanished.

She *may* turn up in New York.

And she might turn up alongside some highway in the mountains, too.

This is one of Fred's few shots of the girls. He hated to disturb them. Actually, The Singer never paid any attention to us or to the other crew, did she, Pete? Mostly, Fred listened to her sing, standing in the crowds in Royalton, Hardburley, Coalville, Chevrolet, Lothair, his camera in his case, snapped shut. Right, Fred? But here, while they sat on a swinging bridge, eating — well, the friend eating, because nobody ever saw The Singer put a bite of food in her mouth, just drink at the mountain springs — Fred got them with his telephoto lens from up on one of those look-offs beside the road.

Kind of grainy and the color's a little blurred, but it looks like it's from a long way off through a fine blue mist at about twilight. Nice shot, Fred.

There's those numbers on my shirt again. What about that? Fred, you want to catch that thing — film flapping that way gets on my nerves.

Personally, I'm glad nobody's got the *end* on film.

Know what you mean, Wayne.

What the papers didn't tell was —

That the boy on the motorsickle? . . .

Wasn't *looking* for the girls.

And he wasn't a member of some wild California gang crossing the country, either.

Go ahead and tell them, Pete.

That's okay. You tell it, Wayne.

The way Fred got the story — Fred, this is one time when I really wish you could speak for *yourself*. Fred was the one who kept his arms around the boy till he stopped crying.

Tell them where it happened.

Outside Dwarf on Highway 82. The girls were walking along in the middle of the highway at about 3 o'clock in the morning and a thin sheet of ice was forming, and this motorcycle came down the curve, and if he hadn't slammed on his brakes —

More or less as a reflex —

It wouldn't have swerved and hit them.

You see, Fred had set out to catch up with them. Me and Wayne'd left him to come back to Louisville alone, because he said he was going to stop off a day or two to visit his cousin in Dwarf, and when he pulled in for coffee at Hindman and some truck driver told him he *thought* he had seen the girl's walking, out in the middle of nowhere, Fred got worried, it being so cold, and —

So he tried to catch up to them.
The girls and the boy were lying in the road.

Kid come all the way from Halifax, Nova Scotia.

Yeah, that's where they got the facts wrong in the paper. Saying he was some local hoodlum, then switching to the claim that he was with a gang from California. The fact is that the boy had quit school and bought a brand new black Honda, and he had set out to see the United States.

Wait a second, Wayne. Fred's trying to hand you a note.

Thanks, Fred. Oh. Ladies and gentlemen, Fred says here that it wasn't *Halifax*, Nova Scotia. He says, "It was *Glasgow*, Nova Scotia. Not that it matters a damn."

A HUMAN

INTEREST DEATH

❊

Edward Savage's father was gassed in World War One. He spent twenty years dying in the veterans hospital at Kingsport, Tennessee. Until young manhood, Edward lived with his mother and his older sister, Helen, on a farm in Cades Cove in the Great Smoky Mountains. His mother was never too severe nor too conciliatory about his needs, his moods, his ambitions. Helen worked in nearby Maryville, a country town fifteen miles from Knoxville, in a dime store, and set aside a portion of her meager salary for Edward's education, to supplement earnings from his rural morning paper route. Declared too short for service in World War Two, he attended business school in Maryville.

In Knoxville, he met a waitress at the Gold Sun Café on Market Square. Anticipating his marriage to Reba, an enormous woman from Hazard, Kentucky, Edward went to work for the Public Utilities company in Knoxville as an accountant, his first and last job.

When Edward's mother died, and Helen moved to Knoxville to be near him, Reba personally auctioned everything off: the mountain farm, the furniture, anything that would bring a nickel. The only thing she allowed him to keep was his mother's wicker rocking chair. But she wouldn't allow that "countrified old rocker on the front porch for all the neighbors to laugh at." Edward wanted to screen half of the front porch with a lattice and let honeysuckle climb it, a reminder of the farm and of his mother and sister, but Reba said, "I'll be damned if you will."

For twenty-five years she would harp on the same theme: "Why can't you move up in the company, up the ladder of success, instead of always quivering on the bottom rung?" Edward merely waited, and things happened to him. He was given a few little raises without asking. He had a son without even trying. He was never able to explain his apathy to Reba, but her constant nagging and his son's sullen contempt were more lucid than any answers *he* could have invented.

Still, he always told himself, his was good, clean, steady, honest work. Besides, look at the next-door neighbor, Jim Logan. An aggressive man, a hunter, a fisherman, a bowler, a poker player, an American Legionnaire. How far had *he* gone? After all these years, Logan was still a bus driver for the Knoxville Transit lines.

But not even having their imbecile daughter Myrna had made the Logans unhappy. When Dennis was in high school and Myrna was growing up (she attained her full height of five-six and a weight of one-ninety by age eleven), Edward would come into the house on a cold winter night to find Reba and Myrna seated before the TV. In the summer, the obese girl would be sitting on the grass at Reba's feet, while she reclined in her deck chair with a Royal Crown Cola, reading *Forbidden Romances* aloud by the failing light that slanted across the lawn. Every morning on cold days, Edward lugged in coal to last until noon. Then Myrna carried in buckets of coal so Denny wouldn't have to do it when he came home from school.

There were times when Edward wished he could go hunting with his son, although even when he was growing up in the mountains, he had not enjoyed hunting. But his son was content to take Reba to ball games, to laugh at her vulgar jokes, to listen to her retell the troubles of the people in the *True Romances*, to fetch her underthings and stockings from the clothes-line.

Edward's house was on the last street along the side of Sharp's Ridge. One night just after he had made love to Reba and was sinking into sleep, a thunderous crash woke him. Naked, he followed Reba through the house to the living room window. They watched a plane high on the ridge burn until daybreak. He asked Reba to pray with him for the pilot, but she laughed at him and pulled a hair from his belly.

A few days later, a telegram came, informing them that their son Alfred Dennis Savage, had been killed in Vietnam "in defense of his country."

The next morning on the bus, Edward watched rain dash against the window. Even for a rainy autumn morning, it was very dark. A kitten, soaked to the bone, was walking very slowly in front of the Methodist Church, which Edward attended regularly, keeping a promise to his mother.

All day, making entries on the books at the Utilities company, Edward thought of the cat. When he came back on the bus that evening, the sky was still gray, and his feet were wet and cold. The kitten was walking in the same direction in front of the church, still wet.

With hasty pity, Edward got off the bus on the corner at Rose's Drugstore. When he stooped down, the kitten walked into his opened arms. Trudging up the hill, he held it inside his overcoat, feeling its icy wetness, its fitful breathing against his heart.

From the bed, where she lay reading *Secret Confessions*, Reba yelled, "Off with them galoshes! You're tracking up my floor." She had not mopped it in weeks. When Edward opened his overcoat, dramatically revealing the little animal, Reba screamed, "Throw that mangy thing out of here!"

"I — I brought him for *you*, honey. To — to keep you company now Denny won't be —"

She laughed contemptuously. He realized lucidly for the first time how much he hated this woman.

But he did not throw the kitten out. Within a month, the alley cat was like a third person in the house, and Reba's baby-talk nauseated Edward.

Myrna often went to the store for Reba. And if she did something wrong, like bringing salt instead of sugar, vinegar instead of Royal Crown, or needles instead of hairpins, Reba was not abusive. But after Denny was killed, she was capable of making her eat the salt, drink the vinegar, and of jabbing her buttocks with a needle. At night in bed, she often bragged to Edward about her hold over the girl, excusing herself on the grounds that Myrna worshiped her and was insensitive to pain and mockery.

On top of Sharp's Ridge a silver tower flashing a red beacon had been erected to warn planes not to fly too low. Edward found an odd comfort in watching it. It seemed a personal sign of everlastingness, a reminder that his heart beat red and wet in the dark cave of his chest, but, also, of his dreary, day by day existence.

Many Sunday afternoons over twenty-five years, Edward went out to the coal house and, in the clothes he had worn every day to work and to church, he sat rocking back and forth, remembering how it had been on the farm in the Smoky Mountains. With the acrid smell in his nostrils, the dry hiss of coal dust under the rocker, he hated Reba for hiding his clean "Sunday best" to prevent him from getting away from her nagging to go see Helen. To dispel the hatred, he imagined the smell of honeysuckle that had loaded the lattice on the porch in Cade's Cove.

One Sunday in early spring, Edward rented a car for an outing in the Smoky Mountains. Reba made him steer clear of Cade's Cove, but she enjoyed the sprawling tourist town of Gatlinburg. Her face seemed the essence of youth and innocence, her stomach was great with child. And he stole fond glimpses of his wife as he drove up into the mountains, covered with wild flowers and budding trees.

After the picnic, he picked some wild roses for her in a thicket by a stream bulging with boulders, and took a snapshot of her sitting, like a girl, on a rock, her feet dangling in the foaming, racing water, the huge luscious roses nodding in her arms.

That night, when they returned home, he paused at the door, pretending to search for the keys, accumulating courage to kiss her. He did kiss her — full on the mouth, then awkwardly unlocked the door. No sooner were they inside than she, confused and surprised by the bold kiss, began to reproach him for not leaving the windows open to let in the spring air, and, with the cat following at her heels, she made a bee-line for the bathroom.

Sitting morosely in the kitchen, he tried to shut his ears to her shrill voice, announcing that he had failed to get toilet paper the day before at Kroger's. The cat was in her arms when she came out, sharpening his claws on the red sweater over her stomach. She strode into the bedroom, slamming the door behind her.

Edward went into the bathroom. Clinging to the inside of the porcelain bowl of the toilet was a wet rose petal.

Two weeks later, after long, agonizing, sleepless nights, Edward walked out of the Public Utilities company building and turned reluctantly toward the Gay Street Bridge. A small crowd was hovering over the railing. Behind them, a motorcycle lay on its side against the curb. Edward, painfully embarrassed to find a crowd, edged to the rail. Below, on the still, brown water, he saw a small object. A fat woman at his elbow said it was a motorcycle cap. Edward got so nauseated by what the people around him said about the man who was somewhere deep under the Tennessee River that he almost vomited on the fat woman's arm.

That night, he thought briefly, and rather nonviolently, of ways to rid himself of Reba. But amid hopeful thoughts of the child, near the threshold of life, he abandoned such furtive thoughts.

For a while, he feared that the child would be a boy, a sort of resurrection of Dennis. When they brought the baby to her, Reba looked at Edward with a new contempt, mingled with bitter resentment, as if to say: So now you are so old and dried up and useless, all you can give me is a girl, instead of a boy to compensate for Denny's death. Edward smiled, faintly. That set her off. She went over each of the baby's features, calmly, in seeming good humor, as any mother might, and for a moment he felt: Perhaps I was wrong about the look on her face and in her eyes. But he heard her saying how peculiar the mouth, the eyes and the chin were, since they resembled neither his nor hers.

Having no answer to that, least of all a smile, he turned and looked out the window, down at the snow on the ground.

Soon after she returned from General Hospital, Reba struck Myrna across the face with a flyswatter and screamed at the top of her lungs, "I don't ever want to set eyes on you again, you fat idiot!" Edward felt for Myrna the pity one feels for an abused animal that seems human. No more did Myrna enter the house with that silent suddenness that had so disconcerted him.

Reba insisted on naming the baby herself. Edward was shocked and then delighted when, in her deliberate ignorance of anything to do with his past, she named the child Lucy, which was also Edward's mother's name. As Lucy grew and her resemblance to Edward was unmistakable, Reba stopped tormenting him with doubts about his paternity, but turned instead to undervaluing the child, remarking that she was getting cross-eyed, that she wasn't bright, that she might even become another Myrna. During these moments he did not speak but fastened his eyes upon Lucy and felt pride and tenderness and joy for the first time in many years. At last, something had come of his marriage that, by virtue of Reba's own crudeness and spite, was his alone. But Reba found many ways to destroy his bliss.

He would look at Myrna's father, Jim Logan, who sat behind the wheel of the bus, and think: Poor man! Yet, he's better off than *I* am. Even though I have Lucy, I can't love her in peace.

He didn't see Myrna very often in the neighborhood for several years. But sometimes, as the bus crossed the Gay Street Bridge over the railroad yards, he caught a fleeting glimpse of her walking down the tracks between the boxcars in the bright evening glow. He would hope: perhaps she is going away, far away and never coming back.

Sometimes at night, Edward heard Jim call to his little boy, Gene, and they would get in the car and go in search of Myrna. Edward imagined them finding her wandering back toward the ridge along Central Avenue, walking as in a trance around telephone poles, and collecting cigar butts from the gutter to give to her father as presents. And Gene, sitting in front, would exchange a look of understanding with his father now and then as they drove homeward with Myrna in the back seat.

But sometimes at night, when Edward went to pull the shade to prevent the red beacon on the ridge from keeping him awake, he saw Myrna sitting in the bushes in the shadows cast by the moonlight, watching the window, even when snow was on the ground. And several times in the morning, when he raised the shade, she was standing just outside the window, and though she looked at him, she seemed to see nothing.

One morning, having abruptly pulled the shade to blot out this terrible sight, he turned to walk out of the room. He happened to catch a glimpse of Reba's sleeping face, and it occurred to him that she resembled Myrna. He stood at the door several minutes, looking at her. Her mouth was open in that perpetual, stupid expression Myrna wore. Having kissed his sleeping child, and put coffee on to boil, he went back to look again because he wanted very much to disbelieve it. He found the cat, lying on Reba's heaving breasts, his green eyes staring, full of indifferent contempt.

When Lucy was three, Helen and "good ol' Bill," her husband, a successful insurance salesman, moved to New York. To Edward, it was as if they had moved to the North Pole. Once in a while, she sent him a letter and reminded him not to forget to put flowers on their mother's grave on Decoration Day. And he felt guilty and ashamed because he had never forgotten, but he had never done it, either, even though he now had a car.

One Sunday, Edward and Reba and Lucy took a drive into the Great Smoky Mountains. It was a very dark but pleasant, cool, starless night in March, the wind singing at the open window. They were just beginning the descent from Clingman's Dome, the highest point in the Smokies. As usual when returning home after having been half civil most of the day, Reba was ridiculing Edward for his failure to become more important in the Public Utilities company and for showing Lucy too much attention while ignoring *her*. Thinking of his child sleeping in the back seat, Edward suddenly trembled with love for her.

And, as usual, Reba told him to stop at one of the pull-offs so she could relieve herself in the darkness behind a tree. Altitude always affected her that way.

Obediently, embarrassed, even in the darkness with no sign of a car, he pulled over, shut the motor off, went around and opened the door for her, and then got back in and started to scoot over under the wheel again when he heard a sharp, sudden scream, followed by a longer scream that tapered off like air going out of a balloon. After almost five minutes, frozen with terror and disbelief, he got out of the car and carefully walked to the edge of the shoulder of the road.

There he found a flat rock. A feeling in the pit of his stomach told him that after that there was nothing for a thousand feet. He did not know how to respond. When a car stopped with a flat tire, he was laughing.

Lucy did not wake up even when the ambulance came and the crowd of tourists became noisy. But with the first glow of morning light on her face, she opened her eyes there in the mountains, and looking up into Edward's weary eyes, said, "I dreamed of fields of yellow daisies."

When she heard of Reba's death — it was a "human interest" death, so she read it in the New York *Daily News* — Helen cabled a bouquet of roses, though Reba had once threatened to beat her to a pulp for alienating Edward's affections. Edward flushed them down the toilet.

As the preacher intoned endless words of praise for "this pious, good woman, this faithful and serving wife," Edward felt remote in mind and body.

The day Reba was buried, he cut up her deck chair for fire wood. He calmly ripped the striped canvas from the frame and tossed it into the cat's box. Then he sat before the fireplace rocking in the wicker chair. The next morning, he found the cloth coiled around his shoes at the foot of the bed. Somehow that incident prevented him from carrying out his intention to call the city pound to take the cat away. The next day, he built a lattice and planted honeysuckle.

A few months later, using part of Reba's insurance money, Edward bought Lucy a new dress and a new tricycle.

Even before he opened the screen door, he smelled the honeysuckle. Overwhelmed, he stood at the end of the long, dark hallway, inhaling, his burning eyes shut. He would not smoke his usual King Edward this evening. He wanted to enjoy the flower's nostalgic odor and the pale yellow blossoms, hanging abundantly from the lattice that walled the porch off from Wautauga Street, while Lucy rode her new tricycle in the front yard. He sat in his mother's wicker rocker and let the coolness of the late summer evening soothe his eyes. His glasses lay on his stomach, the ear pieces held lightly in his fingers.

Rummaging gently among the vines he found a blossom, plucked it, and sniffed it so rapturously that it clung freely to his nostril a few moments. Then he sipped the nectar from the stem. Absently, he put it in his vest pocket next to his watch below his heart.

Through the vines, which blurred the moonlight and the streetlight, he saw Lucy in the fresh cut grass, riding her tricycle in the blended, pulsing lights. Now and then, he heard her soft voice speaking to herself, or to the greenish blinking glow of lightning bugs, gliding on the air, maybe to the tricycle itself. The words blended, too, sounding like a strange, comforting music, along with the crickets and the faint squeaking of the wheels, soothing in the background. He couldn't see her clearly, only her golden hair and her soft, new yellow dress faintly, moving beyond the openings in the tender vines. He knew it was late and she should be in bed, but he couldn't think of breaking the spell.

He wished the red light, blinking over the tower on the crest of Sharp's Ridge like the heart of an animal, worrying the nervous tremor of the stars, would stop pulsing. But as long as it was dark it would not stop. The light intimidated and mocked him. Yet he knew that if it were not there, another plane would crash. His belief that Lucy was conceived the awful night of the crash would not leave him in peace. He was still reminded of it by the black space on the ridge, which five summers had failed to make green. Perhaps the honeysuckle would grow thick enough to shut out the prying eye of the red light, as if Reba were still watching contemptuously his every mood, mocking his contentment. He inevitably lapsed into counting one-two-three infinity, one-two-three infinity, and when he really got started he couldn't stop until it became unbearable. "One-two-three infinity," he began, in a slow whisper, tapping his glasses on his stomach. It made him think now of his work in the office, of the endless years of copying digits into a black book for more ambitious men to give meaning to.

Through the jungle-like growth between his house and Jim Logan's, Edward looked into his neighbor's living room. Even now, looking at this scene disturbed him. Sitting in his own easy chair, Jim smoked one of his many pipes, reading the Knoxville *News-Sentinel* that his young son Gene delivered. His wife, Grace, sitting on the sofa across from him, stopped knitting and Jim looked up from the paper to admire her work. She smiled, and, though the back of Jim's head was toward the window, Edward knew he, too, was smiling, saying something nice to her. That's life, Edward had been telling himself all his life. Some men get all the luck.

He was glad Myrna didn't walk across the room, shattering his contentment with her obesity, her uncannily graceful walk, her long, tangled black hair, her nothing-seeing eyes. He could not be glad enough that Myrna's insatiable curiosity, or whatever passed for it in the warped mind of a sixteen-year-old imbecile, had not embraced Lucy.

A sound like a car back-firing startled him. "Must be those damn little hellions and their drag races! Got to be careful about Lucy playing near the street, wandering out of the yard like she does. Ought to call her in before too long." He thought of Lucy, of her endearing past, of her enchanting present, her glorious future, for the fulfillment of which he would work, aspire, and achieve, save, provide, plan, fight off any and all obstacles.

Aware of the creaking of his mother's rocking chair, he speeded up the tempo, smiling at the fact that no one could nag him out of it. He took the wilted honeysuckle blossom from his vest watch-pocket and sniffed it again. That the fragile blossom had already begun to decay disturbed him. Then his eye caught the red blinker again. "One-two-three *infinity* . . ." He counted until he could no longer endure the monotony, that element in his experience, which, above all else, he wanted to destroy.

Suddenly, he stood up, knocking his glasses to the floor. Groping in the darkness, he found them, not broken. But something green and luminous pulsed on the glass over his left eye. He was still so unnerved by the blinker that instead of immediately brushing the thing away, he counted: "One-two-three *infinity.*" As Edward stumbled into the long, dark hallway, his throat very dry, the firefly flew out into the yard.

He stood leaning back, his buttocks pressed against the sink, a glass poised in his hand, tepid tap water in his mouth. It occurred to him that a good deal of time had passed since he had last heard the musical sounds of Lucy at play in the yard. The cat walked across the hall, coming from Edward's bedroom, going into Lucy's. Something about its arrogant, arthritic stride and the sudden way it turned and looked at Edward, startled him.

Suddenly afraid, he ran out the back door, the glass still in his hand, and descending the steep back-stairs, called Lucy anxiously. He quickly looked in and behind the coal shed, then ran, stumbling in the gullies in the yard, to the front of the house. At the sight of her, sitting slumped over the bars of her tricycle in a posture of sleep, he felt relief coupled with a milder feeling of foreboding.

But as he approached her, he knew something was wrong. Standing over her limp body, he stared at a large dark spot in her blond hair, a thick tendril that spread down her nape and on down her new yellow dress, settling around her small buttocks — a dark red pool on the green metal.

The next day, Edward sat in the living room with a detective, the windows shut, to keep out the suffocating odor of honeysuckle. When someone knocked at the door, the detective answered it for Edward. Jim Logan, his hand on Gene's shoulder, walked in.

"Mr. Savage, my son has something to tell you." Logan stepped backward and leaned against the wall just inside the door and listened with Edward and the detective to what his son was saying.

Gene told of a breach of his father's trust, for which he was very much ashamed, and of the consequences. "Last night I went up on Sharp's Ridge to shoot at tin cans with my daddy's rifle. Halfway up, I heard somebody following me. By the light of the moon and the tower light, I could see Myrna climbing up the path. I told her to go back, but she kept climbing, and it's so steep and loose you wouldn't think she could. She came on up to the top where I was standing, and followed me across the path to the other side, and I told her if she would promise to go back and leave me alone I'd let her shoot first. I gave her the rifle and pointed at a beer can on a log, but she raised the barrel toward the sky with this queer look on her face, like she was scared to death, and she was aiming right at that red beacon light, and she pulled the trigger and missed."

Gene walked over to Edward and stood before him. Looking him full in the face, he told him that he was sorry and that he wished his sister weren't the way she was, so she could tell him herself that she hadn't meant to kill his little girl.

But Edward was only half listening. He was looking at Jim Logan on whose face shone an expression of pride for his son's strength of character, and shame, with forgiveness, for his son's disobedience.

"Mr. Savage," said Logan, "if there's anything in all the world I can do . . ."

That evening, Edward tore down the honeysuckle and the lattice and pulled the rocking chair into the living room. The next day, he buried his daughter. A week later, he took the rocker back to the coal house. The following week, the cat died of old age. Edward is retired now, in excellent health, and he still lives in the house. He doesn't pull the shade against the pulsing beacon light.

THE MASTER'S
THESIS

A sound like the crackling of a fire intruded upon Professor Swinnard's nap. He opened his eyes on a black sweater in full sunlight across the room. Faded and fuzzy, it had a white band just under the V of the neck where red reindeer lifted their feet.

Swinnard became aware that his finger still pointed at the place in *Current History* where he had begun an article by a former student, that his foot, turned inward in the unbuckled galosh, prickled and throbbed, and that a student, without knocking, had entered his office, had taken a chair, and was now peeling the wrapper form a Baby Ruth.

The professor started to speak but closed his mouth when he felt saliva slip down his chin, tremble at his dimple. He swallowed and wiped and settled his glasses in place. "My — my office hours —"

"Yes, sir."

" — are posted on the —"

"Yes."

"Are you in my freshman survey course? Veteran students generally know better than to —"

"Sir," said the young man, uncrossing his long legs, tapping one of the reindeer with the exposed nub of his candy bar, "I am your advisee. I am a Master's candidate."

"What courses have you had with me?" Swinnard relaxed depending upon the effect of his reputation to bring balance to the situation.

"None, sir. I earned my B.A. elsewhere."

The professor blinked. "You expect to *earn* your Master's here?" He closed *Current History* with a slow flourish.

"I can't miss, sir."

Professor Swinnard swiveled in his chair. "I beg your pardon?"

"Can't miss, sir," said the boy, rearranging the wrapper out of which the brown nub of his Baby Ruth protruded.

"Young man, you have already missed a great deal. You will never again invade the privacy of my office. You will knock, you will be granted permissions to enter, you *may* be offered a chair. And you will not, if you please, rattle candy wrappers in my face."

The young man shoved the partially nude candy bar up under his sweater, agitating the reindeer. His eyes pale, his mouth soft, his ears flush from the late September chill, he looked suddenly under sixteen. "My supper, sir."

"Suppose we — start all over again. Or rather, simply start."

"I'll buy that."

"Your name?"

"Philip Hockaday Fonville, so help me God."

"I — I am Professor Swinnard, as you know. Let's see. Ah, yes, here you are — on the list, I see — opposite my name."

"Oh, there's no mistake, sir.

"Did you . . . did you ask for me?"

"Frankly, sir, I had another preference. No reflection — since I hardly know you. But I *had* —"

"What? Whom did you want?"

"Professor Korpmann."

"But he died last summer."

"So, I said, if that's the way the ball bounces, anyone will do."

"I — see. Well, I haven't time this afternoon to engage in a long conference with you. Tomorrow perhaps we can outline your course of study, and once I have had an opportunity to review your work — somewhere near Christmas, I imagine — we may sit down and go over a list of possible thesis projects. I have a good list which has produced a number of —"

"We won't have to sweat that one, sir."

"Mr. Fonville, let me suggest that you . . ."

"No question about the thesis. Square that away right now. Put your mind at ease, sir."

"I'm sure none of us is without his pet topic, Mr. Fonville. We won't be bothered by that. Countless theses have been written. One must review the possibilities . . ."

"No, sir, I'm certain, this is virgin territory. Never been touched, sir. Mine will be an entirely new contribution."

"Your presumptuousness is colossal, Fonville. Perhaps we had best meet tomorrow, when you have had time to —"

"Time? For what, sir? I've chosen the subject of my thesis."

"In my forty years as teaching, I've often stumbled on your sort. Burning with a project that will transform —"

"I realize it will take hard work, sir, and I shall require your assistance at unusual hours of the day and night owing to its nature."

Swinnard was about to say, "My office hours are posted," when the telephone rang. His sister. Calling from her home forty miles away. Wanting to know whether he knew it was raining. He told her he did. Could see it on the window. Good. Just don't forget the galoshes. No. Then goodbye.

Fonville was almost to the door, but turned and pulled out his sweater, dropping the Baby Ruth into his open hand. "Only wanted to let you know I'm around, sir." He nodded, did an obsequious shuffle just beyond the cracked threshold, wandered away.

"Listen, young man, you —" He had to get it settled. But just as he leaned out the door, the red that streaked across the boy's sweater blinked around the corner. Swinnard put his hand over his heart and remembered a hot summer twilight when the ferris wheel jammed and his father kept rocking their chair. Later, as he was approaching the faculty parking lot, Swinnard discovered that he had forgotten to pull on the other galosh

That night Swinnard got out his notes, yellowed and buffed, to review his first lecture. Somewhere in the late Bronze Age, he fell asleep. The telephone startled him awake. When he rose and took the phone in his hand, his notes slid to the carpet.

"You get the news about old Sanford?"

"Who?"

"Sanford, the music teacher. They found him on the bathroom floor."

"Who did?"

"I didn't get you out of bed, did I?" Now Swinnard recognized the voice of the department chairman. "Sanford — they found him dead —"

"No, I hadn't heard. Look — do you know a boy named — ?" Swinnard began to ask, but the department chairman had hung up.

❋

The next morning, the rain had turned to thick fog. In the dark basement hallway, Professor Swinnard almost stepped on the boy. Fonville looked up in the dim light and got to his feet. Close up, his eyes were red.

Swinnard would let the boy begin and at the first opportunity squash him. Not that Mr. Fonville had any kind of upper hand.

"Have a good night's rest, sir?"

"Now look here, young man, once and for all, you will kindly observe a little decorum."

"Sir, I was only inquiring into the state of your health." It sounded to Swinnard like parody.

"Sit down," he ordered. Then he realized he was late for a class and that he had quite forgotten his nine o'clock office hour.

But the boy sat down before he could explain. Swinnard noticed that the boy carried no books. He wore the same sweater, the reindeer crossing the snow to the gentle pace of his breathing.

Swinnard took his notes from the briefcase and tapped them sharply on the desk until they were precisely even. He sought a phrase that would work, but the insultingly eager look on Fonville's face persuaded Swinnard to deal with the boy more roughly. He simply went to class, leaving Fonville to sit in the shadows.

❋

When Swinnard returned from his class to his office, Fonville was there, standing in front of Swinnard's desk with the telephone to his ear. He held it out to Swinnard. Furious, Swinnard jerked it out of the boy's hand and sat down.

It was the president, asking how he was. Fine. How was the president? The president was fine, never felt better, got in some golf before the rain set in last evening. Fine, sir. He had heard some fine things about Professor Swinnard from one of his students there in the office. Said everything was working out just fine. Well, fine. They would see each other soon, of course, and have a nice chat. It had been too long since the last one. In the men's john at a community concert, Swinnard remembered as he hung up.

It felt good to Swinnard to talk to the president without having to play up to him, or feeling as if one had, knowing that one never really had. With one more year, one didn't have to . . . There the boy sat, his slender legs crossed, his palms cupped under his elbows, his chest hairy with the sweater where those reindeer lifted their feet.

"He's a nice guy," said the boy.

Swinnard did not comment. After all, the boy had said something nice about him to the president.

"Now, young man," he said, turning *Current History* right side up and looking for something, anything that he might have misplaced, "suppose we get this whole affair in perspective."

"I'm having it typed up now, sir."

"What's that?"

"The first chapter."

"Come now," Swinnard said, grinning, trying to find some way to attack the problem. "We must be serious."

"Sir, how much seriouser can I get? Up all night gnawing on candy bars to keep up my strength while I struggle with this thing."

"You are actually in the writing phase of —"

"Oh, it's going to be ready before the deadline — way before. Typed up in three neat copies, bound and everything. Neat and crisp."

"I refuse to sit here," said Swinnard, rising, "and listen to you rant in this manner."

"But, sir, as my advisor . . ."

Swinnard walked over to the boy and stood above him. "You will please leave and not pester me again."

The boy looked up at Swinnard and pointed toward the desk. "I'm *on* the list, sir."

"Confound the list!"

"Think," said the boy, standing now, "of the thousands who died building the pyramids, sir."

"To what end?"

"The victims of the plague."

"What has the plague to do with — ?"

"Men die."

"Asssuredly, but I fail to see what this has to do with our graduate program in history." Swinnard moved away from an odor that seemed to emanate from the boy.

"I know how to work in all the footnotes you want, sir. Charts. Tables. Maps, Diagrams." He ticked them off on his long skinny fingers. "Graphs. Indices. Appendices. You name it. I'll whip it up for you in a shake, sir."

"Do you think that makes a thesis?"

"No."

"Then get out."

"I'll see you around, sir. I'll pick up those first pages and shoot them over to you personally."

"You will please not to bother me."

"I can see you're upset just now, sir."

"Not in the least."

"You need to get off your feet, sir."

"I need to be left alone."

"Of course, you're right, sir."

The boy left. In the sudden emptiness of the room, Swinnard realized that he had forgotten something. Yes. The reason for the president's call. Surely not just to ask how he was. Worrying now, imagining, ready to apologize for having cut him off, he rang the president's office.

"No, no, Swinnard, *I* didn't call *you*. The young man in your office called *me*."

⁂

At noon he crossed the campus to the bookstore. He had promised his sister he would bring *Flower Arranging Made Easy* when he came for dinner.

As he was starting up the steps to the bookstore, Swinnard saw Philip Hockaday Fonville running toward him, waving some white sheets, but not calling to him, the faded black sweater with the white band and the red reindeer circling his chest and back as though he were a Greek vase. Swinnard escaped, trying not to run.

✲

The next morning, Professor Swinnard came out of the classroom at the end of the hall, and there was the boy, sitting on the sooty concrete floor, his back against the blighted chestnut office door, his head resting on his crossed arms. Swinnard wedged himself between two students, fell in behind three others, and left the building by another entrance.

Swinnard strolled into the administrative building, glanced at some outdated bulletins, then ambled back to his office. A student leaned against the wall. Fonville was gone.

"Did he say he would be back tomorrow?"

"Who?"

"The boy who was here," Swinnard said.

"Nobody was here."

Then he saw the note.

Dear Prof:

Waited two hours, through your office hours. I hope you realize that I am not an impatient sort, but after all, I am a graduate student, am I not, and should be granted periodic interviews???

Please inform me by student mail as to when you will be available.

Yours truly,
Philip Hockaday Fonville

The three-by-five note card was fastened firmly to his door with a white thumbtack, streaked with red, as though the boy had stuck himself.

Swinnard rose before dawn and went down to the kitchen and leaned against the sink. He drank a glass of water. The moon was a silver bow. There was one glint of light on the clothesline on the lawn. He imagined the bow he once made with a limb from a hedgeberry tree. It had been years since anything had disturbed him. As a child he would stand in his back yard and look up at the sun, upside-down through his legs. He remembered the odd thrill the view gave him. He realized that what he wanted most of all was peace, so, leaning against the front of the refrigerator, he wrote a note that put him face to face with the young man.

To Philip Hockaday Fonville:

Apparently you have been unsuccessful in trying to locate me for an interview. With school only a few days underway, I can't imagine what we would talk about, except a *possible* subject for your master's thesis. Should this be the case, please be advised that my office hours for today are 2 to 5.

Yours sincerely,
Professor Swinnard

Then he slept the sleep of the unburdened.

☀

The Master's candidate hadn't come at two. At four, Swinnard admitted two other students to his office. They would take up the time. He closed the door and sat down with the first student. Something about never being able to remember dates, and Swinnard gave up listening. He thought of Fonville, and then he tried to remember something out of his own childhood. It was when Swinnard heard himself asking the student at his side where he was from that he also heard a light knock on the door.

"Did someone knock?" he asked.

"I believe someone did, sir."

Swinnard had half-risen to leave the desk when the door creaked open and Fonville stuck in his head and saluted with a slim white hand that protruded from the sleeve of his fuzzy black sweater.

"Don't get up, sir. Stay right where you are. Won't take but a minute." Shoving the door open, he swooped, making no noise with either door or feet, only a rattle with the papers in his hand. Swinnard remained half-squatting at his desk. "There we are, sir. Neat as the veritable pin. Chapter One. I'll just place it here and bother you not a second longer." Pivoting, he returned to the door, where he turned, suddenly, and raised his arm, like a child asking permission to speak: "Oh, yes. A report on that tomorrow morning at ten would be of immense help to me, sir. In the midst of things at the moment." He was gone before Swinnard could speak.

The professor dismissed the other student and glanced at the stack of white sheets. The cover page was blank. He locked up for the day. Later, sitting in his car, Swinnard couldn't move. He went back, got the pages, and rammed them into his briefcase.

❋

It was as though he were afraid to let it into his house. At a Chinese restaurant where he occasionally celebrated a birthday, he sat down with orange tea and decided that he would read the piece and find in it such factual inaccuracy and inadequate documentation as could be used against the boy.

But he put it off until he had eaten, and then he opened the evening paper.

❋

That night he realized he had forgotten to read the chapter, that he had, in fact, left it on the table in the Chinese restaurant. He telephoned, and the dishwasher answered. Yes, he had. It was in the garbage, and the garbage was on the truck. Yes, he could read a little English. One word on the second page, "Death," followed by a name in three parts. Swinnard thanked him and tried to sleep.

The telephone woke him. The blinds were still dark.

"Yes?"

"Sir?"

"Who is this?"

"Just called to see how you liked it so far. I'm going full speed on the second chapter."

Swinnard hung up. He turned on the bedside lamp. His wife used to say,

"How can you see to talk in the dark?" He looked at the twin bed where she had died, and all of her unborn children with her.

He went downstairs and made some coffee. He opened the back door and stood behind the screen in the chill air, watching the rain clouds go over the moon.

At ten o'clock that morning he left his basement classroom with the students. Without even glancing down the hall at his office door, he walked briskly out the same way he had used to evade the boy before. But he heard someone call his name. He quickened his stride, his heart pounding hard in the soles of his feet. The touch of fingers turned him. A short, stocky boy, wearing a letter-man's sweater and carrying a load of books under his arm, handed him a note and galloped off.

Dear Professor Swinnard:

Regrettably, I am unable to make our appointment at nine (or was it ten?). Like everyone else, I have my problems. The dentist insists on extracting three of my teeth.

Yours cordially,
Philip Hockaday Fonville

Swinnard crumpled the note and dropped it where he stood. His hand empty, he put it to his head.

*

Professor Swinnard was rolling up the maps after Survey of European History when Fonville walked in, grinning to show where a front tooth was missing. Swinnard, up on his tiptoes to reach the map case, thought he was going to faint. He sat down at the desk.

"Well, sir, everything is now fine. Couldn't be better. Teeth out, pain gone, and here I am for that consultation."

Swinnard began to talk. When he realized he was stuttering, he stood up and looked the boy in the face. "Mr. Fonville," he said, "I have lost your first chapter," and then he turned away to put his notes in his briefcase.

"Sir, this is unforgivable."

"I'm sorry. It couldn't be helped. Now if you'll excuse me."

"But, sir. Think. Think. Where? Where?"

"I — don't recall."

"This means I'll have to write it over, sir. Interrupt my work at its present juncture."

"Don't you see how utterly impossible this whole thing is?" Swinnard blurted out.

"Sir, if you don't mind my saying so, this is a hell of an attitude to take. I come to you with a unique thesis. A little variety. What's impossible about it?"

"Don't raise your voice, young man!"

"Raise my voice? I'm entitled to raise my voice. You've just lost, for no good reason, a thing into which I've put, you might say, sweat, sir! Blood, sir!"

"You will stop haranguing me in this melodramatic way!" Swinnard felt heavy. He backed toward the door. Inside his coat, he was hot. His skull felt numb. The boy kept talking, turning around and around talking, following him, and the reindeer reared up on the white band and the black quivered in the light coming through the tall windows. He reached out to touch the boy, to get him to stand still.

And Fonville was saying, "I am very quiet, sir. I am very quiet now, sir. It's all right. I've forgiven you." Swinnard was in the desk chair, his coat flung back his shirt undone, his tie dangling between his legs.

✳

Days passed with no sign of the boy. In Fonville's absence, Professor Swinnard tried to relax. Dozing off in his office, he would jerk up, anticipating the sound of a candy bar wrapper. He asked around. None of the students knew the boy. Yes, they'd noticed the sweater. He checked the boy's schedule in the registrar's office, but he was down for thesis credit only. That was a technicality Swinnard could use. One had to take certain required courses before even beginning to discuss a thesis.

But as the weeks passed Swinnard forgot that. The boy wasn't registered in the dormitories. The address in the files turned out to be on the other side of town, in a neighborhood with many misleading house numbers. He didn't want to see where Fonville lived. Somehow, the idea of the boy's room frightened him.

Maybe Fonville was ill. The hospitals said no. Or dead. The morgue had never heard of Philip Hockaday Fonville. At night, he would remember fainting in that classroom. He worried about his heart.

One night, he came home to find a note the cleaning woman had propped against the bread box. Philip Hockaday Fonville had called and left a number.

Swinnard couldn't eat supper. When he started upstairs, he remembered the note and decided to make the call from his bed. Instead, he lay down in the dark and tried to sleep. Three hours later, he pulled himself up, went downstairs, and walked out onto the lawn. He looked up at the moon and wondered how the earth, that seemed to curve there in the yard, would look upside-down.

❋

The next morning, Professor Swinnard called the university from a booth on the highway. He said he was sick. He spent the day driving in the country. Toward three o'clock, he felt guilty. He had never lied like that before. He was proud of his perfect attendance record. He would put in an appearance.

Crossing the campus, he saw the boy coming toward him, a huge bundle of papers in his skinny arms. Swinnard ducked behind a massive shrub and cut across the grass, glancing back. The boy was going toward the administration building.

At his office, Swinnard found a slip of paper on the floor instructing him to call the dean immediately.

The dean wanted to know what the problem was with this Fonville youngster. Swinnard's grip on the receiver relaxed. At last they were finding the boy out. But the dean went on to say that the boy had complained that he, Swinnard, was being standoffish. What about that? The president, the dean said, had met with the boy. The president wanted to see that everything was done right by the young man. The boy was right there in the dean's office, very upset, and to tell the truth, hurt. Would Swinnard see him now? Yes, Swinnard would. He hung up.

He wouldn't try to explain. No student was going to do to him what this boy had done to him for almost a month. He would play along. In the end, he would be vindicated.

He sat, waited. After a while, it occurred to him that the boy might be making him wait. Resentment gave way to sleep, as he sat there in his galoshes, the gray light falling through the dusty windows. A light knock brought Swinnard awake with a start. The boy edged into the room quietly.

"I hate to disturb you, sir," he said, very softly, "but as this seemed a good opportunity to have our long-awaited buzz session, I thought I'd come ahead."

"I have less than an hour. I must . . ."

"Oh, I understand, sir. Of course."

Fonville pulled a chair close to the desk until their knees almost touched. Swinnard noticed what tremendous feet the boy had. His galoshes made his own feet look large, but they were small alongside the boy's. Fonville settled himself, but first, Swinnard wanted to know what that odor was.

"Smell, sir?" The boy got up and looked all around the room, sniffing in each corner, sticking his head out the door into the hall, and peeping over the window sill into the yard under the bushes. When the boy sat down, Swinnard realized that the odor was stronger.

They faced each other, ready again for the conference. But the boy didn't speak. He only looked at Swinnard. Then he reached under his sweater and pulled out a Butterfinger and started to split the wrapper with the long, sharp nail of his little finger. "May I, sir? My supper."

Swinnard waited, but still the boy didn't speak. Then he reached under his sweater again and brought out what looked like a transistor radio. The little mechanism glinted like silver. The boy's thumb flicked a tiny switch and Swinnard heard a faint whirr.

"What in the devil is that vicious little object?"

"And I thought we knew each other well enough so you wouldn't shy from it. The quality on the other tapes has been rather sub-standard. My sweater seems to muffle your voice."

"Other tapes?" asked Swinnard, unable to look away from the gadget.

"I've recorded all our exchanges, sir. I believe in getting the full value of —"

"Please go on, young man. What is it you want to talk about?"

"My thesis, of course."

"Then go ahead."

"Me, sir?" Fonville pointed at one of the reindeer with the Butterfinger. "Aren't *you*," he said, pointing the Butterfinger at Swinnard but then lowering it, "going to ask *me* questions?"

"*I* have no questions."

"Aren't you supposed to quiz me, to suggest, to comment, to analyze and evaluate?"

"I haven't the faintest idea what you've been writing."

"Well, now, sir, is that *my* fault?"

"I've heard quite enough of that, young man. I imagine you have written further on your project."

"That's it exactly, sir, sick as I was. Diarrhea. Inflammation of the gums. I'm sorry I didn't keep you informed."

"Quite all right. Turn what you have over to me. In a week or so, we'll meet again."

"You're being remarkably nice about it, sir. Thank you."

"Good, then. I'll take whatever you have."

"Oh, I don't have it with me. It's over at the Ad Building, being run off."

"Run off?"

"Yes, sir. Copies. In case of loss, fire, or something like that. If there's one thing you've taught me, sir, it's to take precautions."

"A very silly idea, Mr. Fonville. An unnecessary expenditure."

"That's okay, sir. I charged it to the department, in your name."

※

Later, Swinnard could not remember what he had said to the boy. No doubt the machine had recorded it.

The professor suffered that night. He could not sleep. His body trembled. He was certain he had a heart murmur. At dawn, the telephone rang.

"Sir?"

He hung up.

An hour later, it rang again. He answered, swaying, his knee braced on the bed that had been his wife's. "Yes?"

"I'll deliver it to your office, sir. You won't even have to speak to me. Goodbye, sir, thank you, sir."

Swinnard held the phone a long time before he hung up.

☼

The turning of the key in his office door set him to trembling. He shut the door. When he heard the light knock, he ran across the room and bolted the door. The knob turned several times. Swinnard waited, knowing that the boy's feet, large as they were, never made noise. He thought he smelled them.

He stayed in the office through his class and heard the students leave his classroom down the corridor, talking loudly, laughing, glad he had not shown up. He tried to busy himself, but the sight of his notes made him dizzy. When he opened a bottom drawer and saw nothing but dust, a few rubber bands, and a rusty paper clip, he wept.

At ten-thirty, he went to the door, listened again. The odor was gone. He slipped the latch and looked out. A piece of cardboard was thumb-tacked to the door.

> Sir: I am looking for you. I must get the finished thesis to you before something happens to it. I'm in the mimeograph room in the Ad. Bldg.!!!
>
> Respectfully,
> P. H. F.

Swinnard returned quickly to his desk and got his briefcase ready to go. His sense of hearing had become so extremely acute that he heard, very faintly, the outside door down the hall open. He rushed to the office door, slammed it, locked it, pressed his back against it. His throat was dry, his eyes burned, his legs were weak, and his heart beat heavily. A light knock. He waited for the knob to turn. A sound like a guillotine, and he looked down.

Between his feet lay a sheet of paper. He picked it up. A brief message informed him that his contribution to the United Faculty Flower Fund had not been received as pledged. Swinnard laughed, sat down at his desk, and wrote out a check. He put it in an envelope and mailed it in the campus box on the way to the parking lot.

He felt utterly calm at supper. Later, he watched television. He even watched a puppet show and smiled. Then he went to bed.

Like a large pimple, a stack of white paper lay on the bed spread.

Fighting an impulse to run, he caught himself, clenched his fists as though arming against some wild creature. The stack was tied with fraying red cord. On top was a note from the cleaning woman.

Dear Prof. Swinnard,

A nice young man delivered this stuff this morning just after you left for the office. He begged me to make you read it tonight because he's leaving town tomorrow. I told him you couldn't possibly finish so much tonight, but he said he'd call you tonight to see what you think of the first part.

Yours truly,
Mildred

Swinnard stepped back and the white bulk bounced slightly where his knee had pressed against the mattress.

He removed the receiver from its cradle, turned off the light, and softly closed the door. Moving through the living room, he lifted the receiver on the downstairs telephone and let it drop into the chair he had warmed watching television. The sound of the kitchen screen opening comforted him.

Standing on the peaceful lawn under the full moon, he knew that, despite the chill in the air, this was what he wanted to do. He ducked under the clothesline. The summer sound of the screen door was still in his ears. He bent over toward the curving grass and reached to grip the backs of his legs. Strands of his thin grey hair brushed the grass. His glasses slid down over the bridge of his nose and dangled from one ear as he peered between his legs, upside-down. The earth turned black, the moon melted, making the sky one white radiance, and in the soles of his feet, Swinnard felt the distant beat of hooves.

OVER

THE CLIFF

✺

When Professor Minitree stepped off the elevator, he saw a man at the end of the hall. He appeared to be standing in front of Minitree's door.

Minitree had awakened in a room which contained nothing but the mattress he had slept on and a view of Barrow Street. Reaching for his trousers, he had knocked over a container of cold coffee which she had brought him. Brenda herself was gone.

Walking quickly through the snow to Eighth Avenue, he had taken a taxi uptown to the Sheraton, where most of the MLA meetings were held. At nine o'clock he was to conduct an interview.

Last night, Brenda had asked, "Have you got anybody to take Mr. Cain's place?"

"Mr. Cain is not replaceable." Surprising himself as well as Brenda, he had admitted that much right away. But not until they had fallen asleep in each other's arms, Cain's name on their lips, had he realized what he had meant.

"Sorry I'm late, Mr. Wheaton."

"Oh, that's quite all right, sir."

Minitree unlocked the door to his hotel room and stepped aside. "Won't you come in?"

"Thank you, sir."

"I arose late and haven't even had time to shave." He noticed the lack of conviction in his tone, then saw the neatly made bed. "Have a seat. I'll be with you in a moment."

In the closet, hanging up his coat, he caught her odor. He cupped his hands over his face and inhaled. The room was so small, the odor would probably reach the candidate before the interview was over, short though it would be. Realizing that the odor must be all over him, he thought, To hell with it, and sat in the chair opposite Mr. Wheaton, who looked nothing like Cain.

"As I understand it, you will receive your M.A. from Princeton in June."

"Yes, sir."

"What's the subject of your thesis?"

"'Verbal Paradigms of Gentility in the Novels of Jane Austen.'"

"I see. I'm an Eliot man myself. George, of course."

"Oh, yes, sir, I just finished *The Mill on the Floss*."

"It stays with you."

"I'll say."

"As I always say, there's an infallible test of great literature: 1) Does the author have something to say? 2) Does he say it well, and 3) Are his characters people you would not be ashamed to have in your home." Mr. Wheaton smiled. "Do you agree?"

"Oh, yes, sir. That's very nice."

"I once said that to the man whose resignation is the occasion of this interview." Cain had given him a novel called *The Cannibal* by John Hawkes. Handing it back to him a week later, Minitree had seized the moment to make what he now thought of as a pronouncement, but which he then regarded as a universal truth.

"Would you like to hear his reply?"

"Yes, sir."

"'Sir,'" he said, "'that dictum rules out more of the world's literature than from which I would gladly part.' Which, of course, was his parody of the way he heard me talk." Mr. Wheaton's face was a blank. Minitree suddenly had an impulse to write something on it. "The son of a bitch was burned in effigy four times before he left the campus, three months after he was hired."

Minitree was delighted with the change in Mr. Wheaton's expression. A sudden intuitive image of twenty-five years of blank faces filled him with remorse for what he had failed to inscribe on them.

"The position, Mr. Wheaton, calls for the teaching of freshman English primarily. Three sections, one of which is remedial. Then there is one section of Humanities. The salary is $15,000, which, for Eastern Kentucky, is about average."

"That sounds interesting, sir."

"Are you married?"

"No, sir."

"Neither was Cain."

"Pardon me?"

"Nothing."

"Sir, I wonder if I might ask a few questions."

"Of course."

"What are the fringe benefits?"

For a moment, Minitree had expected a few questions about Cain. "The usual package. On that we're above average. There's a research fund which may interest you in case you plan to delve more deeply into Jane Austen."

"Oh, no, sir, I'm through with *her*."

"The thrill is gone?"

"Well, you know how it is, Professor Minitree. One has to write on something."

"How old are you, Mr. Wheaton?"

"Twenty-two, sir." He blushed. "I was a little precocious."

"Does your experience range beyond ivy walls at all?"

"Oh, yes, sir. For four summers I worked in a shoe store in Brookline, Mass."

"And what makes you interested in our college, which, as you may know from reading the newspaper articles about poverty, is remote, in time and space, from Brookline, Massachusetts."

"I want to *do* something."

"Well, not to worry. With four courses in English, there's plenty to do."

"I mean . . ."

"Yes, Mr. Wheaton, I know exactly what you mean. Well, Mr. Cain, in a manner quite different from what yours would be, has so raised up the lowly mountain folk — a good number of them, anyway — that if they don't watch their step, they'll go over a cliff — as, I might add, Mr. Cain himself has done."

"This is the gentleman whom you're trying to replace."

"Mr. Wheaton, Mr. Cain is not replaceable."

"And he fell off one of those cliffs?"

"I was speaking figuratively. But you mustn't go away with the idea that Mr. Cain was a lone-wolf peace-corps type out of the Sixties. What I mistook for missionary zeal was simply a cannibalistic appetite for people — in the loftiest sense, of course." Minitree watched Mr. Wheaton's face. In what he was now conscious of as a habitual gesture, he pressed his palms together as though in prayer, pinching the flanges of his nose with his fingertips, but as he released them, he caught his breath at the odor of Brenda's body and scooted the chair back against the window where four inches of snow lay on the sill.

"He came to us from Baghdad, Iraq. Born and raised in Upper Thousand Sticks, Kentucky, actually. Hillbilly, you Bostonians would be inclined to call him. But after graduating from the University of Memphis, he went to teach at the University of Baghdad. Romantic, yes. But not a fresh-out-of-college romanticism, because he was thirty when he got his master's. No stranger to the exotic when he went to Baghdad. At fifteen, he was in the merchant marines, et cetera.

"Only last September? It seems years ago. We had given him up. We'd assumed he had gotten caught in the cross-fire of a revolution. We were re-charting the freshmen, absorbing them into the other classes as an emergency measure. We had been up very late. Classes began that morning, and as I reached for the *Hazard Herald*, there he was, sleeping on our glider, the cushions for which were already in our attic, in winter storage. Stretched out straight as an Indian mystic on a bed of nails, and as lean and famished-looking. Over him he had draped my son's tent, left up since his leaving for prep school in New Hampshire several weeks before. With the beard and the deep tan, I didn't recognize him. His application photograph showed a face much like your own. Except for the eyes and the mouth, which made me a little apprehensive.

"So the man on the glider was a total stranger, and wrapped in the tent, he had the aura of something dislocated in time and geography by some bizarre fluke of night. Then I decided that he must be a hermit from up one of the creek hollows — maybe even a moonshiner — and I became irritated.

"'Get up from there, you,' I said, and tapped his shoulder with the rolled newspaper.

"His eyes opened instantly and I stepped back, a little startled.

"It occurs to me that I may be keeping you from other interviews."

"Oh, no, sir. I mean, there are others but . . ."

"It's only fair to sketch in the situation for you, should you decide to — well, let's not put the cart before the ass.

"To continue."

※

"I say, old man," he said, sticking his hand out from under the tent. "Professor Minitree, isn't it?"

Standing there in my pajamas, I was indeed, or somewhat, Professor Minitree — taking his hand, as a matter-of-fact.

"And *you*, sir?"

"Jack Cain. Just passing through. Thought I'd stop off here in a poverty pocket and teach a little English."

I disliked him instantly. *That* side of him and each of the others, successively.

I told him to meet me in my office in one hour, and excused myself, taking my son's tent with me.

I'm a product of Richmond, Virginia, and I let him know immediately that I do no suffer levity lightly — nor, for that matter, facile alliteration.

The man who appeared in my office, punctually, resembled the man on the glider only remotely. He was, however, the exact image of the young man in the application photo. Under his nose was a tab of toilet tissue that staunched the cut he had made shaving. He wore impeccable clothes, of a modest cut, his shoes were shined, and there wasn't a hair misplaced on his head. For a moment, I had to swivel away from him to regain my balance, but then I realized that this was a victory for me. I had communicated and he had responded; as though aware of what was expected of him, he had acquiesced. That was my assessment.

"I didn't want you to think I'm an aging hippie, sir."

"I got the impression you were a moonshiner held over from the late twenties."

"I can still smell the stuff."

"I beg your pardon?"

"My pappy kept a still. I slept in the fumes half my life. That's why I loved the salt sea air so much, I reckon. I let the beard grow coming over from Baghdad just to see what it would look like. I'm not committed to it. Besides, I hate being classed. Least of all with conformists like hippies."

"I compliment you on the latter, but as to the former, I hasten to stress the fact that you are now a member of the English department, *one* of *seven* instructors."

"I regard the question as essentially an academic one, sir." Which was thrust number one in his developing parody of my manner — not that I quite caught it at the time.

I thought it wise to have him teach in the classroom adjacent to my office.

"Your first class meets in thirteen minutes, Mr. Cain. Humanities 10. Good day."

He went straight into the empty classroom.

While I telephoned Miss Lacey to inform her that I had changed her room, I watched Cain through the little window in the door stride up and down the room, and made a note to tell him to wait until class was assembled before making his entrance. It doesn't *do* to appear so eager.

As the students began to wander in, I began to hear laughter. He had a book open — *not* the text — and with three students he had begun to teach. By the time the bell had rung for class to begin, every student was in a state of — how shall I say — well, I don't know that I *can* say. Perhaps I shouldn't attempt to describe it. Narcosis, trance, euphoria. Rigid elation? No. Well.

Finally, he took up the required text and began to read the table of contents aloud in a tone that had every student convulsed, painfully in some cases, if their faces were any indication, with laughter. And each time he read a title, he ripped ten or so pages out of the book and threw them over his shoulder — the second toss going right into Brenda McClune's face as she entered, ten minutes late, the room. She stopped cold and was held as his pyrotechnics continued without a lag. I, too, was immobile, with shock. I don't recall what he said about each selection as he sneeringly rejected it. Yes. One comment. "And as for Keats' 'Ode on a Mason Fruit Jar,' who needs it?" Finally, he was down to the covers. "Hey, this would make a splendid binding for my *Batman* comics collection." That, of course, got the loudest and longest laugh, on the wave of which I regained enough control of myself to reach for the knob, fairly confident that I wouldn't strangle the maniac before their very eyes. But then I saw that look of infinite contempt on his face that made even me shrink.

※

"Tell me if I'm boring you, Mr. Wheaton."
"Oh, no sir."
"That straight chair must be very uncomfortable."
"Oh, no sir."
"Good."

※

The next thing he did was take out a Bible and hold it casually until each student had taken notice of it and had cut the comedy dead. Then he read the first title. "'Genesis.' You." He pointed at a boy in the back. "You with the All-American half-back laugh. Come up here." The boy, co-captain of our virtually unbeaten football team, rose with a fixed, sick grin on his face and shuffled to the front.

Cain handed him the Bible. "Tear out 'Genesis.'" The boy stepped back, as if about to touch a wasp. Brenda McClune is standing behind Cain, who hasn't seen her yet. In the moment between the boy's shock and his dry-mouthed utterance, "But that's the *Ho-ly Bi-ble*, sir," I could have heard a feather drop — even with the door shut. Brenda's eyes caught me in the window. I ducked. Then remembered that I was head of the English Department, by God. Then the look she gave me — her former freshman English teacher — seemed to say, what do you think of *that?*

"Why don't you tear it out?"
"It's sacred. I would go to hell. God might even strike me dead."
"But you weren't terrified when I tore up Homer, Sophocles, Shakespeare, Dante, Chaucer, Milton, Keats and other rivals of *Batman*." The boy tried to smile. The look of contempt came back to Cain's face. "Hold this." He gave the boy the Bible. "Now start picking up Western Civilization." With the Bible in one hand, the boy began, on his knees. "Isn't anybody going to help him?"

Coming up from behind, on her knees, Brenda startles him. Then others on the front row begin to help. The boy hands Cain a sheaf of pages, a look of shivering hatred in his eyes. "It's a personal matter, isn't it?" Cain said. I knew the boy well enough to know why he didn't respond. He was inarticulate with rage and humiliation — if he tried to speak, his lumpish words would drive him to violence. I hoped it would come to that. "What's your name?"

"Bob Sanford."

"Keep them, Bob. Read them."

Bob turns, the papers clutched in his fist. He stood at the back of the room, staring out the window, unable to trust himself to look at Cain.

Then Brenda starts to hand him the pages she had picked up, saying, "Byron." He asked her name, then told her to keep the pages. She sat on the front row. Cain went through the same routine with each student, and most of them were full of hatred and humiliation.

When they were all seated, he said: "The assignment for Wednesday is in your hands. Read and be prepared to meet God, because you may die before Wednesday."

"But, Mr. Cain," said one brave, though at the moment viciously timid, soul. "These are just fragments."

"Start with that observation and see where you can go from there. See you Wednesday."

"If he isn't dead by then," I heard someone in the hall say.

"Well," I said, as I jerked the office door open. "That was quite a stunt. How long did it take to dream it up?"

"It just happened."

"You realize, don't you, that you've alienated each and every student — not to mention the ones in your other classes, yet to come."

"So now the problem is to overcome the situation."

I didn't stay to observe the next class — I had one of my own in the History of the English Language. It occurred to me as I entered my own classroom, ten seconds after the bell, that I had just confessed to spying on one of my teachers.

✴

Rid of the diffident Mr. Wheaton, who had announced that he had another appointment, Minitree showered, well aware of having betrayed something of himself to the young candidate as well.

Before Cain had had his effect on him, whatever that might prove to be, beyond his behavior with Brenda, Minitree knew he would have felt that he had lost Wheaton. But hadn't he, after all, chosen Cain himself from a field of Wheaton-like candidates?

Turning off the water, free of the smell but not of future possibilities, Minitree heard the door bell, insistent, as if it had been ringing for some time.

A towel around his waist, he opened the door, and there stood Wheaton, impetuosity having clearly erased the diffidence.

"Sorry to disturb you, Professor Minitree, but I'm hoping you are considering me as Professor Cain's replace — for the position, I mean, and so I'd like it very much to know — but, sir, only because you brought it up — what you meant by the phrase, 'over the cliff.'"

"Oh, that. Of course. He ran away with Brenda to New York and then left her to go off to the Artic with Greenpeace to save the whales — and the seals. Leaving Brenda to the wolves, one might say."

And to opportunists like Minitree, he couldn't help but admit to himself.

"Oh, I see," said Mr. Wheaton. "Well, I'll wait to hear from you, sir."

Was Wheaton considering accepting a challenge? Minitree wondered. The challenge of coming in behind a teacher like Cain?

Or the challenge of imitating Cain perhaps?

Maybe the challenge of defining himself by direct contrast with a man like Cain. Whatever the nature of the challenge, Cain would figure in it somewhere, unavoidably.

Minitree faced the certainty that his own teaching would never be the same. He shared Mr. Wheaton's dilemma, facing a range of possible challenges.

And in his life, as well, nothing could be as it had been. Would Brenda want to see him again? When? Where?

Maybe he would take her back to Eastern Kentucky, persuade her to continue her education.

Or whenever he returned to New York, he could see her again.

Staying on in New York with Brenda was a possibility.

Or he could decide about that later, return someday, a retired professor, and run a rare book shop, with Brenda.

The questions, possibilities, and challenges made him a little dizzy. He sat down by the window and looked at New York City.

It was not Eastern Kentucky. Would Eastern Kentucky still be there when he returned?

BY WAY OF

INTRODUCTION

My name is Harold Obolinsky. Or should I first say, Good evening, Ladies and Gentlemen?

When I was allowed to introduce our distinguished speaker, I wondered, Why me? Given the obvious fact that I have no credentials in this field. Nor have I read a single one — my craven apologies — of our celebrated, in some quarters denigrated, speaker's forty-five noted books.

I asked myself, perhaps I was asked to introduce our speaker because, incredible as it may seem to the objective bystander, in all the forty years I have served faithfully on this faculty, I have never been approached to act as introducer of our many visiting speakers.

Mayhap, I was asked to introduce this particular speaker for some light comic effect, incongruity being the very soul of comedy, et cetera, et cetera, et cetera.

Be that as it may, none of these possibilities seemed on target. "On target" is four bulls eyes on the shooting range. Which, truth be told, I have been known to achieve on more than one occasion.

But I stand before you this evening, not to brag about my prowess as a marksman. More to the mark, perhaps, is the little-known fact, but fact none-the-less, that I have speaking abilities not always appreciated in the classroom.

In those forty years, I count one hundred and seven speakers having visited our department, and while I have never before been asked to introduce a single, solitary speaker, despite, I may add, my expertise on several of the subjects on which they expatiated, I have faithfully attended each and every lecture and must confess that I have often had reservations, sometimes severe reservations, about the quality of the speaker and of his or her, as the case may be, conclusions, and have a well-earned reputation for disputation conducted, in a gentlemanly manner, I hasten to add, I think I can state without much contradiction.

Until my dying day, I shall never forget the speaker from Buffalo who regaled us with story after story of his amorous exploits by way of justifying his announced topic of "Henry Miller Unmasked." I rose on a point of personal privilege to denounce him but was shouted down. Some persist in saying, even years later, that I *waylaid* him out in that very hallway — a word I categorically reject as totally inappropriate for an honest intellectual dispute that, through no fault of either contestant, escalated into a shouting match, caught on television and broadcast on our local evening news — not, it goes without saying, because of any fame I can claim for myself, but if you are even the slightest bit outlandish you will willy nilly attract the news media, known far and wide for its chief characteristic, to wit, irresponsibility.

Hence, I am delighted to have this occasion, denied me at the time, to deny that I pursued another speaker to the airport in the a. m. following his speech. In the first place, I sometimes go there for the bargain breakfast and my eyes happened to fall upon the speaker sitting at an adjacent table.

Not to try your patience, as it were, and in the interest of time, which, it is universally recognized, is money, I will dispense with ancient history — in a nutshell, let the past be but the past, a policy that has guided my conduct ever since I graduated from college. Had I survived the hideous tradition of frat rush, perhaps I would have rehashed for you many past frat romps with my fellow frat rats on those numerous occasions when frat brothers meet to rub each other's backs.

My ex-wife was given to saying, with irritating frequency, I might add, that I dwell too much on the past, especially "imagined slights," as she so quaintly put it. She's probably putting it — ye old shaft, I mean — to her new husband, totally unslighted, I'm sure.

Forgive me if I digress. My introduction, I fear, has already exceeded the strict time limit imposed upon me by the program committee. Short and sweet, they cautioned me. I shall endeavor to obey. I am indebted to them for the advice my worthy colleagues have given me over the years, from how to survive divorce, not to mention the sadness that seeps into one's very marrow, when my children stopped coming around, to how to navigate the World Wide Web to how to repair my lawnmower — my high grass, my neighbors have asserted, encourages rats, roaches, and mosquitoes in this climate. Do you think that that is really true? Because it didn't do the trick, so to say. A little humor, in an introduction doesn't hurt either, don't you know?

Well, hopefully, this will be a short introduction so that our illustrious speaker will have time to take questions. I have a question up front, if I may. Why, I wonder, and don't feel you have to answer this one now — even before you start to speak, ha! — Well, no, maybe I would do better saving that one until after. On second thought, that might be one of those questions that get me in trouble. Because, you see — and all you young people especially need to hear this — it is the asking of questions — man the question asker — full of questions, that makes us human. Be but forewarned. 'Tis easier to ask a question than to get an answer. Even such simple questions as, Why is one required by university policy to hold office hours if no one ever darkens your office door? What is my own humble answer to that vexing question? Give me a few hours and I'll show how, at the end of the day, it goes to the very heart of my — our problem as teacher.

On the other hand, who dares even pose the question, If teaching is our mission, why must we who have not published the requisite number of books to become a member of the graduate faculty, teaching a mere two courses, be forced to teach four courses, longevity cast aside. Try it; you'll get the proverbial cold shoulder every time. Take it from a veteran.

While some of us do have to work to keep body and soul together, I doubt that the speaker has ever been called by a person who remains anonymous, the most boring man on the face of the earth. Quote — "Hell is other people." — unquote. I am the first one to admit that Piers Ploughman is not the most fascinating subject, except that we few, we few happen to feel passionately about him — at one time, at least. But I ramble . . .

I see I'm being waved to. Odd, isn't it? The same long-time colleague who doesn't return your wave in the halls of academe doesn't hesitate to wave you on in front of the whole world.

Ergo, I shall indeed turn to my notes so that this welcome task will go more smoothly. And they are only notes. To be sure, I didn't have time to craft one of those shapely, witty introductions. There are only so many minutes in a day, after all is said and done. Come to think of it, what distracted me may shed some light on the announced topic for this evening. I say announced because how many times have you been attracted to a subject announced in the newspaper, gotten dressed, driven across town, only to discover, to your utter dismay, that the speaker has changed topics on you, with no advanced warning whatsoever? Moreover, the speech itself proves to be, in a manner of speaking, a classic stem-winder.

Be that as it may, I am happy to have been chosen to execute the honorable task of giving you just an overview, so to speak, of our speaker's long and varied career. The list of his accomplishments, given the time constraints imposed upon me, is too long to recite here. His who's who is this long. Our speaker attended Harvard. He probably never met one of the earliest Piers Ploughman scholars. That would be before his time. Whatever happened to our own favorite teacher? That is one of those haunting questions to which we may never find an answer. Our speaker's most recent book, I might add, I found, parenthetically, for 99 cents on the remainder table at Books-a-Million, a godsend to underpaid teachers. Suffice it to say, there is great interest in hearing him speak. By comparison, my own credentials are modest. Graduated with honors from an albeit obscure little college in a corner of my home state, earned a doctorate by the sweat of my brow in the state university, published three articles from my dissertation on *Piers Ploughman*, and it should be noted that a university press did send my dissertation out to be evaluated by my peers. Through no fault of their own, they had to abide by the reader's reports, one of which was tinged with a note of jealousy. Connect the dots. In the long run, it matters not.

Although the light on my notes is not up to the occasion, I note, not without interest, that our speaker was born in my own home-town, although his family moved from that city when he was one year old. I wish I could say I have known the speaker all my life, but the fact is that I have not known anyone all my life.

While he would have no memory of the merry-go-round in the park, I would only share this one fascinating episode. My mother put me on the tiger — no, that's too private. Perhaps another occasion . . . I hasten to say, on the other hand, that my father left me an orphan, my mother left me a nervous wreck, the aunt who took me in . . . well, let us not dwell on the past.

Forgive me if I digress (some things are unforgivable). I fully realize that my own history. . . .

I see most of you have removed your jackets, a cue that it is permissible for me, even as introducer, to relieve myself. I have the advantage of access to water, although I seem to have consumed this entire tacky foam cup of water, having hazarded the assumption that since there was a pitcher of water and two cups, one would be for yours truly and one for our renowned speaker.

Time permitting, I might say just a few words about my work-in-progress, the Great American Novel, if you will. But, no, our speaker seems restive. However, if you would like to discuss this matter further, I would be more than happy to meet you one and all out in the hallway. A furtive glance at my watch — which, you will note, is a pocket watch, not a wrist watch — reveals that I have regressed from my main theme. I thought long and hard about the theme or focus of my introduction.

Alas, my time has run its course. Time is of the essence. In my humble opinion, you have been very patient, one and all.

SEVEN FROZEN

STARLINGS

❋

A light wind beginning at dusk, moving swings hanging on rusty chains over non-mopped porches, and then on the lungs of midnight the air was ripe for snow. Pine cones lay under the trees. Leaves fell upon the swings. Snow whispered against frozen windowpanes. The storm came quickly, quietly like a summer rain. Three days the snow fell. The yellow school house was silent by the creek. Foot tracks linked the gap between back porches and wood-sheds. In the square the fountain froze. Then the storm was gone as though a massive door had softly shut.

The fourth morning, shutters and doors opened and sleep-tight eyes blinked at the sun on the snow. Miss Hill, hunching her narrow shoulders, tightly holding the collar of her faded jade coat around her neck, trudged through the snow down Tate Springs Road to the elementary school house. All day, wonder-struck eyes wandered to the window to stare upon the sun-bright snow that lay upon the trees, the housetops, and the mountains rising beyond.

When beyond the leaf-less, snow-barked trees, the sun spread winter water colors of dusk across the sky, Rosemary walked along the road home from school, snow melting in her mouth. The snow, its falling, its blue-white after-math, always filled her with mysterious delight. But snow was sad because it was so brief. With cold fingers she pushed her wild, yellow hair away from her eyes.

Dirt clods clung to the combat boots she wore that were much too large. They had belonged to her brother, and after he was killed across the sea, her father threw them into a shed next to the barn. For a long time, she went into the shed to look at them and hold them in her hands. One day her father found fresh mud on the boots. His eyes were red when he told her never to wear them again. But, avoiding her father, she had worn them every day since school began.

She remembered about her brother only that in the evenings, when he came home from the lumber mill and lay exhausted upon the davenport, she unlaced his shoes, pulled them off, poured the saw-dust onto a newspaper, and, having stuffed his socks into his shoes, looked at his feet, white as the newspaper. His gray eyes looked into her face a long time, without wandering from the sight of her hair-lip.

Down the road a group of boys were throwing rocks at something on the telephone wires. She hated them, who were always together, not only because they shouted jokes about her lip, and in the fall threw rotten persimmons in her hair, but because the sight of them made her see six mangy, red-gummed hounds prowling in green moonlight through a town where everyone was dead.

As rocks struck them, the telephone wires twanged in the white limbs of the sycamore. In ragged helmets and tight, patched jackets, the boys, mouths open in excitement and laughter, thrust their rough, red hands deep into the snow.

When at first she saw the starlings perched on the black, ice-skimmed wire, she foresaw their sudden flight away, and the moans of disappointment from the hounds: cold rocks in their paws: the birds giggling in the twilight sky. As rocks plucked a metallic discord from the wires, the birds trembled on their perch but did not move after the wire was still again. Standing in deep snow beside the road, she frowned.

A rock hit one of the birds on the breast. The boys cheered. But the stone fell into the frozen snow on the road, and the starling remained on the wire, swinging back and forth in short jerks.

Slowly, she realized: during the storm the starlings had paused in their terrified flight to rest on the wire. They had been electrocuted and then frozen. Around the wire their tiny feet, frozen stiff, tightly curled.

Angrily, the boys dug for more rocks. One of them yelled: "Hey, men, look! Ragged mouth, staring like a loon!"

The boys, arms elbow-deep in snow, turned to look at Rosemary, whose stare was buttoned upon the image of the starlings on the wire. Mimicking her, the leader, a fat boy, bugged his eyes and with a dirty finger pushed up his upper lip in the center. "Hey, look! I'm ragged-mouth Rosemary!" The boys laughed and slapped their legs.

The fat boy, his teeth like tiny chips of tree bark, yelled for Rosemary to watch him. Taking careful, elaborate aim, he threw a rock, and a bird fell into the snow. Its yellow, bodiless feet still clung to the wire. The cheering and laughter was slow beginning.

Turning, tightly closing her eyes, Rosemary thrust her long white fingers into her hair and tightly pressed them against her skull to still the throbbing of blood in her head.

"Hey! Ragged-mouth ain't watching, men!"

Arms caught her about the chest, jerked her around. In the darkness behind her shut eyes, she smelled the raw odor of one of the hounds, heard his breathing. Cold fingers pulled her lids up.

"The great, fearless marksman!" one of the hounds yelled. And the rest repeated it together.

In a gray-white blur that wiggled with the flurried movement of the boys, the starlings fell one after another — soft thuds on the snow.

The wire became a sharp black slash across the hard blue sky.

The fat boy hunched up to a slender sycamore, and Rosemary heard hissing and thin blue smoke spiraled into the air, snow turned yellow between his legs.

Wearing an apron, a stout woman appeared on the porch across the road. Rosemary recognized Eddie's face, pressed against the windowpane beside the door. In school, his cow-big eyes always watched her.

When the woman asked them to release Rosemary and go home, the hounds made faces and laughed at her. Wiping soapsuds on the apron, the woman descended the porch steps.

As the woman crossed the road, someone pushed Rosemary into the snow among the starlings. Laughing, barking, the hounds, jumping the mud holes, scurried down the road, yelling rhythmically, in unison, "Ha! Ha! Ha! Ha! Ha! Ragged-mouth Rosemary is a dead bird! My word! A dead bird!"

The woman helped her to her feet and as Rosemary felt the woman's hands stroke her numb body, brushing snow from her coat, she stared at the starlings lying together on the snow, and at the glistening wet streak on the sycamore. The woman was muttering something, a soft sort of drone, when Rosemary broke away and ran down the road, through sedge grass and snow, up the hill, and into the dark woods.

Thirsty, her throat tasting of rust, she knelt at the spring she knew. The water was under a thin spray of snow that concealed her face. Her eyes were open as she bent down her mouth and nose. Her tongue touched water. She sucked it slowly into her mouth. But when she drew away, her face was pale on the water, and a sensation like a lizard skittered up her back. A wild glitter in her eyes, she stood up and ran away from the water. . . . Passing homeward through the woods, hunters wondered at the strange patterns formed by large boot tracks. Often, they encircled a huge tree many times. Stopped at a narrow, shallow branch and began again far down stream. Or they led into thick, darker regions, where the trees stood close, branch-woven, and moonlight barely leaked upon the snow, only to appear again suddenly on the hidden path.

The apple orchard was full of the moon, naked black branches pawed at the stars with the nonchalance of bored cats. The windowpane trembled in the wind.

Nights that put her in a strange mood, Rosemary sat in bed and fashioned her long golden hair into a tent around her head. Staring through the veil of her hair, listening to the wind in the trees, she stayed awake a long time in the cold, damp room. She was very hot for a while, under thick, heavy quilts, but soon chills shook her body.

She crawled from under the quilts and went to the window: her large blue eyes stared back at her. At the sight of her lip, her heart trembled. She felt only hate and disgust for her mouth, as if it belonged not to her, but to one of the naked, black women in the pictures in the dusty *National Geographics* her father kept stacked in the attic. With her finger, she drew on the window a moon around her frost-white face, excluding her mouth from the circle.

She stared at the many-eyed sky. Perhaps the souls of birds were blown in the wind forever before the sun, the moon, and the stars. All birds seemed happy. Yet, though often as many as a hundred flew together, passing like the sound of rain over the trees, each one seemed alone. The soul of a bird must be the loneliest thing God ever made.

She lit a candle and set it on the dusty windowsill.

Under the heavy quits again, Rosemary was lulled to sleep by the flicker of the flame.

The suddenly loud beating of wings woke her. Quickly sitting up in bed, she frightened a tiny white moth that had fluttered out of her ear, brushing its wings against her cheek. Damp with perspiration, trying to catch her breath, shuddering, she watched the moth's frenzied flitting around the candle.

Hugging the combat boots to her chest, she went quietly down the stairs, the smell of fresh-ground coffee rising to meet her. As she passed along the dark hallway, her father coughed in the kitchen.

She heard hounds barking, and now and then lights like sun-blasted cobwebs appeared among the trees on the hills. Hunters. Even after the thick, black woods were behind her and she was in the moonlight on the road, the hounds were not silent in her head.

She walked in deep snow beside the road, brushing her cheek against tall sedge-grass the wind had bowed. All last night her mind had been almost entirely on this road, these telephone poles and wires, and what was lying six in the snow ahead. It was very cold and, wearing only muddy combat boots and a cotton dress, she was aware of her trembling body.

In the pale light of the unseen sun, the six starlings lay under a sprinkle of fine snow, their feet curled tight like wires against their breasts, their black eyes as weird as raisins on the moon. One starling had no feet.

She squatted on her heels, and, her legs apart, fashioned her dress into a basket. As though each were an intangible soul, she placed them in the basket, and her blue-veined hands held the dress above her knees as she dragged her snow-filled boots through the snow toward the schoolhouse down the road.

As she started down the other side of the rutted hill, dawn was yawning sleepy colors beyond the trees. The hounds were silent. Coughing began to wrack her body.

Frost was like breath on the windowpanes. She saw only the white limbs of a giant sycamore through the windows. The schoolhouse was cold. Eddie had not yet arrived, no fire roared inside the rusty swollen belly of the stove in the corner.

Rosemary gently lowered her dress upon one of the desktops. The room began to tremble. Her eyes blinked nervously. She laid her damp, cold hands on her brow, and breathed suddenly, deeply, in a delirium of green semi-darkness, until again she saw clearly the sun, hard and bright on the limbs of the sycamore.

She passed among the sunny desktops, placing the starlings on the desks of each of the six hounds. The last one turned warm in her hands.

A door opened behind her: Eddie, brown eyes staring from behind an armful of short pine logs. He blew his dark hair away from his eyes and smiled hesitantly. Her mouth limp, Rosemary stared, then suddenly sneezed, deeply, loudly, three times.

Eddie began to build a fire in the stove. Rosemary watched him. His movements were awkward, his head bent, as though he were trying not to look at her. He was like all the others. Not that he abused her, but his constant staring frightened her. Yet she was always aware of tenderness in his eyes. And this morning behind his brown hair his eyes were an even softer glow.

But she hated him! Yesterday he had sat in his warm living room and watched the birds fall one by one across the road. Now he was ashamed, for he neither looked at her nor spoke to her.

Sitting at her desk, Rosemary watched Eddie wander about the room, his hands clasped behind his back. When he saw the starlings, he stared at them a long time, frowning. When his hand reached for one of them, Rosemary jumped up and slapped him across the mouth.

"The snow is melting at last," said Miss Hill, coming into the room, stamping show off her galoshes.

Miss Hill would find the starlings lying in the sun on the desks. The hounds would come and there would be no corpses to terrify them. Rosemary and Eddie turned slowly to their seats. Miss Hill, her back to the warm stove, her cob-webby hair tight against her skull, gazed blandly around the room.

Suddenly she walked among the desks. "Eddie, do you know how in thunder these birds got in here?"

Rosemary remained silent, her back to toward the teacher. To stop her lip from trembling, she pressed it against her gum with her thumb.

Eddie cleared his throat in the cold room. "*She* did it."

Not turning, staring into the fire through the little windows in the door of the stove, Rosemary confessed, her voice scarcely audible, trying to explain why she had placed the birds on the desk.

"Of all the –hounds killing birds, souls of starlings — who ever — ? Rosemary, this minute! You get that wastebasket and take those rotten birds down to the creek! You're — I'm afraid to have you in the same room with the other children. Rosemary, do you hear?

Scraping her feet, heavy inside the wet boots, Rosemary went to the wastebasket. She held it while Miss Hill passed with fox-like movements among the desks, dropping starlings with an air of intense disgust into the basket. With each thud, Rosemary became weaker. She began to cough.

"Turn your head, girl! Eddie, go with her and make sure she throws these — into the creek. And don't neither of you come back until all of them are gone!" Miss Hill wiped the frost from a pane, crossed her arms tightly, and stared out the window.

Eddie looked at Rosemary as she paused in the doorway. He put out his hands toward the wastebasket, not touching it, but shaping his hands as though they already held it. Seeing a tear on Eddie's cheek, Rosemary wanted to put the wire basket in his hands, but she kept her arms around it as they went out into the snow together.

Beside the creek under the trees, Eddie asked Rosemary if she would rather he buried the starlings in the snow. She nodded, her yellow hair shaking around her shoulders.

Hot, coughing, trembling, she leaned against a young, white birch and watched Eddie, on his knees in the deep snow, dig slowly. When his hands, turning red, with bracelets of snow, went down into the hole, caressing one of the birds, Rosemary's heart beat suddenly faster: under the snow, their wings fluttering in the cold muddy tomb, the souls of the starlings would bruise themselves against all the earth that covered them.

"No!" Eddie did not hear her. His hands dipped again into the wire basket. "No!" Then his brown eyes looked at her over his shoulder. "No. Drop them in the creek."

Without speaking, Eddie removed the bird from its brief tomb and placed it in the basket with the others again. Passing Rosemary down the path along the creek, Eddie looked without flinching into her face.

She watched his shoes as he disappeared among the naked, thickly standing trees.

Shuddering with a sudden chill, numb with regret for having slapped Eddie, she wanted to run, but it seemed she could not move. Yet when she did try to run her feet trod the snow easily, her body pressing against the still, cold air.

Deep in the woods, stumbling and falling in small gullies, she dragged her feet through the snow. Black, wet limbs slapped across her face. Finally, she came to the spring she loved, into which in the summer she dropped fresh flowers.

She fell upon her knees and leaning over the snow-covered water beat her fists against the ice. Her arms and hands limply struck the ice, no stronger than two stems of sedge-grass against the wind.

SECOND LOOK PRESENTS

The Rape of an Indian Brave

❖

NINE MOTORCYCLES IN A ROW IN BRIGHT SUNLIGHT.
(Song of morning birds)
(David Epstein's voice over) On the morning of July 3, 1976 — a Saturday — nine men, astride brand-new Kawasaki 901s like these, set out from San Diego, California on a journey that was to have ended at a stunt contest in Billings, Montana.

FOUR MEN, HOLDING TO ROPES ON EXTEMELY
STEEP HILL, READY TO CATCH ASCENDING MOTORCYCLE
AND RIDER IF THEY FALL.
(Epstein's voice over, covering garbled voice from loudspeaker) A perfectly respectable — perhaps even middle-class — annual event that attracts far more lovers of the sport than violent gangs. But the nine novice riders did not make it to Billings, Montana. Their journey ended in the San Carlos Pueblo, near Albuquerque, New Mexico.

AERIAL VIEW OF A KIVA, A WINDOWLESS CIRCULAR
STRUCTURE, A LADDER UP THE SIDE, ANOTHER
PROTRUDING OUT A ROUND OPENING IN THE ROOF.
(Song of morning birds)

DAVID EPSTEIN.
I'm David Epstein, and this is "Second Look," a bimonthly special news feature of the Southwest Entertainment Network.
(Flute music over bird song)

A GENTLE BREEZE STIRS LEAVES IN BRIGHT SUNLIGHT.
VIOLETS ON THE BANK OF A SPARKLING BROOK. A MAN,
DRINKING A GLASS OF WATER, STANDS AMONG VIOLETS,
TREES BEHIND HIM, CITY BUILDINGS BEYOND THE
TREES. THE MAN, SPEAKING.

The day has not yet returned when Plainsvillians can kneel beside Sparrow Creek as it passes through its fast-growing business district and drink its waters. But

MAN INHALES.

they can breathe its air without fear of contaminating their lungs.

PLAINSVILLE, CLEAR SKY ABOVE.

(Voice over) Plainsville is a model city in our fight against pollution. Another of American Electric's public service projects.

MAN HOLDING GLASS OF WATER.

Plainsvillians welcome you, but they, along with American Electric, implore you to make the air in your own town

ANONYMOUS METROPOLIS, SMOG LADEN

(Voice over) at least as fresh as the water in Sparrow Creek before you sample *their* air.

GENTLE BREEZE IN LEAVES.

For a free plan of action, write to Model Cities American Electric, Box 5550, Chicago, Illinois, 60611.

DAVID EPSTEIN

A sad fact of American experience in this electronic age is that the average citizen consumes daily far more information than he or she can consciously assimilate, much less retain in memory, and retrieve at will. In this Bicentennial year, we have seen the strange death of Howard Hughes, the Teton River Dam Catastrope in Idaho, the daring raid on Entebbe, the landing of Viking I on Mars, the Legionionaires disease in Philadelphia, Patty Hearst's return home on bail. The Southwest Entertainment Network decided last spring to offer the public a second chance — a second look at events that, no matter how shocking and memorable they may have seemed at the time we first reported them on the six o'clock eyewitness news, have now, months later, faded in memory. Test yourself. Do you remember . . . the rape of an Indian brave?

MARK SANDDANCER, WEARING GLASSES, GOWN, AND
MORTARBOARD IN HIGH SCHOOL GRADUATION PORTRAIT.
(Voice over) Mark Sanddancer was a modern young Tigeux Indian who dreamed of becoming an archeological anthropologist. But he was not just a dreamer. He began as a child to *act out* his dreams. The people of San Carlos Pueblo — those who would consent to speak with us — remember him as not just a child digging in the sand,

SMOLDERING DUMP, A FEW TREES, FIVE LEAN
DOGS RUMMAGING.
(Voice over) but a skinny little fellow who persisted right down deep into the dirt, hunting for relics in the dumping grounds, yelping with delight when he unearthed discarded plastic bleach bottles or some little gadget from a Cracker Jacks box.

MS. HARRIET JACKSON, IN HER ELEGANT LIVING ROOM.
Mark was not an ordinary child — certainly not a typical Indian child. He had the interests and ambitions of a middle-class suburban child of a doctor, let's say, who had graduated from an Ivy League university. My husband and I recognized certain qualities in Mark when we met him at the trading post outside the reservation where he was working at the time. We were on vacation — and there he was. We promised, on the spot, that if he finished high school, we would see to it that he got into college. Well, the child won a scholarship quite on his own initiative and we simply supplemented his stipend.

STUDENTS WALKING PAST A SIGN: UNIVERSITY OF
NEW MEXICO.

MS. JACKSON.

Since that day at the trading post where we bought some moccasins that turned out to have been made in Brooklyn, four blocks from where we live, we haven't laid eyes on Mark Sanddancer.

DAVID EPSTEIN.

It was when nine men on nine brand new Kawasaki 901s laid eyes on Mark Sanddancer that the trouble began.

PHOTO OF MARK SANDDANCER PUSHING A
WHEELBARROW AMONG ADOBE RUINS.

DAVID EPSTEIN.

Mark was a student assistant to the Director of the Coronada Monument State Park.

AERIAL VIEW OF PUEBLO RUINS, SUGGESTIVE
OF HIROSHIMA.

(Voice over) Those hideously memorable but somehow generally forgotten events began here and ended — though not entirely — at the kiva,

KIVA, GROUND VIEW.

the sacred meeting place for Tigeux males only, in the midst of the Pueblo. But let us go back to the beginning —

NINE KAWASAKI 901S IN A ROW IN BRIGHT SUNLIGHT.

as far back as we have been able to go, faced with a scarcity of concrete facts. This second look came close to being no more than a glance. Cesar Valdez. (Birds sing)

SIGN: CESAR VALDEZ'S. 1,000 WHEELS. 1975 DODGE VAN
PULLS UP IN FRONT OF THE STORE. CESAR VALDEZ,
A CHICANO IN HIS MID-THRITIES, GETS OUT, WALKS TO
THE DOOR OF THE SHOP, UNLOCKS IT.

(Valdez's voice) I'd had two hours sleep that morning — up all night assembling the last of the new shipment of Kawasaki 901s to have nine of them ready for

Mr. Jones when he came in, bright and early Saturday morning. And there they were waiting for me — all nine of them, in complete bike outfits, like Evel Knievel. And two of them redheaded twins. And this Mr. Jones, the head honcho — well, anyway, he made all the arrangements, wrote out the one check for the whole fleet. A ten-minute sale, at more than a thousand dollars a minute.

CESAR VALDEZ WALKS INTO HIS SHOP, A THOUSAND
WHEELS IN THE DIM LIGHT. VALDEZ TURNS ON
FLUORESCENT LIGHTS. THE MOTORCYCLES GLEAM.

(Valdez's voice) I mean, he knew what he wanted when he walked in here. None of this endless, aimless wandering around, touching each part of every single bike in the place.

CESAR VALDEZ, IN HIS SHOP.

"I want nine brand new Kawasaki 901s," he says to me — like that. "You want nine brand new Kawasaki 901s?" "Yes." "For nine birthdays in a large family. Right? All on the same day." "No cracks," he says. "How much?" he says. "Let me add it up," I says. Over sixteen thousand dollars in ten minutes! That was the only unusual thing about this guy. Any business man, he could have been any business man on the street — executive type. The suit, the briefcase, the shaving lotion — the whole bit. So what were the other eight? Standing there like that. I mean, all together in this creepy way, but *not* together, know what I mean? Well, you couldn't *tell* what they did in real life before they showed up in those outfits. Every one of them like that.

DUMMY MODEL IN COMPLETE FANCY OUTFIT.

(Valdez's voice over) But not from *my* store. I carry a whole line of accessories, see. From the black-and-white ranger crash helmets like the cops wear, with the Baruffaldi panoramic dual-lens goggles, and the Bates leather motocross pants, jazzed up with your stripes, diamonds, stars, and zippers and pockets all over, to your full-bore touring boots to go with the wheels.

CESAR VALDEZ, IN HIS SHOP.

And each one wore a silver-plated belt made from bike chains around his waist. I stock all that, but they got it somewhere else. The only thing I don't stock is attitudes. That comes with the man. From Cesar Valdez they got no outfits, and only God knows where they got their attitude. Not that they were any trouble to me. They stood there like this dummy — or like this here dummy had just sprung to life and didn't know what to do first. Like zombies, you know what I mean? No, not zombies. . . . Just the coolest damn crew that ever walked in here. Like they was hired to dress up and be cool. I kept rehearsing in my head what I wanted to ask them. Finally, after I'd rolled all nine of the Kawasakis outside — so sleepy I felt drunk from putting them together all night long — I asked this Jones character, "What you fellas going to do now?"

NINE KAWASAKIS IN A ROW.

DAVID EPSTEIN.

Jones — no one knows whether that was his real name — answered, "We've saved up, and we're riding to Billings, Montana. There's a kind of roundup."

CESAR VALDEZ, OUTSIDE HIS SHOP.

They didn't sound like guys that had ever even smelled a motorcycle. Roundup! It's a hill-climbing championship event the Billings Motorcycle club puts on every year. Looks suicidal, but they got these guys holding onto ropes up there that catch hold of you and your bike if you loop at the top or wipe out, and nobody gets hurt much. These guys held their helmets in their hands like fish bowls 'til they all got mounted — sort of awkward, not comfortable in the saddle at all, but a very eager bunch, but still cool, you know, and then all together they put on their helmets. And I says to myself, ain't this a sight? Every one of them with nice boy haircuts — a few sort of long, but done up by some hair stylist with the spray and all. Like they was playing two parts — what they did before they put on the new outfits and what they were trying to do now. I start to go back inside, but Jones calls me over. I didn't want to get near those guys, for some reason. This feeling. But all he did was floor me with this simple question, like some kid. "What do you do to make it go?"

VALDEZ IN FRONT OF THE ROW OF MOTORCYCLES.

So when they left the lot, they looked like a bunch of drunken — Well, they didn't look like what they turned out to be. Now don't get me wrong. I have absolutely nothing against people of their persuasion.

DAVID EPSTEIN.

It should be said at this point that although subsequent events tend to dramatize the possibility that they — or at least some of them — were members of some homosexual club, there is no evidence to prove this claim. The stark fact is that we know absolutely nothing about these men before they appeared at Cesar Valdez's One Thousand Wheels.

CESAR VALDEZ, TURNING AROUND, POINTING
OVER HIS SHOULDER.

Called themselves the Comanches. Had the letters sewed on the back of their jackets.

DAVID EPSTEIN.

And they set out for Billings, Montana.
(Roar of nine motorcycles)
Up through Los Angeles . . .

LOS ANGLES FROM A FREEWAY.
(Roar of motorcycles)
Through the mountains . . .

MOUNTAINS.
(Roar of motorcycles)
Across the Mohave Desert . . .

MOHAVE DESERT.

GEORGE HALL, IN FRONT OF A SMALL FILLING STATION.
Gassed up right at those pumps.
(Roar of motorcycles)

DAVID EPSTEIN.
Through the Petrified Forest . . .

OTIS FERGUSON, NATIONAL PARKS OFFICER,
INSIDE PARK GIFT SHOT
They each bought petrified-wood samples.

DAVID EPSTEIN.

Through the Cíbola region where Coronado searched for the Seven Cities of Gold, and on across the Continental Divide beyond Gallup.

MRS. FRANK NORTON, IN FRONT OF HER TRAILER.

I was washing my hair when I heard them go by, and ran to the door. . . . Well, I've seen 'em pass like that before. Other gangs.

(Roar of motorcycles over)

DAVID EPSTEIN.

And at twilight, Monday, July 5, they rode into Albuquerque.

ELMO PLANK, BEHIND THE COUNTER OF HIS LIQUOR STORE.

Each one of them bought a fifth of Wild Turkey. Stood in line at the counter, like little boys. Polite, but cool.

DAVID EPSTEIN.

Polite, but cool. Everyone who encountered the Comanches testified to that. No one had the least suspicion of what was to happen when nine strangers passed through Bernalillo in the dark. No drunken shouts disturbed the night calm of that quiet little New Mexico town. And in Bernalillo nothing was heard from Coronado monument — before or after the men pulled off highway 44.

PUEBLO RUINS, MOONLIGHT . . .

(Elegiac flute music)

BARE TREES, SMOGGY SKY SHOWING THROUGH. GRASSLESS BANK, OILY, TRASH-CONGESTED STREAM.

BUILDINGS AND STREETS OF A GHOST TOWN.

A MAN SITS ON THE PORCH OF A HOTEL.

I am the only living creature in this town, unless you count the spiders and the ants and the snakes and other creatures of prehistory. Before I came, only silence. I am breaking this long silence to speak to you in the name of the unborn. Don't let this happen to our modern towns. It wasn't pollution that turned Mission City into a ghost town — it was over-reaching human greed. And human greed can work through modern ways to achieve the same end, unless we find ways to stop the misuse of our air — the sky was never intended to become a sewer — and our streams — rivers were never intended to become running sores. As a concerned citizen, you may receive upon request information about how you — and you behind your civic leaders — can create a model city for the rest of America. Write Model Cities, American Electric, Box 5550, Chicago, Illinois, 60611.

WIND WHIRLING DUST IN A GHOST TOWN STREET.

DAVID EPSTEIN.

Ponce de León failed to find the Fountain of Youth in Florida. Searching for gold, DeSoto discovered only the Mississippi River. Then in 1540, Francisco Vásquez de Coronado led an expedition from Mexico City to search for the Seven Cities of Gold, guided by Marcos de Niza, a Franciscan friar who testified to having seen one of the cites from a distance. This most famous and important of the early Spanish expeditions is described by a private soldier in one of the most revealing documents of the conquest epoch. We have more detailed information about this expedition four hundred years ago than about the rape of Mark Sanddancer at Coronado's monument last year.

PAINTING DEPICTING CORONADO LEADING HIS ARMY,
FRIAR MARCOS POINTING THE WAY.

(Voice over) When Coronado captured the first of the Seven Cities, but found no gold, his soldiers were so outraged, the commander had to send Friar Marcos back to Mexico City for his own safety. During the summer and fall, exploratory parties of the Coronado expedition discovered

THE GRAND CANYON.

the grand canyon on the Colorado River in Arizona and explored the Rio Grande pueblo country as far north as Taos.

TAOS PUEBLO.

Coronado established winter headquarters in a Tigeux pueblo on rich land by the Rio Grande near Bernalillo. Actually, archeologists do not know for certain in which of the more than a dozen pueblos in this region Coronado made his headquarters. When the Tigeux pueblos revolted against excessive requisitioning of food and clothing during the hard winter, Coronado put down the revolt so severely, the Indians remained hostile to Spanish soldiers and missionaries for many decades. Still, Coronado is known for his determination to treat the Indians humanely and fairly. When an Indian captive of one of the pueblos told the Spaniards of a very rich country to the east of Quivira, Coronado set forth with his entire army. The Indian led Coronado's army many leagues across Texas into eastern Kansas, where they found vast herds of buffalo, armies of jack rabbits, prowling white wolves, and the Wichita Indians of Quivira living in an areas of rich land, but no gold. The Indian confessed that he had deliberately lied, instructed by his chief to lead the Spaniards out of their territory.

SKETCH OF INDIAN HANGING.

DAVID EPSTEIN

Coronado sentenced the Indian to be hanged. After another depressing winter at the Tigeux pueblo, Coronado returned early in April, 1542 with his resentful army to New Spain, to report his expedition to find gold a total failure. But he had given the Spanish Crown a vast new territory and the priests many Indians to convert. His unintentional gift to the Indians themselves was the horse, a creature they first regarded as a monster of the white devils. But the impact of the horse on the Indian culture was almost as dynamic as the effect centuries later of the automobile on American civilization. And the finest horsemen

PHOTOS OF COMANCHE WARRIOR ON A HORSE.

(Voice over) of the west were the Comanches.

DAVID EPSTEIN.

Nobody knows what drew the Comanche motorcyclists to Coronado Monument. Certainly not Mark Sanddancer. There is no way — known to anybody we talked with — that the Comanches could have known about the existence of that young man. The Coronado Monument is not one of the most famous sights of New Mexico. As far as we know, they had passed up far more enticing national spectacles. So why did they, that night in July, turn off and stop at Coronado Monument? No one seems to know.

SHERIFF TOM GALARZA. PUEBLO RUINS IN THE BACKGROUND.

Whiskey bottles all over the grounds of the monument, mainly among the apartments, as we call them, of the old dwellings. I'll say this for them — they drank only the best whiskey. But a worse bunch of human beings — if they weren't creatures from Mars, and I don't leave that possibility out for one second — never passed through this county under *my* jurisdiction, and I've been sheriff here for twenty years.

SHERIFF WALKS AMONG THE RUINS.

You can see where they was sleeping or laying around — not now, of course, after that record mob of tourists run through here — but they appeared to pair off, two to a section here. . . .Well, two whiskey bottles found in each area. The guard dog must've barked too much to their taste. I found it laying over there, its throat cut. Anybody that would slaughter a dog like that — Well, that's something else. What you want to know from me is what happened here and show you the traces that's left. Well, traces — some, here and there. But what happened? They raped that boy — that's all I know.

DAVID EPSTEIN.

But before Mark Sanddancer arrived at the museum in the state pickup truck that he drove proudly home each evening and parked in front of his mother's adobe — his father was killed in Korea — the Comanches had wreaked a good deal of damage.

MUSEUM BUILDING.

(Voice over) The museum building was closed for repairs. The Comanches opened it up, breaking out the windows, breaking down the door with a battering ram.

POTS AND OTHER OBJECTS.

(Voice over) These pots and other artifacts, unearthed — some of them by Mark Sanddancer himself — on this site, have been reassembled from pieces found shattered on the floor of the building. All evidence indicates that the drunken Comanches had worked up a rampaging momentum some time before the caretaker arrived to open the building for the carpenters and brick masons who were remodeling the museum.

THE CARETAKER, WHO ASKED THAT HIS NAME NOT BE USED. HIS BACK TO THE CAMERA AS EPSTEIN INTERVIEWS HIM.

I'm lucky to be alive today. I'm lucky to be alive today. They jumped me. I walked in — I seen the wreckage outside — I walked in, thinking whoever done it had run off. They jumped me. Had my pistol in my hand. Took it away from me. And that's *all* they done. I want to tell the world — this goes out over the whole world, don't it? — everybody that's listening, that's *all* they done to *me*. I'm just lucky I'm not dead today, after them jumping me. And that's my last word.

DAVID EPSTEIN.

Mark Sanddancer had no luck at all that day. He had felt himself extremely lucky, as an Indian, to have gotten a job through the University of New Mexico's department of anthropology as assistant to the curator of the Coronado museum. His mother refused to talk with us, so we do not know what his mood was that morning — what hopes were highest on that particular morning. His past as an Indian was not happy. Tim Barlow.

TIM BARLOW, BY THE DOOR OF A COCA COLA DELIVERY TRUCK, PARKED IN FRONT OF A TRADING POST.

I was in and out of the reservation for years, and sure, I noticed him. He *looked* different. Not like the others at all. More like a white kid — a book worm, you know. And those glasses set him off. He didn't walk like an Indian. And after about the seventh grade, I'd hear him talking in the trading post, and he didn't even sound — his voice — like an Indian. And I always could tell I wasn't the only one that noticed — all the Indians seemed to sense that he was like sort of a stranger there. I think *he* knew it, too.

DAVID EPSTEIN.

For Mark Sanddancer, the museum, the ruins, were home. He was most at home digging up, dating , categorizing the past. Curator Carl Ellmann.

CURATOR CARL ELLMANN, IN HIS OFFICE.

A likeable enough young man. Yes, I'd say he definitely had a future. But why do we all seem to be speaking of him in the past tense? It's just as likely that he's alive somewhere as that he's dead. Alive, listening to our voices. Alive or dead, I don't expect to see him in this area again.

DAVID EPSTEIN.

The Comanches saw him.

PICK UP TRUCK PARKED IN FRONT OF THE MUSEUM.

(Voice over) He drove up in this truck. Perhaps he suspected trouble as he approached those nine, wildly parked motorcycles — some of them among the ruins, some of them sprawling in the sand. Perhaps he heard the noise of pots shattering inside.

DAVID EPSTEIN

The question has been asked: Why didn't the young man turn around and seek help in Bernalillo? Why did he enter the building alone? To protect his work and the precious work done in the past from vandalism? He had the perseverance and the stamina to dig in the earth from sunup to sundown under the infernal New Mexico sun. But he was known for a lack of physical prowess and for never having had a fight in his life — although he was bullied quite often, even recently, since becoming a young man of twenty-one. Perhaps the same pride that made him refuse an offer of a foster home outside the reservation made him enter the unknown situation in that museum. The caretaker tells us that as soon as Mark entered the building the Comanches set upon him. He broke away from them and ran out into the ruins. It was still dark.

RUINS OF AN ADOBE APARTMENT. MOONLIGHT.

(Voice over) Here they caught him.

The general public tends to regard rape as a sexual assault against a woman. No other word can adequately describe what the nine members of the Comanche motorcycle club did to Mark Sanddancer. Such acts are common in this nations' prisons and jails. The gang rape of a young man outside prison walls — this is rare and so it is a rape of our imaginations. Just as men who are not basically homosexual participate in acts of sexual violence in prison, so it is possible that the nine Comanches were seized with some group compulsion that need not be classified as homosexual. Dr. Albert Steuben, Albuqurque psychiatrist.

DR. ALBERT STEUBEN, ALBUQUERQUE PSYCHIATRIST, IN OFFICE.

Rape is, after all, not primarily a sexual act, but an act of violence — out of resentment, perhaps, or as a release from severe and prolonged repressions.

DAVID EPSTEIN.

As the drunken rampage wound down, the Comanches curled up against the crumbling walls of the ruins and went to sleep.

MOONLIGHT OVER RUINS.

(Sound of motorcycle over)
(Voice over) Toward dawn, one of them was awakened by the sound of a motorcycle blasting the desert calm. One of their own Kawasaki 901s was spinning dust out over the dirt road that runs back to the highway. No one remembers ever having seen Mark Sanddancer astride a motorcycle. Once, he had merely touched his brother's Honda 250 and got such a beating he still bore the scars that night in July. His brother, Felix, was killed in a motorcycle accident just outside the city limits of St. Louis. No one knows what he was doing so far from the reservation. As for Mark Sanddancer's ability to handle a motorcycle, one can imagine that he coveted his brother's bike and continued to nurse a passionate desire to ride and own one, and that somewhere, sometime, he had found a way to learn how to operate one.

GATES OF SAN CARLOS PUEBLO.

(Voice over) The Comanches gave chase, and soon found themselves entering the gates of the San Carlos Pueblo. The sun was just coming up over the Sangre De Cristo Range.

STREETS OF THE PUEBLO.

(Voice over) As they chased Mark Sanddancer up and down the dirt streets of the pueblo, the Comanches did as much damage as they could. Mr. Jones, the leader, had taken the caretaker's pistol and waved it now over his head, screaming, as he led the twisting pursuit of the young Indian. Some of them, growing tired of the chase or thrown off their motorcycles at sharp turns around the corners of the adobes or crashing into the clay ovens that sit outside almost every house, began to run across the flat roof tops, looking for a chance to jump down on Mark Sanddancer as he wove in and out and among the adobes. One Comanche gave chase in a pick-up truck but lost control and it ran

THE RIVER.

into the river. Others opened the gates to the stock pens and turned horses, mules, goats, pigs, and chickens loose in the streets where some of them were run down in the plungings to and fro of the motorcycles. They seemed to behave as if they assumed the Indians would offer no resistance. When a young girl of about fifteen ran into the street to rescue her pet goat, a moving circle of motorcycles hemmed her in and the gang barraged her with obscenities. Still pursued by other Comanches, Mark Sanddancer made a wide sweep around the taunting circle of motorcycles and crashed into the kiva. Somehow he broke away from his tormentors and climbed the ladder up the side of the kiva, but was subdued on the top and thrown down the small round opening.

AERIAL VIEW OF THE KIVA, CIRCULAR ADOBE STURCTURE, A LADDER UP THE WINDOWLESS SIDE, A ROUND HOLE IN THE FLAT ROOF, ANOTHER LADDER INSIDE THE HOLE.

(Voice over) One by one, the Comanches proceeded once again to violate the young Indian, while their very presence inside the kiva violated the sacred place.

TIM BARLOW, STANDING BESIDE HIS COCA COLA TRUCK.
A good way to commit suicide. Why if a tourist even so much as takes a picture of the kiva, the elders come running out waving their arms, murder in their eyes.

DAVID EPSTEIN.
At one point, all the Comanches were down inside the kiva with Mark Sand-dancer, their motorcycles leaning or lying outside all around the kiva. The streets were deserted — the adobes themselves must have looked deserted.

KIVA.
(Song of morning birds)

DAVID EPSTEIN.
When the first Comanche emerged from the kiva, he may have stood a moment in the utter silence of the desert, listening to the morning sounds of nature and the animals settling out of panic, standing up there, looking out over the rooftops of the adobes and beyond at the Sangre De Cristo mountains. Whatever he saw, whatever he heard, he did not see, he did not hear the firing of the rifle bullet that found its mark in his forehead. He rolled off the kiva. There was a long silent pause. Then the Comanches climbed up the ladder one by one, out of the ventilating hole in the roof, and went down the ladder on the side of the building to look at their slain comrade. When only one man remained on top of the kiva, the rifle fire rang out again and the exposed Comanche fell back into the kiva, a bullet in his brain. Sheriff Galarza.

SHERIFF, IN FRONT OF THE KIVA.
The other seven Comanches ran around the plaza in panic among the motorcycles, some hid behind their Kawasaki 901s, some of them tried to mount and ride off. The two red-headed twins tried to double up on one motorcycle, and the sniper got them with one shot in the back. This Jones, the leader, began firing the caretaker's pistol wildly, and he wounded one of this own men accidentally. Some of the Comanches got their bikes going, and the sniper jumped out into the open and ran stark naked down the street, firing a rifle rapid fire. Some of the Comanches tried the doors, looking for places

to hide. But they were all locked. I found several huddled in locked doorways, deader'n doornails. One Comanche tried to escape on a bicycle that had no seat. The sniper shot him in front of the church gates. Jones climbed the ladder up the side of the kiva again and started to jump down inside but the sniper shot him in the head.

DAVID EPSTEIN.

When the sunlight flooded the street, only one Comanche remained alive, the one Jones had accidentally wounded. The naked Indian coolly shot him in the mouth as he screamed for mercy. The slaughter lasted less than five minutes. It was swift. It was accurate. It was deadly. Not a single bullet was wasted. Nine expended rounds were found in the pueblo. And nine dead Comanches.

AERIAL VIEW OF A MAN STANDING IN THE MIDDLE OF THE MAIN STREET OF A SMALL, MODEL TOWN, LOOKING UP.

The lies of a Franciscan Friar and of a captive Indian led Coronado on one of the longest wild goose chases in history, first to the Seven Cities of Gold and then to Quivira. But many fabled cities have lived up to their reputations, and history records ways of life that we do well to regard as models.
(Mayan drums and flutes)

RUINS OF TIKAL, GUATAMALA, MAYAN CIVILIZATION.
(Indian drums and singing)

ACOMA, THE SKY CITY, PUEBLO INDIAN CIVILIZATION.
(Ancient Greek flute music)

RUINS OF ATHENS, GREEK CIVILIZATION.
(Renaissance music)

VENICE, RENAISSANCE CIVILIZATION.
(American folk music)

WILIAMSBURG, VIRGINIA, AMERICAN
COLONIAL CIVILIZATION.
(Rock music)

PLAINSVILLE, AMERICAN SPACE AGE CIVILIZATION.
(Man's voice over) Six model cities in man's history. Coronado found none.
Discover Plainsville for yourself, then make *your* city number seven. Write to
Model Cities, American Electric, Box 5550, Chicago, Illinois, 60611.

DAVID EPSTEIN.
If the caretaker refused to talk to us any further and if no one in the pueblo
would speak to our cameras, where, you must be wondering, did we obtain
such a detailed account of the slaughter itself? The caretaker was forced, of
course, to tell more to the Sheriff than he was willing to tell us. And one
member of the tribe finally agreed to give us some details, provided we did
not give his name nor insist on filming him as he spoke. We have honored
that agreement. But no one could solve for us the remaining mysteries. Who
shot the naked Indian brave who had slaughtered the Comanches single
handedly and with such single-minded vengeance? Our informant claims he
did not witness the shooting. We know neither when nor where it occurred.

SHERIFF SPREADS HIS ARMS, SHRUGS,
THE MOUNTAINS BEHIND HIM.
Your guess is as good as mine — all I know is we found his grave, a decent
burial, in the hills, and traces of black corn near his door that tell me they
gave him the old time sendoff. One thing for sure, he wasn't shot with Mr.
Jones' gun.

DAVID EPSTEIN.
Our information is certain none of the Comanches shot him.

SHERIFF.
Well, *I* don't rule that out. Some people around here — some Indians in another pueblo — think maybe his own people shot him. Why? Well, maybe,

The Rape of an Indian Brave 169

they thought he'd gone berserk and feared for their own lives. . . .Or . . . Well, I just don't know. It's even possible the Sanddancer kid did it. Maybe what he done made the rest of 'em ashamed *they* didn't go after those men.

DAVID EPSTEIN.

One wonders why Mark Sanddancer led the Comanches to his pueblo. Did he expect his people to take revenge upon them, or at least to protect him from them?

AERIAL VIEW OF THE KIVA.

(Voice over) And at what point did Mark Sanddancer emerge from the kiva and disappear from the pueblo and, for all we know, from New Mexico? Our Indian informant did not witness his departure.

DAVID EPSTEIN.

The violation of Mark Sanddancer and the slaughter of the Comanches occurred on July 6, 1976. The bodies of the Comanches themselves were not found until last week, nearly six months after the incident.

AN ARROYO.

(Voice over) A lawyer in Albuquerque, afraid his three boys, who were out hiking, looking for arrowheads, might have gotten lost or disappeared in one of the treacherous arroyos, was searching for his sons, when he saw a hand sticking up out of the sand in an arroyo twenty miles from San Carlos pueblo.

SHERIFF. MOUNTAINS.

While the father was in a state of shock and his sons were feasting at MacDonald's, we dug up the Comanches. These were nude bodies. And the motorcycles had been dismantled and the parts scattered for twenty miles around. No trace of those fancy outfits.

DAVID EPSTEIN.

"Second Look" apologizes for the scarcity of film footage and the imbalance of narration, but as you have seen and heard, the rape of Mark Sanddancer remains an elusive incident. For the past 60 minutes, we have been groping among scattered fragments to piece together something the mind can hold and examine. Perhaps our imaginations take over in those realms where the television camera cannot penetrate. . . . Next week, we will take a second look at Idaho's Teuton Dam tragedy. Until then, this is David Epstein, hoping you have enjoyed this . . . "Second Look."

WE WISH TO STRESS THAT "SECOND LOOK" NEITHER CONDEMNS NOR CONDONES HOMOSEXUALS AS INDIVIDUALS.

CREDITS. . . .

THE RETRIEVER

✳

Stirring the broth, he looked up. A silver car was suddenly out there in the street, coming slowly, quietly to a stop under the wooden trestle. A Mercedes Benz. It was as if the Garden District had followed him over to Spanish Town Bottoms. The driver's door opened. A hand with polished nails set a bowl by the weedy edge of the street. She's brought me the rest of the dog food. When he saw a Golden Retriever pour out the door onto the ragged pavement, he said aloud, "And the damned dog with it."

The Golden Retriever turned in one fluid movement and tried to leap back into the car but the door shut too quickly, and quietly the car glided off between the rows of ramshackle shotgun houses through the mist that was still rolling off the Mississippi River into the bottom.

"You son of a bitch!"

The dog, big but still only a pup, loped jauntily after the car, as if not sure whether to take this as a game or not.

Watching the Golden Retriever chase after the silver Mercedes, he left his fire, parted the tall ironweed, and reached for the brimming dog dish. That dog'll be sitting on the front steps when she drives up, he sneered. Dogs don't know any better.

Back under the trestle at the fire, he poured the broth from the heated tin can over the cold chunks of beef in the dish and sunk his white plastic spoon into it.

✳

Before six the next morning, he was in another part of the Garden District where trash pickup was Wednesday, going from one neat green recycling bin to another, like sauntering down a mile-long supermarket shelf. Sniffing each empty dog food can, he tried to recognize the excellent brand the Mercedes lady had deposited under his trestle. No prices to go by, only computer codes. But in the bins, unmixed with garbage, he could scavenge quickly. The plastic Maison Blanche shopping bag he had filled with empty dog food cans yesterday morning was empty this morning when he left the Garden District and crossed Government into the black section. Yesterday, he had rinsed out each empty can until he had a beef broth. Then the old lady in the Mercedes had delivered the top of the line brand and spoiled him. *Old* lady? He hadn't seen her face. He was remembering the interview on TV several years back with the old lady who was caught stealing cat food and who cheerily declared, "I fed it to my cat for twenty years because it has all the nutrients any animal or human needs and now my cat is dead and I can't afford these high prices!" Her voice had made him sad, sitting in the rec room in the midst of his family, but now he often repeated aloud what she had said because it was so true it almost made him laugh.

Seeing the white-haired, red-faced man coming toward him, he crossed over to the National Cemetery side. He felt the aversion in his very flesh, just as he had felt it when he used to see the man walking as he drove past in every possible part of this area which he himself now walked — or saw him mowing someone's lawn or raking leaves. He was wearing the same business suit he wore winter and summer, immaculate. Probably a miser who emerged every morning from a mansion passed on to him from the Civil War — or stepped out of an abandoned car in Beauregard Town. Always uttering a shrieking, one-note whistle. That nose stuck in the air as if he had everybody fooled. Some time before dark, he knew he'd see red-face again, always coming toward him, never walking away from him.

He followed his daily track. Like a rat. Like a roach. Routine took less effort than venturing outside his habit-determined domain. What would he find beyond the boundaries that he had not routinely found inside? Merely looking beyond the boundaries set up an agitation in his blood until he could taste, like metal, the edge of violence.

The firemen sat on their station porch like housewives taking a breather from Glo-coating the kitchen floor. Even on this familiar street, the sight brought the taste to his mouth. Like metal because of the chair he had thrown across the basketball court at the referee who'd called a game-deciding foul. Men like those firemen would have come to watch the game, watch their kids play, watch skills he had trained them to employ. One such skill — how to repress the impulse to beat the hell out of your opponent when he commits a foul — had failed him that night. The referee showed up in court with ten stitches in his forehead.

Walking among a crew of men installing an elaborate pattern of Christmas lights over the grounds of the state Capitol, he heard a clicking noise on the sidewalk behind him. What he saw when he turned was a Golden Retriever in name only. Its coat was matted with something that — stank like holy hell! He quickened his pace.

⁂

The acres of petrochemical plants upriver blessed Baton Rouge each day like this one with a glorious sunset of burnt orange streaked with baby blue. Every dodging device he could imagine had failed. The stink that had followed him the rest of the day was terrible enough, but seeing how miserable the dog felt had got to him. "Here's *my* contribution," he said to Grandfather Mississippi, rinsing the goddamned Golden Retriever for the seventh time at the foot of the levee where the *USS Kidd* at permanent anchor cast its shadow.

He expected the dog to keep following him, just as it did, because he had rid its coat of whatever cruel concoction some yard-grooming taxpayer had probably doused it with, in mid-crap to send it home to its master with a reeking message to keep it penned up in its own yard. "But that's it, dog. I have no vices. I don't steal. I don't smoke. I don't drink. And I don't talk to dogs. I *do* eat."

So he got back on track, made a stop behind the City Club, hoping for steak instead of the limp quiche he'd had to settle for the last time. Turning from scavenging, he saw it sitting, as if expecting to be waited on. Clean, and almost dry now. He wondered if it could be the same Golden Retriever the silver Mercedes dumped. Another goddamned coincidence. He saw them everywhere he went. He was getting sick of coincidences.

174 *The Retriever*

He flapped the yellow plaid overcoat and yelled, "Git!" It didn't work this time either.

Sitting on one of the benches the city had set out along the median of North Boulevard, under the tiny white Christmas lights strung through the newly planted trees, he nibbled the steak bone he'd found behind the City Club. The landscape designer had called for a red-brick walk that snaked rather than shot straight down the median, making him think of Dorothy in *The Wizard of Oz* that his parents had watched with him on TV and he had watched with his own children religiously each year. Such sudden memories agitated that metal taste in his mouth.

He felt the urge to yell "Go to hell!" into the night to everybody — "You, too!" he said, even-temperedly to the dog — but after the first few weeks on the street, he'd managed to control that kind of spontaneous outburst.

"If I give you this bone, that means I own you, and I do not want to own anything. See this coat? I don't *own* this overcoat. The man who owned it bought it years and years before I was born, and when he died, his relatives cleaned out his attic somewhere over in the Garden District probably to let the St. Vincent de Paul people cart if off, along with everything else. And I found it under the trestle. Some man — or woman — left it in a hurry maybe. Or got tired of it. Or found or stole one that fit better. You get it? I'm wearing it, that's true, but I refuse to own it. Same with these high-tops and this motorcycle helmet. As far as I am concerned, if anybody owns it, the original owners still own it. I don't want to own anything." He handed the bone to the whimpering dog.

"I owned a dog once. Owned a long list of things, and now I'm glad *she* owns them — her and the kids. I owned a house, a car, even saw a sailboat in my future. Owned people, too. A son, a daughter, a wife. They were mine. Not anymore. My students, my team. Now another coach owns them. And the position itself, I worked hard until I owned that. This bench, these lights — the City owns them. I wouldn't rest any easier, while I gnaw on a bone, if I owned this bench, those lights. I don't even own that bone I gave you, like an idiot. And I don't talk to dogs. Git!"

He got up to start out walking to the trestle to crawl inside the big box somebody's Giant Screen TV came packed in while there was still enough twilight to see people by. He saw too clearly that the dog was following him, the bone in its mouth.

He turned on it, cursed it, waved his arms, flapped the wings of the overcoat.

If rich people once owned it, maybe it was trained. "Sit! Sit! Sit!" Still a pup, no discipline.

He decided to teach it to sit, to *stay* on command. Then he would go off and leave it when it was unsuspecting someday.

He was on Spanish Town Road, about to go down into the Bottoms, when a car pulled up alongside and he knew it was a cop car even before he glanced over.

Even before the window got all the way down, the cop was motioning him over with his finger. He doesn't know how easy it would be for me to break his finger, turn it to point the other way.

"Is that your dog?"

"I don't own a dog."

"Then what are you doing with it?"

"You mean what's it doing with me, don't you?"

He saw the cop size him up. The height that helped make him the high school basketball star that got him the scholarship to LSU and then the coaching position at Live Oak High now served to get him out of dangerous situations every day.

"You didn't steal it by any chance?"

"I don't steal. You want to own a dog? Take it."

"No, you keep it."

The window went up and the cruiser took off, red light flashing, a gesture that made him swallow the faint taste of metal.

⁂

Throwing trash toward the dog just to scare it off, only made himself tired. The dog's tail brushing across his face woke him. It was turning around and around to line up its bones just right, then it collapsed, tight up against him. "Git!" On all fours, he shouldered and pushed the dog out of his box. "Git!"

It howled all night like any dog forced out of the house into the night. The dog followed him, more closely every day, as he walked over the Capitol grounds among the people, mostly parents with kids, who thronged to view the most spectacular display of Christmas lights ever seen on earth, he supposed. He had read in a thrown-away *Morning Advocate* that they burned all night long.

As the crowd thinned out to the point where the state trooper cars started leaving, the aura of the lights moved him to crawl up under a live oak whose light-studded limbs swept the ground. He relished the irony that thousands over the past few weeks had come to view the lights, even a week after Christmas was over, as something grand and special, a once-in-a-lifetime spectacle, while he could sleep among these animals and toy creatures traced out in colored lights higher than a house with as much a sense of solitary enjoyment as if he owned them. A flamboyant New Orleans businessman had lent them to the state. But was *he* sleeping in the midst of them, *under* them tonight? Well, while he had always known in the back of his mind that everything was relative, never before had he slept in that knowledge.

But the cold open air and his uneasiness over breaking his habit of sleeping in the TV crate under the trestle made his sleep fitful for a while. When he woke and felt the dog snuggled up to him, he realized that the dog and the lights had been warmth enough to get him through the night.

❋

"Sit!" The dog sat. "Stay!" The dog stayed.

He turned the corner and waited and was glad when the dog did not follow. He'd succeeded in training it to "stay" so he could elude it.

The white-haired, red-faced man in the business suit was coming toward him. Irritated almost to the point of anger, he did not cross the street to avoid him. He stared into his eyes. The old man emitted his one-note whistle but the eyes did not recognize his existence. Stifling the impulse to give him the commands "Sit! Stay!" he walked on past red-face and, feeling the flush of anger on his skin, kept on going, around the next corner and the next and the fourth, and, on an impulse he failed to control, called "Come!"

Seeing the dog running toward him, he was sorry to realize that the sight made him feel glad. "Heel!" And he felt nauseous — knowing he couldn't teach the dog to unlearn commands that made him seem to own it.

But that night, sitting, the dog's chin resting on his leg, on a bench on Riverside Mall uptown, totally deserted, while watching a television in a store window, the sound off, report violence in the Middle East, he realized that what he had read years ago about animals having a calming effect on solitary people was true. In the past few days, fewer and fewer things threatened to stir anger in him. "But I don't own you," he said to the dog, "believe me. I don't own *anything*. . . ."

After his anger launched that metal chair at the referee and he was convicted of assault and battery and the school system fired him and he lost, one by one, most of the things he owned, his wife expressed her desire to own all by herself what was left, including their kids, while also legally declaring that she no longer desired to own him.

When he left the halfway house, owning nothing, not even the clothes on his back, and hit the public streets, his predicament made him see the connection between anger and ownership. Being made to feel that you *must* own things in this world, fight to get them, strain to maintain them in working order, and fight to keep them, made him angry all the time. The ownership of things gets confused with the ownership of people and you feel somehow a kind of valuelessness. To ward off that sense of worthlessness and to avoid anger, he told himself, don't own *anything*. Having seen that clearly, that first day out walking the public streets, he had felt anger less and less often and had been moved to violence not once.

※

It was the huge yellow house on Park Boulevard's turn to lend him the morning paper. In appreciation, he wiped the windshield of the Mazda parked at the curb, but then he saw the yellow dog pissing on the rear tire.

On the front of the Metro section was a photograph of a man and his dog. The man was tall, his back to the camera, following a dog that had stopped and turned to look at him, a Golden Retriever, and up ahead a wooden railroad trestle crossed where the street dipped. Anger rising in him blurred his vision as he read the caption. "A homeless man walks along Spanish Town Road at dusk, his faithful companion making his life just a little easier."

Shot without his knowledge, the photograph made him want to roll the paper the way he did when he was a paperboy and throw it through the big beveled glass window. He picked up a loose brick and kept hefting it all the way across Government Street and into the black district.

He stayed angry for two days, hoping nothing, like the sight of the red-faced man coming too close, would trigger him.

※

When he opened his eyes, he couldn't see straight and his head throbbed with a pain like the time the landing gear of a chopper grazed him in Vietnam. The inside walls of the cardboard TV crate were splattered in full sunlight with blood. He tried to raise his head but couldn't. He tried to call the dog, but only whimpered. When he finally crawled out of the box onto the ground where the ashes of last night's fire were cold, he saw just barely well enough to know the dog was nowhere around. When he could finally call out, the dog did not come.

He staggered around in the noon sun but collapsed in the road and lay there within sight of the trestle. When a train passed over, the noise hurt.

※

"Have you seen The Golden Retriever around here anywhere?" he asked the red-faced man.

"I have rights," the old man said, and let out that high-pitched whistle of his and stuck up his nose. "I have rights. I don't have to answer your questions. I have *my* rights, too."

As red-face passed on by him, he grabbed his coat sleeve and spun him around three times until the old man's shoulder struck a telephone pole.

"If you took it, I'll beat your brains out!"

"You people think you own the world," Red-face said, apparently not even stunned by the impact with the telephone pole, "just because I rake your leaves for you!"

"You aren't senile, you know what I'm talking about, you've seen The Golden Retriever walking with me, and you better tell me if you've seen it! Have *you* got it? Did you sell it to one of your rich customers?"

"If you don't turn me loose," said Red-face, raising one finger to show he meant business, "I will never, never speak to you again."

He turned loose the old man and let him walk on toward the bakery.

Again? This is the first time, you goddamn . . . You almost make me laugh!" he yelled after the old man.

Along his daily track, he looked for The Golden Retriever and asked, have you seen her? of every person he passed on the street or saw on the porches or in the yards or waiting at traffic lights, whether they rolled down their windows or not. He repeated the question in what seemed in his head-hurting delirium to be one unbroken stream. The whole day was the question, only the question, from street to street, until he was wandering late at night in the Garden District along streets that were off his beaten track, seeing no people now, calling, "Ky-le! Ky-le! Kyle! . . ."

A few lights went on in the fine houses on Terrace and on Drehr and, as is on signal, a cruiser was suddenly at his side.

"You! Shut the hell up! What's your name?"

"Kyle."

"Kyle what?"

"Kyle Watt."

"Don't mock me, asshole. What's that you keep screaming?"

"Have you seen The Golden Retriever?"

"No. Is that your dog you're calling?"

"I don't own a dog."

"Yeah, sure. What's its name?"

"Kyle, I call it Kyle."

"I thought that was what you said *your* name was? You mocking me?"

He didn't want to tell the cop Kyle was his middle name, after his uncle, but that his mother never let him use it because she hated her own brother, so that he'd given it to The Golden Retriever. "Have you seen him?"

"No, and I don't want to see you in the Garden District after tonight. You hear me?"

Seeing that gray metal chair slice through the air across the basketball court toward the referee's head, he turned, without replying, and walked toward Broussard, bordering the Garden District, and then cut back up Park Boulevard toward Government and the black district, hoping Kyle had wandered back up that way. He couldn't hold it back long. He wailed, "Ky-le! Ky-le! Kyle . . . !" all the way to the trestle and collapsed exhausted inside the blood-stained box.

*

"I ain't looking for no goddamn golden nothing!"

"Retriever, it's The Golden Retriever," he said, as quietly as he could, looking through the ripped screen door into the front room of the only shotgun house on the street that wasn't nailed up or burnt down, at a room full of men sitting on a sagged-out couch or around the wall, several making noises behind the door.

"The Golden Retriever? Ain't they more than one in this world?"

"Only one."

"Hey, man, ain't you the one that stays in the box under the trestle?"

"I'll ask you one more time, have any of you people seen The Golden Retriever?"

"You *people?* You saying 'You *people?*' Any of you black *people* seen Whitey's *The* Golden Retriever?"

"No, but I seen *The* Golden Beaver," came a voice from behind the flung-back door.

They all took it up, yeah, we seen *The* Golden Beaver, everywhere we go, and pink elephants and purple tigers, and the screen door came flying into the living room skidding to a stop at the feet of the men on the couch.

Not all of them were even able to rise to their feet to come at the door where he stood long enough to punch in the face of the first one to reach him. To keep from breaking bones left and right, he leapt off the slanting porch and ran, putting on some of the speed that won him trophies at track meets in the other life. Once he was out of that neighborhood, across Government on Camelia Street in the Garden District, he let go and laughed till his head started hurting again.

*

Now, somehow, seeing the red-faced man mowing the new spring grass and seeing other characters, homeless and not, with all of whom he implausibly crossed paths almost every day, kept him less agitated, less ready to cut loose at the slightest provocation.

He'd stayed out of jail so far, and he *must* stay out of jail. Too much time would pass before he got out and he might never find Kyle. If he didn't find Kyle soon, he might do something that would put him in prison beyond Kyle's life-span. He'd always feared prison, and felt proud of his ability, except that night at the tournament within one point of victory, to control a temper that his mother used to assure him "will land you in the electric chair." She'd exaggerated just to make a point, but she didn't know, even when he was a kid, how little it took to trigger him and that his keen awareness, almost every day of his life, of how little it took was always a caution and a torment.

So he tried the politeness his mother and grandmother had trained him to show, using a tone that sometimes seemed to put his own family on edge. "I would be very grateful if you would tell me whether you've seen The Golden Retriever?" Calling Kyle by that name with strangers somehow made him safe and alive, just around the next corner, maybe.

When politeness produced no lead on Kyle's whereabouts, the urge to violence took on a sharper edge.

"I ain't seed no gold dog," said a little black boy on a new bicycle during school hours, "but I see a man in a gold-colored van chase a dog and throw him inside and drive off."

"I would be very grateful if you would tell me where you saw this van?"

"Over on Oleander. My daddy pointed him out to me one time and said for me to watch out for him around our dog because he steals dogs and sells them to doctors that cut 'em up and shit."

He ran all over the Garden District, looking, and calling, "Kyle!" but had to lie in the crate under the trestle all night long, alone, wracked with nightmares of bloody mayhem.

❋

The gold van parked beside the mail truck at the Seven-Eleven on Government was empty of dogs, and of the driver until he came out sucking on a multi-colored straw, a Mardi Gras feather in his bill-cap. He knew somehow this was the man, just by the way he walked, sucking on that straw like a winner.

"Where's The Golden Retriever, Dead Man?"

Stopped in his tracks, strangling on Pepsi that had gone down the wrong hole, Dead Man turned on his heel in the gritty parking lot and ran into the black neighborhood.

Taking off the plaid overcoat as he ran, he got close enough to throw it like a tent over Dead Man, who tried to fight it off as he ran into a wall of bone and flesh — two young black men who had been walking toward him. In their iron embrace, Dead Man squirmed.

Dead Man drove with one hand because the middle finger on the other was pressed back in pain just up to the threshold of consciousness.

The makeshift, wire-mesh kennel exploded with dogs moiling and barking but the golden retriever among them was not Kyle.

"Turn 'em loose, Dead Man."

"Just don't kill me."

After the dogs were all out and running, he forced Dead Man to drive him back into Baton Rouge to the river. "Up onto the levee, Dead Man."

Dead Man took commands well.

"Now, aim it."

"My truck?"

"You don't own this truck, I don't own this truck, the city don't own this truck — it's just a truck that will do better stuck in the Mississippi River than driving up to an animal experiment building full of dogs."

He left Dead Man standing on the levee, looking down the slope into the Mississippi River at flood stage higher than it had been since 1927.

※

Roaming the streets, on and off his daily track, he craved the calming stride and faint panting of The Golden Retriever, dreaded the moment that would surely come when the mere look on the face of any one of these people would incite violence again.

Venturing into a classy neighborhood that was strange to him, he started to resent The Golden Retriever for coming into and disrupting his well-regulated life. A tough life, but so was his former life, for a man of his temperament, who, he had always been willing to admit, brought all his troubles on himself.

Up ahead, he saw what he now knew he must see if he was to survive — the silver Mercedes, parked in a circular drive. *The?* That's it! "I know that is the one!"

Despite the bruise under her right eye, he saw that the woman, about his own age, who answered the bell was attractive. Her shoulders cringed like a person whose face hurt.

"Who is it, honey?" asked a male voice, somewhere at the end of the hall.

"Nobody. Just a man who wants to work for food," she called back. "That *is* it, isn't it?"

"Tell him, *no,*" the male voice called.

He started to ask to speak to the old lady, but looking at the long polished fingers holding the door open, he knew they were the ones that had forced the dog out of the car.

"Is The Golden Retriever here?"

"There's no Golden Retriever *here.*" She called back into the house. "Honey, will you talk to this man, please?"

The man was suddenly beside her in the wide doorway, as if slotted in.

"*No,* whatever it is, buddy. We're trying to enjoy a Saturday morning together."

"Did The Golden Retriever come back?" As the anger pumped through his veins, he felt confident he could control it. "Or did you," he looked straight into the man's eyes, "hire somebody to bash my brains in to get your dog back after your wife dumped him on Spanish Town Road?"

"My wife tells me he just showed up again at the front door — *if* that's any of your goddamn business, buddyboy! Brenda, get back inside," as if brushing a fly aside even before it can start landing in your hair.

"You think you own him, don't you?"

"You see what your goddamn father's goddamn dog — ?" he said to his wife. "Vanish, buddyboy, or I'm calling the police."

"To report that —"

"Off my porch!"

"To report that bruise under your wife's eye?"

The barking of The Golden Retriever came from somewhere outside, behind the house.

Even as the husband threw a punch at him, it was obvious he wasn't used to going after another man and, missing, lunging off balance out onto the porch and down the steps where he sprawled out on the walkway like the morning paper that hits and splashes open.

Picking the husband up and dancing him up the steps and through the front door and down the hall to the glassed-in breakfast porch at the back, he kept saying to him and to himself at the same time, "Don't get your blood in an uproar, don't get your blood in an uproar now, just, just, just . . . Okay?"

"Yeah, yeah, I'm okay," the husband kept saying, "I just need to . . ."

"Why don't you just sit down, just the way you were when the doorbell rang, and let Brenda tell me what happened?"

Brenda told him that soon after her father died, her father's Golden Retriever gave birth and she took one of the puppies to remember him by and that her husband screamed bloody murder when she walked into the house with it, and every day she promised to take it back, but despite a bruised face every few days, she kept putting it off, until one day she had to do it, but she knew her mother had had to have the other pups put to sleep and she couldn't bring herself to let that happen, so she thought, she said, of all the poor little black kids who would love to have a purebred Golden Retriever from a good environment. After she left her dog that morning on Spanish Town Road, she felt so guilty she couldn't sleep, and now her husband hit her for moping around the house all the time — he looked as if he couldn't wait for the chance to hit her again — but when she saw the photograph in the paper of the homeless man and his dog, she recognized the dog as her own, and she had decided she had to have her dog back, even if she had to take the beatings with it. "So, I'm ashamed to confess, I paid my lawn boy a hundred dollars to get it back for me, but looking at that wound on your head, I *am* shocked to see that he used such force."

He looked at husband and wife, at the half-eaten breakfast spread on their wrought-iron table in their sunny glassed-in porch, and said, "Nobody owns anything — or anybody," and without looking out into the yard where he imagined The Golden Retriever was penned up, he excused himself and walked out of the house through the front door.

He was halfway to his trestle habitat before he realized that he felt no urge to violence, and not until he was curled up into his crate was he aware that what he felt now was sadness.

A WALK WITH

THOMAS JEFFERSON

AT POPLAR FOREST

A last lingering look at her as she kneels among all the other young people who are digging me up, layer by layer, rusty fragment by rusty fragment, before enough visitors accumulate on the porch to make up a distracting tour group.

That car creeping up the drive seems uncertain, as if this may be the wrong house. A middle-aged gentleman at the wheel, perplexed, a young lady, his passenger, curious. He'll probably circle, then resolutely go back the way they came.

No, he's stopping, looking up the walk to the porch where the docents are telling the visitors the itinerary and the rules. Completes the turn, but passes the drive. Still indecisive, swinging around toward the barn — they must have seen the parking lot — maybe to satisfy her curiosity.

I may as well follow the docent with the least irritating voice on her tour. We are in the dining room, the man and the girl wander in, no docent escorting them.

They stay on the periphery of the group, the girl wanders off exploring, her curiosity scatter-shot, while the man is in an agony of perplexity. They do not behave like father and daughter, nor as if they are lovers, more as if they are married, but I much doubt that.

An old man refuses to stick with the little group, but circles and sweeps past my docent to catch her drift. Makes her nervous. He nods his head, not to what she's saying, but to what he's thinking and feeling, which he'll reveal in his questions and comments. Here he goes. "How long has the house been open to visitors?"

"Less than a year."

"I like it this way. I hope you're not going to restore it too perfectly and fill it with furniture and dishes and stuff from other places."

"Oh, no, we don't intend to do it that way. We want it just as he left it, although, of course, he made changes himself, and after the fire, other changes were made. The private families who have lived here over the years made extensive modifications — dropped ceilings, partitioned rooms, sealed off windows and doorways and archways, and tore down porches and changed the rooflines and even dug a swimming pool out back."

How well I know, how well I know.

"Because this way," the old man presses his point, "you get more of a feel for him instead of the tastes of people who happen to be running the place. You really should leave it as it is, bare, even rough, but restore his architectural features."

As the tour continues, the girl wanders off into the West bedroom and the drawing room on her own but strolls back to ask questions, and I'm waiting for her to discover the window.

"Oh, look!" she cries out, delighted, loud enough to catch the attention of my favorite archeology student on her shiny dark knees just outside, who looks up, into the eyes of the young lady who is, most probably, a college student herself, maybe from the University of Virginia, too.

And the man comes striding over and looks over her shoulder out the window. They share a long moment of felicity.

The Sunday sunlight washes over the diggings where the children — they seem more like children to me — are bent over or kneeling or squatting, very carefully lifting layers, decades, of dirt, hoping to being to light a chicken bone or fork or spoon or button my servants discarded. They toil within a roped-off oblong that encloses the area where I had outbuildings for cooking and ham curing and other work. I wait for the day when she will jump up, holding up high above her head for all the other young diggers to see, some object I lost and don't even remember, some object that will start a flood of memories I have not already gone over time and again.

She reminds me of my favorite granddaughter who stayed here with me when I fled the constant stream of visitors to Monticello for stolen weeks now and then in those last years. My granddaughter seemed to take the fragments of my past and of my present and try to make a picture of them for the future, knowing I wasn't teasing when I told her I wouldn't live forever. My comparison between her and this girl here would have offended her.

I am watching, as maybe my archeologist herself is, the faces and eyes of the man and the girl whose eyes see many things out that window and whose minds are working like lightning in two completely different ways.

The man walks away, distracted, agitated again by the stir going on in his mind, breaking up the picture at the window, but the girl lingers to savor the moment in solitude, moved by the sight of the organized digging outside but now also glancing after the man. The way he walks and talks and observes things makes me feel he is very self-possessed, probably a business man, not an historian, and unlike all the others who come here and to Monticello.

The man and the girl seldom speak to each other — they seem ill at ease with each other, though glad to be together — but I catch a reference to their trip only this morning to Monticello. Not that they have come mechanically from there to my second home. They seem themselves not to have known where they are until now, listening to my docent speak my name, and I suspect they did not even know to buy tickets outside, over by the parking lot. They are here by accident, a happy one to the girl, but one whose consequence for the man has apparently not yet revealed itself.

"This is not the house," I imagine him saying when they were in the car, circling the drive, and she saying, "Well, it doesn't look private, there's a public look to all those people on the porch, maybe it's an estate sale. Let's go see what's going on."

And he complied, seeming as I watch them now to want to please her at every turn, and she seems to take each acquiescence as a gift. They are having a special occasion being together at all.

In the South Portico, the man says, "Let's go outside. I want to wander the grounds a while."

"Can't we see all the rooms first?"

The docent with the least irritating voice surrenders the tour group to the docent with the most irritating voice. "Oh, you must see Mr. Jefferson's basement," she says, her voice suggesting I kept slaves down there for my Sultanic pleasures. She leads them outside and around the house and into the basement and shows them my wine cellar.

And there she will say to them, in an obscenely intimating voice, "Oh, and you must take a peek at Mr. Jefferson's *necessary* at the end of the walkway. He planted trees and shrubs, you know, to screen the ladies as they slipped off to the necessary."

I overcome my reluctance to go down there when she's simpering about, and I can tell the man feels about the way I do about Miss Naughtymouth, and the girl merely tolerates her. On their swing around the house, the group pauses to peer over the rope at the students excavating the outbuildings.

I am very annoyed, my archeologist is very annoyed, when someone says to her at least once a week, as the old man does, "But what did you dig up *today?*"

The group moves on into the basement, but the middle-aged man who is with the girl is itching to slip away and does. He stands just outside, within sight of the girl as if not wanting to worry her by walking out of sight, and gazes off toward the rose garden, shaking his head now and again in that state of agitated perplexity I saw even in his hands on the wheel of his car when they first hove into sight on the drive.

Dangling between the two groups, I wonder what has happened to the picture of the man and the girl at the East Bedroom window in my archeologist's head. Digging up fragments, she must, the livelong day, have in her head and heart a swarm of pictures and thoughts and feelings and now, layered over all that accumulation, this window-framed picture, bright as a new dollar piece.

The girl leaves the group to ask the man why he doesn't come see the wine cellar, but he somehow has persuaded her and they start off, side by side.

"He can't wait to see Mr. Jefferson's necessary!" Miss Naughtymouth tells her obedient charges, and from inside the wine cellar they all turn to look across the floor of the souvenir shop at the man and the girl walking toward the rose garden.

On her strictly measured-off little excavation plot, no larger than an ostentatious napkin, my archeologist has enringed herself with fragments of the day's dig, but her mind seems to wander. Pausing to give her sweaty forehead a swipe with her dark arm, she gazes, as if not for the first time, toward the rose garden where the man and the girl are strolling.

Watching as she does, I see only their heads among the roses and then they are gone behind the brick wall at the back of the garden and we can't see them anymore. She bends her head over her work again but seems present only in the flesh because she imagines the man, in that itchy perplexity, walking erratically about under the great oaks in the cleared space behind the garden wall, the girl not visible to him at the moment. He notices, without being fully conscious of it, a ring of brown grass, marking an oblong plot of new Spring grass. Then he is keenly conscious of it and steps inside the ring and slowly turns, following it, feeling a tingle in the soles of his feet, seeing the little, low shed, off to the side near the brick wall, wonders what it is, or was, and thinks, *a pump*, and she, still on her knees, feels something rise from a great depth, and as two young lovers, naked, embracing, break the surface of the swimming pool, moonlight splashing over the crowns of their head, she utters a cry of exhilaration that verges on pain, lifting, all around her, faces, startled eyes and open mouths.

The girl comes upon the man standing in the middle of the filled-in swimming pool, shaken, breathing fitfully. Concerned, she goes to him, but does not touch him, has not touched him since they embraced yesterday at the reception for parent's day at Sweetbriar College when he told her, "I am your long-lost father," as if out of a luminous sense of the popular assumption that everyone wants to know who his or her real father is, and with a salesman's confidence-inducing smile and spontaneous hug. But a salesman whose office, she soon learned, is at the top of a Manhattan skyscraper.

On the pool site now, she listens to a man full of an emotion he is compelled to talk out, with such fervor he obliterates for her all the sense of him as her sudden father that the past twenty-four hours has made possible.

"This is the very place," he says, throwing up his open hands as if to prove he can work miracles, "where your mother and I conceived you.

"I didn't want to tell you *why* we were driving around the countryside lost because I couldn't remember exactly where this place was, and it was night when your mother brought me out here in her yellow convertible. I don't remember anything of the rest of this place — just that tiny brick building and here where the swimming pool used to be. We didn't even know the house was vacant until later, she a few days, I two years later when I saw her again quite by chance on Lexington Avenue.

"For years, all I remembered was the swimming pool in the dark and a miniature church or temple of brick, with a dome. I wasn't even aware of the mound — too dark, I suppose.

"We had just met. At a party at my fraternity house and she had come over to UV with some other girls from Sweetbriar. Some memory of swimming in the moonlight when she was a child visiting a wonderful old house in the country was working on her, more than my own boyish charms, I can see that now, and she dragged me off into the night in search of that place, and this is what she found.

"It was your mother who wanted to make it a special occasion, a kind of ceremony, by going into the pool in our birthday suits. We dove in on opposite ends of the pool and our fingers found each other underwater and we pushed off from the bottom hugging each other and shot up into the moonlight.

"From naked innocence, it was only a few steps into hidden sin. We found a little brick church or temple with a dome over there, I think, behind that mound. And there we conceived you."

The father is so pleased to be rid of his perplexity and so overwhelmed by memory that he can hardly see the daughter in the evening light as he wanders vaguely away from her toward the mound, hoping to find the temple on the other side.

My archeologist's hands, dark as that dirt, reveals a rusty hinge and as she lays her discovery aside, she catches a glimpse of the daughter walking fast, as if fleeing, through the open field back toward the house alone. She sits back on her haunches and stares until the girl has gone around the corner of the house out of view, then feels in her bones that she will never see her in the flesh again.

Not until the father is inside, under the dome, late afternoon light coming through the stained glass window above, does he feel certain that this is the edifice where they lost their virginity together. But only for a moment, because he discovers, his scalp hot, itching, that what he is standing inside of is the necessary the simpering docent had urged his to take a peek at. As if he has intruded, he quickly backs out. Not wanting to cover the shock with a joke, he turns to his daughter, wondering what he will say to her. She has not followed him and stopped to stand behind him as he has assumed she would.

Looking for her, the father retraces his steps, returns to the pool site where in the fading evening light, the demarcation of the pool's shape is now less vivid. Even a sense of his daughter's presence there moments ago has vanished.

I feel no urge to speculate whether he runs after her in panic to the parking lot, where she drives off in his rented car, leaving him stranded out in the middle of nowhere with a wonderful view of my beloved Peaks of Otter. Maybe my archeologist does wonder, for the daughter walked right past her before she turned the corner of the house.

Watching people turn the corner of a house is sometimes unsettling; maybe that's why I built them hexagonal.

When he walks or runs, in the opposite direction from which he came to the pool site, the father will see a second mound ahead and feel queasy as he comes around it, where a second necessary "temple" will confront him, and as he realizes he will never know in which temple he and the mother conceived their daughter, he will feel a shock not unlike the shock his daughter felt yesterday when the words rushed out of his mouth.

A DEMON

IN MY VIEW

※

In the summer of 1946, in Cherokee, Tennessee, in the Bijou Movie Palace, thirteen-year-old Lucius Hutchfield, a sawed-off, blue-eyed, lightnin'-haired little fucker, stands on the spot in his usher's uniform, gazing, as if in a trance, into the golden outer lobby, and in the Pleasure-Dome of his imagination he watches Billy the Kid walk toward the Tennessee Kid in a duel in Helena, Montana — a story he began writing that day in Bonny Kate Junior High School, certain that by spring he will be a rich and famous writer, while on the screen at his back his hero, Alan Ladd, says to Veronica Lake, "Every guy dreams of meeting a girl like you. The trick is to find you."

※

I usually write in the mornings, but the weekend before I was to set out for Hollywood, I couldn't conjure. Idling past the television set, I punched the *on* button the way you pluck a leaf as you stroll under a tree limb, switched away from Saturday football to Joseph Cotton talking rather condescendingly to Jennifer Jones who was acting uninhibited, unpredictable, and I thought, Ah, good ol' *Portrait of Jennie* (which I adapted into a radio script when I was thirteen), but it began to look wrong for *Jennie* just before Cotton called her "Singleton," and after a Pepsi commercial, the announcer said, "And now we return to *Love Letters*," one I didn't remember. With a faint sneer, I rather reluctantly allowed *Love Letters* to draw me in. I laughed indulgently at its sentimentality, but then it got interesting, despite the passé amnesia gimmick.

Its aura overwhelms me *now*, I forget the details, feel a compulsion to know. I'm going to look *Love Letters* up, again, among the *Screen Romances* I have here backstage.

Love Letters, 1945. Must have seen it at the Hiawassee Theater. Script by Ayn Rand, for God's sake! Alan (Joseph Cotton) used to write love letters to Victoria (Jennifer Jones) for Roger during the war, and Roger won her — the old Cyrano routine. Then one night Roger, drunk and mean because Victoria loves him only as the man reflected in the letters, blurts out that he didn't write the damn things, and beats her, and Beatrice Richards (Gladys Cooper), her guardian — Victoria was an orphan — kills Roger. Thinking she did it herself, Victoria loses her memory, spends a year in prison, and when she gets out, she coincidentally meets Alan. Calling herself Singleton, not knowing who she was before, she falls in love with Alan, but knows he is haunted by the memory of someone named Victoria. Alan marries her. But she traces herself back to Beatrice Richards, who tells her the whole story as Alan overhears.

Among the five hundred magazines I used to own when I ushered here at the Bijou, I had a copy of that very issue of *Screen Romances*. For most of the movies, the pictures were powerful enough to make me feel I knew all about them before they appeared. But *Love Letters* was one of the few stories I read, and the only traces of all those movie magazines to survive my army years away from home were the two covers of *Motion Pictures* — *Gone With the Wind* and *For Whom the Bell Tolls* — and this climactic passage of *Love Letters*, cut out of the magazine and tucked inside a paperback copy of *God's Little Acre*, the first book I ever read cover to cover.

> Slowly, looking straight at her, Alan began to speak words which he knew Victoria would remember now. "I think of you my dearest as a distant promise of beauty untouched by the world. If I never see you again, my last thought will be that I fought for you — and lost. But I fought."
>
> "Alan!" she gasped.
>
> "Do you think you will forgive me?"
>
> For the first time in this room, and slowly at first, her smile broke through. "It was terrible waiting for you. But finding you was such a great miracle that anything I suffered seems only a small payment in return."
>
> And, still with perfect trust, she held out her arms to him.

On the television that August afternoon in Vermont, forty-three years after I first read that passage and copied the lines they quoted to each other from the love letters into the end of one of my own to Raine, the theme music swelled, the camera pulled back in rhythm to it, giving the feeling of a flower bursting from bud to blossom, and I, standing in the doorway between my study and the living room, felt that era go through me in an intuitive rush, like a peristaltic rush, and I started to cry, hysterically, and ran from room to room, raving.

At fifty-five I still dream of opening night in a college play at the Bijou, and no lines learned, a desperate lunge into ad-libbing; dream still of going back to work at the Bijou as an usher after years of being away. That night, though, I dreamed nothing.

I wasn't eager to leave my farmhouse in Vermont and spend four months in Hollywood writing a script from my novel, *The Hero and the Witness*. I was in a state of nervous dread, but thrilled to be fulfilling one of the great ambitions of my childhood. Still, I felt guilty for abandoning work on my second novel.

Monday, the day before my plane was to leave for Hollywood, I got a letter from Momma. Responding reflexively to the assumption that little human interest stories interest a writer, she enclosed a clipping from the *Cherokee Messenger*. It reported that a man was found asphyxiated in his car in the vast parking lot across the street from the Bijou. Snow had fallen the night before and the police assumed the old man had turned on his motor to keep warm. I wondered, to keep warm while doing *what* in a parking lot? You don't *sit* in a parking lot. The car, 1951 Chevrolet, bore Florida license plates. So what was the man *doing* in Cherokee?

I didn't realize then that I had already linked that clipping with the one my mother had sent two weeks before, announcing the imminent demolition of the Bijou, where the new public library was to be erected. A fiend for coincidence, I had already enjoyed the irony of that, for on that spot also Cherokee's first store had once stood, and later a jail, and then, I know now, an inn where General Sanders died in the bridal suite from a Confederate sharpshooter's aim from the tower of "Bleak House" on Kingston Pike.

The old man was on my mind all day, and I began to see the picture. Down in Florida, Miami probably, he too had read about the demolition of the Bijou.

Perhaps someone had sent *him* the clipping. Why? Had he, too, worked there at one time? Maybe he'd been the projectionist. During 1945 and '46 when I ushered there. He'd retired to Miami. Read they were going to tear down the Bijou. Realized it meant more to him than he'd ever realized, then he'd gotten into his car and driven up here. For one last look at the old Bijou. Grown dim in memory. Driving up, he'd reeled off his years as a projectionist. Maybe I was that sawed-off, lightnin'-haired little fucker on the spot, the main aisle. And when he arrived in windy, cold, damp Cherokee, he was shocked to see the complete block-wide spread of concrete where the Pioneer Theater and Max's Restaurant and the Frontier Hotel and the Courthouse Drug Store and other buildings had stood. The parking lot slopes down a steep hill, each space marked in bright white, surrounding a squat little hut. So he arrives Friday night at about six o'clock when the lot is empty and drives right up to the sidewalk in the lot, facing the Bijou, and he sits there staring at the marquee, remembering, starting up his motor every once in a while to feather off the chill, and all behind, around him the lot fills up, people going to the Bijou, to the Tivoli, and the Venice, the only uptown theaters left now, while he sits in the iron cold moonlight, watching his own movie on the windshield, a drive-in memory montage. And the sky clouds up and snow begins to come down and he starts up the motor again to clear his windshield, and the movie patrons return to their cars after the last show, and clear the lot, and snow covers up their tracks, and the old projectionist's car runs out of gas, and the windshield wipers stop flapping, and snow sticks to the windshield, covers the car. Bright and early, the parking lot attendant's footprints squeak over the solid quilt of snow.

In the airport, on impulse, I cancel my plane reservation and plot a trip to Cherokee by train — a complicated maneuver — and leave the mountains of Vermont for the mountains of Tennessee. A conscious romantic gesture. Although I had hopped freights before I was ten, I'd never ridden a train as a passenger before. At a little place near the station, I bought a mangled copy of Thomas Wolfe's *Of Time and the River* to read on my way to the city where I once stole a paperback copy of his short stories, the risk lending greater value to a book by my hero.

✺

Standing on the rear platform, I watched North Cherokee recede as I came closer to the L & N station that would be the starting point of a total rediscovery, re-creation, recapturing. The train was about to go over the Tennessee River to South Cherokee — over the trestle I'd often gazed upon with a thrill of fear and been dared several times to walk across, had often heard tales of boys who got caught in the middle and didn't make it on across, or back, or who dove daredevil into the river and stayed down three days, when the conductor, the spitting image of Elmer Fudd, stepped out, saying, "Thinking about stepping off?"

"Okay if I stand back here?"

"Sure. I always come back here at this point myself." He leaned on the railing, looking out over the June night landscape, deep green, two a.m., foliage, and read semaphore lights. "Notice we stopped?"

"Yeah."

"That's why I come back. 'Bout twenty years ago, we stopped her like that and it black as pitch and two salesmen thought it was their station and stepped off the train. Found 'em two weeks later, downstream in Chattanooga."

The train was moving onto the trestle over the river, a maneuver that enabled it to back into the station. So even though the train *backed* in, *I* entered Cherokee straight on.

When I leave Cherokee, I won't be able to go by train from the L & N. Sharing the fate of the Smoky Mountain and the Southern lines, the L & N ceased not long ago, and they are now demolishing the cathedral-like station. One of the stained glass windows that I salvaged from the wreckage hangs backstage among the movie stills. And I took some good home movies of the station buildings with an old Keystone camera I got from a hock shop (still trying to track down a Keystone projector).

⁂

I checked my bags at the L & N station and walked a mile to the Bijou. Its still slots out front were blank, the marquees stripped to essentials:

FOREIGN FLESH

ALSO CAPTIVE DAUGHTERS

HELD OVER

Seventeen years now, a floozy — showing skin flicks, first tit shows, then "beavers," now, as Leo Gorsey, the leader of the Dead End Kids, would say, "the woiks."

To be torn down for the new library (in the stacks of the old one, yellow marble, I once made love among the W's, Wolfe approving). The wealthiest Methodist church in Cherokee, I've been told, inherited the Bijou and hoped to raze that Tower of Babel, mute its image-flickering tongues forever, not knowing about the seven-year lease, forced to profit now from "porn."

A blue-haired old woman tore off a ticket for me. Inside, stripped, flat, rot-inhibitor pink paint slapped over the walls. Negro balcony sealed off. Drapes in the box seats sagging, ripped, pores loaded with dust. Seats rickety, like riding the streetcar. Stinks like the vanished Smoky Theater on Market Square. Coming out of the men's room on the balcony landing walks the old queer, the Mad Scientist, who haunted the library toilet when I was a kid.

The door to Mr. Hood's old office was open. Two dark, tough Italians with sideburns sat behind and to the side of the desk, filling the small room with cigar smoke. Rock and roll music came from the auditorium.

I asked the manager when the Bijou was going to be demolished.

"They delayed it."

"So you're going to stay here awhile?"

"Naw, we're pulling out. Our lease is up, and business ain't so hot. Movin' on to Asheville."

"When do you close?"

"End of the run of this feature. What's it to *you*, anyway?"

"Used to be an usher here — back in the mid-forties."

"Is that something special to be?"

The men with smoking cigars in their faces permitted me to look around. A mark in the carpet where the still stand once stood in the inner lobby, glowing warmly, orange and green, like a jukebox, illuminating images of Vivien Leigh, Rosalind Russell, Greer Garson, Hedy Lamarr, Veronica Lake, Laraine Day,

Joan Crawford, Ann Sheridan, Olivia de Haviland. Goddesses, untouchables, their smooth marble pussies untouched. Myself, mortal flesh.

Backstage, a trapezoid of uninflected emptiness. Yellow light over the stage door out.

No heart-breaking white legs flaring wide on the front row, spied from the orchestra pit through a rent in the red velvet curtain, my pulse normal now, feeling no fear, forty-three years later — only a bank of whiskered faces, lit by the bright exposure of white bellies, shivering asses, and whirling titties. It's all on the screen.

⁂

I didn't call Momma. I got a room in the little hotel next door to the Bijou that occupies a corner of this sprawling building. The next morning I bought some dark glasses and walked around.

I remembered a photograph of a corpse on a bulletin board in the Sailor's Hotel in Manhattan. DO YOU NO THIS MAN? An old man, face sagging, the sheet peeled down, exposing his nipples. He had died of a heart attack in the Seafarer's International hiring hall in Brooklyn one day when I didn't go in. I was eighteen, waiting to ship out. His face haunted me. I felt guilty for not being able to recognize him, locate his next of kin. Then I noticed the date: December 8, three weeks before. He was already underground in an unmarked grave, nameless. The next day, Christmas Eve, I got a ship to Tal Tal, Chile.

The projectionist's body, too, lay unclaimed on a slab. So I went to the Cherokee County Morgue, hurrying, as if to make it before they carted the projectionist away.

I didn't recognize him. He wasn't nameless, though. Alfred Ford.

I arranged for a funeral. I was the only person at the Greenway Cemetery, where my gran'paw, who shot himself, and my little baby brother, who died of lockjaw, are buried.

I called the producers of *On Target*, their new title for *The Hero and the Witness*, told them I was sick and wouldn't be able to come for another month or so, and they saw no problem in that.

I signed a lease, and a week later reopened the Bijou with a double feature:

A Demon in My View 199

A Song to Remember with Cornel Wilde as Chopin and Merle Oberon as George Sand and *The Blue Dahlia* with Alan Ladd and Veronica Lake.

With money from the option to Warner Brothers, I gradually restored the theater as closely as possible to the way it was in the summer of 1946. I tracked down some old uniforms and hired ushers. I had six months to go until the attack of the wrecking crew.

The old men who congested the hotel next door came — retired railroaders and salesmen and carpenters — and congratulated me for cutting out those dirty movies. I'd promised the church that owned the property to throw in a few DeMille movies now and then to polish up their tarnished image, so I booked in *The Sign of the Cross* with Claudette Colbert and Frederic March.

I moved out of the hotel next door and set up a sort of apartment in the dressing room backstage. After closing time, I'd work in the manager's office on my script of *On Target*, James M. Cain and Raymond Chandler hovering over my shoulder.

I continued to show movies of 1946 and '47 and earlier for about a month, changing programs three times a week. *Leave Her to Heaven, The Razor's Edge, The Postman Always Rings Twice, The Big Sleep, Jesse James, The Maltese Falcon, Love Letters, Duel in the Sun, Portrait of Jennie, The Sea Hawk, Rebecca, King's Row, Now,Voyager.*

But attendance was very light and sporadic, and as I stood outside, under the marquee, rocking back and forth on the edge of the curb, wearing sunglasses and a mustache, it seemed that the people passing felt there was something spooky about the place. Only lonely old men like my daddy — I saw him come in, and hid — came to these movies. I was disappointed and hurt that people my own age weren't interested in seeing the old movies. I knew, of course, that they'd seen them on television, but I'd imagined them secretly yearning for the old setting, the old standard-sized screen. (I'd dismantled the cinemascope screen and brought in one of the old square rigs.)

So, half of my Warner Brothers advance depleted, I closed down the Bijou.

My ex-wife shipped from storage in our house in Bloomington every scrap I ever wrote, in five crates, and they arrived last week — including a few artifacts and mementos — a fat portfolio of drawings, an album of photos, a ribbon, my library card dated 1947, a whole raft of stuff. It's all back there in the dressing rooms, spread out, on exhibit.

When I got out of high school and went to sea, Mammy, my grandmother, let me use the quilt chest I used to sleep in when we stayed overnight to stash my movie stills and books and writings. When she married the Chief, he brought a beautiful mahogany chest into the house and Mammy moved the pine box out to the shed that was originally a circus wagon. When I returned from the army in Alaska and got married, I dug all that stuff out of the box in the shed, and I've put it into many perishable boxes over the years. Out of one life and into another, I've pack-ratted all the writings I've saved — and I've saved everything — from one end of the United States to the other. Boston, San Francisco, Lexington, North Carolina, New York, Oregon — six teaching jobs in twenty-eight years.

My mother is a gypsy, a nomad, too, dragging her junk along from house to house, job to job, city to city, man to man, sickness to sickness, out of the past into the future. When I was a kid, my mother — who still doesn't know I'm in Cherokee — used to wake me up cleaning out her dresser drawers late at night, lights blazing while I was trying to sleep: scratch, rattle, clink. Some of it she has always stored in Mammy's coal house, and she used to go down there three or four times a year to sort out her stuff. Even though this hoarding disgusted and exasperated me, I never throw anything away myself. Not long before my own habit of collecting and transporting and resorting objects imbued with allusions to my life became almost obsessive, I was still pleading with my mother, who was living then in Missouri like a gypsy in two trailers, surrounded by four rickety shacks with leaky roofs containing her belongings, to throw it all away.

With a narcissistic, pack-rat ruminativeness I had often dipped into, read with fixed fascination the stories I wrote. After five years of not looking into them, I've been immersing myself all week. I have never read them all in one groping, but I am now — chronologically. Reading these stories is like making an archeological discovery at a familiar digging site — each story reveals a deeper layer. As I look over these souvenirs, old diaries, old letters, stories, all space and time melt into an ambience. I still wear the gold-plated, radium dial Elgin wristwatch I bought with Bijou usher money in 1948, but the time it tells with hands and numerals is not the one I go by.

❊

Two days ago I set the backstage afire accidentally. I rescued most of my stuff. I'm living in the projection booth now. I've been writing all this in longhand, but today I will begin reading it over into the tape recorders. I'm going to put all my notes on tape, and fragments of thoughts, and descriptions of objects, and I'm going to read some of the stories and story fragments and scenarios and diaries and other stuff into the recorder, too. Writing's too slow. And I feel a compulsion to *tell* it to myself.

※

For two weeks I've been trying to unclog the toilet drain. I've poured burning, smoking chemicals down it, and they just hiss back at me.

This is sort of getting back to the way it was when I was a kid, *telling* stories instead of writing them. Told hundreds for eight years before I ever wrote one. That's who I was, starting at age three. The kid who told stories to other kids. "Tell me a story." That's all it took, and I'd rip one off, tongue clacking as fast as the world champion speed typist. Then got away from telling and into writing. But this is more like way back yonder. Even if it's just telling stuff to myself, I feel strangers hovering around me, and my own words and that winding spool hypnotize me.

※

I've been integrating scraps and notes and fragments and outlines, and scenarios, with their completed stories, to see how the stories developed from ideas. Reading the scenarios in which I projected myself and my sweetheart Raine into the future — "Two People," "Mood of Hunger," "Naked Destiny," "Destroy the Flame," "The Cosgroves of Destiny," "Now and Forever" — I wonder what she and the other kids in them are doing now. A few months after we broke up in 1947, and I'd returned from visiting Thomas Wolfe's home place in Asheville, I had the feeling of tagging along after the Clayboe Ridge gang, tolerated but not wanted. Raine looked back at me as she walked quickly down an uptown street and said, "Stop looking at yourself in the windows, poet!" I skipped toward her twice and, trying to kick her in the tail, slipped and busted my ass on the sidewalk. But she was so outraged by the attempt, she sank her teeth into my knuckles. I carried the scar for two decades, but when I looked one day, sitting in Piazza San Marco in Venice, it was gone. But I see Raine lucidly this instant.

※

The movie stills. Like skin. The magazines a different skin texture. The effluvium of old movie magazines on my desk in the projection booth evokes the aroma of girls' hair, and the starched blouses of the Woodbury-soaped girls was like the new movie magazines on the racks in the drugstore where I used to kneel, waiting for the route man to dump my *Messengers*. With money from delivering papers, I collected 500 movie magazines. Knew all the stars' faces and names, remembered the titles of all the movies I'd seen, many I had read or heard about, until forty-three years later, I have to engage now in complex detective work to deduce the titles of some of these old stills. A girl on my Clayboe Ridge route who looked like Hedy Lamarr bestowed upon me her collection of stills, some sepia-toned by time, dating back to the thirties, as she made a clean breast of it to marry a soldier returning from the European theater of war. I stole some from the Bijou — *To Each His Own, The Postman Always Rings Twice, The Blue Dahlia, Body and Soul*. Put on an exhibit a few years ago in the library of the little college where I taught drama and creative writing and edited a literary magazine, and it was a fantastic success. Left most of them with the editor of *Movie Heritage*, of which I am an associate editor, and he sent them here last week at my request. Some of them I had given Joe Campbell when I was about sixteen. He wanted them because *I* valued them so much, not because he really desired them. While I was away at sea in the Merchant Marine, they were stored in Mammy's coal house in gray flat cardboard boxes, with black tape sides, which I had kept when I used to borrow records from the public library.

I've been trying to get them all back now, round them up somehow. I put an ad in the *Messenger* last week for stills and lobby cards and movie magazines of 1945–46. I retrieved none of the same stills, but from the two people who responded I got six magazines, one of which belonged to *me*. I had written a telephone message to Momma on the back of *Screen Romances*, Tyrone Power and Gene Tierney in *The Razor's Edge* on the front. In the margin of a fictionalization of *The Killers*, with Burt Lancaster and Ava Gardner, I had written: "Life is raw meat slowly cooked by the eye of God."

The more lost articles I recover, the more melancholy I become, and the more I long to touch the things I still can't find.

> Last night I dreamt I went to Manderley again.
> It seemed to me I stood by the iron gate
> leading to the drive and for a while I could not enter,
> for the way was barred to me. . . .

The voice of Joan Fontaine, the opening of *Rebecca*.

※

I used to go to sleep every night after a ritual in two parts: review my life serial fashion, and when I sensed I was drifting off I'd talk to God and go to sleep that way. Later, after I'd begun to write stream of consciousness stuff and didn't believe much in God and was living intensely in my life and my writing, the ritual was simpler in form, more complex in content: I'd let my free will rest and let images of all kinds show up on the movie screen of my mind. Descriptions of LSD trips pale beside my memory of those imagistic orgies — I reveled, wallowed, it was thrilling, sublime, sometimes a little frightening. But I was in control of, if not the content, the method.

※

I've mounted all the movie stills on the fire-blackened brick wall behind the screen, illuminated by two work lights on iron stands, with 200-watt bulbs. They're arranged chronologically. The movie magazines I got from the local ad I ran, and from Larry Edmond's bookstore in Hollywood and from Cinemabilia in New York, are lined up on narrow pine plank all along the wall under the pictures.

I'm trying to put these fragments in order, like editing strips of film. Such parallels charm me, make me laugh out loud. The pattern, irregular though it is, is pleasing, but meaningless. The coincidences that disrupt the pattern are also charming, seem more meaningful. I realize that I'm being too self-conscious on these tapes. I have considered drug-induced recall. Piss on that! The pattern, I know, will, when I get it, explode, and the fallout will produce a truer, richer chaos.

The Fabulous Forties. Hub of my life. The movies and my life — the loving, the writing — always inseparable. Neighborhood Hiawassee Theater, the hub of the early forties, of my childhood, all other theaters spoke out of it, Uptown, the Bijou, jeweled navel of the after-bomb forties, its facets mirroring all Cherokee's twenty-three theaters. Hub of my adolescence. Fuckless forties on screen. Fuckfull in the balcony and backstage of the theaters themselves and in neighborhoods surrounding. My self has been fossilized perhaps, embalmed, preserved, photographed, caught forever on a short strip of film, always there in storage in the film vault of my mind, and it will come when my will beckons, or come of its own power at times when the contexts explain nothing. Is the mind a movie projector gone mad, scrambling all the movies, features, trailers, short subjects, comedies, cartoons, newsreels, throwing on the screen across the Grand Canyon auditorium of the years any image that happens to flit through? What happens to all the stuff that gets edited out, that ends up on the projection booth floor? Can it be reshot somehow, and reintegrated, can a sequence be unscrambled? It's not the metaphor that matters, but the anguish of not being able to do it. Poetically, the image of myself as a child usher is fine: all that he was is compressed into the single charged image that most expresses his essence. But then why the sadness of recalling him only as a fragment? A blinding flash from the projection booth — Hiroshima — he is that shadow upon the wall.

And we are captive under the shattered dome of the Bijou.

WANTED

Ghost Writer

✳

"Wanted: Ghost Writer," Fenton snorted contemptuously, ripped the page in half, wadded it tightly, unwadded and rubbed it to a nap, wiped, buckled, flushed, and left the rest of the *Chronicle* where he had found it.

When he returned to the little park on the east side of the public library, the spaces under the new birch trees were vacant. Convinced days ago that he had finally won their trust, he was hurt to discover that the Family had moved on without him.

Faces exposed to the mild November sunlight, the old men perched along the marble shelf against the library wall witnessed his posture of desolation. Vibrations from the old men of resentment and disgust had pulled the Family like a magnet to the park until it had become their habitual place to groove.

Maybe the pigs had run them off. Ever since the motorcycle dude stabbed Little Luke, the pigs had hassled the Family everywhere it settled. Fenton had noticed one of the old men talking to the motorcyclist, then he had lain back on the freshly cut grass. "You raped my sister!" the dude had screamed, and when Fenton raised his head, the sun in his eyes, Little Luke was sitting under the birch, a pearl-handled knife shimmering in his throat. The old man never returned to the marble shelf along the glaring white wall. Fenton had promised the Family he would find the man and revenge Little Luke's death. Autumn had passed. Now nobody spoke of Little Luke.

Fenton looked down into the Peter Pan family economy size peanut butter jar, half-full of morning sunlight, emphasizing the finger-swipes that had cleaned it, tilted in the grass. Fenton was hurt to realize that the Family had no need of him until he got his unemployment compensation check on Monday. He kicked the jar out of its garland of Hi-Ho cracker crumbs into the street where it volleyed back and forth between the wheels of a bus, then rolled into the opposite gutter unbroken. Behind him, some of the old men laughed, spitefully.

Fenton was older than the rest of the Family, older than they knew, and they seemed to sense he had a history, while the others, even Genesis, had come right out of the straight world of suburbs and high school and maybe a few abortive years of college.

Clouds shut out the sun, and Fenton knew that any day the freak warm weather would turn. Snow. And that deserted building, its windows broken, would be too little shelter. He wanted to offer the Family salvation. Then it occurred to him that if he could buy that vw bus parked with a For Sale sign in front of the Gulf Station, they could escape the winter freezes. Every day the Family passed it, and wished they could get enough bread together to afford it. Remembering the ghost writer ad, Fenton impulsively went back inside the library to the reading room and looked it up.

A block from St. Vincent de Paul's, he used the phone in the sidewalk booth.

"Mr. Hardison?"

"One moment please."

"Jesus, he's got a butler."

"Hello."

"Mr. Hardison, my name is William Cosgrove. I'm a writer, and —"

"Oh, my ad, huh? Good, good. Come right out."

"Yes, sir. You didn't give your address."

"Are you in the city?"

"Yes, sir."

"Oh, I'm *way out*. I'm at 895 Pershing Road. I'll be sitting on the porch, wearing a red scarf. It's gonna turn cold."

Riding buses to the corporate limits of the city, Fenton had to transfer three times. Then he had to walk two miles of rural road. Mr. Hardison must be a gentleman farmer with a grand estate. Straight, conservative, maybe even a Birchite. Worried about his long hair, beard, rummage-sale clothes, and sandals, Fenton hoped the rich old codger would be expecting a writer to look bohemian.

If his bluff worked, Fenton expected to get a fat advance that would enable him to buy the vw bus and move the Family to Tampa for the winter. All he had to do was convince the old man he had written the book he had bought for a quarter at St. Vincent de Paul's second-hand store near the library. *Hollywood's Golden Age* by William Cosgrove.

895 Pershing Road had probably once been an estate but the sign at the gate said: COUNTY HOME FOR THE AGED.

Depressed, he told himself, "Use your imagination, Fenton. Old folks' homes are full of stingy old misers. Take a chance." Stranded without a dime, miles from the last bus stop, Fenton decided he had nothing to lose.

The receptionist in the large Victorian house reluctantly directed Fenton to a white cottage in the rear.

The tableau of old men sitting in a neat row behind a white railing on the gingerbread-embellished porch almost turned Fenton away. As soon as the sun passed over to the west side and the shelf began to turn cold as a curbstone, the old men at the library deserted the wall, but these men, except for their hands and knees, sat in the shadow. Fenton was discouraged. Having taken a chance, he still had to bluff.

As he approached the steps, the old men rose in their rockers and peered stiffly over the railing at Fenton. Not until he mounted the steps could he make out in the shadows a twist of red around the neck of an old geezer sitting at the end of the porch in a rocker set apart from the others.

"Mr. Hardison?"

"Ain't me," declared an obese man at the top of the steps.

"He knows it ain't," said the old man who wore the scarf. "It's my great-grandson come to see me — all the way from California."

That made sense. Fenton was a ghost writer, wasn't he? Disguise.

"Might knowed you'd spawn a swarm of hippies."

As if on cue, all the old men laughed.

"He ain't a hippie. He's a — a — "

"Nark," said Fenton. "I have to dress like a hippie. Undercover agent. Infiltrate."

"Line 'em up against a brick wall and shoot 'em down," said the fat man, his voice deep, booming. "Way we done them Mexicans in nineteen-oh-five. I was there."

"That's in our plans, sir. But first, we're just rounding them up in concentration camps."

Scanning the row of old men, Fenton did not see the one who incited the motorcyclist to stab Little Luke.

"We're the incorrigibles," said a shriveled old man down at the end opposite Mr. Hardison. "Ain't we?"

"Go back to sleep, Sperling," said the fat man, who sat in perfect alignment between the top of the steps and the front door. The handle of his cane was ivory; the others were plain, each tipped with black rubber.

Turning his back on the others, Fenton approached Mr. Hardison, a feeling at his back that all the old men, on silent signal, were rising from their rockers without creaking, lifting their canes in unison to pulverize him.

"Good to see you, Willie!" Mr. Hardison shouted, so the deafest man on the porch could hear. Then Fenton scarcely heard him whisper, "You're a crafty fox, Mr. Cosgrove. They don't suspect a thing. What makes it stick on?"

"Stick on?"

"The beard and the hippie hair?"

"Oh. Used to be an actor. Got into ghost writing for the movie stars. Here's my first book."

"How old are you underneath all that?"

"Thirty-two." The Family seemed to accept his age as twenty-four.

"Then you're too young to remember the days when we flew the mail through sleet and rain and hurricanes and night hazards."

"Didn't Lingbergh used to fly the night mail?"

"Pioneered it. But this is about *me*."

"Fine, fine, Mr. Hardison, but I think before you start, we need to work out the terms."

"Wait till you hear my story, son. All these old liars think *they* got stories to tell — even Sperling. 'I was one of the first this and first that' — all you hear up and down this porch, from sun*up* to sun*down,* but the truth comes out in the AM when they talk in their sleep, keeping everybody awake. Oh, I could tell you a lot about *them,* too."

"Yeah, man, but we need to settle —"

"Don't worry, William. We're going to get rich. And they can read it and weep, the sons-of-bitches."

"As a matter of procedure, sir, I —"

"Want to get rich, don't you? *Every*body loves airplanes. What kid hasn't grown up making models, collecting pictures of war planes, reading about the dare devils?"

"It's the astronauts these days . . ."

"I'm not talking about asshole astronauts. You're talking to a man who's flown the mail in a single engine bi-plane."

"And I'll write it up for all the world to read, sir, but first I have to know what you can pay."

The old man's wrinkles, his yellow eyes and whining voice, the smell of him like moldy salt pork, nauseated Fenton.

"Sit still — that railing'll hold you, skinny as *you* are — and when I'm done, you'll see it's worth waiting for."

"*Waiting* for?

"Yeah, you don't expect an old fart that lives in a bone-house like this to be rolling in dough, do you?"

"You got me all the way out here to —"

"A best-seller! What more do you want? We'll be filthy rich."

"I don't write a word without an advance —"

"Keep your voice down."

" — and if you don't think that's final, watch me split in less than two seconds."

The general repugnance Fenton felt for all these old rejects was concentrated now in Mr. Hardison.

"Okay, how about if I promise to rake it up for you when you come back with the first part written down?"

"How much?"

"Every cent I humanly can. Can't say exactly."

Again, Fenton decided he had little to lose. One more gamble.

※

Pretending to reminisce with his great-grandson, Mr. Hardison started what he called his life story, although he left his first thirty years behind without a trace. "My life began when I flew the mails with Lindbergh."

The years with Lindbergh were so vague, Fenton was afraid he would have too little to hold on to when he wrote up the first chapters. But after George Hardison survived a crash in the Rockies and became director of the air-mail service in Brazil, the story began to take shape.

Hardison was the only American in the service. The pilots were French and Italian. His best pilot, Pierre, was flying in from Peru at about sunset. Two other planes were expected, from Chile and Nicaragua. Then a fourth plane would take off early in the morning for Europe, carrying the South American mail.

There was a storm up ahead but Pierre recklessly refused his wireless operator's advice that they should land this side of the Andes. The sky was full of stars, and it was to fly on such a night that Pierre had stayed in the service despite two crashes in rain and snow.

Meanwhile, at the Rio de Janeiro airport, Hardison was worried about his three planes. But the one from Chile came in safely, and the pilot, Nino, reported he had barely made it through a terrible storm over the Andes. The experience had left Nino badly shaken, but Hardison, who believed in rigid discipline, showed little concern for his pilot's condition. Martineau, an inspector, suggested that Hardison might ease up a little; too much tension on an airstrip was dangerous.

Martineau and Nino went off to town together to have supper. When the inspector returned, Hardison pointed out to him that making friends with the pilots would undermine the discipline he had worked very hard to build up. He had to be cold and objective with men who faced the hazards of night flight. They had to be in absolute control at all times. Personal relationships would complicate and perhaps seriously distract them at critical moments. Hardison explained to Martineau that his conquest over his own injury was a result of Spartan self-discipline. So, regardless of the reason, if a plane came in late, for instance, the pilot forfeited his bonus. Hardison fined or fired his mechanics for the least act of ineptitude. Martineau was convinced, however, that such severity was bad for morale — and in the long run, perhaps, for Hardison himself.

When the bell rang for dinner, the old men rose together. The fat man paused at the floor, stalling traffic, and looked down the porch past the gently rocking empty chairs and said, "Nark, Nark! Who's there?" and went on in, cackling, setting the other old coots off like damp firecrackers. The nonentity on the tail-end of the procession stooped, too, and winked at Fenton. "We're the incorrigibles," he said, and called to the others inside, "Ain't we?"

"That's true," Mr. Hardison told Fenton. "They stick us over here because we don't integrate socially with the rest of the zombies."

Fenton wondered whether Mr. Hardison had pulled his rocker over to the side railing, breaking the spacing pattern of the others, to seclude himself with his ghost writer or whether he always sat apart from the other men.

Fenton agreed to deliver a draft of the beginning chapters in four days, and Mr. Hardison promised he would then fork over a sizable advance payment. Fenton inscribed *Hollywood's Golden Era* and left it with the old man.

Although he managed to hitch a ride back into the city, Fenton still had to walk fourteen blocks to Leafy Bower Manor Estates, the Family's name for the three widely spaced, condemned business buildings still standing in the ten blocks of rubble cleared for urban renewal and an expressway access ramp.

It was dark, it was late when Fenton reached the eighth floor of the Captain Kangaroo building, formerly the Sparks Office Tower. The odor of grass hung over the bare mattresses where the Family sprawled, asleep, Genesis still in his old lady. Picking a broken path awkwardly among them to reach his mattress against the wall, Fenton looked down at their angelic faces, content in the knowledge that one morning soon, he would drive up to the library park in the vw bus and show them that he deserved their acceptance and affection.

For several days, Fenton did not lie among the Family on the brown grass under the new birches, taunting by their very presence the old men along the wall. He sequestered himself in the reference room of the library and wrote Mr. Hardison's life story in Tarzan tablets, then he fed quarters to the public typewriters and made use of the training he had gotten in the business college on the G. I. bill six years ago.

Since Mr. Hardison's own flying years with Lindbergh were so vague, sheer frustration moved Fenton to invent and embroider. To do that, he had to read Lindbergh's own biographies *We* and *The Spirit of St. Louis,* neither of which mentioned George Hardison, who didn't strike Fenton as a memorable person anyway. In the only episode he had told in any detail, Hardison was nothing but a harsh representative of the Establishment. Lindbergh's story so exhilarated Fenton that he forgot to go to the giant window to check out the Family on the grass outside.

⁂

"This what you've done here couldn't be better, my boy," said Hardison. Pretending his great-grandson the Nark had brought him letters from all the family back home, he had read Fenton's first three chapters sitting on the porch.

"I'd 'bout come to think you didn't have no family, Hardass," said Mr. Tate, turning his ivory-handled cane into a mock penis and the row of old men into convulsions of giggles, chortles, and lung-wracking guffaws. "That FBI hippie's the first visit you had since you came here twenty years ago."

"You *hired* those folks that visit you!" said Mr. Hardison, causing all the men to suck in their breath, but not to explode in laughter.

"The day will come," said Mr. Tate, his deep voice booming left and right across the porch, "the day will come."

"To tell the truth," Mr. Hardison told Fenton, "I ain't no good at such talk. I've lived alone too many years."

"What *about* your family, Mr. Hardison?" asked Fenton, really wanting to know.

"The world is waiting to hear the story of my flying days, not boring details about my home life."

Fenton sat at Mr. Hardison's feet on the porch floor, bracing his back against the white wall, while the old man leaned down toward him, away from the others, and his foul breath came out with his whispered story, turning Fenton's stomach.

⁂

Still worried about Pierre's flight from Peru, Hardison called Jacques, the pilot who was to take the mail to Europe. When Jacques reported to the airfield, Hardison chewed him out for having turned back on a flight several weeks ago. Even though he admired and respected Jacques as one of the finest pilots he had ever known, he felt he must be severe in order to keep Jacques at the top of his ability.

Hardison imagined what had happened to Pierre. He must have hit the storm, then searched for a place to land. But the storms had closed all the airfields within his range. Having failed to contact Pierre by radio, Hardison frantically alerted police and airports everywhere in the region.

As soon as Hardison had finished his last call, Pierre's wife, Marianne, called up. They had not been married very long, and when Pierre didn't show up for dinner at the usual time, she had started to worry. Hardison wished he could comfort her with lies, but in the long run the cold truth had always proved the best approach in such cases.

Meanwhile, Pierre must have discovered that the storm had blown him out over the Atlantic; perhaps he had thrown out landing flares and the last one had revealed the endless water. Then he must have turned west again. Perhaps he saw a clearing above him now and then, but beneath him only the solid storm foundation. Then came the terrifying moment when he discovered he had only minutes of gas left — and no airfield clear for a landing.

Beginning to realize that the old man was making an effort to imagine Pierre's predicament in specific detail, Fenton felt less loathing for Hardison.

Then Pierre's young wife appeared at the airfield, almost hysterical. Although he felt compassion for her, Hardison forced an air of icy reserve. Trying to explain to her what it was like to be a fine pilot, he described the dangers that men must face to become monarchs of the air. Pierre, he told her, was like a pathfinder in the old American West. She calmed down, seeming now to understand "what it meant to be a man."

Pierre came through faintly on the wireless, announcing that he was going to descend through the rain clouds. Was he out of gas? Or was he simply hoping to find a place to try a crash landing?

⁂

The ringing of the dinner bell left Fenton wanting to know what happened next. Mr. Hardison smiled, smugly, as if he had planned it that way.

After the last old man had shuffled into the cottage, Mr. Hardison slipped Fenton an old sock, knotted at the neck. "All I could muster," he said, and stuck the sheets of the manuscript inside his shirt against his corrugated chest, speckled with wiry gray hairs, the white skin soft-looking as a baby's.

Down the road, Fenton counted the pennies, nickels, dimes, quarters, Kennedy half-dollars, and bills: fifty dollars.

The sock was too big but it had fewer holes than his own, which he tossed into the gutter.

On the bus back into the city, Fenton wondered whether the old man might not have been famous after all. His story seemed familiar. Maybe he had read about Mr. Hardison. The orphanage had had a ratty little library of donated books that were "good for you": testimonials by men who had risen out of poverty by will power, clean living, and work. None of these things got Fenton out of the orphanage. A lie to the Marine recruiting officer had neatly accomplished that.

Fenton was an MP in Korea before they discovered he was only 17 and kicked him out. He enlisted in the Navy when he was old enough. He enjoyed the routine life of the military. But in college — after Fenton had spent a boring year in a business school — his freshman English teacher "told it like it was" and he dropped out and began to wander. He reached North Beach just as the San Francisco Beat Renaissance was degenerating. Moving on to Greenwich Village just as the new hippie subculture was emerging, he attached himself to one "family" after another in New York, Boston, Vancouver, Seattle, Louisville, New Orleans.

When he entered the room on the eighth floor, the Family was stoned, oblivious to him. Standing at the window, sucking on a joint, he thought he was hallucinating snow. After the others were asleep, he stashed the money in a hole in his mattress.

When he emerged from the Captain Kangaroo building the next morning on his way to the library, snow covered the ruins around Leafy Bower Manor Estates.

The second episode of Mr. Hardison's life story took only two days to write.

※

"You sure you ain't infiltrating us?" asked Mr. Tate, seeing Fenton approach the gingerbread-framed porch.

"You're all wanted for evasion," said Fenton, good-naturedly.

"Evasion of what?"

"You name it," said Fenton, with a sarcastic glint, "and you've probably evaded it."

"Smartass and Hardass, two of a kind."

The row rocked and clattered, rubber-tipped canes thumping.

To avoid suspicion, Mr. Hardison didn't read the second installment there on the porch. He slipped the manuscript inside his black overcoat, next to his red and white flannel shirt. The sun was out, the snow was melting, the air was mild enough.

"What happens next?" asked Fenton, settled now into his corner against the wall where the railing jointed up to the house.

※

When the plane from Nicaragua came in, having eluded the storm, Hardison felt better. The pilot seemed so proud, as if he had proven himself to Hardison, that Martineau, who was sitting in the office, said he thought he understood now that Hardison was not a tyrant but a man who feels so deeply for his pilots and their common cause, that he must exert more control over himself and over them than they can be expected to maintain alone. Rather than show his gratitude for Martineau's understanding, Hardison observed that while his pilots must conquer storms alone, *he* must help them conquer the weaknesses in themselves that might otherwise succumb to such hazards. Martineau declared that he had never before met a man like Hardison.

Finally, the fact had to be faced that Pierre had perished. The remains of Pierre, his wireless operator, and the plane would turn up somewhere in the days and weeks to come. But now it was the business of the survivors to survive. Jacques' plane was warming up for the trans-Atlantic flight. Once Pierre's wife had left the airfield in tears, accompanied by the kindly Martineau, Hardison and Jacques spoke of their lost comrade, Pierre, but without emotion. Sentimentality was off limits to men who had "a journey to make through the unknown."

The only thing that worried Hardison now was whether Pierre's crash would cause the government to suspend night flights.

Jacques headed out over the Atlantic on schedule, and Hardison went back to work, confident that he would turn this momentary defeat into some transcendent victory.

※

On the bus, wearing another of Hardison's socks, Fenton had to admit to himself that, corny as it sounded, the old man's story had moved him.

And as he wrote it out in the Tarzan tablet in the reference room of the baroque library building, Fenton wept a little.

But in the typing room, he prepared the manuscript with a sense of purpose. His mattress concealed two payments; with the third, he would have a total of about two hundred dollars. That, plus a few more such advances and a little bargaining, ought to put him behind the wheel of the v w bus and his Family on the expressway to Tampa.

He arrived at the County Home for the Aged shivering in his Eisenhower jacket. Snow lay over the surrounding countryside and on the roofs of the big house and the cottage behind. The rocking chairs, their seats full of snow, set immobile on the porch, the white wall behind them.

But at the window, Mr. Hardison was watching for him. And when the old man came out, limping painfully, making serious use of his cane (ah, yes, thought Fenton, the crash in the Lindbergh years), he smiled, apparently glad to see Fenton. Has he looked forward to seeing *me*, Fenton wondered, or is he just eager to imagine himself again as the hero of an international bestseller?

Mr. Hardison brushed the snow out of his rocker, sat down, and glanced over his shoulder through the window. "It's okay. Mr. Potter was lying down when I came out," he said, motioning to Fenton to sit in the rocker beside him. "Got to be careful. These old men are lunatics about their goddamn rockers. Makes a man that's soared above the clouds sick to see a rocking chair turned into a cradle. When spring comes, there'll be new men in some of 'em. But I ain't going till I get my due."

"Isn't it bad for you to be out in this cold?"

"Won't be out too long."

"But you got the whole rest of your life to tell."

"Give me the rest of it."

Fenton handed Mr. Hardison the ten pages that completed the episode of the missing pilot. The old man tucked it inside his overcoat.

"Got so I enjoyed your visits, son. That Tate-worm was right, goddamn his soul to hell. You're the only visit I ever had."

"Well, don't talk that way, sir," said Fenton. "We got plenty left."

"No, this is the last of it."

"But that was only one night in your whole life. Except for that collection of bits and pieces during the Lindbergh times."

"Well, that's all I'm telling."

"But what about the rest of your life? Your other adventures?"

"The best part's been told."

"But that — There's got to be — Well, what about your wife and kids, and your real grandchildren?"

"Can't remember them too clear."

"But that's terrible, sir," said Fenton, getting up. He looked down at Mr. Hardison, whose arms were crossed possessively over his chest. "How can you forget the people you spent most of your life with? Your family, your friends?"

"Don't you reproach me, young man. Just remember, you're nothing but an employee!"

"You think that little story about the missing pilot is enough to make a book?"

"The world will be amazed. Besides, it has a noble message."

"Maybe so, but these days a book's got to have more to it. Something else has got to happen."

"Sex? You want sex? Obscene language? And blood and guts? Well, I ain't giving the world none of that to leave behind. Tate-worm would just turn all that into a joke."

"What's *he* got to do with it? Listen, I want to know myself. I mean, I'd like to know what your wife was like and your kids. Your life, man! Your life! Jesus!"

"What are *you* so riled up about, boy? I paid you to do a job and you done it well, and now I gotta be going in to supper. When the royalties come flooding in, we'll divvy up."

"Pay me for this, first."

"Wait for the royalties."

"I need it now."

"I'll give you a bigger cut, if you'll wait."

"No."

"I was afraid you'd grab for the last greasy dime." Mr. Hardison pulled a sock out of his overcoat pocket. The bulge was smaller, but Fenton was too disturbed to argue about it.

"If that's your life, man," said Fenton, his shoulders hunched against the wind that swept snow along the porch and swirled it in the seats of the rockers, "it won't sell."

"It's a great story. You kids today wouldn't recognize a great story if it snuck up and bit you in the ass, 'cause you're flabby and your brains are scrambled with all that rock and roll."

Wind turned tears in Fenton's eyes cold. "Your life stinks, man, and you can just shove it!"

"Why you trying to torment me, son?" Mr. Hardison leaned forward and looked closely at Fenton, breathing clouds of moisture. "You really want to make me bleed, don't you? Don't waste your time, son. I just don't feel it. Sure, I had a wife, I had kids, and they had kids, and all that's just like a parking lot where a factory once stood."

Turning slowly around, the old man became a black form, bent over inside a flap of wool. At the door, without turning, he said, "After Verdun, it wasn't no good no more."

Verdun. The name came back repeatedly as Fenton rode the bus back into the city, watching snow cover the streets and sidewalks and the parking lots in the shopping centers. Verdun. A woman? Maybe the wife of that lost pilot. Verdun. It sounded French. He had heard it before, maybe a girl in some French movie.

Fenton had hoped to reach the room before the Family started getting stoned, but when he walked in, most of them were *up*. He lay down on his mattress and smoked a joint. He managed to sneak Mr. Hardison's third payment into the hole in the mattress, sealing the gash with the sock. He lacked about a hundred dollars to have enough even to bargain for the v w.

Then he got a beautiful idea. A bus with no wheels might sell for a hundred dollars less.

A few cars had been abandoned in the urban renewal ruins. He found a jack. The deep snow left the dark streets and sidewalks deserted. He slogged through the snow to the Gulf station where the v w was parked. A few apartment lights were on, looking both hostile and cozy. As he removed the first wheel, he knew what he was risking. He had served two years in the penitentiary in Montana for stealing a Triumph motorcycle.

Fenton thought about the old man and his life. "Verdun. Verdun. Verdun," he chanted, to take his mind off the freezing wind and his wet, cold feet. One by one, he removed the wheels and rolled them back to Leafy Bower Manor Estates and hid them in one of the utility rooms in the Captain Kangaroo building. Rolling the fourth wheel into the once-impressive foyer of the office building, he remembered having to write a book report in freshman English. He had gone to a reference book in the library called *Masterplots* and copied out a review of a book called *Night Flight* by a Saint somebody, a Frenchman.

Had Mr. Hardison read the novel itself? Or had he, too, simply consulted *Masterplots?*

Climbing the stairs, Fenton felt the old man had betrayed him somehow. Between the third and fourth floors, he heard yelling, screaming, singing, thumping, and banging, as if the Family were dancing, celebrating. Afraid they might attract the pigs, Fenton ran up the remaining four flights.

He opened the door to a room filled with smoke, cotton batting, and bills floating in the air. Strewn out over the floor and the mattresses were pennies, dimes, nickels, half-dollars, quarters. His mattress had been torn to shreds.

"Hey, man, that's *my* money! That's *my* money!"

"Yeah, and you hid it from your brothers and sisters, man," said Genesis, pointing at Fenton through the smoke haze. "He who refuses to share must give all and be vanquished!"

"All, all, all, all, all, all, all!" the Family yelled, dancing around the room, thumping the walls as if they were gigantic drums. Then they turned to beating Fenton with their fists, making sounds with their mouths, as if his body were a drum.

When they saw Genesis rip open Fenton's Eisenhower jacket, they jumped him, chanting, "All! All! All!" Their fingers clawed at his clothes until he was naked, and then at his flesh, and as he bled, they licked, bit, sucked his body and spit on it, and rubbed it with cotton batting and money. Gathering his last strength into a rage, he rose, pushing them back. Hanging on to his arms and legs and around his neck, they staggered with him around the room. Breaking from them for a moment, he backed away into rotten canvas draped over the broken window. As he fell, screaming, looking up into a sky clear of snow, full of stars, a part of him remote from the scream and from the eyes that saw the sky vividly thought, "I dreamed this once. . . ."

※

A few months later, the world — as Mr. Hardison put it — read about a duel which took place on the front porch of the cottage for incorrigibles at the County Home for the Aged: "When J. B. Tate, 73, found his rocking chair occupied by George L. Hardison, 85, he threatened him with his cane. Tensions had been running high in the cottage for incorrigibles, stated the superintendent. Residents had reported a rash of cash thieveries. Hardison was observed by personnel at the home to have exhibited severe despondency in recent months. According to witnesses, Hardison dared Tate to hit him. When Tate raised his cane to strike Hardison, the World War I veteran swung his own cane, hitting him in the ribs. Tate lost his balance and fell backward down the steps, striking his head on the flag-stones. He was killed instantly. Tate is reported to have been the first man to survive a daredevil dive from the Golden Gate Bridge."

LYING IN WAIT

As I said before, it's just to rule you out.

Yes, but . . .

Now you said earlier that you arrived on the sixteenth of July. Correct.

Yes, correct, and again correct.

That you had no idea —

No idea she would be waiting for me.

Because?

Same answer as before. I didn't really know.

But you had some idea, some inkling.

Yes, but I didn't use that word exactly.

And that she said — Please repeat what you remember her saying to you.

She said, in so many words, I have missed you.

And if I recall correctly, you said . . .

Why me? There were others.

But you were always the one?

Yes, she said. You were always the one. And then she laughed.

Which you interpreted as meaning what?

That she was happy she was telling me that.

Now, I believe you said that you went for coffee in a little shop nearby, and that you fell into a long conversation about the meaning of life, or some such topic.

That's right.

And the marriage took place a year later?

A year later. We weren't so sure of ourselves.

Okay. So now I have to ask you, why did you not want the baby?

We were too young, and I was just entering my freshman year.

At the university. And she?

She what?

And what about her? After the decision not to bring the baby to term, what did she do with herself, so to speak?

She just sat around the trailer.

This was a trailer where?

On my father's farm.

Was your mother with your father?

No, they were divorced. She lived a long day's drive away.

How often did you see her?

When we were living in the trailer?

No, before that. How old were you when they got divorced? Who divorced who, by the way?

She divorced him when I was seven. Said she was not cut out for life on a farm, the loneliness, she said. I saw her, to answer your question, once a month maybe. He, my father, would drive me down there and wait in the truck.

Were they friendly with each other?

Oh, yes, that's what confused me. Son, he said, if I go in there, you know what will happen. As if I knew. I guessed he meant — well, later, I saw them, accidentally, and they were, well, extremely affectionate.

Did you miss her?

Very much.

Did your wife miss *you*? Lonely in the trailer, I mean.

Lonely? Well, I guess she was. She never complained. She read all nine or so volumes of Proust. I quit after ten pages.

So you had little in common?

I didn't say that. We were compatible. After the first year, we moved into the city.

The one where your mother lived?

No, the one where I was in college. And then she worked nights at a convenience store.

To help put you through college?

I guess you could put it that way.

Did *she* ever put it that way?

Not in so many words.

How many words did she use?

None that I know of. She was, I guess, long suffering.

And what was the exact date on which your wife got shot?

November 22, 1992. I remember because it was the date Kennedy was shot.

And your wife 28 years later. And you stated that she survived, but that they could never remove the bullet, is that correct?

That is correct.

Okay. This brings you to areas not covered earlier. After she recovered, did she go back to work with that bullet in her chest?

Yes, but a day job, as a filing clerk.

And what was she reading after the Proust?

Anything she could get her hands on.

Did you read some of the stuff along with her?

No. I was in marketing.

What did you two do together, then?

Not much.

But you were compatible. Is that it?

Yes, comparatively.

As compared with what?

With other couples we encountered.

How do you mean, 'encountered'?

Encountered, saw, me in school, her in the office where she worked. And, you know, watching couples in restaurants and such.

Did you take her to the movies?

Now and then, yes, when we could afford it.

How would you sum up that period in your life?

Oh, I guess, 'placid' would be the word, except for the stress of school work.

When it was just the two of you, it was placid?

Yes.

Did you ever use that word with her?

Not that I remember.

What word or phrase did *she* use to you to sum up your lives together?

Once or twice she used a lot of words, some of which I didn't know the definition.

For instance?

I remember this one time. She said, 'You know, we almost, almost live lives of quiet desperation.' I didn't quite get it, but her tone was not sad exactly, so I guess I kind of shrugged it off.

Do you recall another time?

Yes, I even memorized it because I used it on some acquaintances of mine. It was after I was in the business and she was a senior in English literature. 'Polymorphous perversity.'

And this was how she summed up your lives together at that juncture?

No, she was talking about not just us, but everybody, nationally. So I used it on my partners at Monday morning meetings a time or two.

It does have a ring to it. But moving on. So, your wife, did she graduate and if so, what kind of work did she get into?

English, of course, teaching English at the community college, because we could only afford so far as a master's, and she planned to go on for her doctorate later on.

Did she?

No, she loved teaching so much she didn't want to stop and go through that long process of getting a doctorate.

Did she want to write books, be a scholar?

Not really. It was all about teaching for her.

With that bullet in her chest all this time?

With that bullet in her chest.

So she, at least, was not living a life of almost quiet desperation and certainly not one of polymorphous perversity?

No. I am certain of that.

Were *you?*

I don't know. I never thought about it in those terms.

Thought about what?

My life, I guess you meant.

What terms did you use?

None, that I can put into words. I mean, feelings about myself, my life.

Did you envy her in any way?

Maybe. I don't recall.

Did she envy you your success in business?

No.

Did she get pregnant again?

Yes.

Did you want her to have the baby this time?

I was all for it.

Did *she* want to have it?

I got the impression she wanted to.

When it was born, was she happy?

She looked happy to me.

Did she miss her teaching?

I never asked her. I thought a baby would make her happier than teaching had.

But did she ever say so?

Not in so many words.

Did she seem to love the baby?

Looked to me like she did.

Did *you* love the baby?

Of course.

Why that choice of words?

I mean, sure.

Did you change her diapers?

No, I think she was too embarrassed.

No, I don't mean your wife. We'll get to that later. Did you ever change the baby's diapers?

No. I could never get the hang of it.

Did your wife miss teaching?

She never said. She kept reading those books. Milton, I think. And some French writer. Sims, I think. No, Simpson. I seem to remember some of the titles, *The Snow Is Black* and *The Man Who Watched the Trains Go By*. George. With an S . . . Simenon! A hundred of them by him. She looked like she was drowning in them.

Did you ever steal money from your business?

Is that what this is all about?

Please answer the question.

No.

Did you ever think about stealing from your business?

Every day.

Why didn't you?

Weak, I guess. Scared. Not that I needed the money. We are okay. It's just that it's there and you think, why not?

Did you ever think of killing your wife and child?

No.

Did you ever think of suicide?

Doesn't everybody?

Please just answer the question.

Yes, but only fleetingly.

At what points in your life?

When I was seven and when I was a junior in college and maybe another time later.

What other time?

I can't recall just now.

Does your wife ever talk of suicide?

No, but I imagine it's an option for her.

Have you ever had an affair?

Now, that one . . .

You understand, I have to ask these questions, just to rule you out.

No affairs, per se.

One night stands?

Yes, at almost every convention.

What category of women?

A girl in the office, actually an older woman. A colleague from another city in the room next to mine that time in Cincinnati. Mostly girls of the night, as they used to call them.

Did you use protection?

Of course. I mean, out of consideration for my wife.

How is your child taking it?

It?

Your wife's illness.

She's not the talkative type.

Based on your own observations, how would you say your child is taking it?

I realize that I should pay more attention. I do what I can. I provide for her. I do all the things her mother used to do, things I can fit into my tight schedule.

Do you wish you could do more?

Yes. Definitely.

And what do you do for your wife?

As I say, I do everything I can, given my busy schedule.

Except change her diapers?

Yes, except change her diapers.

Would you do that for her if she could no longer do it for herself?

I'll have to cross that bridge when I come to it.

How soon do you think that might be?

They say she has eleven months. But she says she intends to fight it to the very end, so I can't really say. But —

But what?

Hospice normally takes care of such things.

What would you do without her?

Well, so much of our life together has been me watching her read and her watching me come and go.

Another bridge, another time?

You could put it that way.

How about your little girl?

What about her?

Will you act as both father and mother when your wife is gone?

If my wife is ever gone. She says she will fight it to the bitter end.

Please answer the question.

My mother is willing to take her in.

Why not stash her away in the trailer on your father's farm?

Now you are being sarcastic.

Is your father still living?

Yes. Barely.

Do you visit him often?

Why put it that way? Often? How can I, given my schedule? Yes, as often as I can.

Which is how often?

Once or twice every year or two. My mother visits him.

Is your mother married?

Yes, ever since the divorce, I mean two years after. He took me down there once a month, and that's when, one of those times, I walked in on them.

Would you say, even now, years later, she still loves your father?

You could call it that. Nothing I wouldn't want to walk in on, but she does come up to visit him.

What is the relationship between your daughter and your mother?

She's her grandmother.

I am asking about the nature of their relationship.

Good.

Do they call each other?

Not in my presence. Maybe she calls her on her cell phone.

Your little girl has a cell phone?

Yes, just in case.

Does she call her mother from the school bus or at recess?

I sometimes hear them talking when I can get away to check on her.

So you have one of those family cell phone deals?

Yes. It's very convenient.

Have you ever wished your wife had not survived that robbery?

No. But I wish they had been able to get that bullet out of her chest.

Why? Has it bothered her much over the years?

I think it has bothered me more than her, knowing that it is always there.

Have you ever considered ending your wife's suffering from the cancer?

Not really.

If she asked you to do it, would you do it?

I would consider it, but then again, there would be a penalty, I think. I need to look into that part of it.

Would you hesitate because of your little girl?

She's only nine. But then, she could go to live with my mother. They get along pretty well, so far as I know.

At this juncture, I wonder if you have an observation about your life that you would like to make on your own behalf.

Well, no, unless it might be that all my life I have felt that something has been lying in wait.

Explain that, please.

I can't. I never put it into words until just now. Let's move on.

I have to ask this. What do you feel most passionately about?

I never thought about it. What do you mean by that?

What, for instance, do you hate the most?

Nothing.

What do you love the most? Or who?

I would have to think about that one.

Take your time. You understand, I have to ask these questions in order to rule you out.

Ask a different question, will you?

All right. We can come back to that one. Actually, we will be coming back to all of these questions, again and again, until we have ruled you out.

THE HEADLESS
GIRL'S MOTHER

❄

We parked in sawdust again in the midst of what looked to be another used car lot. The smell of sawdust and recent rain, and tents and animals and sultry human bodies, and cotton candy and hot dogs was strong in the air even before we got out.

We walked fast, me holding her hand to keep her from going off wildly in six directions at once.

"Hold onto me now, Arabel. That dog is somewhere in this crowd and he's liable to be on us 'fore we know it. Just keep looking around you and don't lose control of yourself. I know how you feel, honey, but we got to be calm and search this place with our wits keen. Stop that crying now. You can't see with your eyes full of tears."

"I feel like a chicken with its head cut off." She squeezed my hand to let me know she wasn't going to act like one.

We went over every inch of that midway, watched the Ferris wheel go round twice, tried to see the faces in the tilt-a-whirl, waited till they skinned back the caterpillar, watched the dodg'ems, pushed through the crowds watching the geek eat chickens live and spit up the guts on the back of his hand and hurl the heads at the hecklers.

We looked among the children hanging over the monkey pen, looked among the crowd standing around the motorcycle pit, coughing at the exhaust smoke and blinking at the sparks, and we barged in on the fortune teller who called us sons-of-bitches, till we had looked everywhere but the sideshow.

231

The ticket taker wouldn't let us in till the barker had finished his harangue to the crowd. So we stood in front of a bunch of people who were clustered around the platform outside the tent. He was luring the open-mouthed, frog-eyed people with a sample of the freaks on the inside. For a moment we got caught up in his ranting and in the monster he kept pointing to — a headless shape covered with a white sheet, surrounded by huge jugs of what he called blood — long, coiled tubes jutting out from under the sheet where the head should have been. Pale, delicately blue-veined hands and dirty, bare feet were all that stuck out from under the sheet. A bird's claw design clutched a quartz ball at the ends of the arms and the legs of the chair. The hands curved over the balls at the ends of the armrests, one hand twitched that wore a turquoise ring. The blood bubbled in the jars.

The barker looked like a gypsy — tall, skinny, skin dark, eyes black eyes, black hair slicked back, combed close to his skull — and he wore a tight, double-breasted, gray, pin-striped suit and black and white shoes with points to the toes. And as he talked and as he gestured, the rings he wore and his black eyes glittered in the colored lights that hung on cords between the sharp tent poles. And back of him as he moved, lurid, fading banners fluttered in the little night breeze that had come up — freaks fluttering on the banners — petrified man, hermaphrodite, armless, legless fat man, two-headed pony, sword swallower, monster fetuses in formaldehyde.

The people around us forced our bodies together. "I'm getting sick, Frank. That thing without a head! Look at that blood trickling into her neck! And that man looks like a snake. His skin looks greasy and his eyes are so cold — like black ice."

"She can't help it, folks!" The barker leaned far out and rared far back. "She was born this way! She come into this cruel world without no head. She is ninety-nine percent helpless. Her life hangs by the hair. Only the miracles of modern science and the grace of God have kept the blood beating in her frail body. Blood is her only food — blood sold to us by poor, homeless, wandering tramps who were so hungry they had to sell their blood. Only your generosity can keep her alive. The midway can't afford to keep those bottles full. Four gallons a day must go into that poor girl's body. I know you folks are aware of those animals screaming over there, and you feel a little nervous. Imagine how she must feel! It is the blood they smell. You can't smell it because you are human, but at night when the lights are out and the tents and the rides are empty, they cry for it. By the grace of God she can't hear them, but she is human and we can only imagine that she must sense, must feel the restlessness of the animals. She cannot live much longer. This is your one and maybe your only opportunity to see her up closer on the inside. When you come back tomorrow she may not be with us. Some of you may doubt she is alive even now. Watch those pitiful hands twitch with the grateful beating of blood in her body. That's no electric current doing that. You there, you, big fellow! Come up here and touch her and testify to the folks that she is alive!"

As he came down on the steps of the platform, pointing at me, his black eyes stared into me, and the people looked up at me.

"Let's go, Frank!" Arabel pulled on my hand.

"Go ahead, buddy! She's harmless!" someone yelled, his own flesh crawling, most likely.

Arabel screamed in my ear, I turned, and her mouth was open, her teeth blue with stain from what we picked in that berry patch, and she sent a long scream up into the air over the midway.

I saw the dog's long silver snout, the lips curled back over the red, glistening gums, the teeth glowing in the colored lights and a leather thong around her neck was pulled taut by a hand sticking out of the crowd.

The crowd twisted, stirred and surged back, people screaming and yelling as the dog leaped up the steps.

The gypsy turned on the steps and ran and spun around on the platform and staggered back against the headless girl's chair, and one of the jugs got jolted off its stand, shattered beside the chair, the red fluid gushed on Lucius' feet as he came up behind the dog, the dog pulling at the leash and him stumbling.

The sheeted thing rose suddenly like a Jack-in-the-box when the jar fell, its arms spread, and it pushed back against the chair. The dog's snout darted into the folds of the sheet and its teeth ripped it. The gypsy was nimble on his feet and they were all zigzagging around up there, and then he hit the dog on the head with his fist and kicked Lucius between the legs, making him double up and clutch at the chair. Lucius still held the leash. But the dog had the sheet in its mouth and it ripped it off the body it hid, and first a golden mass of hair, the head thrown back, emerged.

A girl jumped up on the seat of the chair, her arms swinging at nothing and everything, knocking the jugs down crash on the floor. Lucius caught the gypsy's coattails with one hand, a long knife held high, poised to plunge, in the other hand. The gypsy kicked and turned, his whole body limp and loose in fear. The light glanced off Lucius' black glasses as he flung back his head, yelling a nasal, spit-garbled flood of gibberish. And the dog snapped at the girl's bare feet.

She was frozen in fear and mashed her tiny body against the back of the chair, the chair quivering backward on two legs. And then Arabel's fingernails finally drew blood in the palm of my hand, and she got her throat unclogged of shock and fear and horror enough to scream, "Avis! Avis! Avis! Avis!"

Two cops got up on the platform before I could even see them go up. They struggled with Lucius and he struggled with the dog's leash because he'd gotten tangled up in it.

The gypsy whirled on the edge of the platform and fell over onto the sawdust at our feet. He thrashed around as though in a fit and then he crawled under the platform, and I saw him run into the tent.

The crowd made a great roar, falling in against itself, a mass confusion of faces and limbs and scattering of sawdust. The cops struck the dog with their pistols and one of them fired, but the bullets sputtered and splintered into the planks. Then Lucius lost his balance and fell and pulled the dog down after him.

Arabel tried to break away from me to get up on the platform to Avis, but I held her tightly to me.

And one of the cops had Avis around the waist. She kicked her legs out over the platform. "Rago! Rago! Rago!"

She cursed the cop and bit his wrist, and he slapped her. Lucius was pulling the dog under the platform. The other cop came down the steps after Lucius, but the crowd had surged in again and he got tangled up in it.

All this took about three minutes, then it calmed down. The cop had Avis gripped tightly around her waist. Her long, blonde hair flared out wildly around her hot face. The mauve, silk blouse she had on was pulled up under her tiny breasts, and her tight blue jeans had slipped down over her hips, the white of her panties showing above a wide, black belt with green, blue and red studs on it, and her navel showing in the white flesh of her belly. She gritted her teeth and her large blue eyes burned. Even so, she was the most beautiful, wild, little creature I had ever seen.

A siren came, louder and louder, until it burst into the midway area, and a patrol car rolled, bounced across the sawdust, skidded in the mud at the platform. Two cops jumped out.

I glanced around for some sign of Lucius and the dog. All I saw were the black glasses — smashed into the sawdust, blood from the jugs dripping on them through cracks in the platform.

"Get back, you two! Get back with the crowds!" One of the new cops started pushing with both hands. But I was rooted to the spot.

Arabel put her face up to him, her eyes full of tears.

"I'm her mother! I'm her mother, you hear me?"

Well, he was deaf if he couldn't.

"Whose mother? That little girl's up there?"

"Yes, damn you! Get the hell out of my way!"

She jabbed me in the ribs with her elbow, and I let go and slipped in the mud trying to catch her again. The cop was doing a polite sidestep, but she didn't even notice because she pushed him against the edge of the platform, knocking his cap down over his face. She went up the steps, mad as a bumblebee, into the arms of a cop up on the platform.

The other cop had Avis in his lap on the chair now, trying to keep her fingernails away from his face.

I went up the steps, trying to catch Arabel.

"Let her go to her mother." The cop was trying to keep Arabel away from the chair. "She's the child's mother."

"You her daddy?"

"No. That was him with the dog." He stepped aside to let Arabel pass.

"Hey, Earl! Did you find that bastard with the dog?"

"They took off, Ralph!"

"Well, get after 'em, goddamnit! And find that barker, too!"

Arabel reached out to touch Avis, she drew back over the arm of the chair, still held tightly in a double vise, clasped in the cop's arms and clamped between his knees. She shut her eyes and shook her head and screamed, "Rago! Rago! Rago!"

"You better leave her alone, lady! That dog must have bit her! She's gone hog wild!"

"Bit her? Avis, did it bite you?"

"No. She just acts that way. The little bitch is trying to gouge my eyes out!"

"You call my child a bitch, I'll bust your head wide open!"

"Get her in the car, Cecil!" The cop who seemed in charge of the chaos pointed at the car. "Get her away from her. Now, lady, keep away from her. You may be her mother, but if you want to see her, you'll have to come to the juvenile home. They's too much hell going on here. Just calm down now. You can see her later."

The cop named Cecil carried Avis down the steps, trying at the same time to keep Arabel's hands off her.

I grabbed Arabel and held her. "Now, honey. Let him take her. We'll go to the juvenile and see her there."

She didn't resist. She sank against me, and I held her while two of the cops got in the car, one behind the wheel, the other in the back with Avis. The doors slammed and the wheels spun in the mud and sawdust, and then the car shot forward, got going through the crowd.

"Now what started this?" The cop in charge looked up at me as though he thought he had the right man.

"Man, can't you see she's sick? Let me take her home."

"No! Take me to see Avis."

"Okay, honey. Okay, honey, just don't worry."

"Who was the man with the dog?"

"The wrath of God. Ain't that obvious?"

"Hey, you want me to drag you around this midway a few times?"

"You'd just wear yourself out."

"You look like the guy we're looking for. You that private detective we — Were you over at the — ?"

"That's me. I was trying to track down the man you just let get away."

The cop named Earl came loping along between some tents, and when the cop standing before me turned and looked at him, Earl spread his arms and shrugged his shoulders, shook his head.

"Couldn't find hide nor hair of any of them!"

"Look. We'll be at the juvenile home. Could I talk to you there?"

"Yeah, go on. I'll call Cecil and he can ask you some questions. Things are so wild I won't get away from here for an hour."

I took Arabel to the car and she fluttered back against the seat like a butterfly pinned in a frame alive.

"Did you see the way she looked at me?" She was slow, sluggish with the horror of seeing it again in her mind. Then she breathed in jerks and her face trembled.

"W — w — what's wrong? Something's w — w — wrong! What was s — s — she doing like th — th — that?"

"We're going to see her, honey. Now try to get hold of yourself. Both of you are in a state of shock. Ever' thing'll fall to pieces between you."

"Oh, Frank. If you only knew. If you only knew."

I didn't ask her if I only knew what, because she was slowly getting calm. As calm as you could expect of a woman who had just seen what she had just seen. By the time we got over there, Arabel was fairly calm.

The juvenile home sets on a mound-like hill that's completely covered with kudzu. A cold, brick building inside a diamond wire fence, barbed wire running along the top at an angle, and although very few kids try crawling up that fence, the vines do, and they spill down the hill to the edge of the street. Weak, naked bulbs strung through the trees lit the driveway up to the gate.

"How do we get in? The place looks closed up." The windows were barred. You don't have to commit a crime to get in there. Some kids just commit the crime of getting conceived in the wrong bed, and this place becomes a way station between what they had for a mother and a charitable institution.

We parked beside the police car and got out and walked to the gate. Crickets sang in the trees around us. The heat was sweltering. Arabel pushed a buzzer beside the gate. "I've been here before. Used to come to see my brothers, Troy and Lennis, before they grew up and got to be respectable crooks."

A door opened, and a stout woman appeared in the doorway, a pale orange light behind her.

"What do you want?" She weaved her head about, trying to see us. Then she came down the walk, stopping every few steps. The sight of me got into her tone of voice. "What do you want? It's nearly midnight. No visiting now."

"I'm Avis Satterfield's mother."

"Well, you get yourself in here, and maybe you can do something with her. Never in all my born days I seen a child so wild." She scratched among a bunch of keys on a ring and unlocked the gate. "You must be the people them policemen are waiting to see." She stopped and looked back and up at me over her shoulder. "You her father?"

"No, ma'am. Just a private detect — just a friend of the family."

"Must be some family."

She led us down a passageway to an octagon where four corridors met. It was a pool of very pale gold. The two cops leaned against the two-toned wall, dark green below, light green above, smoking cigarettes, their palms riding their pistols. Two closed doors painted silver had wire meshes over the windows in them.   Arabel stopped at the edge of the octagon and blinked her eyes. Avis sat drawn into herself on a long bench that stretched the length of one wall, her head back against the wall, her eyes staring up at the ceiling. Her blue jeans were so tight her knuckles were shaped out perfectly in her pockets. One of the legs was cocked up and the sole of her bare foot rested on the edge of the bench. The mauve silk blouse hung loosely on her, ripped down one side, showing her ribs and the white of her brassiere and the soft curve of her breast. The red and green glass studs on her black belt glittered.

The stout woman stood in front of one of the silver doors. Her breast flabby, her lips looked like they had never tasted anything but lemons.

Planted right in front of Arabel, staring down at her, was a tall, thin woman, her arms crossed over her flat chest. Her blue-tinted hair flared out around her head.

The two cops had been watching us come down the dark corridor. "Okay, buddy, you and the lady ready to tell us what brought all this on?"

"I'll tell you ever'thing I know, but let her see her daughter. How about it? Hasn't seen her in two years."

"Okay, you'll do. Who is Rago? She keeps screaming Rago. Nothing but Rago."

I backed into the corridor a ways so I could get them out of there. The walls and the floor were bare and moist from humidity. I leaned against the wall where I could watch Arabel with Avis. I told the cops everything I knew, and when one of them recognized me, I had to elaborate on how I came into all this as a case getting out of my control.

But I kept watching all time what was going on between Arabel and Avis. Nothing was. For a while, Arabel tried to get close to her, and I could hear her mothering voice murmuring. But Avis pulled her legs up against her breasts, gripped her knees, her hair falling down over her arms.

The stout woman stayed in front of the door and the thin one in the middle of the octagon. They both looked disgusted and took turns saying stuff like, "Speak to your mother, Avis," and "Can't you even speak to your mother, you little hellion?" with "mother" sounding as nasty as "hellion," and Arabel would look up sharply at them, hurt in her eyes and then she'd go on talking softly to the head of blonde hair. Finally, she sat beside her on the polished bench and kept trying to touch Avis' hair and her wrists and to stroke her feet, but she would flinch and huddle in the corner. When I looked again, Arabel was at one end of the bench and Avis at the other. The two women glanced at them, whispering. And Avis had sat up now, her legs stuck out stiff and spread apart, her bare heels on the floor, her shoulder blades propped on the low back of the bench, arms crossed, and the ring shining in the yellow light.

Arabel just looked at her, bewildered and hurt, and she would glance at me and I looked between the two cops at her and Avis, and the cop who wasn't talking would look around to see what I was looking at. Our talking was the only sound, except I heard the echo of a girl's coughing ring along a corridor behind one of the silver doors, and one of the matrons heard it, too.

Cecil kept showing me the bites and scratches Avis had given him, saying, "She kept grabbing at my cods, trying to put me out of commission." He was a little in awe of it, but laughing.

I heard a hiss sound and looked into the octagon again. Avis held a burning match in one hand, a box of them in the other. She let it burn down to her fingers. Arabel and the two women watched her. From the look on their faces, I reckon they thought she was going to let it burn into her flesh, but she dropped the curled, black stub on the floor.

"You pick that right up!" The tall matron spoke slow, through her nose, pointing at the floor.

Avis didn't even look at her. She took another match from the box and popped it into flame on the ruby stud on her belt, her body still propped in that slanted position. And she let it burn the same way.

The tall one stepped toward her. "You give me them matches!"

Avis stuck the match out toward the woman's stomach. She did a quick little dance backward. Avis snapped another match.

"You want me to stop her?" The offer came from the cop at the edge of the light. Not Cecil. He knew better.

"She is in our care now. If her mother'd just go on home, we might could handle her."

"Let her go ahead." The stout one huffed up her shoulders. "She'll run out d'reckly and then we'll take her inside."

"A fine job you done of raising that little brat." Cecil knew I wasn't her daddy.

"I told you. I'm not her daddy. He's the one with the dog. The one you oughta be out trying to find, before he sics that dog on somebody else or before Arabel's brothers shoot him down."

"You hear him, Jack? Now he's trying to tell us how to do our job."

"No. No. Hell no." I was exasperated now. My stomach growled for food. The cops looked at me.

"What did you say?"

"Nothing. Not a damn thing."

We watched Avis strike the matches, hold each one till it sputtered at her fingertips and then drop it at her feet. All six of us watched her, fascinated, each time sure she was letting it burn into her flesh. She stared at the matches very seriously as though this was what we had brought her here to do. Then the matches were all black and cold around her feet, and she closed the box very carefully as though it were a miniature coffin and the viewing was over, and then she flipped it at the tall matron and it hit her where her breasts should have been and bounced and plopped on the marble floor. The two women, looking a little scared, moved slowly in on her, and pounced on her as Arabel rose, trembling, putting her hands out to touch her.

"Need any help?" It made Jack laugh.

"You two apes get out of here." The stout one waved them away, fumbled at the door and opened it. The two women went into the cell-block, and the door slammed and they were gone.

Arabel didn't say anything on the ride across town. I drove her to her house on Buckeye Street and parked where I had before.

I reached in front of her and got the gun out of the glove compartment. "He may be around here someplace. I'm gonna get you safe and locked in the house before I go."

We walked in the moonlight up the path to the dark porch, and I opened the door, and she still didn't speak. She went right to the bedroom and laid on the bed and kicked her shoes off and crossed her arms over her face and cried softly. I looked in all four rooms and on the back porch to make sure.

Then I went back to the bedroom and looked down at her. "Want me to make you some coffee?"

She didn't say anything but I couldn't hear her crying anymore. The moonlight fell across her through the window. I looked at the side of Mrs. Cabbage's house, milky white.

Then she took her arms down and looked up at me. "You still haven't eaten anything, have you?"

She smoothed back her hair, her mouth open a little and moist. "That's what my stomach keeps saying." She reached out and took my hand. "Poor little thing."

"Poor little thing? With all you got on your mind, you calling me poor little thing?"

"Hush. If I don't stop thinking about it, I'll go stark, staring mad. Stay with me awhile." She swung her legs around and sat on the edge of the bed and pulled herself to her feet, holding my hand. "I'll fix us something to eat 'fore we both drop in our tracks." She walked listlessly into the kitchen. She hadn't even turned on the lights, but the moonlight glowed softly in the rooms. "You lock the front door?"

"Yeah."

She pulled the light cord and the kitchen was bright, a little closed-in place with another day just getting born outside. "You know how to build a fire?"

"Yeah."

I built a fire in the cook stove while she got the coffee ready to boil.

"Now what else?" She stood in the middle of the kitchen with her thumb between her teeth thinking. Then she looked around in the cupboard. "Salt and pepper."

"Salt, with pepper on it. Sounds good."

"I'll look in the icebox." She went out on the porch, and I stood behind the screen door and looked at the way the moon was shining in the mimosa tree in the backyard.

"Here's some pinto beans I can warm up. And a couple of pork chops. I tell you what. I'll just fix us a real supper."

"At one o'clock in the morning?"

"Why not? Ever'thing else's turned upside down."

"True."

"You like to have some nice sliced tomatoes and some onions fresh out of the ground with some corn bread?"

"Does a chicken have feathers?"

"Come help me round up some fresh tomatoes."

I went out on the porch and followed her into the yard. The grass was wet and crickets were singing and fireflies were pulsing.

"Watch the clothesline." She ducked under it. I ducked too, thinking of Lucius and his seeing-eye dog.

Up and down behind the houses, all the backyards were lifeless, pearl gray in the moon. I felt the gun in my hip pocket.

She glanced around, too, watching the shadows to make sure they didn't move. Just under the limbs of the mimosa tree the little garden patch started. Fluffy pink and purple blossoms lay in the grass and among the tomato plants. Everything smelled strong and fresh and good.

"Is that green beans growing up those sticks?"

"Uh-huh. And I got lettuce and they was some strawberries but they're all gone now. And over by the coal house is some poke greens but they take too long to cook. I'm hungry as a wolf myself. You, too?"

"Now, ain't I?"

"You come Sunday and I'll fix us the best Sunday dinner in all Knoxville. Just you and me and Avis."

"I'll be right here."

She squatted among the tomato plants and her hands moved among the leaves and she had her head to one side, trying to find some ripe tomatoes. I sat on my heels beside her in the soft earth. The aroma of her hair and of the tomato vines was too much. Too much!

"Man, o'man, it sure smells good out here!"

"See if you can find some nice onions over yonder, 'stead of breathing on my neck. I'm about to lose my balance."

I stooped among the plants, looking for the green spears of onions.

"Did you hear something?"

I stopped and listened, an onion plant dripping dirt from my hand.

"Naw. Just us, scratching in the 'mater patch."

"Let's go in." She had one tomato in her upturned hand and three laid out along the inside of her arm up against her belly. Under the mimosa tree she stopped and looked around. Not looking for a sign of Lucius and the dog, but letting the night soak into her. "Frank, don't it seem like we're the only two people awake in the whole city?"

I smiled and nodded and kissed her cheek.

While she fried the pork chops, I sat at the table and drank her coffee and watched her walk about the kitchen. She got the oven hot and made us a batch of cornbread. She told me to slice the tomatoes and wash the onions.

We ate and didn't talk much — just felt each other near. And she'd get a faraway look in her eyes and notice me looking at her and say, "What's you looking at?"

"You."

And we wondered why we hadn't heard from Lennis and Troy and then we thought maybe they hadn't heard about us finding Avis at the midway.

"Well, let's not talk about it," she said. "Tomorrow I'll go get Avis, and 'fore too long ever-thing'll be all right."

She got down some peach preserves and we had some with country butter on the crisp cornbread.

"You think you ought to stay alone here tonight?"

"What do you think? You think he'll try — ?"

"Never can tell. Look at your hands. You can hardly light that cigarette."

"Well, dammit, you're s'pposed to light a woman's cigarette for her."

"I know it. I just like to watch the way you do it."

"I hope you get your eyes full."

"You go like this . . ." I tried to imitate her. "And I get butterflies."

"Aw, shoot a monkey, Frank. You lie like a —"

"Well, I do. Do I make you feel any certain way?" She looked at me through the smoke. "You make me feel you ought not to stay here much longer."

"Come over here."

"What for?" But she was getting up, dragging on the cigarette. When she got under the light, she threw back her head and blew the smoke up at the bulb, and reached up and yanked the cord.

I put my hands on her waist and drew her down on my lap. "Let's us just sit here in the dark." She spoke so low I hardly heard her.

We sat quietly, and I ran my hands up and down her back and over her ribs and she hugged me around my neck. "Your breath smells like peaches and cornbread."

"Well, I been eating cornbread and peaches."

"You have, haven't you? Do I smell of peaches and cornbread?"

"Your breath smells like peaches and cornbread."

"Yeah. And you got the smell of the whole summertime on you."

"I wish you'd quit sneaking your hands down there. If you'd just go ahead and put 'em back there, maybe your big o' heart'd stop pounding against me so hard." I did what she told me. "I wish it would rain again. It's so sticky, and I'm so tired and weary and sad and blue. I'd just love to lay on the bed and listen to it rain — to ease my jangled nerves."

"Maybe if we lay on the bed and listen hard enough, like when we used to lay our ears on the tracks to hear the vibrations of the train coming, maybe it will rain."

"Well, I can see I'm gonna have to get up off your lap." She got up and blew cigarette smoke in my face. She was facing the front door with her back to me and I saw it stiffen.

"What is it, honey?"

Her hand reached back and her fingers clawed into my shoulders. "Look! Standing on the porch." Her voice was in a deep husky whisper.

I looked. The bent, black shape of a man stood at the window in the door. Suddenly, another shape rose up beside him in the gray light. Its pointed ears were black and sharp, and it was looking in, trying to see us. I heard the shrill screech of claws on the glass.

THE LAST

BIZARRE TALE

※

On July 23, 1921, a young Italian troubadour came rolling into the East Tennessee mountain town with a one ring circus and by nightfall lay with a
tent stake in his chest. On August 14, 1990, he was to be buried in a hillside
cemetery by the railroad tracks.

The young man mowing grass had never heard of the murder nor did he
know why the man on the hillside below was breaking the rocky ground with
a spade. The sun rising, he was wondering why he had accepted this job one
day instead of going back home to Bristol.

He didn't want to be reminded of Ricky. Things like the mausoleum were
what had driven him over the mountains into this remote and very different
region. He did not mind remembering Ricky's funeral. But without ever seeing
it, the mausoleum Ricky's mother had erected had disturbed him.

What kind of mind and heart, he had often wondered, did it take even to
imagine a replica of Ricky's room inside a mausoleum? Doing it took a year
and almost wrecked the family business and Ricky's parents' marriage. On the
day he would have graduated from high school, it was ready for Ricky's mother
to enter. Over the past year, she had visited it, sat in the room, according to
talk around Bristol, and kept it clean herself. Jeff would go out of his way to
avoid even passing the gates of the cemetery. Of the five in the car, Jeff alone
had survived the crash. He sometimes wondered how he would survive in a
world where people like Ricky's mother did such bizarre things.

Precariously riding the mower across the hillside past photographs of the
deceased set in the gravestones, past urns of plastic flowers, Jeff could not

help but imagine Ricky's mausoleum and wish all the harder that there had been a job opening for him when he arrived in South Mountain yesterday afternoon.

Word had reached the streets of Bristol that the South Mountain city fathers, with help from the Federal government, had funded the restoration of the town as a way of drawing tourists off the major artery that came from Washington, D.C. down the Shenandoah Valley through Bristol to venture over two-lane mountain roads to South Mountain. After a year of indecisiveness, he needed to make some money so he could make a move — into the university to study engineering or into Europe for a bike tour so he could think over possibilities. No money at all left him open to the temptation to join the Air Force to learn how to fly a helicopter.

He had delayed too long, the jobs were all taken. But as he watched men tearing up the streets and laying brick sidewalk, he heard two other unemployed men saying they'd rather starve than cut grass in the cemetery on an open hillside in the hellfire of August. Jeff asked where to go, and got the job. So far, the morning heat was bad, but not horrendous. Being forced to imagine Ricky's mother's private freak show was.

Jeff wondered why the man digging the new grave below by the railroad track kept looking up at him. Maybe he's just suspicious of strangers. Or maybe I'm cutting into his work.

After three passes above where he was digging, the man yelled up at Jeff, "You be careful now!"

"I am, don't worry!"

"You the one better worry! The regular mower tipped it over on himself and he's in intensive care right now!"

Jeff felt a chill in his scalp.

"Where's your cap?"

"Don't have one!"

"None of my business, but that sun'll turn your brainpan into a hot skillet fore you even know what hit you!"

"Hope not!"

"Come take mine! I'm used to it!"

Jeff said no thanks, but the gravedigger insisted so bossily, he caved in, parked his mower, left it idling, and trounced down the steep hillside to level ground by the railroad track.

"Three years in 'Nam will climatize you for the rest of your life," the grave-digger said. Long exposure had burned him dark, but his hollow eyes and sharp jawbones made him look like death warmed over, as Jeff's grandmother used to say.

Jeff took the cap the Vietnam veteran handed him and putting it on, asked, "How long does it take to dig a grave?"

"Forever, seems like, but by noon it'll be ready for him."

"Who's that?"

"Old Spaghetti."

"Did you say Old Spaghetti?" Jeff always played along with older people who liked to talk that way.

"Called him Spaghetti cause he was a wop."

"Not many Italians live around here, I bet."

"Right. But this one didn't live here either. More like here was just where he was being dead all these years."

"Well, how old was he?"

"They say he was twenty-one when he was killed, but if he had lived, he would be about ninety by now."

This man is not worried about whether I have a heat stroke or not, Jeff thought, he just wants somebody to tease. If I were twenty-one he probably wouldn't do it.

"I don't get it."

"Where you from anyway?"

"From over at Bristol."

"Tennessee or Virginia?"

"Virginia side. What difference does it make?"

"Makes all the difference in the world, but either side, you bound to have heard of Spaghetti."

"Never did. Or if I did, I forgot."

The vet went back to digging and Jeff sensed that telling it would take him awhile. He wished he had turned off the mower. The sound of the motor forced him to strain to hear and the exhaust drifting down the slope stung his eyes.

"Well, he was a wandering singer and violin player who took up with a little one-tiger circus and come rolling into South Mountain July 23 in 19-and-21 and they found him that night dead out back of a tobacco warehouse that used to be on the west side of town. Somebody had stabbed him in the chest with a spare tent spike, they never knew who. Didn't nobody know his name, but they knew he was Eye-talian, so they just called him Spaghetti — Well, that was later because at first there wasn't any reason to call him anything. He was just your everyday corpse lying at Smythe's Funeral Home on the third floor of the Smythe building over Smythe's hardware store by the railroad track where nobody paid any attention at first. No reason to.

"The circus broke camp and moved on and sent word to the young man's father in Chicago who promised to send money to ship him home."

Suffering the heat of the rising sun, Jeff watched the Vietnam vet, the digging and the telling synchronized.

"Didn't come, and it didn't come, so there being a law you had to bury him or embalm within three days, Smythe embalmed him and left him in the coffin, hoping the money would come after all. Them Smythes. They're the ones behind this restoration scam. Who's gonna come to see it? They used to come to see Spaghetti all the time, though.

"After about a year of laying in that coffin an turning black as a Nigerian, they couldn't spare the coffin if they was to stay the richest family in the county, so they trussed him up on wires against the wall." His digging-talking rhythm seemed hypnotic. "That's how the choo-choo train curving over the trestle threw its beam through one bare window and out the other, swooping across the room, exposing, only to the engineer, of course, what they called the Mummy of South Mountain. That light like threading needles. The engineers carried it from town to town, and this is a major line, you know, from Richmond, and so it got to be a scary story that got all over in those days, until the engineers would let you come up there with them in the cab so you could see what they saw, for a price. But the railroad made them cut it out after a few years.

"By then, you know, the word was out and some folks passing through would get out of their cars or off the bus or even off the trains and show up at Smythe's hardware store and ask could they see it. Why, sure, they could see it. And they would climb up to the third floor and look at it, and look out at the tracks to see how the light they had heard about must have shot through the windows. And those Smythes would ask for a donation to help send Spaghetti back where he come from. They say it was some sight."

Jeff was appalled by what he was hearing. "Did *you* ever see it?"

"No, I never got to see it because by the time I come along they had quit showing it except for a select few and my folks were not among the select few. And after I had been to 'Nam and back, I didn't have any desire to look at it. I've lost my interest in human interest sights like that."

"So you're digging his grave now?"

"I'm digging Old Spaghetti's grave, because the town wants to turn into something cute and mummies ain't cute no more, and tomorrow the new Mayor and some state representative from Memphis who's a relative of the dearly departed and a few others will come here for a little ceremony, and after the grave settles, in about a month, they'll erect a monument to him."

"Do they finally know his name?"

"Yes, I heard it said, but I can't recall it. You'll have to stick around or come back and read it for yourself right where you're standing. No, don't move. You're casting a nice shady shadow on me."

"Well, what I don't understand —"

"What don't you understand? What? What? What?

"Mind if I ask?"

"No, just run up there and turn off that damn mower. My nerves is frayed enough just on general principles. And that exhaust is too much."

Jeff gladly did it.

"What don't you understand?"

"Well, how the law would let them do it, for one thing."

"Do what?"

"Let him just hang there, wired up to a nail in the wall that way for the whole world to see."

"Smytheses was, is, the law. They're in everything around here. Some say they're even in the Klan. Guardian of morals right up to now. They want to censor the videos, they —"

"But didn't the singer's father ever send for him?"

"Never did. Maybe he died of a heart attack. Who knows? In the twenties, some said it was the Mafia that sent a hit man down here to do it. See, it all depended on when you were born. Different generations had different attitudes about it. Like when I was growing up, it was a dirty little secret. People were ashamed of Spaghetti. Nowdays it's just P.R., pure and simple."

"And how about the church people? Isn't it blasphemous or sacrilegious or something not to bury somebody?"

"Probably, but that's just for homefolks, not for a double alien like he was. Eye-talian plus being circus scum was the way they looked at it."

"But would they have let that happen to a criminal?"

"Never did."

"Or even a lynched black man?"

"Of course not. Inhumane."

"Then I don't understand."

"What's there not to understand? People are crazy, don't you know that yet, boy?"

Jeff watched him digging, thinking of Ricky's mother, sitting this very minute, it being Saturday, in the replica of Ricky's room, inside a mausoleum in the Bristol city cemetery.

He wondered what the Vietnam veteran would think of that bizarre tale. Bizarre tales. Jeff felt stuffed full of them, from infancy on to this new one. The bizarre, violent past. The Civil War tales. The World War I tales. The World War II tales. The Korean conflict tales. The Vietnam stories on TV that he could now barely remember. The folksy tales of the Southern Appalachians, full of cruel jokes. Backdrop to the blandness of the past ten years of his own life. The blank of his future. A profession in engineering? Helicopter school inspired by this gravedigger's era? A bike trip through Europe, on an off-the-deep-end impulse? A crazy world to have such people as these South Mountain people in it. All those generations of mummy showoffs.

"Yeah, boy, the sooner you realize that people are crazy the better off you'll be."

"Hearing this story doesn't really make me feel any better off, I'll tell you."

"It's just a story."

"No, it's not just a story. That man once breathed this same air like you and me. First, somebody murdered him, and then the whole town took away his dignity as a human being."

"A corpse ain't got no dignity. Now listen to what I'm telling you. See this hole? All corpses go in a hole just like this hole. Or they burn and blow away. Get used to it, boy."

"Don't it make you feel bad? Thinking of him all those years, naked, on exhibition like a freak in the sideshow?"

"Why would it make me feel bad? And he wasn't naked." The vet handed Jeff the shovel. "Here. Hold this a second." He pulled out his wallet and dug in it and came out with a photograph. "See?"

Jeff saw an almost naked, very skinny, coal-black man, with a huge white smile like the janitor of his grammar school had, and he wore a kind of diaper. "What's this?"

"See, he's wearing a thing like an Indian to hide his ding dong of doom."

"That's Old Spaghetti?" Jeff regretted saying his nickname out loud. "He looks real."

"Used to be a lot of barroom jokes about what sex was he. And writing on the latrine walls, even in my grammar school, I remember. Smythe had to keep his eye on the kids, of course. But, hell, the Smythes tell it that they caught some of these high society ladies peeking up under his flap to see what it looked like after all that time."

"Who's that standing beside him?"

"That's my only surviving picture of my daddy."

"Your daddy? Why would he want his picture taken beside — the — ?"

"To show off to his buddies in his outfit. He was home on leave. That's my only picture of him. He was killed in the invasion at Salerno."

Jeff wondered whether the vet showed the photograph to his own buddies in the Vietnam war as a joke. He wanted to ask, hoping not.

Jeff handed the gravedigger his shovel.

"Well, hold it till I get it put away." The vet put the photograph back, took the shovel, and continued to dig.

Nauseated by the heat and lack of food and the last bizarre story he ever wanted to hear, Jeff started to walk away.

"So now do you understand?"

"No."

"What more do you want to know?"

"Nothing."

"Don't go away mad."

"I guess you need to finish digging and I need to finish mowing. . . . Here's your hat."

"You need that hat."

"No, I appreciate it, but I got a handkerchief I can rig up — tie it at four ends and fit it over my head. It'll do. Thanks."

On the mower, Jeff tried to go over his options for the future again, imagine how each might work out, but the young Italian singer stayed on his mind. He tried to fend off images and thoughts of the murder and the desecration that followed, year by year. The young man could have lived on to this very day, a ninety year old man who had experienced the world as all those who had lived had experienced it. The Roaring Twenties. The Depression. The World War II Era. The Atomic Age. The Space Age. And some faint taste of the present vanilla age. Was the man who embalmed him still alive? Probably not. No, he didn't want to dwell anymore on those people, the curious who came by foot, and wagon, and car, and bus, and train, and airplane, who passed through here to take a look and go away to tell the bizarre tale, call attention to themselves as the source.

Mowing, mindful of the danger of tipping over, mindful of the steady rhythm of the vet's digging down by the railroad track, the same track that crossed the trestle past the third-story window of the building where the singer once hung by wire from a nail in the wall, he tried not to let the questions sink their hooks into him. Did a fellow Italian put a curse on him? The evil eye? How many thousands of photographs like the one of the World War II soldier, father of the Vietnam vet, had been taken with the mummy singer and put away in drawers or albums all over the world? Japanese, Germans, Russians, one or two at least, may have passed through here and heard about it and asked to see it and asked to be photographed so they could show it back home. Like those lawmen photographed with the corpses of the Younger brothers and later Dillinger's.

Did Ripley's *Believe It or Not* mummify him in a book? Wasn't it a violation of all known burial rights or rites in the recorded history of mankind? And yet he vaguely remembered that one of the bizarre tales his kin thrived on had been about the custom of hanging the family dead in remote mountain villages in the barn in cold weather until the ground was soft enough for grave digging. And didn't one man keep his wife hanging in the barn because he hadn't the heart to part with her? Or had he dreamed that? And yes, they had in one town many long years ago hung a lynched black man in the show window of a millinery shop on the town square for public display but only for three days, not for half a century. Why were other unclaimed bodies not treated that way? Thousands of funerals and decent burials over the many decades had taken place here, while the singer hung naked. Grave robbers and cemetery vandals had been sent to jail over the years. The banality of evil — he had heard that somewhere about the Holocaust and why and how it could have happened.

Maybe I shouldn't judge them by present-day standards. But he didn't want to condone that prolonged act of desecration. If he was to live in this world, he needed to understand how such things happened. Something in human nature made it possible? What? Too blazing hot to think! He would be delirious even before he realized it.

But he could not stop trying to see. The vet had talked about generations. Something happens to each generation. The generation in place when the singer was murdered allowed a process to get started; so that in the Depression years, the original generation had been displaced, time-the-neutralizer had dehumanized them, made them into clichés, stereotypes — all the people, and the singer with them, turning him into Old Spaghetti, a joke. But underneath it all must have been a steady sense, like the one he felt now, of nausea. Time displaced the mummy, too, and people living here and coming through could think of him in the same way you think of the Egyptian mummies on display in the Museum of Natural History in Washington, D.C. Even Boris Karloff as the mummy.

The present generation feels shame, tires to bury the past, but it comes too late to rectify. Rest in peace, among the unloving living who are all in love with death.

Jeff stopped the mower. He had moved aslant, not straight across. He shut off the motor. He staggered down the hillside to the gravesite, where only the Vietnam vet's cap showed above the rim of the grave.

"Hey!"

"You scared me half to death," he said, putting on.

"Do me a favor. Tell the keeper I quit. He doesn't owe me anything. See you."

Jeff walked down the railroad track toward the next road that would cross it, wherever that might be.

A road was not far ahead. And he caught a ride as soon as he stuck out his thumb. Coincidentally, the man was headed for Bristol. Jeff felt it would probably turn out to be a damned bizarre coincidence. The man asked if Jeff were from around South Mountain and he said no, Bristol, the Virginia side.

They lapsed into silence, and he was thankful. Weak from the heat and lack of food, he tried to sleep to keep from thinking about the singer who would be buried tomorrow. He felt guilty for not being there to pay his respects. But he was so glad to get out of that town, so glad. And when, six hours later, he knew he was only five miles from Bristol, from home, he was so glad to have put that town and those people behind him, and even Ricky's mother seemed likely.

But he kept thinking of all the people who had passed through that town and collaborated with the townspeople in the desecration of the young circus singer. But wait, he thought, what about me? Don't I count? If I feel bad, that means one person on this earth feels something, whatever it is, for the wandering singer. But that prideful revelation made him feel ashamed of himself.

Wait now, if I feel that way, there must have been other people who did, too. Who went to see him eagerly or even reluctantly but did go, and then felt, when they actually saw him on exhibit, some compassion, and went away imagining him as a real human being who had lived and been murdered and then desecrated by his fellow man. Enough people like that after all, men and women, young and old, who did not laugh or feel a cheap thrill. Who resurrected him in their feeling of compassion and in their imaginations as they walked away, rode away — and some who lived on in that town — to all points, North, South, West, East of the world, with images in their heads, stories in their mouths. And so the singer has had a life in those responses, a life he wouldn't have had even if he had lived to this day, or tomorrow. The rush of energy he felt, seeing that, had been loosed into the world many times before by other people, hadn't it? Mind and body, he was totally awake. He felt too confined in the car. He had to get out and walk.

The man stopped and he got out and the car sped on ahead and Jeff continued on foot, walking, walking fast, feeling an intuitive sense of there being images of the singer in the heads of people in every corner of the world, as far as India, even as far as the South and North pole, passed on from generation to generation. A sudden feeling that the singer lives everywhere, more intensely than Ricky had, than Ricky's mother, than the Vietnam gravedigger, than all those townspeople, than Jeff himself, lifted him into a leap of exhilaration.

ACKNOWLEDGMENTS

The author and editor thank editors of the following journals for granting permission for these stories to be reprinted.

"The Singer." *The Kenyon Review* 28 (1966): 79–107.
"The Master's Thesis." *Magazine of Fantasy and Science Fiction* 33 (July 1967): 87–99.
"A Secondary Character." *Cimmaron Review* 20 (July 1972): 5–19.
"Wanted: Ghost Writer." *Epoch* 23 (Fall 1973): 44–59.
"Second Look Presents: The Rape of an Indian Brave." *Fiction International* 4–5 (1975): 81–92.
"Lights" by David Madden, Copyright © 1984 by David Madden. First published in *New Letters* 51, no. 2, Winter 1984–85. It is printed here with the permission of *New Letters* and the Curators of the University of Missouri at Kansas City.
"The Last Bizarre Tale." *Contemporary Southern Short Fiction: A Sampler* (Texas Review Press, 1991).
"The Retriever." *Louisiana English Journal* 1.1 (Oct. 1993): 25–30.
"Over the Cliff." *Southern California Anthology* 12 (1995): 2–10.
"A Walk with Thomas Jefferson at Poplar Forest." *New Millennium Writings* (Fall–Winter 1996): 104–11.

Other reprinted stories, the rights to which are retained by the author, appeared in the following journals.

"Hurry Up Please It's Time." *Botteghe Oscure* 24 (Autumn 1959).
"The Headless Girl's Mother." *Adam* 11 (1967).
"A Human Interest Death." *Descant: The Texas Christian University Literary Journal* 14 (Spring 1970).
"Seven Frozen Starlings." *Twigs* VII (1971).
"The Demon in My View." *The Southern Review* 25 (Spring 1989).
"James Agee Never Lived in This House." *The Southern Review* 26 (Spring 1990).